KIDNAP.org

By Peg Herring

Gwendolyn Books, USA

KIDNAP.org

Printed in the USA

KIDNAP.org is a work of fiction. The names, characters, and incidents are entirely the work of the author's imagination. Any resemblance to actual persons, living or dead, or events, is entirely coincidental.

Cover art: Phillips Covers: http://phillipscovers.com

Editor: R Hodges

ISBN: 978-1-944502-07-2

Chapter One

Robin was taking her second shower of the day when her phone played a few bars of "Fat Bottomed Girls." As the ringtone sounded a second and third time, she leaned out to see the caller ID, but clouds of steam obscured her view. As Freddie sang out a fourth time she stepped out of the stall, dripping water and soapsuds onto the fleecy bathmat. Taking up the phone, she stabbed the connect button and said, "Hello." It was more of a challenge than a greeting.

"Um, Robin, this is Carter. Your friend from down the hall?"

She suppressed a sigh of irritation, in no mood to chat with a neighbor who was eccentric, to say the least.

It's not his fault you're upset.

A glance at the mirror revealed a face still blotchy from tears. Despite aroma therapy promises, her lavender-scented soap had not relaxed her tense muscles. After the worst morning of the year—make that two years—she wasn't in the mood for people, not even harmless guys like Carter.

Still not his fault.

The voice that often spoke in her head tended to be argumentative, making Robin doubt even her best intentions. Still, it was correct in this instance. Her disastrous day wasn't Carter's fault.

Grabbing a fluffy, pink towel from the bar, she dried her face with her free hand as she tried for a normal tone. "What's up?"

"I—I shoved a guy and then I locked him in the trunk."

Robin stopped toweling, and her own concerns slid into second place. "What?"

"We had a fight and I pushed him and he fell into the trunk and I closed the lid and I drove away and now he's real mad." Carter's voice rose a tone as he asked, "Should I let him out?"

Be careful. When Carter's nervous he chokes up, and you'll never get a straight answer.

A year before, when he moved into the apartment down the hall, Carter Halkias had briefly stirred Robin's fantasies. Tall, dark, and handsome enough to model for romance novel covers, he'd carried in large items of furniture as easily as if they were toys. It had been disappointing to learn he operated at about the level of a ten-year-old. Though Carter managed simple life tasks like paying the rent and purchasing groceries for himself and his ailing mother, he had few social skills and seemed unable to fathom the world of adults.

They'd become acquainted in the building's uninspired but adequate workout room, where Robin pedaled the stationary bike in an attempt to keep extra pounds from attaching to her thighs and butt. Each morning as she sweated and the bike hummed, Carter lifted large weights and recounted his achievements on various video games, complete with sound effects. Apparently, tossing out an occasional "Wow!" had made her a friend in Carter's mind.

"Robin?" Worry came through in his soft Georgia accent. "Should I open the trunk and let the guy out?"

Now there's a question I never imagined being asked.

"Where are you now?"

"You know the empty grocery store on Twelfth Street by the green church? I parked behind it so nobody can hear the noise he's making." His voice rose. "What should I do, Robin?"

Toweling more vigorously, she replied, "Don't do anything, Carter. I'll be right over."

The outside temperature wasn't too bad for February. After putting on soft jeans and a long-sleeved shirt, Robin added a light jacket and slid her feet into flats rather than her favorite flip-flops. Since her hair was still wet from the shower, she covered it with a hat, and since the heater in her car was almost non-functioning, stuffed gloves into her jacket pockets. After a few irritating moments spent locating her wallet and keys, she was on her way.

Cedar, Georgia, was a city whose fine old bones were fast succumbing to inferior replacements. Buildings that had once held dignified offices now rented to tattoo parlors and vape shops as wealthier tenants moved to multi-story buildings downtown or branches in the suburbs. As she steered her battered CRV through streets too narrow for the traffic they carried, Robin's thoughts jolted, stopped, and swerved like the vehicles around her. She tried to push her bubbling cauldron of worry to the back of her mind and concentrate on driving carefully. It wouldn't do to have a cop notice some minor infraction and follow her to where Carter waited.

If Carter thinks I can help, he obviously doesn't know me very well. Her eyes filled with tears for the third time that day. *I can't even help myself!*

She replayed the conversation with Carter, imagining what she *should* have said instead of what she *had* said.

"Robin can't come to the phone right now. Call someone else."

"I'm in the shower, Carter. Can't hear a thing."

"Robin moved to Seattle to experience Puget Sound and the Cascades."

"You'll have to move to Tibet, because no one here can help you."

"I'm your neighbor, not your keeper, your mother, or your friendly neighborhood 9-1-1 operator. Take your body in the trunk and stuff it—somewhere else."

She couldn't have said any of that. Carter was a nice guy with problems he wasn't equipped to handle. His mother's death a month before had no doubt contributed to whatever he'd done today. If she explained to the man in the trunk about Carter's mental challenges, his shallow understanding of societal norms, and his recent bereavement, she could smooth things over. She was likely to have better luck fixing his mistakes than she ever would with fixing her own.

***

Carter stood next to a vintage Lincoln Continental whose rear end protruded slightly from behind the abandoned grocery store. Even if she hadn't known there were problems afoot, she'd have detected stress in his repeated gestures: mussing his hair and wiping his hands on his shirtfront. Full-blown panic wasn't far away.

As soon as she got out of her car, Robin heard curses coming from the rear of the Lincoln. The voice sounded tired, as if the speaker no longer believed his threats would come to anything.

"Who's in there?" she asked.

His beautiful brown eyes avoided hers, but that wasn't unusual. "Mr. Barney Abrams. He's a Cedar County commissioner."

Great! Why didn't you choose a decorated war vet or a homeless six-year-old?

"You attacked a county commissioner."

He looked at her briefly before his gaze slid to the side again. "I guess."

Staring at the trunk Robin repeated, "Barney Abrams, County Commissioner."

Though she wasn't politically aware, an overly-smiley face plastered on billboards around town before the last election came to mind: HONEST ABRAMS. Despite the epithet, Robin recalled the man being accused of corruption more than once. He'd wriggled out of it each time, claiming the charges stemmed from misunderstandings or personal vendettas. Once when undeniable proof of wrongdoing was offered, he'd blamed it on a mistake and fired some nameless staffer. Her bosses at the law firm sometimes commented on Abrams' "acumen," which she read as "ability to make big profits while not getting arrested."

"Tell me how Mr. Abrams got into the trunk."

Carter rubbed at his chest as if he had some weird kind of rash. "Remember I told you I had to see about a mistake with my mom's property?"

She recalled him saying something about it, but the clanks of lifted and dropped weights had interfered with her hearing. She'd been impressed though, because Carter usually wasn't willing to interact with strangers. The matter must have been important to him.

"You went to take care of a problem and this is how things ended up?"

"I can hear you, young woman." The voice from the Lincoln was scratchy but loud enough to make her scan the area for passers-by. "Explain to your retarded friend that he will never breathe air outside an institution again!"

"Let's move over there." She led Carter to a spot some distance away, where his prisoner couldn't hear. He glanced back at the Lincoln nervously, and she realized he needed time to collect himself. "Wait here." Crossing the street to a gas station, she bought two sodas and hurried back. Ice sloshed in the foam cups as she held them out, allowing Carter his choice. After he chose the Pepsi, Robin sipped at the Sprite. "Tell me about the mistake."

Taking a long pull on the straw, Carter swallowed and began. "Mom, Dad, and me lived out in Westfield my whole life. Dad was a farmer, so we had a lot of property."

A farm family. That explained some of Carter's discomfort in social settings.

"Dad died two years ago. Then Mom got sick, so we moved into town so she'd be close to the hospital for chemo and stuff." He took another drink, which seemed to calm him. "After she died I found out she sold the farm."

"Without telling you."

His eyes went sad. "She used to cry about how I wouldn't have anybody to take care of me. I told her I can do stuff myself, but I guess she didn't believe it."

"She did what she thought was best."

"Except she got cheated."

"You're sure about that?"

Shifting his muscular shoulders, Carter nodded. "At the funeral, one of our old neighbors said our place is gonna be worth a lot of money soon. He hoped Mom didn't sell too cheap."

"Why will it be worth a lot?"

"They're going to build a mall out there, and I guess our farm's the best spot for it."

Robin's gaze shifted briefly to the Lincoln. "Abrams bought your mom's farm?"

"Somebody else did." Carter's dark eyes clouded. "But Mr. Abrams came to our apartment one day back in November, when I wasn't there. He told Mom I'd need money for her funeral and stuff. He said the farm wasn't worth much but he knew a guy who'd take it off her hands."

She pointed at the Lincoln. "This guy got your mom to sell her farm to a different guy?"

"He says he never, but Mom's letter says he did."

"Letter?"

"Mom wrote a bunch of stuff down for when she was gone and I couldn't ask."

Robin pictured Mrs. Halkias, a tiny, slightly querulous woman who'd tapped her forehead one day as she told Robin, "My boy is different. The Lord gave him to us because He knew we'd take good care of him."

Had a couple of local crooks cheated a dying woman and her special son?

She thought about what had happened to her earlier that morning. *It must be open season on people who can't fight back.*

"So you went to ask Abrams about the land deal. How did he end up in your trunk?"

"Not in *my* trunk." Carter's tone implied that would be silly. "The car is *his.*" Robin couldn't think of anything to say to that, but he went on. "The lady at his office said Mr. Abrams wasn't there, but I saw him go in. She was real snotty about it, so I decided to wait outside until he went to lunch and talk to him then. Around noon he came out and headed for the parking ramp. I followed him to his car, and he opened the trunk to put a suitcase in there. When I tried to show him Mom's letter, he grabbed it right out of my hand and tore it up."

For the first time Robin felt empathy for Carter, not just sympathy. "He destroyed a letter your mom wrote to you?"

Carter's gaze stayed just to the left of Robin's. "He started yelling at me, and he hit me on this shoulder." He touched the spot as if the location of the blow was crucial to her understanding. "He poked me with his finger a couple of times. It didn't hurt because he's kind of blobby, but he wouldn't stop, even when I asked him nicely."

He scrubbed a hand through his hair, leaving a curly clump at the crown that made him look like a kindergartner just up from his nap. Though Robin didn't know what his mental capacity actually was, Carter's axons obviously fired in a whole different way from those of most people.

She squeezed his arm, finding steely muscles that contradicted his childlike demeanor and hesitant manner. "We'll tell the police you didn't mean to kidnap the guy." Five minutes after meeting him, a cop would understand Carter had trouble making decisions under pressure.

"He said he'll have me put in jail." Again Carter's eyes met hers briefly. "I wouldn't like being locked up, Robin. I need to go outside sometimes and look at birds and stuff."

"He threatened to have you arrested for asking questions?"

"Yeah. He took out his phone and said he was calling the cops." Carter sniffed, trying to hold his emotions in check. "That's when I got scared and kinda mad, and the next thing I knew, I shoved him and he fell into the trunk, and I—I shut the lid." The words came out in a rush.

"Is he hurt?"

"I don't think so. He started making noise right away, kicking and hollering. I thought somebody might walk by and ask why he was in there."

And well they might. “What did you do?”

“When I shoved him, his phone went flying and his keys fell on the ground. I picked them both up, and then—” He paused before the next admission. “—I got in his car and drove away.”

Changing the crime from simple assault to kidnapping. “Why did you do that?”

Another hair tousle. “I thought if I drove around for a while, he’d calm down and listen to me. Whenever I get nervous, I go for a walk or a drive and it helps a lot.” Carter paused, genuinely unable to see where he’d gone wrong. “But he just keeps getting madder.” A sharp thump from the car trunk verified the statement.

Oh, my Great Aunt Fanny.

“Did he actually call the police?”

“No. He just waved the phone around like he was gonna call them.”

A bluff? If Abrams wanted to scare Carter but didn’t want a cop to hear what he had to say, could she use that against him somehow? She rolled her shoulders in an effort to ease their tension.

“The phone works, even after it dropped on the concrete,” Carter said. “I’ll give it back when he feels better.”

Great idea, neighbor, but it’s hard to say when that will be.

Had Carter actually uncovered a plot between Abrams and a second man to cheat an old lady out of her property? It seemed improbable, but working at a legal firm had opened Robin’s eyes to how heartless—and how devious—people could be when large sums of money were involved. “You said your mom should have gotten more for her land. How bad was it?”

"She sold a hundred acres for ten thousand dollars." His mouth twisted sideways as he added, "Ms. Kane says we got screwed because my mom was a dodo who lived in the past."

Emily Kane lived across the hall from Robin and next door to Carter. Though about the same age, she was the opposite of Carter's mother, sharp-minded where Mrs. Halkias had been vague, and opinionated where the other was self-effacing. Robin wondered how the two women had become acquainted, but infirmity might have created commonality. Mrs. Halkias was weak from cancer, while Ms. Kane thumped around the building with a cane due to a bad hip.

A practical question occurred to her. "Don't car trunks have escape buttons these days?"

The tension in Carter's face cleared. Cars were something he could talk about all day, and he was far more comfortable with facts than feelings. "Since 2001 they have to, but this is a 1996 Lincoln Continental 75th Anniversary Edition. It's got leather seats, voice-activated cell phone, JBL audio system, auto electro-chromatic dimming mirror with compass, and traction control. He updated it with some really cool stuff too. It's got remote access and starting—"

"We don't need the Wikipedia version." Another thud sounded from the Lincoln. "Can he breathe in there?"

Carter pointed at the car's rear end. "He punched out the tail-lights on the way here."

She stared at the trunk as another thump sounded. If Abrams had read internet advice on how to behave when kidnapped, he'd soon start waving his necktie through the opening.

Not funny, Parsons. The man had every right to have Carter arrested. Things she might have suggested two hours earlier, hiring a lawyer or contacting the press to address her neighbor's grievances, weren't possible anymore.

"He said the sale was legal and I should get over it." Carter's brow knit as he struggled to recall Abrams' exact words. "I need to accept the way the world works."

Robin cringed as the phrase she'd heard so often growing up came into play for the second time that day.

The way the world works. Grow up. Face it. There's nothing you can do to change it.

Brushing at her forehead as if to push the words off to one side, she focused on Carter's situation. "Abrams tore up your mother's letter, and then—the rest of it happened."

"Yeah." His hands flew out from his body and back in like frightened birds. "I tried to tell him I'll let him out if he'll be quiet, but he keeps swearing at me." He gave the trunk a chiding glance. "It isn't nice to swear."

As Robin stood debating, Carter dragged the heel of his shoe across the concrete. "I don't want to go to jail, Robin. You're a lawyer, so I thought you'd tell me what to do."

Returning from her own dark thoughts, she corrected his misconception. "I'm not a lawyer, Carter. I work at a law firm." Grimacing, she added, "I did. I got fired this morning."

"How could you get fired?" He scowled at the air. "I bet you were really good at your job."

"Really good isn't enough sometimes."

Wiping a hand on his shirt, he struggled to comprehend. "You helped me with the landlord."

"Her so-called reason for raising your rent after your mom died was a crock. I told her I worked for a law firm and let her draw her own conclusions."

Gesturing toward the Lincoln he asked, “Can you fix this for me like you fixed that?”

If her boss hadn’t given her the ax that morning, she’d be receiving a paycheck right about now. If she’d been busy at work, she wouldn’t have answered Carter’s phone call. Someone else would have dealt with the commissioner in the trunk.

Why me?

She tried to focus. “Did you say he put a suitcase in there?”

“Yeah, and this was on the car seat.” He handed her a paper sleeve that held a boarding pass for the train to Atlanta at 2:34 that afternoon. One plus in a day of minuses: no one at his office was expecting Abrams back after lunch.

“He said he had a busy weekend coming up.” Carter cleared his throat. “He didn’t have time to explain a business deal to a retard.”

Though her anger boiled up again, Robin struggled to remain logical. She couldn’t let herself get so emotional that she did something crazy for a second time in a single day.

She took Carter through the story again, looking for any hint of dishonesty or exaggeration. His account remained the same; in fact, he seemed incapable of changing it either to gain sympathy or to excuse himself. Carter knew the difference between how much his mother had been paid and what the land was worth. Abrams had taken advantage of a sick, dying woman, but he’d underestimated her son’s ability to spot a bad deal. Faced with his crime, Abrams had tried to stonewall Carter. The resulting trouble had engulfed them both.

If he hadn’t overreacted, Carter might have gone to court and claimed his mother wasn’t in her right mind when she signed away her property for a pittance. His halting speech and delayed thought process would have worked against him, but he’d have had a shot. Now he'd committed a crime against a local dignitary and stood little chance of being heard, much less forgiven. She imagined the lawyers at her former firm reading accounts of Carter's arrest for kidnapping and commenting, as they often did, on the need to "lock up the crazies."

Little-boy eyes looked at her from an oh-so-manly frame. "What are we gonna do, Robin?"

A year ago, a month ago, even a day ago, she'd have said something completely different. Now, as she thought about all those who suffered at the hands of small-time grifters and big-time crooks, she replied, "We're going to teach Mr. Abrams a lesson."

Chapter Two

Leaving Carter with instructions to buy a bottled water and stuff it through the damaged tail light, Robin went shopping. A plan had formed in her head—crazy but irresistible.

It was wrong, so wrong. She shouldn't do it—shouldn't even think about it. But Carter was in trouble because he appeared too weak to fight back. *And buddy, do I know what that feels like.*

Entering the first home store she found, Robin thought of the cheaters she'd encountered in her lifetime. First and foremost was her father. She lived with the damage Dear Old Dad had done to her self-confidence every single day.

Next came the drunk who'd killed her mother. Though his license had been pulled years before for multiple violations, he'd been driving under the influence when he ran a stop light and T-boned her car. Six months before that, her brother had been critically injured in a petroleum-based war nobody with an iota of common sense thought the U.S. could win.

How do so many bad things happen to people who don't deserve it and so many good things happen to those who keep getting away with stuff they shouldn't?

If only Carter hadn't asked for her help on the very morning she'd screwed her own life up like an out of control power drill.

She'd been twenty minutes late that morning getting to work. The bosses never arrived until nine, and none of the office staff said anything. By 8:25 she was at her desk, transcribing handwritten notes that looked—and smelled—as if wine had been spilled on them. In several places she had to guess what it said. It was a good bet the job hadn't originally been hers but had been passed down the pecking order to the last hired and the least likely to squawk, due to her aforementioned tendency to arrive late.

Though Robin was cordial to her coworkers, the fact that she was years younger than the others and unmarried meant she was regarded with suspicion, as if she might steal their jobs—or their husbands. Her lack of interest in office gossip didn't endear her to them either.

When Mr. Eldon Green, Esquire, arrived, the chirping of the other women quieted and the atmosphere in the dark wood-paneled offices became sedate. As he passed, Green called to Robin with a terse, "Parsons. Come in." She followed him into his inner sanctum, where even darker wood and deep carpeting created the feeling she was entering a giant coffin.

Dubbed "Grass Green" by the staff to differentiate him from partners "Pea Green" and "O.D. (Olive Drab)," he took off his Burberry and hung it on the wrought-iron tree beside the door. She caught a whiff of the Dior knock-off aftershave he bought from Smelz-Like-It.

Boss, you really need to know: it doesn't.

Robin waited a few steps in, tablet in hand. She'd learned not to get too close, since Green often "accidentally" bumped her chest with a hand or arm. He always apologized, but insincerity was evident in his eyes. She always accepted, hiding the disgust in hers.

Taking off his suit coat, Green hung it over the back of the chair, adjusting it so it wouldn't get wrinkled. That done, he pulled out his leather chair and sat down, wriggling his large posterior until he found the most comfortable spot. Though she couldn't help thinking he looked like a toad in a Brooks Brothers shirt, Robin kept her expression neutral and her eyes alert.

"Ms. Parsons," he said without asking her to sit. "I won't keep you in suspense. We're letting you go."

She stood there with what was no doubt a stupid look on her face, temporarily unable to fathom the meaning behind the words. There'd been no hint of impending layoffs, no dissatisfaction expressed with her job performance.

"Mr. Green, if this is about the times I've been late, my car is—"

A shake of his head stopped her. "It's nothing like that."

"I'm signed up for more classes next term. If I made mistakes—"

This time he raised a hand, his expression faintly irritated.

Robin stopped talking. It was one of her weaknesses: a tendency to explain too much and take blame onto herself that didn't belong there. She struggled to find an argument that would let her keep her job.

Don't they know my car's about to fall to pieces and my rent is three days late?

Folding his always-damp hands on the smooth desktop, Grass said in what she thought of his smarmy voice, "We're sorry to lose you, of course. It's this awful economy." He attempted a sympathetic expression, and she was reminded of times she'd watched him lie to clients about how terrible he felt about problems he had no intention of addressing. "Of course we'll provide you with excellent references. A talented worker like you will soon find something else."

Are you going to pay my credit card bills till then? She tried to recall how much money she had in her bank account. Six, seven hundred dollars, maybe.

Surprise began turning to anger. She'd sacrificed for this job, studying at night and working all day. Her social life had sunk to the level of a Benedictine nun's. She'd told herself it would lead to future advancement. It wasn't just the amount of work she'd done that fueled her outrage either. She'd lost tiny bits of self-respect every day as she dealt with clients and her bosses, all of whom lived for money and gloated about how cleverly they went about getting more of it.

Still, she needed both the references Green mentioned and the pay she'd earn in the two weeks they were required to give her before a layoff. Digging her nails into her palms until it hurt, she stared at the bland wall over her boss' shoulder and managed to say almost nothing in response to his insincere comments.

Don't think about it right now. Think about pillows and rocky road ice cream.

When Green finally dismissed Robin, her legs didn't want to work. Her chest muscles seemed intent on squeezing the air out of her lungs. Only a month ago she'd finished paying off her mother's debts and the funeral expenses that had kept her at starvation level for the last year and a half. Now, when the light at the end of her particular tunnel had begun shining ever so dimly, Green, Green & Green had stepped in to unscrew the bulb.

Forcing herself to walk slowly and keep her head up, she made it to the bathroom before tears overcame her. Locking herself in, she tried not to sob too loudly. Were the others aware of what had happened? Were they sorry or glad to see her go? Either way, she fell back on the only worthwhile lesson she'd ever learned from her father: *Don't let the hurt show.*

Once she recovered, Robin returned to her desk and went through the motions of her job, filing, typing, and texting, almost unaware of what she was doing. Her mind buzzed with questions that had no answers. At 11:00, when the lawyers retreated to O.D.'s office, one of the women hurried over to speak to her. Eileen was the friendliest of the staff at Three G's, not because she was a nice person, but because she loved to spread gossip. Squatting beside Robin's desk she said breathlessly. "It sucks what they're doing to you."

"What do you mean?"

"You got laid off, right?" She glanced around to make sure no one else was listening. "O.D.'s golfing buddy came in last week, and I happened to overhear their conversation. His daughter just got an associate degree from some business school, and he asked them to find a spot for her." Eileen raised drawn-on brows. "Apparently the girl needs experience."

"Experience?"

Eileen deepened her voice in a parody of a father's tone. "'Her mother and I want Daphne to go on with school, but she says she's tired of studying. It's time the girl learned about the world of work.'" She glanced around the office as if imagining the future. "His baby girl probably never had a real job in her life. The rest of us will have to pick up the slack."

"They'd do that?" she asked. "Replace me with some girl they don't even know?"

Pushing long bangs out of her eyes Eileen replied, "The other Greens weren't thrilled, but when I saw the look on your face this morning, I figured they did it." She leaned in close, and Robin smelled Scope. "Did he bring up all the days you've been late?"

"No. It was pretty much 'Here it is. Deal with it.'"

Eileen shook her head, causing her bangs to slide back over her eyes. "You're a good worker. It's just that if you questioned the layoff, they could say you're late a lot."

"Is that why they picked me to boot out?"

"Well, sometimes you're not very respectful when you talk about clients."

"Only the ones who are scumbags."

The bangs fell back down and Eileen brushed at them again. "It isn't our job to judge them."

"I can't help it. I hate dishonest people."

"I get that, but the bosses decide who we deal with, not us."

Robin blinked away fresh tears. "Why'd they pick me?"

Eileen was only too happy to tell. "I happened to hear O.D. say that an attractive woman like you can always find a husband with a good job. Then you wouldn't need to work."

"Prince Charming rescues Cinderella?"

"It didn't work for me," she said ruefully. "But men like the Greens still think that way."

When Eileen retreated to her desk, thrilled to have delivered devastating news, Robin sat stunned. "I'll fight them," she muttered, but it was an empty threat. The Greens were lawyers, after all, and it wasn't like there was a union supporting the rights of mistreated office workers.

Nobody was going to listen to her complaints. Nobody was going to save her job.

I have no power, so I lose.

Warmth spread through her chest, up her neck, and into her cheeks. As anger surged through her like a tide, she dropped her pen, rose from her desk, and headed for O.D. Green's office. Without knocking, she threw open the door so hard it banged against a filing cabinet. The three men looked up from restaurant flyers they'd been deliberating over.

"You're laying me off so you can hire someone else." Robin fought to keep her voice under control, but it shook with rage. "That's not fair."

"Miss Parsons—" Pea began, but she paid no attention.

"I've worked hard for you people, and this is what I get? You're disgusting!"

If Grass resembled a toad, Pea was a slightly confused owl who molted his way around the office, leaving dandruff and dry skin cells everywhere. "Miss Parsons, please calm down."

"Nobody should be treated this way!"

O.D. Green (who, to continue the animal analogy, reminded Robin of a boar) spoke in a growl, his eyes hard and his lips tight. "Young woman, this business belongs to us, and we'll run it as we see fit. I advise you to grow up and accept the way the world works."

"You make me sick!" She was yelling now, loudly enough that the whole office would hear. Stalking away she stopped at her desk, snatched up the few things she wanted, and turned her back on the Green Law Firm forever, ignoring the surprised looks on her coworkers' faces. She meant to slam the door as she left, but the hydraulic closure prevented it. Instead of a bold punctuation mark, she heard only an unconvincing hiss of air behind her.

Hurrying to the car with her Minnie Mouse stapler and her essential oils diffuser, Robin had consoled herself by imagining the good old boys at 3 G's learning on Monday morning that no one else in the office knew how to make coffee in the new brew pot or change the toner in the copy machine. And Grass would have to hope the new girl wouldn't mind if he "accidentally" brushed her breasts or touched her butt.

Which doesn't change the fact that you're broke and out of—

"Excuse me?" The voice, coming from only a few steps away, startled her so much she jumped and had to grab her purse to keep from dropping it.

A man in an orange apron regarded her with a concerned expression, and she realized she'd been muttering under her breath.

"Can I help you find something?"

She took a deep breath. There wasn't much she could do to fix her own situation. But she had an idea how she might fix Carter's.

"Yes, you can," she replied. "Where can I find the duct tape?"

Chapter Three

Robin planned to take Barney Abrams somewhere private and present him with evidence of his wrongdoing. Face to face with the victim of his scheme, he'd see how unfair his action had been. Once he admitted guilt, they'd demand he make amends. Carter would receive what was owed to him. Abrams would keep quiet about being locked in the trunk in exchange for their silence about his cheating a cancer patient in her last days of life.

There were two problems: first she had to find a setting where Abrams couldn't shout for help or run away from them. That part she had figured out. She'd use the storage unit a few miles out of town where she kept her mom's things. Mom had been a pack rat, and it had taken months to decide what to keep, what to sell, and what to donate to charity. The unit was mostly empty, but it was still hers.

The second problem was hiding her identity. Abrams knew who his kidnapper was; that couldn't be helped. But if she remained anonymous, she'd be in a better position to protect Carter if things went wrong.

Robin bought four clamp-on trouble lights and a roll of duct tape. As she was about to check out, she recalled that her storage unit had no electricity to power the lights. Heading down another aisle, she bought the smallest portable generator they had in stock. Though it was expensive, she figured she'd return it tomorrow and say she'd found a better one.

As she loaded her purchases in the trunk of the Honda, she noticed a toy store a few buildings down. That gave her an idea, and after a short search down a novelty aisle filled with things that lit up or twirled around or made strange noises, she found exactly what she wanted.

A half hour later, she pulled in at the Ur-Place Storage Lot. Four rows of identical buildings stood out like an island archipelago in a sea of red Georgia soil. An acquaintance had told her the distinctive soil in the Piedmont area was composed of iron, aluminum, and silica, was very old, and had been subjected to intense weathering for a long time. "It just looks odd to me," she'd replied. "In Indiana we have dirt-colored dirt."

The lot had no visible surveillance equipment, which she guessed meant there was none. Nor was there a person who monitored the comings and goings of renters. Though the facility was surrounded by cyclone fencing eight feet high, there was no barrier at the top to prevent people climbing over it. Ur-Place was not a particularly secure property. Today that was exactly what Robin wanted.

Mission Impossible—or at best, Mission Improbable.

Robin's unit was in the row farthest from the road, #121. Opening the roll-up door all the way, she moved the few things still inside to the back corners, except for her mother's cheapie plastic lawn chair. She had plans for that. Calling Carter, she gave him directions to the lot. While she waited, she duct-taped the four trouble lights to the door frame, making sure they didn't interfere with the door's operation.

Fifteen minutes later Carter arrived in Abrams' car. Directing him to pull the car inside the unit, she closed the door, shutting out the daylight. Setting the lawn chair near the trunk of the car, she focused the lights on it. In whispered tones, she told Carter what they were going to do and switched the lights on one by one. As they hummed to life, the rest of the 10x20 space became so dark she couldn't see Carter's face. That was good. She didn't want to know if he approved of her plan or thought she'd completely lost her mind.

When all was ready, Carter pressed the button on Abrams'

key chain that opened the trunk. Robin's hands shook as she set the voice-changing device she'd bought against her neck. Planning this had been one thing; actually doing it was much scarier. She wondered if it was too late to back out, but of course it was. She had to do it—she *wanted* to do it. They were striking a blow for anyone ever mistreated by crooks and charlatans.

A few seconds after the trunk clicked open, a wilted Commissioner Abrams sat up. Short on shoulders but amply supplied in the waistline, he looked like a garden gnome peering over the edge. His expression was unpleasant, but she couldn't fault him for that. Three hours in a car trunk would make anyone testy.

When no one said anything, Abrams slowly put one foot onto the floor of the unit, then the other. Grasping the car's frame while his legs got used to holding him upright again, he squinted into the bright lights. When he spoke, his voice was raspy from shouting. "You are going to be sorry for this, Halkias."

Robin called up the anger that had brought her this far. She couldn't let Carter down. She couldn't let this guy off the hook. Taking a deep breath, she let it all out, something her speech teacher had claimed calmed tonal tremors. Her voice came out low and growly. "He's the least of your concerns right now."

Abrams turned toward her with a glowering scowl, and she noted signs of dissolution: puffiness along the cheekbones, broken blood vessels on the nose, and red-rimmed eyes. *They must use a lot of makeup when they film those* VOTE FOR HONEST ABRAMS *ads.*

"Sit down in the chair, please."

He looked at it briefly before returning his glare in her general direction. "No."

The refusal surprised her. If she'd been kidnapped, held in a trunk for hours, then ordered to sit, she'd have done it.

"Who are you?" Abrams demanded.

She forced a commanding tone. "Sit down."

He thought about it for a moment then, with exaggerated slowness that signaled disdain, moved to the chair. Testing the seat, then the arms, he pulled it across the floor a few inches as if choosing the most comfortable spot. The scrape both irritated and discomfited Robin, which was no doubt what he intended. Turning toward her with a smirk, Abrams sat. "Happy now?"

"Satisfied," she responded.

"What's this about?"

"It's about a county commissioner who cheated an old woman out of her land."

Abrams made a tent of his hands and rested his chin on it. "Which commissioner would that be?"

"You."

He waved a hand. "I assume you can prove this allegation? An old, sick woman with a morphine pump says I came to her home to personally persuade her to sell her run-down farm?" He waggled a hand to indicate instability. "Poor thing probably thought she spoke to the President in her final days too."

Then how did you know she had a morphine pump? She chose not to argue that point. "You took her land and paid her almost nothing for it."

"Did I?" His round face creased in a smile he no doubt practiced before a mirror. "You won't find my name on any paperwork associated with that particular transaction."

Of course he hid his involvement in the deal. I should have done some research.

Robin was starting to doubt her plan, but she tried to regroup. “We know you’re behind it, no matter whose name is on the deed. Mrs. Halkias recognized you from the news.”

Abrams shrugged. “Everybody in Cedar County recognizes me from the news. That doesn’t mean I visited some crummy apartment to offer a real estate deal to a drugged-out old woman.” Perhaps sensing that came out too harsh, he softened his tone. “The lady was mistaken, but she’s no longer with us, so we can’t explain it to her, can we?” His sigh was unconvincing. “I guess we’ll never know who talked her into selling.”

In the scenario Robin had imagined, they’d accuse Abrams to his face and he’d admit to his crime, maybe even show remorse. It wasn’t working out that way. Behind her Carter’s feet shifted nervously, and she almost turned to snap at him to keep still.

How do the cops on TV make it look so easy to get someone to confess?

Sensing his advantage, Abrams went on the offensive. “Who are you, anyway?” His glance went to the floor, and Robin looked down to see that her shoes were lit in the glow of the lights. “Well, what do you know? The retard’s got a girlfriend.”

She tried to keep her voice calm. “We’re a group of citizens that has had it with crooks like you.”

Abrams’ piggy eyes squinted even more. “Tell you what. Why don’t we go to the police? You can tell them how a perfectly legal land sale was made to someone who isn’t me, and I’ll tell them how your special friend assaulted and kidnapped a county official with your assistance.”

At his mocking tone, the heat rose again in Robin’s neck. He was supposed to admit what he’d done, but instead he was almost amused. If he won the debate, she and Carter had put their futures at risk for nothing.

It isn't a debate, her mind whispered. *You're no longer playing by his rules.*

Standing straighter, Robin firmed her voice. "We're not presenting evidence in court, Dirt-bag. We want justice, and we're going to get it."

Something in her changed demeanor caused Abrams to lick his lips. "What does that mean?"

"You're going to explain exactly how you cheated Mrs. Halkias."

After a moment he went back on the offensive. "I don't think so."

If it had been a Bruce Willis movie, they'd have come to the part where the stressed-to-the-max good guy beat a confession out of the rotten-to-the-core bad guy. There was no way Robin could do that, physically or emotionally, nor could she order Carter to.

But you can convince Abrams you're capable of it. "Do as we say and we let you go. Say no and you die."

The man's lip rose in a sneer. "You're a couple of amateurs who've made the biggest mistake of your lives. You're nuts, but I don't think you're capable of murder."

"Listen—"

"No, you listen!" Abrams stamped a foot, and the chair back clanged against the bumper of the car. "I'm an elected official of this county, not some punk you can scare with lights and a creepy voice. I intend to see that Halkias spends the rest of his life in an institution for retards with violent tendencies." He stared into the darkness, and it felt as if he could see Robin there simply because he wanted to. "You'll get a long stretch of jail time too, Missy. That's how the real world works."

The real world is exactly why we're here.

Again Carter moved nervously in the shadows, but Robin made a calming gesture. Abrams' comment had reminded her how men like him operated, cowing others with their willingness to lie to get what they wanted.

"You're going to tell us the truth about the land deal. Then you'll pay a fine for what you've done."

"Fine?" He sounded genuinely confused.

"To ensure that we don't expose your crimes to the public."

Abrams made a dismissive gesture. "Your so-called proof is the ravings of a terminally ill old woman. I, on the other hand, can prove I was kidnapped and held against my will."

Her stomach churned. With a crook's sense of crookedness, he'd concluded they wouldn't follow through on the threat she'd made.

Robin chewed on her thumbnail, trying to see a way forward. Should they give up and let Abrams go? Should they call the police and hope someone would at least investigate the land deal? If they were lucky enough to get that far, would the investigation turn up evidence to support Carter's story? Even if it did, would kidnapping a prominent citizen be excused? Did one crime justify another?

She shook her head, impatient with her own doubts. The man was scum, but that didn't mean a thing if she couldn't make him admit it. *If only I believed in waterboarding!*

That brought to mind something she'd once read in a novel, a trick that made an innocent act seem like torture. Could she trick Abrams into doing as she demanded?

Squaring her shoulders, Robin wiped her soggy thumbnail on the back of her jeans. "Hold Mr. Abrams' head still and cover his eyes," she said to Carter. "Let's show him we mean business."

After a moment's hesitation, Carter stepped toward the chair. Taking off the knit hat he wore, he pulled it over Abrams' eyes then took hold of the man's head, one hand under his chin and the other on the top. Once Abrams was immobilized, Robin located the duct tape she'd used to secure the lights and tore off several strips. As the tape coming off the roll made its unmistakable sound Abrams stiffened, but Carter held him tightly while she taped his arms to the chair.

When she finished Robin glanced at Carter, who seemed concerned. *Me too, dude. Me too.*

Returning to where she'd set her drink, Robin fished out the only remaining chunk of ice. "You will talk, Mr. Abrams," she said, making her mechanical voice slow and ominous. "Here's a taste of what's in store." Though her stomach heaved in objection, she set the ice against the skin of Barney Abrams' plump neck.

His body tensed as he tried to pull away from what felt like cold steel. "Hey, don't do this! Don't!"

"Are you ready to tell us how you got Mrs. Halkias to sell her farm?"

In a last bit of resistance, Abrams hesitated. Pressing her lips under her teeth, Robin drew the ice a couple of inches along his skin. On contact with his warm body the ice melted, creating the feeling he was bleeding.

Abrams screamed in perceived pain. "All right, all right—I'll tell!"

Robin backed away, aghast, but her other half asked: *Which is worse—scaring a creep or lying to terminally ill old ladies?*

She felt like a creep herself, but Abrams' arrogant confidence had deserted him. Carter surprised her by displaying a grin and an awkward thumbs up.

It's role-playing for him, like his games. She took a deep breath to relax her shoulders. *That's how I need to look at it. We aren't hurting the guy, even if he doesn't know that.*

Abrams panted, "You cut me!"

"I warned you. We're not joking, and we're not all that patient, either." Robin hoped one scare was enough, because she wasn't sure she could repeat the move without throwing up. Besides, the piece of ice was rapidly turning to water in her hand.

"What do you want to know?"

Pressing the *record* button on her phone she said, "Tell us how you got Mrs. Halkias to sell her property and how you benefited."

When Abrams said nothing she hesitated, unwilling to repeat the terrible thing she'd done. Her father's favorite saying came to mind: *In for a penny, in for a pound.*

She laid the ice against his cheek. "Spit it out."

He slumped in the chair like a deflated balloon. "Because of my work on the county board, I sometimes hear about future events before they're general knowledge."

"Like the mall they're going to build in Westfield."

"Yes. My cousin Donnie buys the land and we split the profits."

"Your part was to convince Mrs. Halkias to sell."

Again he hesitated, and Robin set the last bit of the "knife" at his Adam's apple, near the jugular vein. She'd just have to throw up later.

"Old people worry about medical bills," Abrams said in a rush. "She had no idea what her land was worth. I looked up what her father paid for it in 1965 and doubled it."

No doubt he'd also played on Mrs. Halkias' fear that her son couldn't handle the responsibility of owning a farm. Robin didn't want Carter to hear that part. Drying her hand on her jeans, she ended the recording. "Okay. That was step one."

Carter released Abrams' head and at a nod from Robin, cut the tape that held his arms. Putting a hand to his damp neck, Abrams frowned. "What the—?"

She ignored his confusion. "Now that you've confessed, you're going to pay us to keep it quiet."

"What?"

"We all know Mr. Halkias deserves more than the ten thousand dollars you paid his mother."

He squinted into the lights. "How much are we talking?"

Again Robin wished she'd had time to research the amount, but she chose a low-end figure, hoping Abrams would absorb it and keep quiet rather than going to the cops and taking the chance his misdeeds might come to light. "Fifty thousand dollars."

Abrams' expression went from disbelief to relief. "Fifty thousand?" The word *only* was clearly implied.

Too late to raise the amount. "Now."

Abrams' smirk was back in place. "I need to make a phone call."

"Here." She tossed him his phone and watched as he pressed a few buttons. "I need fifty thousand in cash. Put it in a bag and bring it to—" He put the phone to his chest. "Where?"

"Leave it in the bushes at the west gate of Veterans' Park, near the sign about picking up after your dog." With a little more confidence she added, "Within the next hour."

Abrams nodded, repeating the order into the phone. "Move your ass." Ending the call, he ran his tongue over his teeth. "Shouldn't take long."

In seventeen minutes less than the allotted hour, his phone rang. "Put it on speaker," Robin ordered.

With a grimace of irritation, he complied. "Abrams."

"It's done, Mr. Abrams," a young woman said. "Is everything okay?"

"Yeah. I'll see you Monday." He set the phone in Carter's outstretched hand. "Go get your money."

"Thank you." *That didn't sound very tough.* "Now here's the last of our demands. You will not tell anyone about this—ever. You won't mention Mr. Halkias to anyone, and you'll hide where the 50K went."

Abrams shrugged. "My people know better than to ask. And Halkias?" He leaned in Carter's general direction. "If I ever lay eyes on you again, you're going to wish I didn't."

Swallowing the fear that clawed at her chest, Robin said with as much confidence as she could muster. "If anything happens to him, recordings of the confession go to the state police and the media."

Abrams touched his neck where the cut should have been. "Tricky, aren't you?"

"Get back in the trunk." When he seemed about to object, she barked, "Do it!"

Muttering under his breath, Abrams obeyed, his short legs

making it an almost comical effort. Robin stood in the shadows while Carter stepped forward and closed the lid. She should have worn a ski mask, she thought, but at best Abrams got an impression of height and body shape. He couldn't identify her.

She was surprised when she opened the unit door and realized it was still daytime. The sky wasn't exactly sunny, but it was much brighter than her mood. She had the distinct impression it should be four o'clock in the morning instead of four in the afternoon.

Before leaving she warned Carter, "Don't say a word to him, and stay inside the unit so nobody sees you." Carter nodded, his expression serious. As she drove toward the park, Robin wondered how he was taking all this. He'd seemed at various moments scared, confused, fascinated, and even pleased. Did he comprehend what they'd done? It occurred to her that while she was gone, Abrams might try to trick Carter into revealing their location or her name. She pressed a little harder on the gas pedal.

By the time she reached the park, the anger that had carried her through had dissipated. She was weak and shaky; in fact it felt as if someone had strung an electrical wire up one of her arms, through her chest, and down the other. Breathing in through her nose and out through her mouth, Robin calmed her overstressed nerves. First she scouted the area, doing warm-up stretches as if she were going for a run. Nothing unusual. In fact, she saw only two teenagers so wrapped up in each other—literally and figuratively—that she could have been wearing a bomb strapped to her chest and they wouldn't have noticed.

Once she was fairly sure there were no cops hiding in the azalea bushes, she jogged along the path that circled the park's exterior. The first time she passed the spot where the money should be, she didn't slow her pace, though her gaze darted everywhere. Making a complete circle, she stopped to retie her shoes and check again. There was no one. She made one more circuit, feeling better as fresh air and movement calmed her nerves and loosened her tense muscles. The last time around she paused near the spot, leaning against a tree trunk and stretching her calves. Again she scanned for trouble. The park was deserted. Four-thirty was early for after-work runners and late for moms with kids. On the final circuit, she reached into the clump of greenery behind a sign that said *CLEAN UP AFTER YOUR PET*, pulled out a black gym bag, and sprinted for her car.

The calm she'd almost achieved from running turned quickly back to fear with the presence of fifty thousand ill-gotten dollars in her back seat. Her heart pumped overtime all the way back to the storage unit, and she was once again a mess. Under the fear, however, was a tiny gleam of exhilaration. She and Carter had made a crook pay. They'd pulled it off.

Almost, she reminded herself. *We still have to give the guy his life back.*

They waited until dusk, ignoring Abrams' intermittent demands that he be released. When they were sure the parking garage at the county building would be largely deserted, Carter drove Abrams' car to the top level and backed it into a stall. Robin followed in her car, waiting on the exit ramp one level down. As she'd instructed, Carter walked as far away from the Lincoln as the remote signal would reach and clicked the trunk button. The chirp resonated along the concrete walls, and a metallic clunk followed as the lid lifted. Carter tossed the keys toward the car. Before the sound of metal skittering across the concrete had dissipated, he was sprinting around the corner. Hurrying to Robin's CRV he climbed in, and they were out of sight seconds after Abrams realized he was a free man.

On the bottom level, Robin let Carter out near the ancient Pontiac he'd left there hours before and led the way back to their apartment building. Parking in her usual space, she turned off the engine and let out a long breath. It was over. They'd gotten away with it.

Or had they? What have you done?

Numbly she climbed out of her car and started for the door, swaying a little as she went. Carter stood on the sidewalk with his back to her, looking up at the plain brick building as if he'd never seen it before. His posture was as upright as always, and his hands hung limp at his sides. Was he thinking that the person he'd called for help had made everything a hundred times worse? That he'd have to leave Cedar now, since she'd added extortion to his original crime. Robin felt as if a damp blanket had dropped over her head, and it was suddenly hard to pull in air. Two people who'd led blameless lives until today had used violence—at least the threat of it—to get money from someone who, though a criminal, was now a victim as well. Carter was no doubt regretting it, as she was.

When he turned toward her, however, he was grinning like a little kid. "That was so cool!"

"Carter—"

"You were awesome, Robin." He gestured at the bag. "He cheated my mom, but you fixed him."

"I fixed him, all right." That was when the world went funny. She felt herself falling. Then she felt nothing.

She came to in Carter's arms. He held her clumsily, squashing her face into his shoulder as he made measured grunts of exertion. The sensation of climbing told her he was carrying her up the stairs.

"Carter?"

"You fainted, I guess." He stopped and relaxed his arms enough that she could look up at him. "I thought I'd better get you home before anybody saw you."

"That was good thinking. You can put me down now."

He stopped on the landing and set her on her feet, holding his hands on either side of her in case she wasn't able to stand. "Are you okay?"

"I think so. It's a delayed reaction to stress. I never know when it's going to hit."

"When we get upstairs, you can rest for a while."

"Yes." Still woozy, Robin literally pulled herself up the last flight of stairs. On the third floor she opened her apartment door with hands that shook so hard the keys sounded like wind chimes. "Come in."

He followed her inside, glancing around. "You have a really nice home," he said, using the good manners he'd obviously been taught.

"I'm glad you like it," she replied, "because you're going to have to stay here."

He turned, his eyes wide. "Why?"

Groping her way to a chair, Robin leaned her weight on the arm and settled her rear on the seat like an old, old woman. Supported by its strength, she counted her fears on her fingers. "Abrams has probably called the police by now. They'll check the surveillance cameras in the parking garage. The money could be marked. People might have seen you or me or both of us acting suspicious. Abrams knows your name and what you look like. You can't go anywhere the police can find you, especially not home."

We're dead meat.

Carter surprised her with convincing counterarguments, stuttering only a little as he spoke. "Mr. Abrams isn't g-going to call the police, because you recorded him confessing what he did to Mom. If the police don't know what happened, there's no reason they'd look at surveillance tapes. And he didn't tell anybody to mark the money. We heard him." He frowned briefly. "He acted like fifty thousand was nothing, didn't he?"

Humiliation laid a shadow over her worry. She'd taken a huge chance, ruining Carter's life and possibly her own, for an amount that seemed like a joke to the commissioner. Carter was owed a lot more than she'd figured.

Still, he'll have money to start over somewhere else.

"Abrams will say he thought we'd kill him unless he said what we wanted to hear," she told Carter. "Even if he doesn't go to the police, he could hire someone to find you."

Carter's eyes widened. "You mean like a hit man?"

She didn't really know what Abrams was capable of, but she didn't want Carter to panic. "If anyone comes here looking for you, I'll say I don't know you that well, which is kind of true."

She expected further discussion, but Carter merely looked around. "I don't see any video games. Are they in a closet, or should I go get some of mine?"

***

Barney Abrams was still in a foul mood on Monday when he came down to breakfast. After the two morons released him Friday night, he'd sat in the empty parking garage for almost an hour, chewing on his problem. In the end, he decided to continue with his weekend plans rather than explain why he hadn't. He caught a later train to Atlanta and spent two days and nights at a conference that was little more than an excuse to eat too much, drink too much, and sleep too little. It wasn't enjoyable, since he stewed about what had happened to him the whole time. Friends made joshing remarks about his distracted manner, but he couldn't forget the dark space of his car trunk, the smell of the spare tire at his back, and the boldness of the amateur terrorists who'd tricked him, humiliated him, and taken his money.

As he faced a return to the parking ramp where he'd been attacked and abased, Abrams found his anger almost choked him. He forced himself to down the eight crisply-fried links, half-plate of hash browns, and four fluffy eggs his wife set before him. It wouldn't be good to have the Dragon start asking how much alcohol he'd consumed while he was away.

The pair who'd waylaid him—despite their claim of being a group, he doubted there were more than two—had caught him off guard, which was how they got the better of him. Now they had a record of him admitting impropriety. If it ever became public, he'd claim the confession was obtained under duress, but it was damning, nonetheless. Detail made the story ring true, and the cops could easily find more examples of land parcels his cousin had bought cheap due to Abrams' knowledge of county business. The old guy in the nursing home who'd been thrilled when a local luminary stopped in to say hello. A landowner desperate for cash who'd been assured Abrams was looking out for his interests. Most of Barney's victims didn't even realize they'd been cheated. But if Halkias released the recording, the purpose of the commissioner's caring visits to select constituents would become clear. He'd lose his seat for sure, and possibly his freedom as well.

Who'd have thought the retard had the ability to cook up a plan and carry it out? Maybe the girl was the brains behind it, but between the two of them, they'd put old Barney in a spot. He'd have to curb his financial shenanigans for a while, though there were more pickings out in Westfield he'd had his eye on. In a sudden burst of anger, Abrams threw his cup across the room, splashing coffee onto the wall and the draperies beside it.

"What happened?" his wife called from the kitchen.

"A little accident," he replied. "I'll take care of it."

She leaned into the doorway, a concerned frown on her plain face. “Did everything go okay in Atlanta?”

“Yeah, fine.”

“You didn’t drink too much, did you? It messes with your metabolism and you get all out of whack.”

“No, we were too busy working to do much drinking.”

“That’s my Barney. Always wheeling and dealing.”

“It’s what they pay me for.”

“Good for you, hon.” She disappeared again, and the slosh of dishwater in the sink sent his level of irritation even higher. *I buy a house with a perfectly good dishwasher. I hire a woman to come in and clean. She does her own dishes, by hand, like it’s still the 1950s.*

Drops of coffee dribbled out of the remains of the broken cup and onto the rug. *If Halkias shares what he knows, everything I’ve got could drip away, just like that. What am I going to do?*

His mind answered the question almost as soon as he formed it. *Find them. Stop them.*

No one could know why he was looking for Halkias, but once he located him and the girl, he’d find a way to silence them. Then things would get back to normal.

Happy with his plan, Abrams’ mood improved. He even hummed a little tune as he picked up the pieces of the broken cup and tossed them into the garbage.

Chapter Four

On Monday Robin was still a nervous wreck. She'd spent most of Saturday and Sunday at the large window in her small living room. She watched the sun rise over the buildings opposite, turn the parking lot below them to brilliant white, and retreat until street lights made circles in the darkness of night. No one came to arrest them.

That didn't make her feel safe. Carter was guilty of kidnapping. She'd aided and abetted him, adding to the seriousness of the original crime. They were in possession of fifty thousand dollars that wasn't theirs, no matter how moral their actions had been.

Still, it felt kind of good too. Robin Marie Parsons had struck a blow against corruption. She'd made a greedy, conniving businessman pay—not enough, apparently, but something.

What should she do next? The money was still in the black bag, stuffed at the back of her bedroom closet between her winter boots and her vanilla-scented sachet from Mexico. They hadn't even counted it, though Carter had checked the stacks to make sure they were real. "Hundreds," he reported. "We should have asked for fifties and twenties."

She almost laughed out loud. *That was the least of what we should have done.*

Every possibility she considered created new fears. Robin herself was fairly safe, since no one knew she was involved, but she felt responsible for Carter. He'd started the mess, but she'd dragged him farther in.

She might open negotiations with the police on his behalf. He hadn't meant any harm to Abrams, and they'd probably take his mental difficulties into consideration.

And lock him up as a violent mental defective, if Abrams has any say in the matter.

Could she take the blame onto herself and go on the run? Her career was in ruins anyway. She could start over somewhere new, and Carter could have his life back.

But Abrams knows Carter was there. He'll insist Carter is punished, no matter what I say.

Robin wished she had someone to talk to about it. It would have to be someone who knew what they were faced with. Someone who knew the law.

That was it! She needed to find a lawyer and pay him a retainer. Once hired, he'd have to provide advice but couldn't turn her in to the cops.

While Carter played *Mines under Therla* (which she'd gotten by sneaking into his apartment at three a.m.), Robin went through a mental list of the lawyers she'd met since moving to Cedar. The Greens were out, since they were jerks, mostly concerned with corporate law, and mad at her.

A man had come to the office once, a criminal lawyer who worked mostly for poor people. She'd pegged him as an old hippie, the kind who never trusted anyone over thirty until one day he woke up and realized he was twice that. He hadn't looked particularly impressive, but from the grumbling the G's did after he left, he'd managed to best them somehow.

What was his name?

Taking up her phone, she typed in *LAWYERS, CEDAR GA*. She got a long list, and after scrolling for some time, stopped at a name: *R. BUTLER MINK*. How could she have forgotten a name like that?

***

Butler Mink had an office downtown, up a flight of stairs and over a bakery. The odor of freshly-baked bread from below must have made it hard not to gain weight. Robin climbed the narrow steps to find a half-dozen people seated on battered folding chairs in the reception area. Beyond them the lawyer stood beside a metal desk in a closet-sized room with the door open. He had risen to escort a tough-looking young man out, and when he saw Robin in the entry, he waved her in, closing the door on the scowls she got for moving to the front of the line.

"I don't get many appointments," Mink said, waving at a slightly crooked wooden chair opposite his desk. "Mostly people just show up."

The office smelled of perspiration and desperation, as if those who'd occupied the chair before her left the scent of their fear behind. Mink was friendly and reassuring, and she imagined him calming nervous parents and worried wives with his knowledge of the system and concern for their welfare. Though he was much as she remembered him, Mink seemed more at home here than he had at the Greens' office. He wore corduroy jeans with a Falcons jersey, but on a hook near the door was a tweed jacket, a rather beat-up white shirt, and a plain black necktie. His hair was buzzed to an easy-to-keep half-inch on top, but a thin braid about a foot long ran down his back. His graying beard was trimmed short, and half-glasses sat almost at the end of his nose. Taking them off, he tossed them on the desk. "Have we met before?"

"A year or so back. I used to work for the Greens."

One eyebrow rose. "Used to?"

"I got pushed out so they could move someone else in." The confession and the bitterness in her voice surprised her. She hadn't even told her brother yet about losing her job.

Mink touched a yellow legal pad near his right hand. "You want to sue them?"

"No. It's something else." Now that she'd come, Robin didn't know how to begin. Mink waited, a look of polite interest on his uneven features. She guessed plenty of people had trouble getting started, probably because they knew they were guilty.

Just like I am.

"I want to hire you." Opening her purse, she took out ten one-hundred dollar bills she'd taken from Barney Abrams' bag. "Here's a retainer."

He glanced at the money and returned his gaze to her face, studying her for a moment. With an abrupt motion he slid open the center desk drawer, causing a metallic grate, rummaged in it until he found what he wanted, and slapped a receipt book on the table. He picked up the glasses and put them back on, squinting despite their helpful power. Scribbling an entry, he tore the white copy out of the book and handed it to her. "There. I'm officially your lawyer. Now you can say anything, and unless you're planning a future crime, I can't tell a soul."

"I have no plans for crime in the future, but I need to tell you about the crime I did commit."

She told the story she'd concocted, a blend of truth and fiction. A friend had been cheated. She'd found out who cheated him and got revenge by waylaying the cheater and making him pay a fine in return for his freedom. Unsure if lawyer-client privilege extended to Carter, she made herself the lone criminal.

It did no good. "Who's this friend?" he demanded.

"I can't—"

Mink regarded her over the glasses. "I need to know everything if I'm going to help you."

She set her lips. “I don’t want to implicate anyone else.”

The huff he made might have been humor, might have been disgust. “Okay. Tell me the real story this time, but use...um, Bozo in place of the other person’s name.”

“The clown?”

“I’ll picture him with a white face and a crazy hairdo.” He leaned back, folding his arms on his chest.

The papers hadn’t reported that Abrams was kidnapped. Robin had given a false name when she made the appointment with Mink, and she’d paid in cash. He had no way of knowing what they’d done, no way to learn her identity.

Too late she recalled mentioning she’d worked for the Greens. *Operating outside the law is harder than I imagined.*

Rubbing her hands together, she gave Mink a second, more truthful account, this time admitting she hadn’t instigated the crime but merely exacerbated it. When she finished, he asked questions that were perceptive, to the point, and probing. She thought about each one before answering, trying to be as honest as possible without revealing details that might identify Carter or Abrams.

“So this person you and Bozo kidnapped and held for ransom. He’s important?”

“Um, yes. You could say that.”

“And now you’re afraid he’s going to call the cops on Bozo.”

“Yes. The man knows Bozo’s name and address.”

“But you recorded his confession.”

“Yes. But Bozo is...different. He couldn’t stand up to this guy in any sort of verbal battle.” Robin scrubbed a hand across her forehead. “I’m afraid he’ll end up in some institution, and that’s not right. Bozo isn't violent, and he's actually pretty smart as long as he can take things slowly and do them his own way."

Mink turned his chair from side to side for a few seconds, causing the oil-parched base to make cries of distress that were almost human. Just as Robin concluded she'd made a mistake showing up there, the lawyer's face broke into a grin. "Miss Polk, you're a heck of a woman."

She sat up straighter in the chair. "What?"

"Don't get me wrong. The courts in this county would string you and your friend up for this, calling you vigilantes and worse. But sometimes I don't think much of the way the law operates these days. We protect the privileged and squirt grapefruit juice in the eye of the poor." Leaning one elbow on the opposite arm and setting his chin on his fist, he asked, "You didn't set out to commit a crime, did you?"

"Well, no."

"And you didn't hurt the guy."

"Of course not."

"Then I say, 'Good for you.' You let him know he can't always get away with crap." Mink frowned. "Now if it had been me, I'd have demanded better behavior in the future." Apparently speaking from experience he added, "It's all well and good to teach guys like that a lesson, but the lesson doesn't stick as often as we'd like to think. In a month or six, he'll be at it again."

Robin grimaced, conceding the point. "I wasn't thinking of anything but getting justice for—Bozo."

Mink waved dismissively. "Your guy probably laughed out loud the next morning when he woke up in his own bed, still owning land he's going to get rezoned commercial and sell for a million dollars."

She bristled a little at the implied criticism. "We didn't do it for the money."

Mink's expression turned serious. "Right, you were helping Bozo. If the police weren't called, that's good, but there's no guarantee the, um, target won't arrange to get back at Bozo some other way."

Robin shuddered. "That's why I've got him hidden."

His nod signaled cautious approval. "But what's your long-term plan?"

"I guess that's why I came to you. I don't know—" She stopped and smiled sadly. "I don't even know what I don't know."

Mink covered the whole lower part of his face with the palm of one hand then slid it down to his neck. "You say the guy's got no relatives?"

"Nor friends. That's why he called me when he needed help, though we're just neigh—acquaintances."

It really is hard to be consistently dishonest.

He ignored her mistake. "If he had a new identity, could Bozo relocate and live on his own?"

The suggestion surprised her. "Is that possible?"

The lawyer—*her* lawyer—picked up a spongy stress reliever shaped like the head of former President "Dubya" Bush and began squishing it in his right hand. Robin wondered if he was feeling torn between his obligation to the justice system and his desire to help her.

"I have a former client who deals in such things." He shifted in the dilapidated chair. "Of course I can't give you his name, because I'd be encouraging a criminal act for both of you."

Robin had felt a ray of hope when he mentioned a new

identity for Carter, but the ray faded.

Mink stared at the ceiling as he squished the ex-president's head. "This former client's name is in my address file there." He pointed at what was possibly the last remaining Rolodex on the planet. "At least I think it is. I'd better check." He flipped through until he found the name he wanted, picked up a pencil, and jabbed it between two cards. "There. Now I can call him later and see how he's doing." His eyes said what his voice didn't, and the ray began to shine again.

Rising, Mink said, "I need to go out and bring in my next client. I'll be gone a few minutes, so you should gather what you need and be on your way." Stepping past Robin, he pulled the office door closed with a parting comment. "Fifty thousand dollars will buy Bozo a lot of anonymity."

Chapter Five

To Robin's surprise, Mink's forger was neither sleazy nor creepy. Andy was a slightly nerdy-looking college student with sloping shoulders and the squint of someone who spends too much time staring at an electronic screen. On the phone they'd arranged to meet at the university coffee shop. Feeling overly dramatic, Robin arrived in dark glasses and a wig she'd bought for a Halloween party.

The place smelled like pepperoni and had a constant hum of movement. Andy sat at a corner table, looking like a dozen other students there to use the free Wi-Fi, but he wore the Padres ball cap he'd told her to look for. He was open about his sideline, explaining he earned tuition money by providing documents for a select list of clients. "I know it sounds like a bad thing, but if people deserve a new start, guys like Mink send them to me."

"And you trust them to send only legitimate cases?"

He sensed disbelief in her tone. "The last person I helped was a seventeen-year-old girl whose parents are in a religious cult. They planned to marry her off to the leader, who already had six wives." His expression revealed what he thought of the parents, the leader, and the cult itself. "I get a few domestic abuse victims and some who hate their lives and want to start over." He added a warning. "I don't help if the cops are involved."

Keeping her tone neutral Robin said, "There are no arrest warrants out for my friend."

Not yet, anyway.

She'd brought along things Andy requested: three small, clear pictures of Carter's face, his physical information, and notes on his age and ethnic background. Glancing at the information,

Andy chewed his lip. "The guy's twenty-two and he's never had a job?"

"He grew up on a farm." She wondered whether to explain why Carter needed a new identity, but it seemed like one of those less-said-the-better times.

"Does he have skills I can put into his background, so he can get a job somewhere?"

"Um, nothing I know of." She supposed feeding chickens and planting onions weren't things one listed on a CV. According to Carter, he'd been home-schooled after second grade because his mother didn't like how the other kids treated him. "He can read and do basic math. He knows a little about government and he watches a lot of TV, so he is familiar with social issues." She sorted through what she'd learned about Carter. His knowledge of practical things surprised her. Using a knife from her kitchen drawer, he'd fixed the dripping shower head she'd been bugging the maintenance guy about. Shocked that she didn't own a hammer, he'd tacked down a loose corner of carpeting with one of her stiletto heels. Was ingenuity something you could put on a résumé?

"Ask about cars or farm machinery and he can tell you anything. Mention Shakespeare and he'll probably ask who that is." When Andy just looked at her, Robin raised her hands in a helpless gesture. "He knows a ton about video games. He won't eat Chinese food because his mom said they use cats instead of chicken."

He rolled his eyes. "I'll see what I can come up with to fill in the gaps."

An idea occurred to her. "From what I saw, he took great care of his mother in her final days."

"Okay. We'll give him a few years' experience as a private

caregiver." Sliding the envelope into his backpack, Andy rose. "Meet me here at noon in two days and I'll give you the basic documents. In a week or so he'll be a new man, with credit cards, a debt history, and all the rest that goes with being an American."

"Thanks." Robin fiddled with her fake hair, feeling silly about the distrust that had caused her to wear it.

"No problem." He waved casually as he walked away, his tablet tucked under one arm.

And it wasn't. When next they met, Andy gave Robin a driver's license in the name of Cameron Phillips, along with a believably battered birth certificate and a plastic-encased Social Security card with one corner bent, as if it had been stuffed into a drawer or wallet. "They look real," she commented.

"As good as, unless you get the FBI involved." He handed her a slip of paper. "The credit cards should arrive in the mail at this postal box, which I rented in Cameron's name. He can have stuff forwarded from there to wherever he ends up." He pointed. "The combination's on the bottom."

"You're amazing."

He regarded Robin as if deciding whether to say something. "I don't usually give advice, but here's what I've learned from watching clients either succeed or fail. To be a new person, your guy has to be willing to give up everything in his past. If he collects Fatheads, he has to stop. If he reads the *New York Times*, he should switch to the *Washington Post*. He can't hold onto anything from his past, and that includes you."

"Me?"

"He's going to have to give you up, unless you want me to make you a new identity too." Andy scratched at the back of his neck. "Judging from his photo, he's quite the specimen, but you're a good-looking girl. You'll find someone new once he's gone."

The day was chilly, and as she shivered her way to her car, Robin considered Andy's advice. He was wrong, of course. There was nothing between her and Carter—*Cameron,* she corrected herself. They'd spent over a week together in her apartment and had hardly touched in passing. Apparently she wasn't his type, and she'd known for some time that he wasn't hers.

That didn't mean Andy's advice was bad. This new man, Cameron Phillips, had to leave everything behind. After a sheltered life on a farm, could a guy with developmental problems carve out a spot for himself in a place where he knew no one?

"What would I miss?" Carter replied to the question as he examined his new driver's license. "Mom and me only lived here since November, so I don't know anyone except you and Mrs. Kane. I missed the farm at first, but they're going to build a mall on top of it, so I can't go back there anyhow."

"But Carter, you'll never see your friends again."

"You're supposed to call me Cameron now, right?" Frowning, he explained, "I only ever had one friend of my own. His name is Jerry, but he moved to California last summer to get into show business."

"Show business?"

"Yeah." His eyes remained focused on the screen. "I got a Christmas card. That's the last I heard of him."

His cheerful acceptance made Robin wonder if her secret roommate had any idea what his future would be like. Still, she didn't see any other way to protect him, and besides, a change might be good for him. In a new place, Carter could open up to the world and make friends of his own.

Robin thought for a moment about leaving Cedar herself. She, her mom, and her brother had come here to get away from her abusive father, but even after more than a decade she wasn't particularly attached to the area. She had friends here, but not close ones, and that was mostly her own fault. Years of hiding secrets – bruises, fears, and actions she was ashamed of – had put her in the habit of keeping people at arm's length.

Yes, leaving Cedar was a good idea, she decided after some soul-searching and two glasses of white Zinfandel. Once she got Carter—Cameron—settled somewhere, she'd be done with taking risks and breaking laws. She could start over.

***

Robin was unloading the dishwasher and considering life in Arizona—her third choice in the last few hours—when her brother called to say he had a layover of several hours in Atlanta. Thrilled, she offered to drive over and meet him. Metterino's Restaurant was Chris' favorite place to eat in the city, so she planned to take him there and celebrate his twenty-eighth birthday a few days early.

The newly-christened Cameron claimed he'd be fine alone. To herself Robin admitted she could use a break after a week of having a 24/7 guest in her apartment. Not that Cam was intrusive; he played video games, watched TV, and had little to say, though it wasn't difficult to learn what he thought about things. Cam was completely honest, without concern for anyone's feelings. Robin learned that she was too skinny (his mother had said it so it must be true), the postman had really bad breath (she'd noticed), and boxers are much more comfortable than briefs because "your boys need room" (way TMI).

Cameron's lack of concern for his safety was about to give her an ulcer. At least once a day, Robin cautioned him to stay away from the window. Each time, he backed obediently away, saying things like, "I was looking at the trees and birds and stuff." He missed his evening walks, and Robin wished he could take one, if only to give her a little space.

The problem wasn't Cam, really, it was Robin herself. Used to being alone, a couple of times she'd almost come out of the bathroom nude after her shower, forgetting she had a roommate. Though Cam avoided her bedroom as if it were a radioactive zone, it was weird living with a relative stranger.

Even weirder was all that cash sitting on her closet floor. Cam urged her to take whatever she needed, and she'd used it to pay Mink's retainer and Andy's fee. Those things were for Cam's benefit though, and she thought of the money as his. Still, she talked herself into taking a few fifties from the bag before she left for Atlanta. Dinner with her brother would run late, so after he went on to Indianapolis, Robin decided she'd spend the night in a motel. Time alone would allow her to think things through, and if she and Cam ended up in prison next week, at least she'd be able to say she benefited once from their ill-gotten gains.

Robin picked her brother up at the airport, setting his travel wheelchair in the trunk of her car after he hefted himself into the passenger seat with powerful upper body muscles. The sight hurt every time, but she was proud too. Chris faced the latest blow life dealt him as he had others, with humor and hard work, making himself as independent as possible. Facing the same obstacles, Robin feared she couldn't have been as upbeat.

Once they were in the car, she leaned over to hug him, feeling the scratchiness of the reddish beard he'd let grow to lumberjack length. "Good to see you, Older Brother," she said.

"Same here, Baby Sister."

A horn sounded behind them to hurry them along. Navigating the maze of airport roads, Robin and Chris caught up, falling into the emotional shorthand those who've grown up together often use, where a word or a look tells more than any words can. It would be just the two of them at dinner, since her sister-in-law was a U.S. Navy nurse currently stationed in Bahrain. Though Robin liked Annika, she looked forward to having her brother to herself for a couple of hours. As kids she and Chris had united to protect themselves and their mother from the man neither of them called Dad. Their father had simply been "Mark" or "He" when they spoke of him, which they hadn't unless it was absolutely necessary.

Chris and Robin were still close, but their lives had gone in different directions. Though she'd had boyfriends along the way, no one she met inspired Robin to get married. Chris was disabled military, with a wife who adored him despite the fact he'd been blown literally to pieces by an IED and now lived in a wheelchair. Their story was one of those hospital romances paperback readers love, where nurse and patient fall in love despite his terrible injuries.

Robin's precarious financial position was due in part to the fact that after their mother died, she'd lied to her brother for the first time in her life. Miranda Parsons, never one to think ahead, had left no money, no arrangements for funeral expenses, and plenty of credit card debt. Believing Chris had all the mental, physical, and financial problems he could handle, Robin had paid the bills herself, assuring him their flighty mother had gotten her act together in her last few years.

They arrived at the restaurant, and Robin stopped out front and retrieved the chair. Chris maneuvered himself into it and went inside while she parked the car. When they were seated, they consulted the menu and ordered, chatting the whole time about their health, the weather, and people they both knew back in Indiana. Once they'd caught up Robin asked, "How is the work going?"

After his injury, Chris had created a website meant to expose corruption in business and in government. “Hardly worth mentioning. I can’t get anyone interested in stopping the crap that goes on.”

“You will.” The waiter set a metal basket of rolls between them, and she peered under the napkin. “Of all the people I know who are capable of spotting cheaters, you’re my number one choice.” She chose a popover, adding, “You stood up to our own personal flim-flam man, and you’ll always be my hero for that.”

Chris’ smile was tinged with sadness. “He’d have beat me to a pulp if you hadn’t threatened to bean him.”

She tore the roll in half and buttered it more vigorously than was necessary. “We stuck together, Chris; that’s what sent him on his way.”

“I’m not sure Mom ever forgave me,” he said, “but it had to be done.”

Images of what they’d lived through as kids occupied her for a moment. Mark Parsons, a charming con man, had insisted his children assist in his schemes. If they did as he wanted, he told them how clever they were. If they failed to perform to his standards, he smacked them around. “The smartest and strongest are meant to survive, not the nicest,” he’d often told his family. “It’s how the world works.”

Their mother, a sweet but weak-willed person, accepted her husband’s faults with a shrug and a comment: “At least he provides for us.” Even when he slugged her for not getting his eggs right, she seemed unable to imagine life without him.

When Robin was thirteen, she’d come home to find her fifteen-year-old brother toe to toe with her father. Their mother sobbed in the background, one eye almost closed from a blow she’d received. Chris ordered Mark to leave and never come back, but he’d only laughed in response. Terrified for Chris, Robin had picked up the nearest weapon—a frying pan—and threatened to smash in her father's skull if he hit Chris or her mother again. He hadn't taken her seriously at first, but when she and Chris stood together, he'd stormed out, calling them "ungrateful bastards" and predicting they'd soon beg him to come home. It was the last time any of them ever saw him.

Her brother's comment about forgiveness rang true. Though she loved her pretty, clueless mother, Robin knew Min Parsons would have stayed with Mark no matter what he did. When Chris took his stand, she'd had to move away from Indianapolis, get a job, and raise two kids on her own. Somehow she'd blamed her son but not her daughter for her changed life. It was no wonder Chris joined the military as soon as he possibly could.

Chris' thoughts were focused on more recent history, and his voice brought her back to the present. "I went to Richmond yesterday to meet with a whistleblower, but the whole trip was a bust."

The waiter set drinks before them, and Robin sipped her wine before asking, "Why's that?"

Chris tasted his beer, sighed with pleasure, and wiped foam from his lip. "There's a state senator who seems to be selling his votes to the highest bidder." He arranged the condiments on the table more neatly as he spoke. "He has an exorbitant life-style and a drug habit. My source was supposed to provide evidence."

"The guy was going to help you nail the man he works for?"

"It's a woman," Chris corrected. "She claims he'll be paid to torpedo an upcoming bill in committee." His brows descended. "The proposal is to build a new veterans' center in the western part of the state, so you can guess it interested me."

"What happened to change your whistleblower's mind?"

He shrugged. "She won't take my calls, so I can't even ask

her."

Robin felt a familiar sense of outrage. "What do you have on him without her help?"

"Just old allegations. Nothing I can prove." Chris folded his arms at his chest. "This was a chance to actually catch him with his hand in the cookie jar."

"How can one guy kill a bill?"

Chris made yapping motions with his fingers as he parodied politician-speak. "'It's fiscally irresponsible to begin new projects in tough economic times.'" He bit into a breadstick with more than necessary ferocity. "They send guys like me to get blown up in foreign countries but claim the support we need afterward is too expensive for overburdened taxpayers. Apparently we can afford fancy planes and lots of bombs, but not wheelchairs and prostheses."

"Sounds like a great representative for the people of his district."

The waiter brought their salads, and when he'd set them down and moved away, Chris returned his silverware to exactly ninety degrees from the table edge. "I can't prove what I know, so there's no sense talking about it."

Robin took up her fork. "He'll slip up someday, and you'll be there to catch him."

"Who'll even notice?" Chris asked. "People are sick of all the mud elected officials throw at each other for political gain. They stop listening—stop caring."

"Can you blame them? Lies get picked up by the media and tossed around for days or even years because they're supposedly 'news.'" She made quotation marks with her fingers.

Chris brushed a few breadcrumbs from his beard. "This guy—

Buckram—will look sad and tell how his conscience dictated his vote, but it will all be a lie."

Robin leaned her elbows on the table, suddenly tired. "Is our government really that terrible?"

"No. There have always been people who get away with stuff they shouldn't, Rob. You know that."

She frowned. "Who bribes a senator to stop a veterans' center from being built?"

"Well, fiscally conservative groups don't support any new spending, but beyond that, you'd be surprised."

Her mouth full of salad, Robin made a rolling hand gesture to indicate, *Explain.*

After a sip of beer, Chris obliged. "If the government has decent, well-administered programs for vets, there's no incentive for donors, big and small, to support private organizations."

"Those groups that make TV ads showing disabled vets that break your heart?"

"Exactly. Some are legitimate, but others spend way too much on 'administrative costs,' huge salaries for their top people and big bucks for celebrities who make more of those heart-tugging commercials."

"Using veterans to make money. Yuck." She deepened her voice to approximate Mark Parsons' tone. "Life isn't fair, kiddies; never has been, never will be. Grow up and deal with it."

Chris smiled ruefully. "We can't fix the world, Rob, so let's just enjoy our meal."

As if on cue, the waiter arrived with their entrees. Shifting his wheelchair closer to the table, Chris said, "Steak. Can't beat it."

"Pasta," Robin replied in a familiar refrain. "Better than dead cow." Her meal smelled divine, and she took a moment to savor it.

As they ate, she told Chris about losing her job, admitting she'd given in to rage and said things she shouldn't have. "I ruined any chance I had of getting a decent reference. It was dumb, but I couldn't believe what they'd done."

His eyes had turned hard. "They let one worker go so they can hire someone else. Can they do that?"

She shrugged, trying to keep her voice light. "They did."

"I'm really sorry to hear it, Rob, but that job wasn't for you anyway—making nice with people who've got more money than humanity. Take it as an opportunity to find what you really want to do with your life."

"Yeah. The Greens did seem to believe I wasn't quite human, being female and lacking a law degree." She washed down some noodles with wine. "It's still not fair to screw someone over like that though."

Chris salted his carrots as he talked, and she winced at how many shakes that required. "People shouldn't be able to use their position to hurt others." Setting down the salt, he took up the pepper. "I hate that the bad guys win way more than they should."

Robin was tempted to tell Chris about the blow she'd struck for justice, but she didn't. He'd worry if he knew she'd committed a crime—actually several crimes. And besides, she had to protect Cameron.

A thought tickled the back of her mind, but she brushed it away. It was dumb.

The thought fluttered back. *You did it once. You could do it again.*

No.

Chris' hard work would achieve results.

No!

Chris is here, eager to share what he knows. It can't hurt to talk about it.

Setting her wineglass gently on the tablecloth, Robin smiled innocently at her brother. "Tell me more about the senator with the drug problem."

***

After a semi-restful night in the motel, Robin returned home to a crisis. At first things seemed normal enough. TV gunshots rang out as she unlocked the door, and she guessed Cameron was watching a cop show. When she entered, however, she found him perched nervously on the edge of the sofa, turned away from the screen. Facing him, her back perfectly straight in Robin's saggy old recliner, was their neighbor, Ms. Kane.

"Good morning, Miss Parsons." The old woman's voice approximated the sound of a talking crow. "Carter and I have been waiting for you."

Robin began explaining, mostly to give herself time to think. "I drove to Atlanta to meet my brother then spent the night at the Hampton Inn. The traffic this morning was brutal."

"I see."

Emily Kane reminded Robin of a teacher she'd had in middle school who could make the most innocuous comment seem like an accusation. With iron-gray hair and a chin that suggested silliness would not be tolerated, Ms. Kane wore glasses a decade out of style and spotted with what was possibly white paint. She hobbled around the building, speaking to other residents in homey clichés about rain coming down in buckets or sun so hot one could fry an egg on the sidewalk.

Ms. Kane smelled of arthritis cream and wore polyester everything: pants that bulged at the waist but drooped in the seat and pullover shirts in solid colors, always with a collar and two-button placket. She was seldom seen without a cardigan sweater, and today's was navy blue. Sometimes she wore the garment; other times it draped over her shoulders. Today it lay folded over the arm of the chair. Apparently her body temperature was subject to frequent, violent changes.

There was a moment of silence as Robin considered her options. Carter/Cameron seemed frozen in place. Emily Kane waited, her mouth a straight line above her long chin.

Finally Robin chose her course of action. "Well, *Carter*, I want to thank you for checking on the apartment for me." Turning to Ms. Kane she confided, "I'm kind of a baby about coming home after a trip. I always imagine someone has broken in while I was gone and—"

"He's been living here."

"Oh."

Oh-oh.

"You're not a couple." She nodded at the blankets Cameron slept in, neatly folded at one end of the sofa. "He told the landlord he'd moved to California."

"Colorado," Cameron supplied, but a glance from Ms. Kane caused him to clamp his lips together and look down at his lap.

"My hearing is excellent, and your television has played for days, all day, even when you're out. I saw him leaving here late last night." One gray brow lifted slightly. "I get up several times at night to pee."

Cameron turned to Robin, his expression guilty. "I needed to get outside for a while. I didn't think—"

"It's okay." Turning a resolute face to Ms. Kane she said, "What he and I do, where we sleep, and how much TV we watch is none of your business."

Surprisingly, the old woman nodded agreement. "That's correct, except for two things. First, a man has come around asking about Carter."

"Cameron," he said helpfully. "I changed my name."

Don't tell her that!

Before Robin could decide how to react, Ms. Kane said, "It isn't what they call you that matters, I suppose. It's what you answer to. All right then, Cameron. The other reason for my concern is your welfare." She adjusted her glasses, though when she finished they still sat crookedly on her ultra-thin nose. "When I moved in here, your mother was good to me."

Cam nodded. "She said you were odd as two sticks but nice enough. I-I think that means she liked you."

Ms. Kane accepted the comment with no apparent rancor. "She was a little drifty, your mother, but she had a good heart." Turning back to Robin she said, "I won't have Doreen Halkias' only son used for some purpose of yours that will break his heart or his bank account."

"It's nothing like that, Ms. Kane."

"From what I understand, it's worse." Her cane thumped sharply on the floor. "Carter tells me you're hiding him here so he won't be taken to jail."

Feeling trapped, Robin gave the briefest possible explanation. "Cameron had an argument with someone—a misunderstanding really—and things got a little rough. The other party is kind of a big shot, and he's liable to press charges. Since jail wouldn't be a good place for Cameron, I decided to let him stay here for a while."

"That's why the private detective is looking for him? To charge him with assault?"

"I guess so."

Ms. Kane studied Robin with faded-blue eyes. From the way her lips twitched, it seemed she was thinking.

Robin was thinking too, wondering how fast Andy could make her a new identity. *We'll take a train to D.C. and lose ourselves there. Or maybe we'll take a bus west, to—*"You haven't done badly for amateurs," Emily Kane said, "but you still need my help."

What?

"Help? Um—"

A bony hand stopped her protest. "Do I look like I just fell off a turnip truck?"

"No, but Ms. Kane—"

"Then don't try to string me along. And call me Em, like the aunt in *The Wizard of Oz*." She squinted toward Robin's tiny kitchen. "You'd better make a pot of coffee. My life story takes some telling."

Having no idea what else to do, Robin rose to obey. Digging her almost unused coffeemaker out from under the sink, she located a packet of Hawaiian coffee she'd received as a Christmas gift from her Secret Santa. As the aroma of the brew filled the apartment, she put sugar into one plastic storage container and poured a half cup of milk into another, creating an impromptu condiment set. As Robin worked, Emily Kane talked.

"I retired from the FBI in 2006, after thirty years on the job. I spent most of my career in the Midwest, Michigan, Wisconsin, and Ohio." She glanced at the snowless expanse outside the window. "I moved here so I'd never see another winter." Her lips tightened. "Snow is pretty, but I miss that bitter cold about as much as I'd miss a chapped hind end."

Robin was trying desperately to decide if Em Kane's background hurt or helped the situation. If she'd spent years enforcing the law, her sense of duty might overcome any fondness she felt for her neighbor's son. Hoping to generate amity, Robin said, "You must have had some interesting times."

Em chuckled. "I certainly did. Female agents had to prove we could cut the mustard every single day."

It was hard to imagine the seventy-plus Ms. Kane kicking down doors and chasing bad guys through the streets of Cleveland. *Still,* Robin reminded herself, *old is what everybody gets to be if they don't die first.*

Pouring a cup for their guest and setting the sugar, milk and a spoon on the end table, she wondered if politeness demanded she have coffee too. Having never developed a taste for it, Robin instead got sodas for herself and Cam. Popping hers open with a hiss she asked, "What did you mean about us needing your help?"

"The private detective is good at his job, and he's as determined as a blue jay at a bird feeder. He's all over the building asking questions, and he's come to my door twice." She raised one gray brow. "I didn't tell him anything, but I doubt he'll give up easily."

"Ms. Kane—Em—Cam plans to relocate soon. If you could keep his presence here a secret for a few days longer, he'll be gone and the detective will go away. "We hate to ask you to lie, but—"

Em Kane's smile was slightly feral. "Oh, I don't mind lying, Honey, as long as it's in a good cause."

***

Robin went through the rest of that day and the night that followed with a war going on inside her head. The idea of subjecting the senator Chris had described to the same treatment they'd given Barney Abrams was crazy. But the lawyer she'd consulted hadn't seemed outraged by her actions, and Em Kane had calmly offered to help Cam avoid the private detective who'd been poking around. Though neither of them knew all of it, the support of objective outsiders made Robin believe that her actions had been laudable, though certainly not legal. The next question was could they possibly get away with taking action against a second target? It meant they'd both have to go on the run, but they might accomplish something good in the process.

Senator Buckram was a con man who cheated others the way her father once had. Though Robin had felt sorry for her father's victims, she'd been unable to help them. She guessed Chris' current crusade to expose corruption stemmed from the same feelings of guilt and shame she had about their past. Now Chris had discovered a crook he really wanted to take down, but he was at an impasse. Robin wasn't sure she was capable of following through for her brother, but she wanted to try. And that meant she needed to ask someone for objective advice.

Someone who will talk you out of this.

Robin took a seat on the same battered wooden chair in Mink's cluttered office. In the outer room a couple argued in tones that suggested the disagreement was old and well-rehearsed. When Mink had peered out to see her in the waiting room, his weathered face creased in a smile, and Robin saw—hoped she saw—sympathy in his gaze. Maybe the lawyer felt sorry for everyone whose lives hadn't turned out the way they imagined.

"Would you be interested in hearing a story, Mr. Mink?" she

said when he was seated behind the desk.

His brow furrowed. “A story?”

“It’s a suspense novel I plan to write.” She swallowed. “It’s about clowns who want to fight corruption and dishonesty in America.”

Mink’s face lengthened as his brows rose. “You’ve come here to tell me a story?”

“Yes.” She met his gaze directly. “I need legal expertise in order to make the plot believable.”

He tilted his head to one side. “All right. Let’s hear this fictional tale.”

“My main characters are two clowns,” Robin began, “Bozo and, um, Clarabell. They have an acquaintance who’s in a position to hear of corruption in business and government. We’ll call him Ronald.”

“Of course.”

Her smile was brief. “Ronald doesn’t know he’s providing a basis for the actions of the other clowns.”

He nodded. “Is Bozo aware of Ronald?”

“Not specifically.” She made a waggling gesture with one hand. “Bozo pretty much trusts Clarabell to make decisions for both of them.”

Mink regarded her for a moment with his head tilted to one side. “Miss Polk—”

She almost turned to see who’d come into the office but realized after a moment that *Polk* was the name he knew her by.

“—are you certain this is a book you want to write?”

Silence stretched between them for perhaps thirty seconds.

Mink waited with a patient expression. When she finally spoke, Robin told him something she'd never told anyone before.

"My father was—probably still is—a con man, a grifter, whatever you want to call it. He's always on the con, and he doesn't do it because he needs money or sex or your grandmother's brooch. He does it because it makes him happy to take something away from someone else." She stopped, but Mink remained silent. His expression revealed interest and nothing more, neither the disgust or the pity she'd feared.

"When I was a kid, he used to make me help him." She paused to choose a typical example. "We'd go to a rest area, and he'd tell me to stand by the entry door and cry." Her hands clenched in her lap. "If I couldn't cry, he'd give me something to cry about." Now Mink's eyebrows approached each other, but he said nothing. "Sooner or later someone would stop and ask what was wrong. That's when Mark would hurry over, put his arm around me, and explain that I was sad because my mom had been in a horrible house fire. He'd smile this really sad smile and tell them we were on our way to see her at the burn center when our car broke down. Then he'd look embarrassed and say he didn't have any money, since payday wasn't for two more days." She brushed a hand through her hair. "At that point he'd manage a tear or two of his own, and seven times out of ten, the person who'd stopped forked over a twenty—sometimes a fifty."

Mink leaned his face on his fist. "You felt like you helped him cheat those people."

Robin gave a sniff that was half anger, half determination to keep from crying. "Mark had a dozen different scams, and we—I—was part of half of them."

"So your, um, book is about righting your father's wrongs?"

She shook her head. "I don't think the things he did can ever really be made right, but I'd like to do what I can—in my story, I mean—to stop people like him."

"What's the next chapter going to be about?"

Robin described her "antagonist," a politician who used his position to line his pockets. While she recounted the scenario that would bring the man face-to-face with his deeds, Mink listened, leaning back in his chair with a sneaker-clad foot on the handle of his desk drawer. "Just the two clowns plan to accomplish this?"

She smiled. "Well, there's a lawyer whose advice would be useful."

"And the lawyer's job will be what?"

"Consultant." She leaned forward in her chair. "In the first chapter, the clowns made mistakes. From now on they'd like to avoid them if possible." Scooting the chair closer, she punched Mink's stress toy with a finger and watched it return to shape. "You've seen criminals come and go. You know what works and what doesn't."

Mink's expression seemed doubtful, and Robin said, "It's all fictional, so you aren't responsible if Bozo and Clarabell get caught." When he still didn't reply, she added, "Of course, I expect to pay for your advice."

"Will the clowns demand money from the target?"

"Yes," she replied. "For two reasons. First, they need money to get started in a new place. Second, when a person has to pay for something he's done, the lesson is more likely to stick with him."

Mink smoothed his ponytail with one hand. "Indulgences."

"What?"

"In the Middle Ages, priests made sinners pay for forgiveness. Most today see that as corruption in the church, and they're probably correct. But the priests might have known what you just said: losing something he cares about—money, for example—as a result of wrongdoing makes a person less likely to sin again." He chuckled. "At least he'll be more cautious about it."

"These clowns aren't priests," she cautioned.

"True." His tone turned warning. "They have no structure supporting them, and society is against vigilantes, though some see the value of, um, *de facto* justice if it's applied with caution."

Robin felt some of her tension dissipate. Her idea wasn't crazy—well, it was, but not so crazy that Mink couldn't see the value in it. "I like that. *De facto* justice."

His manner turned businesslike. "Since money has never been my reason for doing what I do, I'll advise your fictional clowns *pro bono*." He reached out a hand, and they shook to seal the deal—his cool, dry palm meeting Robin's warm, slightly damp one.

"We—the clowns—have agreed to give half the money to charity. Anonymously, of course."

"What part of your novel do you want advice on?"

Now that they'd agreed to work together, Robin wasn't sure how to begin. "What's your first concern when you look at my plot?"

"Amateurs," Mink replied without hesitation. "Your clowns were lucky the first time out, but they simply don't know much about being criminals. How will they stay out of police data bases? How will they avoid facial recognition, which grows daily in scope and sophistication? If one of them is caught, will that lead to the capture of the other?" He spread his hands. "It doesn't take much effort to *become* a criminal, but it takes a great deal of effort to *be* a criminal who remains uncaught."

"All right," Robin said thoughtfully. "I'll work on those things. You said something before about telling the target that we—the clowns—will be watching them."

"Yes. The clowns might claim they'll monitor electronically or say they've bribed someone on the target's staff to tattle if he returns to his old ways. That will depend on the situation. The prospect of electronic bugs is unnerving, and not knowing who can be trusted among his own people would make anyone think twice." He considered for a moment. "You might want to establish some sort of communication that requires them to check in with you periodically. It's easy to backslide when one doesn't think anyone is paying attention."

"Okay, so we need an email address or something where they have to report in. What else?"

Mink tapped his chin with his fingers. "They need an escape plan that covers all possibilities. Most criminals are caught because they simply can't imagine things won't go as they expect."

"All right." She rose. "I might not see you again, Mr. Mink—"

"Tell you what," he interrupted. "If you need to speak with me, send me an email or a text with—" He scribbled some letters on the blotter until he found a combination he liked. "Put *KNP* in the heading. That way I'll know it's you, no matter what address or phone number it comes from. I'll respond as soon as I can."

"Great. Thank you very much."

As they shook hands, he met her gaze. "Be careful,, Miss Polk. I'd hate to see your book end in tragedy."

Robin promised she would, but she left Mink's office with more questions than answers. How was she supposed to devise some genius escape plan? How could she set up a system that could track Buckram's behavior after they released him? And how goofy was she, agreeing to secret codes and cloak-and-dagger conferences?

By the time she got home, Robin was half-angry with Mink. *He could at least have* tried *to talk me out of it.*

Chapter Six

A knock on the door at ten the next morning caused both occupants of the apartment to start in surprise. Since Cameron came to stay, Robin had avoided contact with both friends and neighbors. At a glance from her Cam followed the plan they'd devised, switching the TV to a news channel and hiding the video game controller in the end table drawer before hurrying into Robin's bedroom and closing the door. When they discussed possible visitors, Cam had proposed the bathroom as his hiding place, but she'd answered that a guest might ask to use it and there he'd be, his six-foot-four frame looming over the five-foot shower door. As Robin went to answer the knock, she heard the louvered closet doors in her room close behind him.

Peering through the peephole, she saw a man of about thirty whose erect posture hinted at both a military background and zero tolerance for things and people that made him wait.

"Who is it?"

"Thomas Wyman from Terra Investigations, ma'am." He held up a leather wallet with an I.D. card.

Robin's pulse rate increased dramatically. The man who'd been hired to find Carter Halkias.

She could say she was busy, but he'd only come back later. Best to do this now. Her hands shook as she opened the door, but she lectured herself the way Em would if she'd been present. *Be casual, a little curious, and willing to talk.*

The first thing she noticed with a full view was that the corduroy jacket he wore had an empty sleeve. Wyman was missing an arm. Knowing how Chris hated people staring at where his parts should be, she focused on her visitor's face. He had a stoical aspect she'd noticed in many ex-soldiers: observant and confident in his worth. "Yes?"

Wyman offered a business card with his left hand, which was scarred and missing the last finger. Ignoring the injury, she took the finely-embossed card and read the information: TERRA INVESTIGATIONS, THOMAS WYMAN. There was a downtown address. When she looked up again he asked, "May I come in, Miss Parsons?"

Robin backed away. "Of course." Wyman was about her height, five ten, with a wiry build, gray-blue eyes that might be termed steely, a strong chin, and high cheekbones that gave his face a chiseled look. A scary man, Robin decided, though she admitted she scared easily these days.

"Have a seat," she invited. "Can I get you a soda or something?"

He sat on the edge of a chair, spine erect and feet flat on the floor. "A glass of water would be good."

Probably lives on whole wheat toast and tap water. As he glanced at her cluttered apartment with its girly kitsch and Nicki Minaj posters, she imagined his place, probably empty except for an army cot and a weight bench.

Moving into the kitchen, Robin felt Wyman's gaze follow her. To get control of her nerves, she fiddled with her guest's drink, taking an ice tray from the freezer and dropping cubes into a tall glass. Wyman frightened her but made her angry too. What business did he have tracking Cameron down like a runaway dog?

It's what he does for a living.

Well, it's mean. People shouldn't have to be afraid all the time.

That's what "people" get for being criminals.

She poured water over the ice, which cracked and hissed as it broke into chunks and shards. When she returned to the living room, Wyman had risen from the chair and gone to examine a row of caps suspended from a wire across one wall.

"Baseball fan?"

"My grandfather got my brother and me hooked as kids. I still see a game or two each season."

He tilted his head to study her before making a guess. "Braves?"

"Are you kidding? Pirates all the way."

Wyman shrugged. "I'm more of a football guy."

You prefer games where people knock people down. There's a surprise.

"Was there something I could help you with, Mr. Wyman?"

Nodding as if to acknowledge she didn't want him hanging around, he said, "I'm wondering what you can tell me about your neighbor, Carter Halkias."

"Carter?" She tried to look surprised. "I'm afraid I don't know much. He moved in a while ago with his mother, but she passed away, last month maybe, or the month before. We sometimes meet in the workout room, but we don't talk much." Trying for a light tone she added, "I'm usually too out of breath to chat."

Wyman ignored the joke. "He never shared any personal information with you? Friends? Girlfriends?"

Keep to the truth as much as possible. "I know what kind of movies he likes. That's about it."

Wyman sipped the water and set the glass carefully on a coaster. "He ever ask you out?"

"No."

When she didn't elaborate he said, "A nice-looking woman just a few doors down, I thought he might."

Surprised by the comment Robin said, "I was busy with my job until recently, but I'm not working anymore." *Now why did I tell him that?* To avoid blurting out more personal information she finished, "I haven't seen Carter in at least a week."

"I've been told he moved out, or at least he's in the process."

She nodded as if that were news. "That explains it."

Wyman's gaze held hers, and she clasped her hands in her lap to keep from twisting them. "Nobody I've talked to has seen him since last Thursday," he said. "The landlord got an email saying he'll be gone at the end of the month, but he hasn't come to clean out his place or drop off his keys."

Robin tried for a casual expression, but her lips felt like concrete. In her head she was berating herself for letting Carter's situation drift along in limbo. Wyman's repeated visits to the building should have warned it was time to commit to Carter truly becoming Cameron and leaving Cedar for good.

"You have no idea where Halkias is right now?"

She was starting to feel like a mouse dropped into a boa's cage. Was the guy trying to make her nervous, or did he always look at people in a way that practically accused them of lying?

Rather than answer his question she asked one of her own. "Why are you looking for him?"

Wyman's brow furrowed briefly. *He doesn't like it when people don't jump when he says jump.* "It has to do with his mother's medical treatment. He doesn't owe money or anything, but they need some signatures."

"Someone hired a big investigations firm for that?"

"It's not a big firm." He glanced at his empty sleeve. "When I left the army, I was sort of at a loss. A woman I knew in criminal investigation offered to train me with the idea I'd eventually become her partner."

"How is that working out?"

His tone turned cold, Robin guessed she'd stepped over some unseen boundary. "I don't think the partnership is going to work out."

Robin had learned from Chris' situation that even though many employers say they want to help wounded vets, they often doubt their physical or emotional ability to do a job.

Wyman glanced over her shoulder as if seeing into the future. "Finding Mr. Halkias would go a long way toward convincing the businesspeople in Cedar to trust me with other cases."

The client's an important man, like a county commissioner maybe. Crossing her arms, Robin said, "Sorry I can't help. Like I said, I haven't seen Carter in a while."

A hundred-eighty seconds or so. That's a while.

Wyman stood. "Well, then, I won't take up—"

A thud from the direction of the bedroom caused him to stop. After her heart skipped a beat or two, Robin managed a tinny laugh. "My cat is terrified of visitors. He hides in the closet and knocks stuff over."

"Thank you for your time, Ms. Parsons." Wyman didn't offer to shake hands. "If you should hear from Mr. Halkias, will you ask him to call?" He gestured at the business card she'd laid on the coffee table.

"Of course."

He didn't move toward the door but stood looking at her in a way she couldn't fathom. Curiosity? Amusement at her pathetic attempts to lie? Robin bit her lip to keep from filling the silence that stretched between them. Wyman probably hoped she'd blurt out something useful under the pressure of his steely gaze. She crossed her arms in front of her chest, surreptitiously wiping her palms on her sleeves.

"It was nice to meet you," Wyman finally said.

Moving to the door, she opened it as encouragement. "You too." *Please—just leave!*

When he was gone, Robin set her back against the door and breathed in and out a few times. Cam emerged from the bedroom, his mouth open to apologize for the noise, but she shushed him. When Wyman appeared on the sidewalk below, she said, "It's okay. I told him I have a cat." Accepting her word for it, Cam dropped back onto the couch, retrieved the controller from the drawer, and returned to his game.

Robin stood at the window, unobtrusively watching the parking lot as Wyman drove away in a sporty-looking black car. The visit had unnerved her, but Cam didn't seem perturbed by it at all. When nothing bad happened, he'd set the matter somewhere outside his consciousness.

That wasn't possible for Robin. She needed to talk with someone who understood what *might* have happened. Crossing the hall, she knocked on Em's door. When the older woman answered, she hurried inside.

Em's apartment was spare, with only essential furnishings. The stiff-looking couch that sat along the picture window looked like it had never supported a single rear end. The end tables matched neither each other nor the coffee table between them. One comfortable chair sat before the TV, and beside it a knitting bag overflowed with yarn in various colors. Even in her disturbed state, Robin had a momentary, depressing image of the old woman sitting there, day after day, with nothing to do but knit.

"What's wrong, Sweetie?"

"That detective was at my place. I told him I don't know Cam very well, but I don't think he believed me. Then Cam made a noise, and I said it was the cat, but what if he knows pets aren't allowed here? What if he noticed the game sleeve on the coffee table? It's something with *Blood* in the title." Her voice rose higher. "What if somebody else saw Cam outside the other night? What if Wyman comes back?"

Em put a weathered hand on her shoulder. "Take it easy, Hon. He's just a guy doing a job."

Robin went on as if she hadn't spoken. "Why did I think I could get away with this? I'm an out-of-work secretary. My partner in crime is somewhere on the autism spectrum. My support group is a hippie lawyer and a—" She managed not to say "a senior citizen," but she'd begun crying, so the last few words were incomprehensible anyway.

"Hey," Em comforted. "Jesus was a carpenter who picked a bunch of fishermen and a tax collector for support. It's how you use what you've got that makes the difference."

Leading Robin to a chair, Em ran a glass of water at the sink. "Drink this and stop that god-awful bawling." She sat opposite Robin and set her bony elbows on the fake-maple tabletop. "Tell me exactly what you two did last week. No more bull about a misunderstanding with a nameless bigwig. I want names and details."

Gulping tepid water between sentences, Robin obeyed. When she was finished, Em tapped a fingernail on the tabletop for a moment. "I can't believe you two pulled it off, but it's like they say—even a blind squirrel finds an acorn sometimes."

"Except Abrams has sent that private detective looking for Cam."

"Yes," Em said thoughtfully. "Let's go over exactly what Mr. Wyman asked and what you told him."

Robin obeyed, fully trusting her neighbor now that the dam had broken. Em stopped her every few sentences to question how Wyman had reacted and even where he'd looked as he spoke. When Robin had reported everything she could think of, Em said, "If Abrams knows there was a woman involved, Wyman probably suspects it was you. It's not like Cameron is acquainted with a whole string of girls."

"I know! That's why I have to—"

"Don't get your panties in a twist! There are some things we can do to throw him off the scent."

"We? Em, you can't be involved in this."

She raised a hand in a commanding gesture. "You're planning to do it again, aren't you? You've got another crook in mind that you want to set straight."

Robin looked down at her nails, which were badly in need of attention. "Maybe. I mean, we've talked about it, but it isn't for sure. Not at all. I mean—"

Em interrupted her. "You'll be starting a life that's different from anything normal people understand."

"Normal people?"

"Do you know anyone else who's guilty of kidnapping and extortion?"

Good point.

"There are things you have to think about before you take another step." Em raised a finger. "First you have to learn to be *aware* of possible consequences but not *terrified* by them. You're a worrier, and worry gives a small thing a big shadow."

Mink had warned that being outside the law wouldn't be easy. Never again could she assume no one was watching her. Never again would she be an innocent bystander. Any infraction of the law could bring discovery. Standing in a crowd that was being filmed or near a group posing for a photograph meant her image could be searched out and analyzed. She had to learn to hide her identity while disguising the fact that she was doing so.

Em patted Robin's arm with cool fingers. "You've probably never played a role before, but now you have to, every single day."

Though Robin didn't argue, she *had* played a role for years. In public, she and Chris always pretended their home life was okay. They'd both been ashamed to tell anyone their father beat their mother whenever it pleased him and turned on Chris if he tried to stop him. They'd kept quiet about the cons, too, embarrassed by their participation in the duping of innocent victims. Only Robin's best friend Shelly knew anything about Mark's evil side, and she had never pressed for details. She'd just been there when Robin needed her, no matter how far apart they lived.

If she could pretend her father was a decent man back then, she could pretend to be anything she needed to now.

Unaware that Robin's thoughts had wandered, Em went on. "A lot of what we did in the Bureau required the same skills you need now: making people believe what you tell them and hiding the fact that you're so nervous you might throw up any second." She paused. "Getting away with things is 90 percent inside your head. If you make yourself believe what you're projecting, others will believe it too."

"Okay," Robin said. "What else?"

"You have to control your emotions. You can't operate from anger—or from fear, for that matter." She tapped her forehead. "Cultivate a cool head and an analytical mind."

"But it makes me angry that there are so many jerks in the world."

Em frowned. "Every two-bit crazy with a gun claims he just couldn't take anymore. If you're the girl I think you are, you don't want to just react to evil. You want to make things better, which means you can't go off half-cocked, like you did with the commissioner."

Robin turned defensive. "It turned out okay."

"Which was mostly luck," Em responded. "There were a hundred times you might have been caught, and you still might, if Wyman has his way. Take my word for it, fear and anger aren't your friends. You have to play it cool. That comes from knowing you're doing the right thing and you're prepared to do it right."

"I'm not much for playing it cool." She tried for a joke. "I'm usually more like stressed and self-doubting."

Taking the empty glass from her hand, Em rose and set it in the sink. "With a little practice, I think you can." She patted Robin's shoulder, adding, "The possibility of prison time is great for motivation."

Chapter Seven

Tearing off the top sheet of her notepad, Robin read through her new list.

DISGUISE KIT

1. NO CAPES OR TIGHTS (Cam had suggested it, though she thought he'd been joking.)
2. DARK, SHAPELESS CLOTHING
3. WIGS, BEARDS, MUSTACHES?
4. EYEGLASSES?

She'd made a dozen lists, trying to think of anything—everything—that might happen if they went after Senator Charles T. Buckram. She'd looked at Buckram's recent votes, which were all over the place with no apparent belief system behind them. Though he had detractors who pointed out his inconsistencies, "Buck" Buckram's folksy, brash manner resonated with voters. "He listens to his conscience," one interviewee gushed.

His voting record told a different story. Anti-smoking bill? Yes. Continued tobacco subsidies? Yes. Encourage the establishment of new banks? Yes. Allow existing banks to buy up smaller ones? Of course. Buckram didn't listen to his conscience. He listened to whoever offered the most money.

Watching video clips of Buckram's public statements, Robin thought she detected the look of want seen in addicts' eyes, although her perception might have been colored by what her brother had said. His vague resemblance to her father made her prone to dislike him. Even taking those things into account, Buckram needed to face his dishonesty and do something about it.

The rattle of cereal into a bowl alerted Robin to Cam's

presence in the kitchen. They'd fallen into a routine. He got up early, used the bathroom (which he left so neat she was amazed), and made himself breakfast. Robin remained in her bedroom until she heard him rummaging in the refrigerator and then took her turn in the bath. By the time she was ready for the day, Cam was on the couch with a breakfast Pepsi, in his mind the ultimate indulgence. His mother had been adamantly in favor of grapefruit juice for growing young men.

Though their time was spent mostly in companionable silence, they had discussed what they would do, could do, and should do. Robin now understood that Cameron's dull aspect was largely due to a need for a second or two to process what was said to him. While information percolated through his unique brain, Cam's expression went blank, causing the appearance of no thought at all. Once she learned to wait a few seconds after each utterance, she found him more capable of logical thought than she'd imagined. He even had an odd but enjoyable sense of humor.

Robin suspected Cam's development was limited by overprotective parents as much as by his disability. His mother had decided when he was very young that since he was "different," he should avoid the very things that might have helped him adapt and grow. Cam had never been to a museum, live theater, or a sporting event—beyond a few weeks in Little League where he'd failed miserably due to his slow reaction time. His idea of a family outing was a trip to a mall that had an arcade and a food court.

The idea of a KNP, as she'd begun thinking of it, appealed to Cam, who viewed kidnapping "bad guys" as a big adventure with a noble purpose. While Robin agreed their purpose in capturing Buckram was noble and would undoubtedly be adventurous, she had a hard time picturing success. It was great to fantasize about teaching the crooked, druggie senator a lesson, but that fantasy lived in her dreams, not in the realm of possibility. It had been a mistake to tell Cameron how she thought it might be done, because now he was so thrilled with the idea of striking a blow for Truth, Justice, and the American Way that he paid no attention to counterarguments.

She set her list aside. "Maybe we should forget this and find you a new place to live, Cam."

"We can do it," he insisted. "I'll catch the guy, and you'll talk to him, like you did Mr. Abrams."

"We're not even sure we got away with that," she argued. "The guy who's looking for you, Wyman—"

Cam dispatched an on-screen zombie with a squishy thud. "Em told him I moved, and he went away."

"But it has to be Abrams who hired him."

He shrugged it off. "He didn't find me, so he gave up."

"I hope so, Cam. I really hope so."

Robin's efforts to dissuade Cameron were weak because despite her doubts and fears, she wanted to go ahead with a second "KNP." They'd bested one crook in a spur-of-the-moment, sloppily-planned event. This time, with advice from a lawyer and an ex-FBI agent, she dared to hope they might do it again. She'd already asked Andy, Mink's forger client, to make a new identity for her. When the KNP was over—*if* she decided to go through with it, she and Cam could relocate together, maybe as sister and brother, and start new lives. She could tell Chris his hard work had paid off, and he'd be inspired to continue the work he was so passionate about.

Could they really do it? At times the answer was a resounding yes. Who'd suspect two people from Cedar, Georgia, of attacking a politician in a state they had no connection to? If they acted boldly, as they'd done with Abrams, it would be over in a couple of hours.

On the other hand, they were amateurs who'd been lucky once. That didn't mean luck would be with them a second time. Someone might witness the abduction and call the police. Buckram might fight them off and escape. One of them might lose the nerve the job required and freeze when the moment to act arrived. The task sounded noble and worthwhile. It might end up pitifully comedic.

Picking up her pen again, Robin added another note: CHEEK & JAW PADS. To cope with alternating excitement and dread, she'd begun making list after list. Items they might need. Possible scenarios. Escape plans. She did research on Chris' research. She read everything she could find about the area where Buckram lived and his habits. Following Mink's advice, she tried to think of everything that might go wrong and what their reaction should be in each instance. She tried to look at the task as a mathematical problem, requiring certain steps to achieve a final, correct answer. That meant setting aside her anger at the senator and even her pity for her brother. After looking at it from every angle, she concluded the KNP was doable. With the evidence she had compiled, it was also likely, though not certain, that the result would be worth the effort.

At the slightest hitch, she promised herself they'd abort the plan. If it was early in the process, they'd simply leave Richmond. If they were compromised, she and Cam would drive to Mexico, cross the border, and from there head to a country where they could disappear forever. She looked up from her notes. "Cam, if we have to run, would you like to go somewhere with a tropical climate?"

An on-screen ammo dump blew with an echoing boom. "Probably not. I hate snakes."

"My sister-in-law says Bahrain is nice."

"Okay."

She studied his serene profile. "Could you really leave the States and never come back?"

He shrugged. "They got grocery stores there?"

"Uh, yeah."

"And Wi-Fi?"

"I suppose so."

"Then, sure."

Robin wished for a moment she could adopt Cam's linear way of thinking and shut out the "what ifs?" Of course she was the one who would actually make the decision, so she had to ask those questions. Before attempting a KNP on Buckram, she needed first-hand knowledge of the situation. She had to go to Richmond, scout the location, and gather evidence that would convince Buckram he was vulnerable to exposure. The most likely source of help there was the person who had backed out of talking to Chris.

Picking up her phone, she made a call. "Hey, Elder Brother. How are things in Indy?"

"Good," Chris replied.

She wanted to make her call seem casual, so it took a while to work around to the senator with the drug problem. "That guy you told me about at dinner. Is it true he carries a concealed weapon?"

"That's what I've read." Chris' tone changed. "What are you up to, Rob?"

"I've been thinking a lot about Mark lately."

That brought a disgusted grunt. "Why would you waste your thoughts on our worthless old man?"

"That guy you told me about, Buckram. He seems to have a lot of the same qualities."

"If you mean an inflated ego, a lack of compassion, and a talent for manipulating others, I agree."

"The night he left for good, Chris. What were you and he fighting about?" The lack of answer told her what she'd long suspected. "About using us in his schemes?"

Chris sighed before replying. "I told Mom everything, all the stuff she didn't want to know about how he made us help him scam people. She hated it. I thought she was going to put her hands over her ears and go "NANANANANA!" A grim chuckle, and then he added, "She was as mad at me as she was at him."

"She had to face what he was. We had to be free of him."

"Mom wouldn't agree with you. She'd have put up with all of it: the lies, the petty crime, even the infidelity. When I laid it all out she was forced to face what he was, but she really didn't want to." His voice went wobbly. "And look what it got her."

"A beating, but it was the last one. Once we all stood up to him together, he was done."

"I just always knew some part of Mom resented it. She had to move. She had to get a job. She had to live without a man."

"She was better off, even if she didn't see it. And as for me—Brother, you saved my life."

He bowed, acknowledging her candid statement. "What's brought all this thinking about?"

"Like I said, this Buckram reminds me of Dear Old Dad. I'd like to do something to stop him."

"Like what, Robin? I've put the info I have on the net, but no one seems to care."

"I need to know the name of the source who changed her mind about telling you Buckram's secrets, and don't ask why, okay?"

He thought about that for a long time. "She won't talk to you."

"If she doesn't, she doesn't," she said. "But I'm going to try."

***

Em Kane stopped by most afternoons, and Robin got the sense the older woman was both lonely and bored. She claimed she knew no one in Cedar except doctors, and any mention of the usual socialization opportunities offered to senior citizens brought disparaging comments. "Bingo, for crying out loud!" Em snorted. "Every mark some old codger makes on a card gets him one square closer to the funeral parlor."

Em sat in the most comfortable chair, in deference to her hip. She had taught herself to knit in retirement, so she usually arrived with her bag of yarn, needles, and some half-done project. Her needles clicked softly as she talked, manufacturing colorful clothing that would seldom, if ever, be worn.

It wasn't that the things Em knitted were badly done. She made fine, even stitches in complicated patterns and worked with amazing speed. The problem was the color combinations she chose, which were nothing short of hideous. A muddy-looking scarf in purple and brown was followed by a red, yellow, and green vest that seemed unable to decide if it was celebrating Easter or Psychedelic Tuesday. Robin had received the vest and Cam the scarf, and for once Cam hadn't spoken his mind. He'd thanked Em politely, and when she was gone told Robin, "Mom said just say thanks. The only explanation she could think was

Ms. Kane is color-blind."

Em became their instructor on how law enforcement operates. Cam played *Dragon's Revenge* as she talked on and on, but Robin listened eagerly, determined to learn everything she could about real police procedure. Em said to ignore the fanciful stuff of TV drama. "There's a lot less DNA testing and CODIS searching than most people think, due to cost, volume, and the lack of sophisticated equipment in most police departments. You'd have to come to the attention of someone with the resources and the determination to track you down." Em sipped at the coffee Cam had made for her. "Your best protection is that your targets don't want to bring in those resources, since their own dirty tricks might come to light."

Thomas Wyman's face appeared in Robin's mind. He seemed pretty determined. If he located her or Cam, what then? Would he report to Abrams and walk away? Turn them in to the police? Or was he more sinister than she'd imagined? Was Wyman's job to eliminate her and Cam for Abrams and erase the chance that his crimes would ever be exposed? Em dismissed her fears with a puff of air. "Finding Cam is just a job for him. When it's clear he's left Georgia, Wyman will lose interest and move on to other cases."

Robin and Cam began closing their affairs in Cedar. She took her decrepit car to a local garage that reconditioned vehicles and sold them at discount prices. The man gave her the best price he could, which wasn't much with all that was wrong with it. When Em offered the use of her car whenever they needed it, Cam also sold his mother's Pontiac, letting Robin handle the deal when a couple arrived ready to buy.

Working quietly after midnight, Cam had gradually taken his clothes and the few other things he wanted from his apartment. They discussed what to do with what remained, and Robin warned gently that the plaid recliner, floral couch, and mismatched pressed-wood tables wouldn't bring much if he offered them for sale. "Call the Salvation Army," he suggested. "They say on TV they'll come with a truck and take everything."

He was right, and Robin was able to drop his keys in the landlord's mailbox with a note severing Cam's ties with Munson Apartments.

Em picked details about the second KNP—which Robin still insisted on referring to as *tentative*—out of Cam every time she got him alone. If Robin went to the grocery store, a frequent necessity due to Cam's healthy appetite, she'd come home to find Em sitting at her kitchen table. The coffee pot now sat on the countertop full time, and the smell of freshly-made no-bakes, apparently Em's only culinary accomplishment, accompanied the smell of percolating coffee. Cam waited on Em the way Robin imagined he'd waited on his mother. He always glanced helplessly at her when she came in, as if to say he didn't know how to deny Em's visits or refuse her brusque commands.

Em had no intention of telling anyone they'd kidnapped Commissioner Abrams. In fact, she seemed to see it as an achievement. "When I was at the Bureau," she told them, "too many got away with stuff because we couldn't prove what we knew they were up to." Setting her knitting in her lap, she sipped at her coffee. "If I were twenty years younger, I'd jump into your scheme with both feet."

"I bet you put plenty of criminals behind bars in your day."

"And then it was over. You don't miss the water till the well runs dry, Kiddo." Picking up her knitting, Em started work again. "This bum hip stuck me behind a desk, and I didn't feel like I was really on the job anymore. I decided to get out before they tossed me in the trash like a used sheet of Bounty."

Robin wondered if Em's limp was due to an on-the-job injury, like a bullet wound or a fall from a roof while chasing a bad guy. While she often told stories of old cases, Em never gave specifics about her own exploits. She also never mentioned a husband, kids, or family.

"Have you considered a hip replacement?" Robin asked.

Her smile was bitter. "Baby-doll, this is what I get *after* a hip replacement. There's no more they can do."

"I'm sorry."

She sniffed dismissively. "The old gray mare just ain't what she used to be."

What had it been like to fight crime in Chicago or Detroit in the last millennium? Had Em actually met J. Edgar Hoover? Had she tucked a spare gun in her bra or strapped it to her ankle? "At least you're out of the nine to five grind."

Em made a derisive sound. "Let me tell you something, Chickie. You spend the last third of your life trying to find something to do with all that time you saved rushing through the first two-thirds." Her needles clicked faster. "Ever wonder why so many old people work so hard for a church or a charity? It gives them a reason to get out of bed in the morning." Pressing her elbows into the chair arms, she shifted her hips to a more comfortable position. "I used to do things that mattered, and if I had my way, that's what I'd be doing now."

Robin wanted to say she was sorry but knew her neighbor wouldn't appreciate pity from her—or anyone.

Em abruptly shifted topics. "Cam says he's pretty sure you're going ahead with your new plan."

Scrambling for a kernel of truth, Robin said, "It isn't decided. I mean, there's someone who needs a lesson, but I'm not sure we're equipped to handle it."

"What would this lesson entail?" Robin hesitated and Em

said, “A burden shared is half the weight.”

Haltingly at first but gaining confidence as she spoke, Robin described the “dishonest governmental official” they’d zeroed in on and outlined the plan they were considering.

“Sounds pretty good,” Em said when she’d finished. “I’d add a few touches to make it run smoother, but I think you’re onto something with this kidnapping thing.”

“So I’m a pretty good criminal mastermind. Should I be pleased or horrified?”

Em ignored her little joke. “You’re getting a new identity. Can you use it so no one looks at you twice?”

“What do you mean?”

“Well first, you and Cam should travel as husband and wife, so you blend in with all the other couples on the road every day. When you get your new documents, you need to learn to be casual about using them. When you get nervous, you explain way too much.” She made a huff of derision. “That first day you babbled on about meeting your brother in Atlanta and staying at the Hampton Inn. That kind of thing can give you away.”

“I don’t see—”

“If a clerk says, ‘How was your trip?’ and you say, ‘Traffic on I-85 is really bad,’ you reveal the direction you came from. Get it?” Receiving a doubtful nod, Em gave the table two little pats to emphasize the differences in her next statement. “You have to be alert all the time, but you can’t *look* like you are.”

Robin had begun to understand she’d have to give up things she’d always been—honest, open, and law-abiding—to become someone who lied as a matter of course, kept secrets from those she loved, and broke laws, big and small, every single day. It wasn’t lost on her that her father had done those same things. At times she felt ashamed of herself for dragging Cam into her schemes. Still, their cause wasn't selfish, as Mark's had been, and Cam was enthusiastically gung-ho. Their new life was scary, but scary exciting too.

When the Buckram KNP was over, could she become the old Robin Parsons again? Would there even be a way to do that? Asked that question, Em would probably quote Wolfe: "You can't go home again."

Em seemed to read her mind. Spreading the piece she was knitting on her lap and smoothing it with her hands she asked, "Where will you go once you've pulled off this Richmond caper?"

He even blabbed the location!

"*If* we do it, we'll stay mobile for a while afterward," she replied. "To muddy the trail."

"A complete break is probably wise." Despite the words, Robin saw disappointment in Em's eyes. She'd been getting a vicarious thrill from hearing their plans and giving advice, and the prospect that it would soon end saddened her. "You're going to need a base of operations eventually."

Robin blinked. "Base of operations?"

"A safe spot to go between jobs."

"Em, this isn't a long-term plan. I—"

"Honey," Em interrupted, setting her knitting in her lap, "The world is full of wicked people who never get caught. Anything you do to stop one of them is good."

"I'm not sure we can convince this target to confess to anything."

Cam spoke without looking up from his game. "What if we follow the senator and get a shot of him buying drugs? If we have a photo, he'll have to admit what he did."

Em's eyes lit with interest. "A senator, eh? Quite a step up from a county commissioner."

"We're 95 percent sure he's crooked," Robin said defensively.

Possibly as incentive for more sharing of information, Em said, "That private detective showed up again. I sent him off on a tangent."

"He was here *again*?"

"Told you he was an eager beaver." She wriggled her brows comically. "I said I heard in the elevator that Carter Halkias was living in Denver with a girl he met at the laundromat."

Robin relaxed a little. "Thanks, Em."

The older woman smiled. "By the time he chases that dead trail, you'll be packed and out of here."

"Robin," Cam said, "Maybe Em could go to Richmond with us. She could—"

She cut him off. "Cam, we can't ask Em to do more than she's already done."

"Why not?" Em demanded. "You'll need a driver. I can do that in spite of this stupid hip."

"No."

A third person would be helpful.

The plan—*if* they proceeded with it—was to grab Buckram during his evening walk, but Robin worried that seeing a man Cam's size coming at him would put the senator on guard. Since he was likely to be armed, things could easily escalate. Cam was no Jason Bourne, Robin wasn't Lara Croft, and neither of them wanted to hurt Buckram. She'd been trying to figure out a distraction that would make the grab easy and quick. If Em helped, Robin and Cam's chance for success would increase exponentially.

Not that I'm sure we're going to do this. It's a scenario, not a plan.

Em watched Robin, her eyes eager. "At the very least I could go with you—in case the poo hits the fan."

"*If* you came, it would be to provide a diversion. You might walk by and say something to the guy to turn his attention away from Cam and me. Then you'd keep walking, no matter what happened."

"Sure." Em's analytical mind almost ticked aloud as she considered. "We need a dog."

"A dog?"

"People can't resist them. They stop. They pet it. They ask questions." She grinned knowingly. "And even if your senator isn't an animal lover, dogs are known for being curious."

"Where would we get a dog?" Robin asked.

"There's a stray that hangs out by the trash bins. I'll see if I can make friends."

"No pets in the apartments," Cam reminded Em soberly.

That brought a sarcastic salute. "Breaking the building rules is the least of our worries, Handsome." She turned to Robin. "When is this going down?"

Glancing at the calendar, she licked her lips. "The legislature is taking a recess on Friday. I was going to go to Richmond on Tuesday and meet with—a person who could help us confirm that Buckram is taking bribes."

"It would be best if we travel together. Then we can make a

decision after you meet with your source."

Robin felt control slipping from her hands. "I haven't even—"

Em paid no attention to her objection. "What do we know about this senator's evening walks?"

"Every night around seven he leaves by an alley at the back of his building. Satellite view shows we could pick him up before he reaches the street, where there's probably video surveillance." In consideration of Cam's suggestion she added, "I guess it would work if I followed him to see what he's up to on his walk. We could still catch him in the alley on his way home."

"Too bad we don't have a computer whiz to help out." Robin wondered when Em had become part of *we*.

"Yeah," Cam said from the couch. "Like controlling the traffic lights so we can get away from the cops."

"That isn't as easy as it looks in movies." Em kneaded her elbow. "But a guy who knows his way around a computer would be good."

Robin raised a hand. More people meant more risk, another person she had to trust not to slip up. "Let's not get ahead of ourselves."

"Yeah," Em agreed. "Where would we get a geek willing to risk life in prison for thrills and chills?"

Though Robin continued to tell herself the KNP was tentative, Cam acted as if they were going ahead with it, and now Em seemed just as certain. Though she wanted to proceed, Robin wrestled with the questions Mink had raised, most importantly, what would they do if things went wrong?

Get arrested, probably.

She realized she was chewing her thumbnail and reminded

herself she didn't bite her nails anymore. It was chilling to think she might have to go on the run, even leave the country. She'd never see her brother or best friend again. They were all she had, but that was a lot.

Don't think about that right now. Think about polar bear cubs playing with a beach ball. Anything but pursuit, harassment, and prison time.

Chapter Eight

Senator Charles "Buck" Buckram tried to sit still as the chairwoman droned on about states' rights and the president's inexcusable habit of tromping on them. Though Buck was feeling agitated, he made a conscious effort to keep his hands still, to stop his right cheek from twitching, and to avoid sniffing back the moisture that gathered in his sinuses and dripped out his nose or down the back of his throat. As a member of the majority party, he had to at least maintain the illusion he cared what others on his side said—over and over and over.

He needed a little something.

Disguising his hyperactivity as necessary movement, he reached for a pad of paper and a pen and pretended to take notes.

Jeez Louise, does she ever shut up?

"We must work to protect the people of this great state from government overreach," the chairwoman was saying. "We will not allow our constituents' rights to be ignored and abused."

Except by us! Buckram laughed aloud at his own joke but covered it with a cough.

A few people glanced at him briefly, but he arranged his features into an expression of interest and stared at the speaker as if enthralled by her words.

I need a little something. Just a little help to get me through today.

Buck often promised himself he'd get off the stuff. He could; he was absolutely certain of that.

I can quit anytime I want to.

It was just that he was so much better with a little jolt of coke in his system. His enthusiasm for the job returned. He was able to concentrate better. It was great.

He worried sometimes about the chances he took, but the benefits were so worth it. And he really could quit whenever he chose.

Just not today, he admitted as the speaker droned on. *Today I need a little something.*

***

Robin, Cam, and Em began their trip to Richmond in Em's 2006 Buick (which Cam referred to as a "grocery-getter") with the stray dog Em had befriended in the back seat with her. The creature wasn't well-bred, literally or figuratively, but he was docile as long as Em was near. In fact, he looked at her as if she were Mother Teresa.

On the way they bought a gray panel van Cam spotted when they stopped for gas. Since he wasn't comfortable dealing with strangers, Robin did the talking, which made the process odd, to say the least. The owner kept directing his comments to Cam, only to have Robin reply. In the end, Cam examined the vehicle thoroughly, took it for a spin, and said, "He didn't take very good care of it, but I can work on it." When she was done blushing, Robin went inside to seal the deal, and Cam followed them in what she thought of as "the Kidnap-mobile" the rest of the way.

They chose a motel on the outskirts of Richmond, a small, non-franchise operation. It had a large parking area out back where the owner said Cam could work on the van as long he did it during daylight hours and didn't leave a mess behind. Once Em and Cam were settled in separate rooms (Robin registered as Cam's wife but shared with Em), it was almost five thirty. Taking Em's car, Robin drove downtown to meet Jessica Quern, Senator Buckram's public relations manager.

At the agreed-upon restaurant, Robin asked for a table facing the entrance, wanting a chance to examine the woman before she put on whatever game face she might employ at their meeting. Quern had once been willing to tell Chris the senator's secrets, so his illicit activities must bother her. Something had happened to change her mind, and Robin guessed it had been something frightening.

When Quern entered, Robin recognized her from online photos of Buckram's staff. Everything about Jessica Quern was "done," from nails to hair to face. Her clothes were expensive and stylish, her body toned and tan. Still, as Ms. Quern stopped to speak to the hostess, Robin thought she detected an air of defeat. A flat look in her eyes hinted Quern no longer believed things always work out well in the end.

Robin had called posing as a writer planning a magazine article about Senator Buckram's good works. Though Quern sounded surprised by that, she'd agreed to meet her at a restaurant along the Bottom, Richmond's trendy riverside area. The "reporter" had said she'd be wearing a green headband.

When Robin waved discreetly, Quern strode toward her. The defeated look was replaced by professional confidence she wrapped around herself like a shawl. A waiter trotted behind, and before she sat down in the chair opposite Robin, Quern ordered a glass of brut white wine, the go-to choice for dieting drinkers. The young man hurried off as if he were afraid she'd swat him if he tarried. Quern's smile had a hint of satisfaction. Someone was eager to do her bidding, even if it was in hopes of a generous tip.

"I'm so happy you agreed to this interview," Robin began after they'd introduced themselves. "We plan to spotlight leaders who work to improve the lives of their constituents, starting with Senator Buckram."

The waiter brought Quern's wine and set it before her like an offering. She thanked him without looking up, raised the glass to her bright red lips, and took a long drink. "Why him?"

Robin played dumb. "To be honest, I didn't choose the subjects. I guess my boss is impressed with his grasp of the needs of our state."

Quern had taken a second drink, and she seemed to have trouble swallowing it. Setting her glass on the mosaic table surface with a clink, she examined Robin closely. Finally she said, "You look like him."

"What?"

"Chris Parsons. He mentioned he had a sister somewhere in the South." She smiled at her own cleverness. "When you speak, you move your mouth the same way he does."

Robin hadn't considered the physical resemblance between her and Chris would give her away.

Quern's smile wasn't a sneer, but it wasn't happy, either. "I can't believe he told you about me."

Knowing it sounded defensive Robin said, "Chris wants to stop men like Buckram."

Quern's mouth curled sardonically. "Me too, once upon a time."

"He scared you into keeping quiet."

At first she shook her head, but Robin waited expectantly. Quern seemed torn; she wanted to tell someone. "Are you taping this?"

"No."

"No recording of any kind?"

"None."

"Legally, if I ask, you have to tell me the truth."

"I am telling the truth."

Quern nodded as if reassuring herself. "I won't testify or even speak to the police. If you repeat anything I say, I'll insist you made it up. And I can't give you documents." She glanced around the room. "Snooping in someone's files looks easy in the movies, but it's scary when you actually try it." She pulled her lips over her teeth before adding, "I probably telegraphed guilt all over the place."

"You tried to get the evidence Chris wanted."

"I did, and Buck caught me. He just—went off." Quern rubbed her arm absently, and Robin got a mental image of it being twisted cruelly behind her back.

"Did he hurt you?"

"I thought he was going to strangle me for a minute." As if recalling rough treatment, she smoothed her hair with both hands. "I managed to convince him I was gathering quotes for a press release, but he's suspicious now. If word gets out, he'll see that I never work in this town again."

Robin wanted to ask if a person's soul was worth a job, but it seemed that bargain had already been made. Quern drained her glass. "I've told you this so you understand that we won't be talking further." She pushed her chair back. "You can pay for the drinks."

Despite Robin's hopes, the interview was over less than five minutes in. As Jessica Quern rose to go, Robin put a hand on her arm. "Give me something—anything that might help us."

Quern shook her head then apparently reconsidered. "I can give you a name."

***

Patrick Delacroix was a junior state senator and a veteran of the Afghan War. He seemed the polar opposite of Buckram, certain of his position on the issues and able to explain clearly why he held them. Since Delacroix had introduced the veterans' health bill Buckram was "considering," she hoped he'd have incentive to help her.

"It's hard to imagine him just agreeing to give us dirt on a colleague though," Robin said to Em.

"The kid's new and innocent." Em wriggled her brows. "He might be dying to tell somebody his troubles."

Delacroix certainly looked like a straight arrow. Comments they found on various websites told of the junior senator working tirelessly to help constituents navigate the maze of governmental roadblocks and red tape. One writer wrote, *Senator Delacroix has a mature grasp of what government is supposed to be.* After some research, Robin had to agree. With time running short before she had to make a decision on the KNP, she decided to simply show up at Delacroix's office.

To get past the gatekeepers, she invented a story about a suicidal brother with PTSD. The receptionist, a sweet-faced woman with glasses the size of New Jersey, gasped in sympathy and promised the senator would see Robin if she could wait. They'd squeeze her in between appointments.

It took almost two hours of listening to canned music and checking the news on her phone, but eventually Robin was escorted into Delacroix's office, a second-class space with mismatched furniture and no windows. Along the wall, books and papers lay stacked on chairs, on tables, and in corners. Many were marked with sticky notes and colorful arrows to locate spots he wanted to return to at some point.

The senator was as baby-faced in person as he looked in his pictures, with a lock of hair that refused to stay off his forehead.

He'd taken his jacket off and rolled up his shirt sleeves, and he stood to shake Robin's hand with a friendly, no-nonsense manner. "Please, sit down, Miss Jackson. I understand you need help with medical benefits for a veteran."

Robin glanced over her shoulder as she took a seat in front of the senator's desk, making sure the receptionist had left the room before she spoke. "Actually, no."

He looked surprised. "I must have misunderstood."

"I lied," she admitted. "What I'm looking for is proof that Senator Buckram is corrupt."

Delacroix glanced at the door, then at Robin, then at the phone console on his desk.

"Please don't call security yet. Give me two minutes." She wiped her sweaty palms on her pants. "I've got no weapons and I have no intention of hurting anyone. Please let me tell you why I'm here."

He nodded, but his eyes remained wary. Robin leaned forward, speaking quickly but softly. "I'm part of a group that tries to curb the influence of men like Buckram. We work behind the scenes, and we have a good record of convincing them to change their ways."

That isn't a lie. We're one for one, as far as we know.

The senator was unconvinced. "Miss, I can't—"

"No one will know you helped us." She met Delacroix's gaze. "He's going to kill the veterans' bill you introduced. He'll claim he's taking the moral high ground, but you know that's complete gibberish."

Delacroix shook his head. "We can't force an elected official to change simply because you or I disagree with his position."

"He hasn't got a position and you know it. The reason he's stalled this long on the decision is to see if your side can outbid the other side."

The senator's face seemed to age a decade. "I won't plot against a fellow legislator. The bill will proceed or it won't. If it doesn't, we'll try again."

"Listen to me. He's being paid to kill your legislation. It won't even be considered unless we stop him."

Delacroix's expression became even more morose. It was time to offer reassurance.

"We don't hurt people." Robin held her hands up, palms out to emphasize her point. "We just insist they face their misconduct and reconsider the paths they've taken."

An eyebrow quirked as he considered her words. "How do you do that?"

She paused, unwilling to give up the cautious agreement she saw in his eyes. "Our methods are unorthodox, I admit, but the senator will not be harmed." She waited, giving him a chance to think it through. "You know he's as crooked as a tree branch."

"What do you want from me?"

"Something tangible we can present to Buckram, something that proves his wrongdoing."

A rueful smile appeared on the man's face. "Don't you think if I had proof I'd have used it?"

She leaned back in her chair. "Not necessarily. First, you have your career to consider, and whistle-blowers are seldom popular. Second, you might know something that isn't convincing by itself, but we put together bits and pieces from many sources." Seeing the slightest of nods, Robin went on. "And finally, you're a person of conscience who doesn't want to destroy another man's career.

That's noble, but we aren't looking to destroy Buckram. We'll give him every chance to change the way he operates. All we ask is that he represents the needs of the people and not deep-pocket special interests."

And get off the drugs, Robin added to herself. There was no need to share that with Delacroix.

After a long pause the senator said softly, "A man named Nathan Blume is a big supporter of Buckram. He claims to be a businessman, but his business doesn't always smell so good, if you know what I mean."

Robin felt a little thrill of triumph. "My source mentioned Mr. Blume."

Delacroix fiddled with some papers on his desk. "I accidentally saw a text message Buck received the other day. He's a bit of a Luddite, and he was having trouble sending a photo from his phone. While I was helping him with it, a message showed up on his screen." He blushed. "I didn't mean to read it, but there it was."

"They do just pop up."

The reason for the blush became clear as he went on. "I forwarded the message to myself. It wasn't ethical, but I needed time to think about what it meant." Reaching for a folder at the corner of his desk, he searched through its contents until he found what he sought. "I thought we could use it to prove he takes bribes, but my advisers say it isn't specific enough. If I share it, I open myself to criticism for snooping in another official's private correspondence. If it helps you..." He handed Robin a sheet of copy paper. It was a screenshot he'd printed of a message from Blume to Buckram: SD-20K ON DEFEAT.

"If I read this correctly, someone—SD—offered to pay Buckram to work against your bill."

Delacroix smiled ruefully. "You're taking it the way I took it, but there are a dozen other possibilities. I think SD stands for Soldier Distress, a private group that claims they fund research for traumatic brain injuries." His tone turned disgusted. "They spend a lot more on administrative salaries than they do on research."

"Yes, my br—informant mentioned groups like that."

"SD could mean other things," he warned, "from South Dakota to ScanDisc. But my guess is that Blume works as intermediary between Buckram and those who bribe him, to blur the money trail." He gestured at the paper she held. "That doesn't mention my bill. It's just something I felt in my gut."

Folding the paper, Robin put it into her purse. "This will help when we approach the senator."

He reached across the desk in an unconscious gesture, as if he wished he could take back what he'd done. "You won't tell him where you got that?"

"No." Standing, she put out a hand. "I admire your efforts to serve your constituents with integrity."

Delacroix smiled grimly as they shook hands. "A lot of Americans don't believe there's such a thing as an honest politician, but we're here. We just don't make as much noise as the dishonest ones."

Chapter Nine

After talking with Delacroix, Robin called Chris and told him about the message taken from Buckram's phone.

"I know about Buckram's old friend Blume," Chris told her. "A real piece of garbage. Let me work on this for an hour or so."

While she waited for Chris' call, Robin wandered the hotel room. Cam was hard at work, adapting the van they'd bought, and Em had taken the dog for a walk. The mutt didn't seem to mind Em's slow gait, and she claimed they'd practice their role in the caper along the way.

Robin took the time alone to do some tidying up, stuffing her dirty clothes into a plastic bag and going over what she'd brought for the still-tentative KNP for the thousandth time. As she passed the window, she stopped at the sight of a familiar-looking black car. Her breath caught in her throat as one of her inner arguments began.

There are lots of black cars in the world, Robin.

Yes, but that detective, Wyman, drives one that looks a lot like that.

You're suddenly a car expert? You don't even know a Ford from a Chevy without checking the logo!

She stood there for some time, but in the end there was nothing to be done. She'd be crazy to leave the room and try to get a look at the driver. Motels weren't allowed to give out information about who was staying there, and they hadn't used their real names anyway. After a while she went back to folding clothes, and when she looked again, the black car was gone.

It couldn't have been Wyman, she told herself. *There's no way he could know we're in Richmond.*

After half an hour of biting her nails then reminding herself she didn't bite her nails anymore, Robin got the call from Chris she'd been waiting for. "Buckram received a $20,000 donation to his re-election fund last week from Nathan Blume. It looks like he's serving as middleman so Soldier Distress doesn't appear as a Buckram donor."

That was when Robin stopped telling herself the KNP was tentative. Cam was almost finished with the van. Em and the dog were ready. She'd rented a storage unit in an out-of-town facility. It was time to act.

***

Just after seven p.m., Buckram left his building by the back door and started down the alley, his steps purposeful but not hurried. He looked behind a few times out of habit, but his posture was relaxed. It was clear he'd done this many times without attracting attention.

Four blocks away was a small park surrounded by a low wall of red brick. Buckram entered through a wrought-iron gate, and as Robin followed, she smelled some sweet-scented, early-flowering shrub. A brisk walk down a path that cut diagonally across the park led to a small fountain where water spilled noisily onto water. Buckram stopped there, apparently to enjoy the evening air. Robin slid into the shadows, crouched down, and crept forward, her phone in one hand.

Buckram walked around the fountain twice before a woman approached from the opposite side of the park. For a drug dealer, she was surprisingly normal-looking in jeans, a puffy coat, and expensive boots. It took Robin a second to shake the stereotype formed from watching too many cop shows.

The woman joined Buckram with a casual nod of greeting.

She was more watchful than he, no surprise given her profession's inherent risks, and her gaze flickered to all sides. Taking his cue from her, Buckram examined the darkness, head tilted as he listened for sounds in the night. Though Robin's haunches were starting to burn, she lowered her face and let the darkness and her clothing hide her from sight. Satisfied they were alone, the woman said something to Buckram, who answered with a question.

Robin couldn't hear the conversation, but she video-recorded the meeting. Buckram gave the woman something, money, she guessed, and in return received a packet he slid into his coat pocket. Though they used their bodies to shield their actions from view, the clandestine nature of the exchange was obvious.

As soon as their business was concluded, the woman melted into the darkness. Buckram returned through the gate he'd entered, passing Robin's hiding place without once glancing her way. His step was light, and he whistled as he walked.

He's gotten away with deceit for so long he can't imagine he won't keep doing it.

She'd prepared two messages for Cam, a go and a no-go. Scrolling to the one that said, *WE'LL DO IT*, she hit *SEND*. Sliding her phone into the zippered pocket of her jacket, Robin followed the senator out of the park.

When Buckram entered the alley leading to his building's back door, an old woman wearing a long, dark coat and a wildly colorful scarf came toward him. Beside her was a scruffy-looking dog of mixed breed. "Nice evening," the woman said in the casual way of neighbors. The dog jerked on its leash, trying to sniff the newcomer, which caused the woman to lurch sideways and bump Buckram's arm. "Sorry," she apologized. "Cuddles gets excited when we take our walkies." Hardly bothering to nod in response, he moved on.

A gray van sat parked ahead, its motor running. As the senator neared it, Em let go of the dog's leash and the mutt bounded back the way he'd come. Alerted by the sound of paws on cobblestone, Buckram turned, picking up his pace when he saw the dog coming at him.

He wasn't fast enough. The dog jumped, knocking him against the brick wall of the building. As its intruding nose snuffled at his coat, Buckram flailed at it. "Get down! Go away!"

The dog ignored the command, licking noisily at the gob of beef base Em had smeared on his sleeve moments earlier. Setting its front paws on Buckram's arm, it licked at the sleeve as the angry man slid along the wall in a vain attempt to escape.

While the senator shoved at the dog, Cam approached from behind and grabbed his arms. Catching up at a run, Robin punched Buckram hard in the stomach, knocking the wind from his lungs. Fumbling at the holster at his waist, she took his sidearm and stuck it into her jacket pocket. Next she located his phone and took that too.

While the senator fought to get breath back in his lungs, Cam lifted him off his feet and propelled him through the open van doors. As soon as Cam stepped back Robin closed the doors, hearing the latch click a half-second before Buckram's shoulder hit the other side. The force of it shook the van—and Robin's confidence—but the doors held.

After a quick look to assure there were no witnesses, Robin threw herself into the driver's seat. Cam got in the passenger side, watching nervously as she missed the ignition several times before successfully inserting the key. As they pulled away, Em gave an enthusiastic thumbs up. Less than four minutes later Robin, Cam, and their unwilling passenger turned onto the freeway ramp and headed out of the city.

The back of the van sounded like it was under attack from

gremlins. Between blows at the door that no longer had an interior latch, Buckram promised the full weight of the Commonwealth of Virginia would descend on them, along with the FBI and Homeland Security. "You'll rot in prison! Hell, you kidnapped a government official. They might even send you to Guantanamo." Robin forced herself to concentrate on driving. Cam seemed to have retreated to a place in his mind where sound didn't penetrate.

When they reached the storage unit Cam got out and made certain no one was around. Removing the padlock, he opened the overhead door. After Robin backed the van inside, he pulled the door closed and set a block in the latch so the door wouldn't open.

Without interior illumination the space was inky black, and they moved around using headlamps. A lawn chair was already in place at the back. A video camera and a stack of documents were laid out on an empty cardboard box, within easy reach. They were ready. With a deep breath, Robin pulled her mask back on and switched on the trouble lights. "Let's do this."

When Cam opened the doors Buckram barreled out like a rampaging gorilla, sending the chair flying against the wall. The lights blinded him and he stopped, shielding his eyes with a hand. "What the hell is this?"

Robin turned on the device at her throat and spoke commandingly. "Pick up the chair and sit in it."

Buckram peered into the lights. "You're crazy! I won't—"

"Bozo."

Cameron stepped into the light, completely covered by his ski mask, canvas jumpsuit, dollar-store tennis shoes, and brown garden gloves. He set the chair in place with a firm clank, took Buckram by the shoulders, and set him in the chair as easily as if he were a rag doll.

Robin approached with duct tape in hand. When the senator tensed she warned, “Sit still, or Bozo will show you how.”

Glowering, Buckram let her tape his arms to the chair. “Do you know who I am?”

“Yes, Senator, we do. You’re going to confess your crimes to us. Then you’re going to atone for them.”

“Crimes? What the hell are you talking about?”

Robin consulted her list. “Let’s start with Nathan Blume, who paid for that Lamborghini you’re driving.”

“That’s not true.”

“It is so.” Cam’s voice came from the shadows behind. “It’s an Aventador two-door coupe worth $400,000. That thing is sweet!”

At a gesture from Robin, he suppressed his rapture over the senator’s car, and she went on. “You can’t afford that car. It’s an illegal and unethical gift.”

The chair rails scraped on the uneven concrete floor as Buckram’s weight shifted. “I make investments—”

“You take bribes. You’ve broken every promise you made when you got elected to the state legislature.”

His expression turned pious. “I do what’s best for my people.”

“You do what’s best for Nathan Blume and his cronies.”

He set his jaw. “I have great respect for Mr. Blume’s business acumen.”

“He’s been investigated for everything from money laundering to murder.”

The senator closed his eyes for a moment. "He's an acquaintance. I don't really know him that well."

"He's paying you to work against the new veterans' center."

Buckram tried to raise a hand, but because of the duct tape, he managed only a finger. "It would be a waste of taxpayer funds. We have excellent veterans' centers in other parts of the state."

"Not within three hundred miles of the proposed one."

He leaned forward to make his argument. "That's a good thing. People pay better attention to a doctor's orders if it takes a lot of effort to see him."

"That's the stupidest argument I've ever heard."

His face took on a superior expression. "That's because you don't understand human behavior like I do."

Shaking her head in disbelief, Robin tried to get back on track. "You're a crook who takes money from other crooks. Illegal contributions—"

"My friend," Buckram interrupted, "you don't understand the way things work. I comprehend the system extremely well, if I work it better than the next guy, that just proves how much smarter I am than everybody else." The finger waggled again. "I'll bet you've got no proof I've done anything illegal, so if you call me a crook in public, I'll sue you into the poorhouse. And let me just say this: I believe in hitting back as hard as I get hit—maybe harder."

"You'd sue someone for telling the truth about you? That's priceless."

One of Buckram's brows rose. "I bet Delacroix put you up to this. I gotta tell you, he's a nut case. I call him Nutty Delacroix, because he makes stuff up."

"We don't deal with political rivals," Robin said to dispel his suspicion. "Too subjective. What we did notice was that you were all for a veterans' center six months ago. Then suddenly you were against it. How did that happen?"

"I'm friends with the head of Veterans' Affairs. He told me we don't need another center in Virginia."

"Are you saying the Secretary of the VA doesn't want this center? He said that to you directly?"

Buckram's lip jutted. "In a private conversation."

"Where? When?"

The man's his head shook so hard the chair wobbled. "That doesn't matter."

"I want to know when you spoke to the head of Veterans' Affairs."

There was a pause. "In the capitol. We were waiting for an elevator."

"Right after you both commented on the weather?"

"We had a really good talk. It wasn't very long, but I grasp new information very easily. That's when I changed my mind about the bill, because I listen and I decide with my brain. I have a very sharp mind."

Is the guy delusional or has he just lied so often he can't stop?

"Let's talk about your problem with cocaine."

His chin rose. "I don't use drugs."

She navigated to the video she'd taken earlier. "Then what's going on here?"

Peering at the tiny screen, Buckram frowned. "That woman

asked for a handout, and I gave her a few bucks." He made an attempt at a pious expression. "I'm a Christian person. I believe in the Bible and the New Testament. Both of them."

"One of our people is interviewing her right this minute." *If you can lie, Bubba, so can I.*

"I don't know what she'll say. People tell lies about me all the time."

Reaching into his pocket, Robin found the bag he'd purchased and held it in front of his nose. "You use cocaine, Senator. A lot of it."

Buckram sniffed. "It's hard, what I do. Sometimes I need help to get through the day, but I'm no druggie."

"What would your constituents think about the 'help' you need to do your job?"

Buckram fought his way back to denial. "Nobody will believe you. People like me. They call me up all the time and they're telling me I'm a good person. The voters know how much I—"

In an action so sudden it surprised even her, Robin tore a strip of duct tape from the roll with an abrupt rip and slapped it over Buckram's mouth. "Stop spewing lies, Senator, and for once listen to the truth."

Buckram's eyes widened, and he roared behind his duct-tape gag. He half-rose from the chair, apparently ready to attack Robin, but Cam reached out a hand and set him back down. For a few seconds Buckram struggled to rise, but Cam held on. Looking into Buckram's eyes, Robin realized he wasn't trying to attack her. He was desperate to avoid facing the truth. Though he finally gave up his efforts to move away, he refused to look at Robin, staring at the floor while she read his crimes from the list Chris had compiled. It was a combination of suspicions, accusations, and hints gleaned from the media, public records, and documents covering official investigations into Buckram's conduct. Not one item was provable in a court of law, but the list was impressive.

As Robin read, Buckram's head drooped almost to his chest. For years he'd prevailed by bragging, boasting, and shouting down opponents. Forcing him to listen—though it took duct tape to do it— made him face what he had become. When she came to the last item, the email from Blume offering the bribe to vote against the veterans' center, she saw a hint of shame in the senator's eyes.

How long will it last? A lifetime of avoiding self-examination wasn't likely to be cured in one evening. For the moment, Buckram accepted his guilt, so they had to move quickly. Robin explained the requirements for his release and their silence. "Delacroix's bill will be sent from committee and given a chance," she ordered. "You can vote your so-called conscience when the time comes, but don't stand in the way of a fair hearing."

He nodded numbly, and she went on. "You will not take bribes from now on, from Blume or anyone else. Live within your means, and get into drug rehab—anonymously if you like, but do it. We will be watching." Taking Buckram's phone from her pocket she finished, "Now about the fee you're going to pay for our silence."

***

Once the situation was clear to him, the senator called an employee and directed him to bring the payment to a nearby rest area. When a young Asian man dropped the bag of money in a trash can outside the men's room, Robin had Buckram instruct him to get back into the car, turn it toward the exit, and wait. She retrieved the bag and checked to assure that the money was there. When she signaled, Cam let the senator go, and he hurried to the car and got in the passenger side.

As the senator and his man drove away, Robin became aware

that Cam was standing behind her, very close. She looked down to find his hands extended around her like a personal force field.

"What are you doing?"

"I'm ready to catch you when you faint."

Robin took stock: heart rate, okay; lungs, functioning. "Aside from a need to visit the rest room, I'm good."

"Seventy-five thousand dollars." Cameron counted it as they headed for the state line. "We did it!"

Robin checked the rearview mirror for the twentieth time. "Think he'll do what we said?"

"He has to, or we'll send the stuff to the newspapers. That was smart, telling him we'd be watching him."

"It wasn't my idea," she admitted. "I guess people like Buckram need somebody like us standing over them in order to straighten up and act like decent human beings."

Cam gave her a look. "Sounds like we might do this again."

Robin sighed. "I think I like kidnapping bad guys."

Chapter Ten

"You want me to pretend you're living here?" Robin's best friend spoke over measured chops as she cut up vegetables. Already soup stock bubbled on the stove, sending mouth-watering smells into the air.

Robin had arrived in Green Bay with a small bag of essentials and a plan to stay ahead of Wyman or anyone else who might have been looking for her. Now she had to decide how much to tell Shelly about what she'd done and what she intended to do. Involving her best friend in her crimes was wrong, so she figured the less Shelly knew, the better it would be for her if everything went sour.

"I want my mail to come here," Robin told her. "If anyone asks, I'm doing real estate appraisals, so I have to travel a lot."

"Why do you need to pretend to be in Green Bay when you aren't?"

"Honestly, Shel, it's better if you don't know."

Shelly folded her arms. "Does this have anything to do with the beautiful hunk who got off the plane with you and is now staying at the Holiday Inn?"

Robin gave the easy answer. "He's part of it, yes."

"I knew it!" Shelly gave her an enthusiastic hug. "Go wherever you need to, but I want a phone call every week. Whatever you and he are up to, someone needs to keep track of where you are."

You won't really know, Robin thought, *but it's nice that you care.*

The rest of Robin's visit was spent working out the details. Most of her things had been stored in the unit outside Cedar, but she'd left several boxes at the FedEx store. Once Shelly agreed to her proposal, Robin called and had them overnighted to Green Bay.

Having sworn off men after her divorce, Shelly now lived alone in a three-bedroom house. When the boxes arrived, Robin unpacked them in the guest room, taking what she would need for a couple of weeks on the road and leaving the rest to make it appear Shelly had a roommate.

Next they drove to a mall where Robin bought two cell phones, a tablet, and a laptop computer. When she paid with cash, Shelly's brows twitched, but she didn't say anything. Robin was satisfied when she tried the phone and the ID came up *GREEN BAY WISCONSIN*.

That night she called her brother to tell him she was moving in with Shelly until she could figure things out. Chris asked the questions she'd expected, but overall he sounded relieved. Robin made a date for lunch, promising to tell him all about the move.

After three days, Robin Parsons split into two people. Imaginary Robin stayed on in Shelly's guest room. Real Robin left Wisconsin, traveling as Lynn Taylor, landscape photographer. Ms. Taylor traveled with her husband Richard, who was a metal artist. They carried little with them in the secondhand blue RAV4 they'd purchased, planning to buy what they needed along the way.

Cam had enjoyed his first time alone in a hotel, and he told Robin all the wonders he'd experienced, like room service and "really nice ladies" who made his bed. When they merged onto 94 South he asked, "Where are we going?"

"Indianapolis," Robin replied. "We're going to find out who our next target is."

Used to each other's company, they didn't talk much on the drive. Robin stopped at places Cam liked for meals, which meant fast food. He didn't like waiting to be served, and he liked the fact that food came packaged separately. He couldn't abide it when segments of a meal ran together on his plate. Robin missed the finer side of dining and disliked the monotonous offerings of such places, but she told herself she could visit sit-down restaurants by herself once they were settled somewhere.

As long as it isn't in a holding cell while we await our trial.

Em had advised staying in small, privately owned motels in order to avoid national data bases. Some of them accepted cash in payment, which left even less of a trail. When they stopped at the Woods Motel west of Indy, however, their stay required a credit card. "Been burned a few times," the owner said.

Cam carried their overnight bags down the slightly musty-smelling hallway. They'd taken one room, and Robin was relieved to see there were double beds. Though she'd become used to having her former neighbor close by, sharing a bed was beyond what she was willing to endure for the sake of their cover.

Cam didn't seem concerned. "Is there Wi-Fi?"

"The sign said there was."

Going to the ancient wooden desk, he set the new computer on it and opened the case. The laptop hummed as it booted, and Cam located the signal, logged in, and dropped into his techno-world. He'd quickly become bored with "shrink-wrapped games," which offer limited options for competition, but Robin explained that his online identities might lead Thomas Wyman to them. Somewhat reluctantly, Cam had given up his impressive history of high-scoring games and begun creating new avatars and building different worlds.

As the laptop flickered and phaser fire sounded, Robin staked her claim to the bed on the far side of the room and began setting out her things. To support their cover story, she'd bought a Pentax camera, and she practiced with it a little, taking shots of the room and the view out their window, a barren field with a few abandoned lawn chairs for interest. In her only year of college, she'd taken a couple of classes in photography and one in computer graphics, so she possessed enough surface knowledge to make her "I'm an artist" lie believable.

Uploading the pictures, she examined them on the screen of her tablet. They weren't great art, but she liked the angles she'd chosen, which emphasized the room's smallness and the field's wasted expanse. Maybe she'd take online courses and learn how to set up better shots.

Yeah, right. Between kidnappings and running from the cops, I'll have lots of time for snapping pictures.

***

The next day Robin left Cam immersed in *Lightning War* and drove into Indianapolis to meet Chris. Spring was not as far along here as in Georgia and Virginia, so she wore a sweater under her light jacket for extra warmth. She and her brother had agreed to meet for lunch at an Irish pub near Monument Circle. Having downloaded a parking app before leaving the motel, she easily found the spot she'd reserved for the car and walked toward the State Soldiers' and Sailors' Monument, a 284-foot limestone obelisk visible for some distance in downtown Indy. As she approached the street that encircled the monument, a carriage passed, the horses' hooves clopping noisily on the pavement. Inside rode a young woman in a huge white dress, surrounded by attendants arrayed in shades of blue. Robin smiled as the bride waved enthusiastically to the people on the street who weren't fortunate enough to be getting married on this cool but sunny spring day.

Marriage was a topic she didn't often contemplate. Though Chris and Annika were happy, Shelly had found only heartache. Thoughts of marriage made Robin remember her mother, cowed by her husband's ugly temper and tentative in everything she did. If that was what it took for a woman to have a husband, Robin thought she'd pass. *If I ever find a prince, he'd better be a charming one.* So far, no man she'd met qualified.

The pub was a block from the downtown circle. Entering, she saw Chris at a table to one side. "Hey, Sissy!" he called loudly enough to make everyone in the place turn to look at her. Robin shook her fist at her brother, bowed to the lunchtime crowd, and bumped her way through the customers to join him at the table.

First she asked about Annika and when she'd be finished with her deployment. Then they moved on to the subject of the dogs, who were more like children to the couple than pets. Chris went on for some time about their antics, and Robin laughed to hear him tell about the smaller dog, Bo, dominating the larger one, Terra, through sheer nerve.

When the conversation fell into a brief lull, she took a breath. *Time to get down to business.* "What are you working on now?"

He examined his hands. "A couple of things, actually."

"Any interesting bad guys?"

Tilting his head to one side, he said, "Rumor says a certain senator has gone into rehab."

"Huh," she said blankly as the waiter set a basket of peanuts between them. "Must have hit rock bottom."

"I got an interesting email from Jessica Quern, thanking me for my help." Chris met her gaze. "Are you responsible for Buckram's change of heart, Rob?"

She felt a thrill of pride. "Maybe."

"What did you do?"

Expelling air out her nose, she tried to decide how much to tell. "Let's just say I've found a way to apply pressure to people who misuse positions of trust."

"People, as in more than one person?"

She held up two fingers. "Nobody's been hurt. We—I give them a chance to straighten out their lives and incentive to do it."

"Incentive."

"That's all you need to know, Chris. Anything more would put you in a bad position."

"I see." He'd never looked so serious. "What if I chose to be in that position?"

Their waiter returned, and Chris ordered the corned beef sandwich. Robin asked for a salad, and they each chose a different craft beer so they could exchange tastings. All the time she was thinking. Would her Jarhead brother agree with what she was doing, or would he demand she stop? Once the waiter left, she lowered her voice and said, "You've been working for two years to stop abuses in the system. You've had some success, but there are people you can't get to. We—I mean, I can."

Chris shook his head. "You've stumbled twice on the we/I thing, so I know you're not working alone."

"Okay. I have friends with similar goals. We work together."

He lightened a question with a childhood rhyme. "Are your friends big and tough and hard to bluff?"

She thought about that. Cam was strong. Though not big, Em was certainly strong-minded. "One's ex-FBI and the other is a martial arts expert." *Cam has to be learning something from all those video games.*

Their beers arrived, and they compared, deciding they liked Robin's Rebel Red better than the Pale Ale Chris had chosen. Once that was established, she got back to the point. "We have a lawyer on call too."

Chris took a drink. "If you're messing with corrupt people, Rob, you're asking for trouble."

"We're all willing to fight for this." *Possibly not able, but certainly willing.*

"I'd like to help," he said after a moment, "but I don't suppose I can do much from this chair."

She grinned, relieved to be past the stage where he'd try ordering her to give it up. "But you can, Chris. You've worked hard to develop sources, so you know who breaks the law and how they get away with it. Give us their names and information about what crimes you suspect them of, and we'll go after them."

The manager came by with the inevitable question: "Is everything tasting good?" Chris was thinking so hard he seemed unaware of the interruption, but Robin answered for both of them, and the man moved off.

"What do you say?" she prompted. "Do you have any cheaters on your radar?"

Chris chuckled grimly. "That list is endless. It's not a war you'll ever win."

"So we strike where we can." She leaned toward him. "I know you hated what Mark used to make us do. This could take away a little of the shame, a little of the guilt. I need to do it, and I think you do too."

"You can't go off like some comic book hero and fix the world, Rob. It could get you in trouble with the law for sure, and it might even get you killed."

"Don't you think we haven't talked about it for hours and hours, Chris? We know what we're doing, and we're going to do it. The question is are we going to do it with or without you."

He looked at her for a long time before he spoke again. "There's this judge who abuses her position."

Robin laid her hands on the cool, smooth table surface. "Tell me about it."

"Her name is Beverly Comdon, she's a canned vegetable heiress from Louisiana, and she's creepy."

"What do you mean?"

"Judge Comdon takes a special interest in certain young men who come into her court, usually first-time offenders accused of a serious but not necessarily heinous crime."

"Such as?"

"Wrecking a car while intoxicated. Injuring someone in a fight. Sex with an under-age girl."

"Crimes where the judge has leeway in deciding punishment."

"Right. Say a guy gets drunk and rapes an equally drunk co-ed at a frat party." Chris shrugged. "That's a rotten thing to do, and in today's climate of non-tolerance of the whole boys-will-be-boys argument, he could be punished to the full extent of the law. But hey, he was drunk too, so the judge offers him a deal. He can redeem himself by completing her program, Rehabilitate Louisiana. That's where the judge takes advantage of the accused."

"How?" The look on his face stopped her. "They have to—?"

"They don't *have* to. They can choose to do prison time and come out with a felony record." His expression turned thoughtful.

"Did Mark ever make you help him get women?"

The memory hit her like an ice cube in the heart. "Twice that I remember. I was supposed to cry about my dead mother."

"He made me do that a lot, at least until I got too old to get away with it." Chris fiddled with his wedding ring. "This woman does something similar, pulling her victims in like a spider in a web."

"How?"

"Rehabilitate Louisiana is supposed to be like community service. Men are 'confined' to the judge's estate, where they do tasks that teach them 'work skills.'" He made imaginary quotation marks. "From what I gather, they live high on the hog but serve as the judge's boy-toys."

"Don't people suspect this is going on?"

He fiddled with a lever on the side of his chair. "The men aren't objecting, and as for those involved, professionals tend to protect their own. Corruption in the ranks makes them look bad."

"Yes, I ran into that with—I know what you mean."

Meeting Robin's eyes to let her know he saw her equivocation, Chris took a drink of beer. "I first read the accusation on a blog, and when I looked at the judge's candidates for rehabilitation—well, you'll get it when you see them."

Robin leaned back in her chair. "She sounds like a possible KNP target."

"And what does KNP stand for?"

She tilted her head to one side. "Maybe once we nail this judge, I'll tell you."

***

When she got back to the motel room, Robin began looking at internet articles about Beverly Comdon. She'd occupied the bench in her Louisiana parish for thirty-two years, and her website claimed "Judge Bev" worked to bring "strong, law-based justice" to the people. That got her re-elected term after term.

Robin read an opposing opinion on-line. In a post titled *About a Certain Judge,* an angry writer accused "a so-called" lady named Bev of being a cougar. Despite misspellings and almost non-existent punctuation, the piece resonated with truth, claiming that Rehabilitate Louisiana needed to be investigated. Since the site operated under a pseudonym and the comment section was disabled, she was unable to learn the blogger's identity.

The land-line phone on the desk beside her rang, making Robin jump. Guessing it was one of those annoying calls where the management asks if the room is satisfactory, she picked up the receiver and responded with a curt, "Hello?"

"Mrs. Taylor?" The voice was light, the *r*'s elided. "I'm calling about a crime you recently committed."

Robin's throat closed like a clenched fist. "Excuse me?"

"I am aware of what you did in Richmond."

Her lungs seemed to be filling with cement. "I don't know what you're talking about."

"We need to meet face to face."

"Um, I don't see any reason to—"

"I'm downtown," the caller interrupted, and something about the *o*'s said he wasn't a native speaker of English. "I am sitting on the steps of the monument facing Starbucks. In half an hour I will call the local police and tell them everything I know."

She gripped the receiver so hard her hand hurt. "I don't have a clue what—"

"Talk to me or to the police, Mrs. Taylor. Discuss it with your husband if you like, but don't take too long."

"Listen, I don't know—"

"I'm wearing an orange leather jacket." The call ended.

She stood holding the handset for some time. Should they run? Though her imagination conjured a statewide manhunt, she decided no. If the caller wanted justice, he'd have told the police where they were. He'd called her because he wanted money.

She set the phone in place. "Cam, I need to go back downtown."

For once he sensed the tension in her voice. "Should I come?"

It was a difficult question. He was big enough to scare the man away, strong enough to fight if the need arose. Still, if the police were waiting to arrest her, she wanted Cam to have a chance to escape.

"Stay here. I'll call if I need you."

She put on her jacket and gloves slowly, trying to decide what to do. Demanding a meeting didn't feel like something a cop would do, but if this guy knew about the KNP, why hadn't he called the police? Would he offer the chance to turn themselves in? That didn't feel right. It had to be money he was after.

As she left the room, Robin picked up the bag that held their remaining cash. If she had to, she'd give the mysterious caller all of it, come back for Cam, and get out of Indy. She checked to make sure she had her room key. Cam was already focused on his game again.

Be ready to run if I call. She didn't say it aloud. She just closed the cheap wooden door with a scrape.

Chapter Eleven

When the guy said his jacket was orange, he wasn't kidding. Robin saw him from some distance away, a small figure on the steps to the monument, about halfway up. Though the air had been crisp all morning, the sun had warmed the afternoon. In spite of that, the man's shoulders were hunched and his head pulled into the jacket in a turtle-like pose. He seemed totally engrossed in watching the traffic circle, but when she started up the steps, he stood and made a polite nod that was almost a bow. "Mrs. Taylor." Up close she recognized him as the one who'd delivered the ransom and taken Senator Buckram home.

If he'd meant their meeting to be discreet, he hadn't dressed for it. In addition to the jacket, which was by no means a subtle shade, he wore mustard-yellow sweat pants, a green scarf with gold leaves scattered across it, and eyeglasses possibly inherited from a long-dead ancestor. "I'm Hua." Shyly, he extended a hand, which she grasped only long enough to be polite. She didn't ask if the name, which rhymed with *rah*, was his first or last name. They weren't going to spend enough time together for that to matter.

"You wanted to speak with me about something, Mr. Hua?" She tried to sound as if she had no idea what his call had been about. *He knows that's a lie, or you wouldn't have come.*

"Please sit down."

Robin obeyed, and the cold stone immediately leached body heat from her thighs. Sitting down beside her, Hua spoke in a tone that wouldn't carry to the sidewalk below. "You kidnapped Senator Buckram and took a great deal of money from him."

"I—" Dread stopped her voice, and she had to try again. "I—"

He waved a hand like a magician promising a wondrous trick. "The senator says two men in a gray van took him to a storage unit and demanded money for his release, among other things. He is fairly certain they traveled on the freeway. I called storage places outside the city and asked if someone driving a gray van had rented a unit within the last few days. Once I found the lot, I hacked nearby traffic cameras and found the van stopped at a light just minutes after the abduction. That gave me the license number. The photo showed me the senator was wrong: he was not abducted by two men, but a man and a woman."

All those mystery shows on TV, and I didn't remember to obscure the plate with dirt!

"The registered owner of the van reported he recently sold it to Richard and Lynn Taylor. The Taylors were gone from the Merry Motel by the time I located it, but yesterday their credit card was used to book a room near here." He raised his hands in a "ta-da" gesture. "I called the front desk and was connected to your room."

"Why did you bring me here?"

"I arrived this morning on a Greyhound bus. I have no vehicle and very little money. By consulting a helpful tourist map posted on the station wall, I saw I could walk to this landmark. I also felt it would be easy for you to find, even if you didn't know the city well."

"You're pretty smart." *A little flattery can't hurt.*

"Yes. I have learned quite a bit about your activities. What I don't know is why you did as you did."

She wasn't about to tell a stranger the senator reminded her of her scumbag father. "I want to make cheaters pay for what they do to good people." She met Hua's gaze, hoping he'd see it was an honest answer.

"And what did you do with the money?

"We kept half of it. The other half went to charity."

They'd made a game of it, letting chance decide which nonprofit would get the donation. Em had chosen a time and Cam named a TV channel. The first charity mentioned after seven a.m. on Channel 6 on Saturday morning had received thirty-seven thousand, five hundred dollars, mailed from a West Virginia post office in a Priority Mail box. They'd handled the money wearing gloves, but she doubted the Meals on Wheels program of greater Richmond would look that particular gift horse in the mouth.

Hua's brow furrowed on hearing of their donation, and Robin felt a tiny glow of satisfaction. There were *some* things he didn't know. If she convinced him her motives were honorable, might he keep what he'd discovered quiet?

"You mentioned calling the police. Is that negotiable?" She'd prepared a text message before leaving the car, simply the word RUN, and she had her phone in her pocket. If there were cops waiting at the base of the monument to arrest her, she'd send the message and give Cam the chance to get away.

"There will be no police. I only said that to assure you would come."

"What do you want from me?"

"Saturday morning, Senator Buckram ordered me to learn who kidnapped him and took his money."

"And you've done that." Some of her nervousness bubbled out in anger. "I guess that makes you a great employee, but I have to tell you. Working for a corrupt man makes you a corrupt employee."

Something flashed in Hua's dark eyes, but he answered

calmly. “You misunderstand, Mrs. Taylor. I am not the senator’s employee. I am his property.”

“What?” It came out louder than Robin intended, and she glanced around to see if anyone had turned to look at them. No one had, so she asked, “How?”

Hua’s lips pressed together briefly. “I was brought to this country nine years ago by...businessmen who deal in such things.”

“They sound like human traffickers to me.”

Hua nodded, allowing her to put her own label on it. “I was one of four orphans taken from my village in Thailand. Our caregivers were told we would receive an excellent education and worthwhile employment.” His lips tightened. “Our friends were happy for us. They thought we were lucky.”

“Instead you were sold as slaves.” Robin was aware that many of the world’s sex workers, domestics, and farm laborers were people tricked into servitude with promises of a better life. She touched Hua’s arm, all thoughts of the police and what might happen to her melting away. “I’m sorry.”

Scratching at a spot on his jacket sleeve with his index finger Hua said, “Senator Buckram was fascinated with the idea of having a houseboy, a servant who was completely devoted to him.”

“Like some millionaire in a ’40s movie.”

“I suppose so. My handlers saw that I was trained to his express wishes. For years I took care of his clothing, kept his apartment tidy, cooked his meals, and even helped when he entertained guests in Richmond.”

Robin rested her chin on her knuckles. “How did he explain your presence?”

"The senator has a pleasant story he tells visitors. In this tale we met when he visited Bangkok. I was a street child who tried to steal his wallet. Despite my thievery, he took a liking to me and offered a job and a home." Hua rubbed at his smooth chin. "People often remind me to be grateful for the senator's generosity."

"What does Mrs. Buckram think?"

Hua's opinion flickered briefly in his eyes, but his voice remained flat. "We have never met, though I suspect she knows about me. I remain at the Richmond apartment, which she never visits."

"Has he—Does he...?" She didn't know how to put it, but Hua got the idea.

"The senator does not love boys. He only loves the idea of owning another person."

"You've been a prisoner for years and people either don't notice or don't care?"

His smile was tinged with bitterness. "People see what they will. You yourself have probably seen slaves in your lifetime, but because you are unaware, you fail to notice the signs."

That she understood. Her own experiences caused her to notice the signs of abuse: odd bruises, eyes that avoided direct contact, children who didn't cry when they fell or got hit by a baseball. Mark had often warned, "Keep your mouth shut about what happens at home." Being his kid had been a lot like slavery.

"Does anyone else know your, um, status?"

"The senator's security expert does. He finds my state amusing. Another man, Senator Buckram's business manager, felt sorry for me, but he feared losing his position if he questioned the senator."

"A coward."

Hua shrugged. "Mr. Dotsun had a prison record and therefore could not find honest work. Senator Buckram hired him to 'cook the books.' Is that idiom correct?"

"Dotsun keeps the senator's secret books?"

"Mr. Paul Dotsun died suddenly a year ago." Hua put a hand on his heart. "I took his place."

"You?"

Hua spread his hands. "Mr. Dotsun was an excellent teacher, and I have some affinity for both numbers and computers."

"But you're just—I mean, how old are you?"

Hua smiled. "I am not sure. Perhaps eighteen."

"At 'perhaps eighteen' you're Buckram's houseboy and his book-cooker. Very economical for him."

Hua's eyes clouded. "After I replaced Mr. Dotsun, my life with the senator became less—troublesome. He trusted me more and even taught me to drive his vehicle, because it was worthwhile for him."

Do what I say and I'll be good right back at you, Mark used to say. Buckram was like her father in more than just looks.

Suddenly Em's voice replaced Mark's in her head. *Don't fall for a hard luck story just because it reminds you of your own!*

Robin forced herself to focus on facts. "Once you had access to a computer, why didn't you call for help?"

Hua's expression said she couldn't possibly understand. "The senator often said since I am so small, my body could easily be concealed in a trash can."

Even during the worst of Mark's tirades, Robin hadn't faced

the threat of death. She'd had Chris and her mother for support while Hua had been a child alone in a strange country. "Sorry. Stupid question. I can't imagine what it was like for you."

He bowed gracefully. "Thank you for understanding." Rubbing his hands together he began, "On Friday night the senator called me to deliver the ransom you demanded. He did not want others to know what had happened."

Robin smiled for the first time. "You chose the fluorescent chartreuse backpack?"

"Did you like it?"

"A little showy, but it worked."

Hua pulled his jacket tighter as the breeze swept over them. "I do not think Mr. Buck knew how much he revealed on the way home, but as I listened I thought, 'Promises of better behavior? Required to enter drug treatment? Unusual in a kidnapping.' I decided that once I found these criminals, I would study them."

"Study us?"

"I believe your gang has admirable motives." He turned to Robin. "Is this an insult, to call you a gang?"

She chuckled. "I'm not sure what to call us."

"No matter." Hua's posture straightened—not that he was a slumper—and he made a formal statement. "Mrs. Taylor, I would like to join you. I believe my skill with computers can greatly benefit your work."

She took a moment to let that sink in. "I don't think you know what you're volunteering for."

"Do you attempt to stop those who prey on others?"

"Well, yes, but—"

"That is what I am volunteering for. I told Senator Buckram I could find no trace of the people he seeks, and I erased all records of your visit to Richmond. Once that was done, I escaped."

"Escaped?"

"When the senator leaves Richmond, I am locked in my room. There is security, but a window in my bathroom is thought too small to require an alarm." He grinned. "You have noticed I am not a large person, so I was able to exit there."

"That wasn't easy, or you'd have done it before this."

He considered. "It is eight floors up, so there were precarious moments."

"You crawled out a window eight stories high?"

"There was a balcony below, and another below that one, and so on. In the end I reached the ground, shaken but feeling rather satisfied with myself." He tugged at his jacket hem as if reliving the moment it had taken to recover. "I walked several blocks before asking a passerby how to get to the bus station."

"So you could come here and join our gang?"

"Once I satisfied myself that your intentions are truly good."

She closed her eyes for a moment. "*I* think they are, Hua, but we're not what you imagined. Our organization is...loose, and our plans are pretty vague."

"But they are worthwhile plans nonetheless." His dark eyes met hers. "Mrs. Taylor—"

She waved the name away with a gesture. "Call me Robin."

"Mrs. Robin, whether you take me into your gang or not is up to you. If you have no place for me, I will continue on my own. However, I can help you succeed, and I am terribly weary of working for the bad guys."

Chapter Twelve

Robin wanted badly to believe Hua. She was aware, however, that childhood memories of her father's tyranny colored her judgment. Shared past abuse didn't mean Hua should travel with her and Cam. She needed someone objective to advise her.

Taking Hua to a nearby hotel, she paid for a night's stay. He was awed by everything he saw on the way. Though he'd lived in a luxurious apartment in Richmond for a decade, it was clear he hadn't gotten out much. At the hotel she showed him the basic amenities, much as she'd done with Cam a short time ago, and instructed him to use room service for meals and stay put until she returned. When she left, Hua was unwrapping the soaps and sniffing the complimentary body lotion.

At the motel, Robin told Cam what had happened. "I can't confirm he's telling the truth," she finished, "and even if he is, what would we do with him?"

Cam accepted Hua's story at face value. "Who'd make up something that weird?" he asked. "You said you wanted somebody who could do computer stuff. It sounds like he could."

"But he thinks we're a gang." She made ironic quotation marks around the last word with her fingers. "He has no place to live, no money, and no documentation. We'd have to take him with us."

That brought a frown. "You mean, he'd, like, live with us?"

"Yeah, I guess." She thought about what that meant. *Another person I'd be responsible for. Life dealt him a bad hand, but that doesn't mean I can fix it.*

Cam's brow furrowed. "What if he won't take a bath? Mom

said those people—"

A look from Robin stopped him from repeating his mother's xenophobic prejudices. "Hua could have screwed us big time, Cam. Instead he kept his mouth shut and ran away to join us."

"Yeah," he agreed. "That does sound pretty cool."

Unable to decide what to do, Robin messaged Mink, using the KNP subject line they'd agreed on. When he called a few minutes later, she said, "I'm considering adding a computer expert to the story." She gave an account of her meeting with Hua, framing it in terms of the story arc.

"If he's working for one of the clowns' targets," Mink cautioned, "he could be setting them up."

"I know. He might be sent to infiltrate the organization and get all the clowns arrested."

She grimaced at her own words. *Infiltrate the organization?* They were a couple of ordinary people with big ideas taking advice from two experts past their prime. Hua's skills seemed cutting-edge, but Robin reminded herself she was one of the "everyday idiots" Em claimed were clueless when it came to detecting hidden motives.

"I'd advise the clowns to keep him in the dark as much as possible," Mink said. "And watch to see if he communicates with anyone."

"He already knows a lot. I—the clowns—doubt they can keep him in the dark for long."

When her conversation with Mink didn't provide a satisfactory solution, Robin called Em. As the phone rang multiple times, she pictured Em making her way across the apartment to wherever she'd left it. She answered on the seventh ring, and Robin asked if she'd told anyone about her recent trip to Richmond.

"Nobody has a clue where I go, and nobody cares," Em responded. "What's the problem?"

When Robin told her about Hua and his request to be part of their "gang," she became irritated. "Do you listen to me at all, girl? You should have played dumb and refused to admit anything."

"Em, he knew which motel we stayed at, what we were driving, and the names Cam and I are using."

"And how many Taylors are there in this country? I told you—until the police get involved, deny, deny, deny. When the cops arrive, demand to see a lawyer."

"He seems sincere."

Em made a rude sound. "I hear Ted Bundy came across as a real sweetheart—until it was too late."

"What should I do?"

After a moment's thought she said, "Put me in touch with the guy. If he's got an agenda, I'll figure it out."

Somewhat reluctantly, Robin provided her with the phone number listed on the hotel receipt. Em wasn't likely to be gentle, and it seemed mean to let her browbeat an escaped slave. Still, Em was an experienced interrogator. "He's in Room #31."

"I'll get back to you."

An hour later, Em called back. "Hua is in," she declared. "I think he'll be a real asset."

"What made you decide he's the real deal?"

"In the first place, he speaks Thai like a native, so that part of his story is true."

"You speak Thai?"

"You don't?" Em snorted a laugh at her own joke. "I served in the military near the end of the Vietnam era. Spent some time in Thailand."

Robin played devil's advocate. "Okay, he's Thai. That doesn't mean he's not lying."

"The computer expertise is real too. I can't really do much with the dumb things, but I can make it sound like I do. Hua came through that part of the test with flying colors."

"So we know he's Thai and he's a computer whiz. That still doesn't prove he's on our side." When Em paused in surprise, Robin said, "You keep telling me not to be naive, so I'm questioning everything."

"That's good," Em acknowledged. "My third test was loyalty to Buckram. I asked for a great deal of information about the senator's affairs, and Hua gave me enough to boot the senator out of office and into prison if we wanted to use it." She made a *tsk* of disgust at what she'd learned in the interview. "If Hua were a plant, he couldn't afford to go as far as he did."

"So Hua is what he says he is, but he's an asset who will also be a liability. What do we do with him?"

Em chuckled. "The guy's too good to lose track of. Whatever you have in mind for yourself and Cam, I suggest you add Hua to it."

***

The addition of a third active member to the group increased the need for a permanent base. Two men traveling with a woman was more noticeable than a married couple. To make matters worse, Cameron was becoming restless. The motel had neither workout equipment nor a decent place to take a walk, and she'd noticed him stuttering more often. He needed a space to call his own.

Robin fetched Hua and brought him to their motel, telling him a little about the goals of KNP as she drove. Explaining her desire to make a difference caused a question to come to mind. “Maybe we could get back at the people who took you from home and sold you to Senator Buckram.”

He was horrified. “No, Mrs. Robin. This would be something very bad for you to attempt. They are not merely crooks like the senator. Those people are killers—very dangerous!”

“I get it,” she said soothingly. “It was just a thought.” *We might not be ready yet, but someday.*

At the motel Robin led Hua to where Cam waited, glad their room faced away from the office so the owners weren’t likely to see the new arrival. When he saw Cam Hua said, “The senator said you were a big sonofabitch, which is very correct, Mr. Cameron.”

“Not Mister,” Robin corrected. “Just Cameron. Or Cam.”

Hua nodded soberly, and Cam asked Robin, “Do you think he likes Pepsi?”

“I haven’t got a clue. Why don’t you ask him?”

There was a long pause before Cam stuttered, “W-w-would you like a Pepsi?”

Hua glanced at Robin before answering. “No, thank you. Maybe I would like some later.”

Cam turned again to Robin. “He seems okay. I mean, he’s polite. That’s good, right?”

“It’s pretty important.”

“Do you think he likes the same video games as me?”

Robin sighed. "Ask him."

Cam turned to Hua, who seemed confused about whether to look at him or at Robin. "What's your favorite video game?"

Hua frowned. "I was never allowed to have such things."

Cam's eyes clouded as he pondered that atrocity, but after a few seconds a smile lit his face. "You can play all the games you want to now, can't he, Robin? I'll show you how."

***

She left Cam and Hua alone for a few minutes, sensing they'd get to know each other more easily without an observer. Since Hua hadn't eaten since leaving Richmond and Cam would eat as many times a day as food was offered, Robin went to buy sandwiches. She returned to find Cam and Hua playing some game that involved navigating a field of meteors. They were laughing and punching each other on the arm, so she guessed things were good on that score.

Once each man had a sandwich in hand, Robin opened the atlas she'd recently bought and turned to a map of the continental United States. "We're going to buy a house, and it needs to be centrally located." As she spoke she drew two vertical lines on the map, marking the nation's midsection. "Em says rural areas are easier to hide in if you convince the locals you're not very interesting."

"How do we do that?" Cam asked.

"We'll work on that later." She handed Hua her laptop and a list she'd made. "Find houses like this."

He scanned the list. "In the country. Near an airport. At least three bedrooms."

"More if possible." Robin rubbed her cheek. "Who knows who'll want to join our merry band next week?"

In less than twenty minutes, Hua had three possibilities: Des Moines, Iowa, Oklahoma City, Oklahoma and Kansas City, Kansas. They agreed to start with the closest one, a short drive north of Kansas City.

"Shall we go look at it first thing in the morning?" she asked.

"I offer my services as driver for our gang, Mrs. Robin," Hua said eagerly. "I am very competent behind the wheel of an automobile."

"It's not Mrs. Robin. It's just Robin. And in public, try not to say our names at all.

"I understand." Hua tapped his lips with a finger. "We are incognito, yes?"

"But we got good reasons for lying to people," Cam cautioned. "We make bad guys straighten up."

Right. A couple more superheroes and we'll be the Justice League of America.

"Where can he sleep?" Cam asked.

Hua pointed to the couch. "It will be much more comfortable than a closet floor." His casual tone made Robin wish she'd punched Buckram in the nose a few times when she had him taped to a chair.

Cam located the extra blanket in the closet, gave up two of his four pillows, and made a neat bed on the sofa for their guest. Hua seemed both pleased and embarrassed by the attention, and Robin guessed it had been a long time since anyone took pains to see to his comfort—if anyone ever had. As she left to get take-out for their dinner, Cam was explaining the basics of *Jupiter Astronauts* to Hua. "You have to kill the bad aliens," he said as she closed the door, "but you don't want to hurt the alien mothers or their babies."

Very early the next morning, they loaded their belongings in the RAV and started for Kansas. Robin typed the address into the GPS, and it indicated they would arrive at the property just after 11:00 a.m.

As soon as they were out of the city, Hua began noticing things he'd never seen before. His bus trip to Indianapolis had taken place mostly at night, so the sights along the way were a delightful surprise for him. "Look!" he'd say, pointing out the window. "That is a horse!" or "Goodness! Do you see how flat the land is?" Hua tended to steer in the direction he was pointing, so what should have been an uneventful ride turned into an hour of terror. Twice Cam took hold of the wheel to keep them in their lane, and several times Robin grabbed his shoulder, urging, "Watch the road!"

"Of course, of course," he said each time, but that lasted only until he saw something else new to him. After a herd of llamas that almost led to a collision with a rest area sign, Robin suggested they stop. When they'd visited the bathrooms, she claimed it was her turn to drive. Quick on the uptake for once, Cam agreed, as if taking turns was their long-established practice. After that it wasn't so nerve-wracking to have Hua point out flowering trees or ducks on the roadside ponds. Still, he kept rolling his window down to "smell America," half-freezing his companions. His behavior led Robin to choose *Bubbles* as Hua's clown name.

"In this gang we are clowns?" he asked.

"Cam is Bozo; I'm Clarabell. Our lawyer is Pinky—because he had on a pink shirt the last time I saw him—and our researcher is Ronald, because he has red hair."

"So red?" Hua asked incredulously.

She laughed. "No. Just reddish."

"I like Bubbles," Hua informed them. "Like them, I do not weigh much but still I am very pretty."

Twenty minutes north of Kansas City, they left the freeway and took a state highway east. There was nothing at the exit but an abandoned gas station, but a sign said, GARDINER, TEN MILES. Cam, who had taken over driving duties at the last stop, followed GPS directions down a narrow paved highway for two miles and turned down the even narrower Bobby Road. He steered down the center, avoiding the worst of the potholes.

"Arriving at destination, on left," the voice announced, but there was nothing around them but trees.

"What now?" Cam asked. Hua's window hummed as he opened it and stuck his head out like a curious cat.

"Keep going," Robin advised. "Some rural places aren't in the GPS memory."

"This could be very advantageous," Hua said. "Hard for others to find, yes?"

They drove on for perhaps half a mile, seeing nothing but fields and trees. The road was built up like an old railroad grade, the land around it flat and muddy with spots of leftover, dirty snow tucked in depressions and corners. Slashed cornstalks stuck out of the ground, their dull gold turning to rotted black at the bottom.

"I don't see any houses," Robin said. "Should we—"

"There!" Hua interrupted. "That is a driving way, yes?"

It was and it wasn't. A turnoff sloped drastically downward in the faintest resemblance of a driveway. At the bottom of the incline, a large puddle of melted snow covered an area at least twenty feet square. Beyond the water was a long patch of slime that brought to mind mud-run courses Robin had seen online.

"Can we make it through that?"

Farm boy Cam took her question as a challenge. Shifting into low gear he said, "No problem."

Robin grabbed the hand-hold and Hua gasped in dread as they descended toward the mud hole like a theme-park gondola hitting the water course. "You gotta give her gas and keep going," Cam said, his eyes focused on the way ahead. "If you stop, your tires sink in and you're stuck." As he spoke the car bogged down, shuddered briefly, and caught on something solid enough to propel it forward. Sloshing sounds indicated water hitting the vehicle's sides. The car slewed and bucked, but Cam kept steady pressure on the gas pedal. At the far side of the puddle the tires began making sucking sounds, and clods pelted the undercarriage as their rotation released mud from the treads. The ground ahead rose. They were safely through.

The driveway cut through the stand of maples that obscured their view of the house. "When there's foliage, this place will be completely hidden," Robin commented. Trees that hadn't been trimmed in decades scraped the roof of the van.

When they reached their goal Cam turned off the engine, and they sat for a moment, taking it in. The hulking, dismal structure brought to mind the haunted mansions from Scooby Doo cartoons. Made of red brick, it consisted of a large, three-story square with single-story wings on either side. Several chimneys, black with old stains, were visible along the roofline. The dignified architecture had seemed attractive in the on-line picture, but the photographer had wisely taken the shot through the trees in high summer. The photo was romantic. Reality was starkly different.

"It's kind of r-run-down." Cameron rubbed his hands over his jacket front.

Robin sighed. "We can go on to the next one."

"No, no! This house is very perfect!" Hua gestured expansively at the windshield. "Very big! Location is excellent! And you have the senator's money. You can buy what we need to make this a very good home."

Robin wished they hadn't given away half the ransom. Making this house "very good" would eat up their remaining funds in an unbelievably short time.

Hua sensed her lack of enthusiasm. "Let's look in the windows. Maybe we will like it very much."

Leaving the vehicle they approached the house, sidestepping puddles and a stubborn, gray-tinged snowbank in a shadowed corner. The air smelled of wet nature, not unpleasant but not exactly fragrant. Robin's mom, a real estate appraiser, had often commented on what was important about a property. "Don't look at the pretty details," she used to say. "Look at the bones." The frame of this house, its "bones," seemed solid. The main roof was in decent shape. There were no telltale droops in its line, no bricks lying on the ground.

A sign nailed to a tree advertised the property's availability for purchase, but the sign was almost as decrepit as the house itself. Realtors had long ago given up on this sale: too far out, too far gone.

The first-floor windows sat high enough off the ground that neither Robin nor Hua could see in. "Empty," Cam reported. "I see a fireplace but nothing else."

Robin could see corniced windows and fancy ceiling molding. "Nice detail in the trim."

"I guess." Cam was clearly unimpressed with architectural flourishes.

Hua had disappeared around the side of the house, and he called, "Here! We can go inside!"

Cam and Robin followed his wet footprints across what had once been a courtyard. Its cobblestone bricks had rolled as the earth moved below them, and they had to step carefully so they didn't trip. At the end of the west wing, a set of French doors stood open. Inside, Hua gestured an invitation like a friendly doorman.

"This was unlocked?" When he hesitated, Robin frowned. "You broke in."

"I did not break anything," he said indignantly. "I have, um, talent with latches of simple construction."

Reminding herself she was guilty of crimes much worse than unlawful entry, Robin stepped inside.

The room they entered was large, with high ceilings and tall, thin windows lining the south wall. Some of the panes were broken, and leaves and grime had blown inside, landing in dirty piles in the corners. Opposite the windows, three doors lined the north wall. Robin opened the center one and found a bath with connecting doors on either side. The bath was a mess, but the mess was old, so the smell was only faintly offensive. On either side were larger rooms, perhaps ten by ten, and she guessed they were meant as bedrooms with a shared bath. Servants' quarters? Overflow for the children of a large family? It was hard to tell.

When she returned to the main room, Hua stood at the windows, looking out. The courtyard was overgrown with weeds, dead and brown at this time of year. Beyond the paving, several dozen trees edged the courtyard. Robin didn't know what kind they were, but from their shape and size she guessed fruit of some sort.

"This view is very nice most times of the year, I think." Hua's face glowed, but Robin had begun a mental tally of what it would cost to make the place habitable. The list was long and depressing, and she tried to find the words to tell him the next house was sure to be better. Cam would back her decision; there was no way to—

"Robin! Hua! Come see this!" Cam appeared at the top of a short, sloping hallway, beckoning furiously as if to hurry them along. Together they followed him up a short ramp that led to the main part of the house.

The room they entered was circular, with a wide stairway in the center rising dramatically to the second story. At the front were the double entry doors they'd seen from the car. Around the staircase, doorways led to rooms of various sizes. Peeking through open double doors, Robin saw what had once been a formal living room. In the center of one wall was a brick fireplace someone had painted an ugly shade of green. Several of the mantle's trim pieces were missing, and the hearth looked as if it had been battered with a sledge hammer. Wind whistled noisily down the chimney, suggesting missing or broken parts inside. Such willful damage led Robin to conclude the house had at some point been turned into rental units. It was sad to note its descent from elegant family home to cheap apartments to its current state, a derelict visited only by vandals and vagrants.

"The kitchen's back here," Cameron called.

"Coming!" Robin and Hua passed what had probably been the dining room and entered the kitchen, where Cam was exploring cupboards. In one corner she noted a mouse nest, and the scarred countertop was littered with what appeared to be squirrel poop.

"Those are antiques." Robin frowned at the harvest gold refrigerator and stove combination. "Seventies, maybe earlier. And there's lots of animal activity."

"Mice, for sure," Cam said agreeably. "A possum too, I think."

Hua seemed to be observing on a whole different level. "Lots of room for things," he said. "I am an excellent cook, if the stove can be made to operate."

If you cook like you drive, we're in trouble.

"I bet this place doesn't have a single outlet that can handle a microwave." She looked at the ceiling, where several acoustic tiles hung half out of their frame. "I doubt it's been occupied since they were invented."

They continued around the staircase, passing a room lined with shelves that looked like a large closet. "Pantry," Cam announced. The next two rooms had probably been parlors, and after that was a large space with empty bookshelves. On its floor, a few mildewed books lay scattered, their pages torn out and spines broken. A creaky, flimsy door under the staircase opened to reveal a bathroom obviously fashioned from a former closet. Though cramped, it had all the requirements: a sink, stool, and the smallest shower stall Robin had ever seen.

Next they went upstairs, stepping carefully over spots where the boards had rotted, leaving gaping holes in a few spots. The second story consisted of four rooms, two of them spacious and the others smaller and further reduced by the slant of the roof. In the center was a large bath, complete though hardly modern. The fixtures appeared to be lilac, though it was difficult to tell through the dirt.

"Every room of any size has a fireplace," Cam noted. "I counted twelve so far."

"Most of them in bad shape." Stepping carefully, Robin started back downstairs. "It was a beautiful house once, guys, but now it's a wreck. No central heat, no air conditioning, antiquated appliances—" She pointed at evidence of rodent activity on the next-to-last stair. "—and lots of holes where critters can come in."

Hua disagreed. "To an American it is old, perhaps, but in my country it is only a baby." He gestured widely. "It is dirty, but what is dirt? It is big enough for us and more." He pulled on the newel post. "It is a strong house, and the many fireplaces will allow us to heat only the rooms we need."

Robin tried to see the place from Hua's viewpoint. His original home was a remote Thai village. His second was an elegant prison. Any house where he was free was a palace to Hua, but he didn't understand how much money it would require to make the place livable.

"Hua, I don't—"

Still exploring, Cam had opened a set of pocket doors that led to the east wing. He turned to them, his eyes alight. "Can I have this part, Robin? I mean, I can share it, but it's really cool."

Robin and Hua followed as Cam went down the ramp. The wing was similar in construction to its opposite, but someone had turned its walls into pencil art. Rendered in black on the cream-colored base, bigger-than-life-sized figures ran, flew, and stood in heroic poses: Superman, Batman, Wonder Woman, and others Robin struggled to name. The Hulk, she thought. Another might have been Thor. Though they weren't badly done, her first thought was that a coat of paint could fix it.

Cameron stood in the center of the room, turning slowly. "Isn't it great?"

"You like it?"

He stopped, confused. "Sure." Turning to Hua he asked, "Don't you think it's something?"

Hua's response was circumspect. "You are exactly correct, Cameron. It is something."

"I wonder what the other rooms look like."

"I can hardly wait," Robin murmured. Like the other wing,

there was a bathroom between two rooms on the north wall and windows along the open area to the south. The comic art continued, with a Mickey Mouse theme in the bathroom and more warrior types in the others. “A guy could really relax in here.” Ignoring the cobwebs, Cam touched a figure that might have been Genghis Khan. “Too much color makes it hard for me to think.”

Action heroes done in black and white. Perfect for a guy like Cam.

Hua turned to Robin. “See? Cameron sees good things in this house. He likes it too, very much.”

“Are we going to take it?” Cam asked, his expression hopeful.

Robin sighed. *Two against one.* “We’ll see what kind of deal we can get.” She glanced into the woods that surrounded the house on three sides. “This certainly isn’t a spot anyone would think to look for me. With all these trees, I feel like I’m in a scene from *Friday the 13th*.”

Chapter Thirteen

At a hotel near the Kansas City airport, they got two hotel rooms. Though Robin disliked spending the money, she was almost desperate for some time to herself. Cam and Hua were willing to share; in fact they seemed to have lots to talk about. Hua was patient with Cam's hesitant speech, and Cam gravely taught Hua life hacks like how to operate a vending machine and take pictures with a cell phone. Either Hua liked playing one video game after another or he pretended to for the sake of politeness.

With a few hours to herself, Robin took a long shower, noting she was almost out of her favorite coconut-scented conditioner. *Have to pick some up soon.* As the hot water ran, she hung a clean but rumpled outfit in the bathroom so the steam would dispel the wrinkles. Her carry-on was meant for weekend vacations and wasn't nearly big enough for life on the road. She kept a plastic tub in the car and took clean clothes from it as she needed them.

I should get a bigger suitcase next time I'm near a mall.

After the shower she filed her nails, which were sadly neglected of late.

Need to get an emery board and some polish when I see a drug store.

She read a little of the novel she'd downloaded to her phone, sometimes napping between chapters. The hours flew by, and soon it was time to dress and find dinner for herself and the guys.

At four they knocked on her door, showered but otherwise looking the same as they had when she saw them last. For Cam that was normal; he favored boot cut blue jeans and T-shirts with a single front pocket. Hua had nothing but what he'd escaped

Buckram's building in. Robin added getting clothes for him to her mental list.

We're living like hobos. We could all be arrested at any moment. And I'm planning a shopping trip?

Hua was excited about the shampoo provided by the motel. "It smells like ginger," he said, offering his head for her to sniff. "Is it permissible to take these small bottles away with us?"

Robin assured him it was and gave him her own bottle as well, adding ginger-scented shampoo to her mental shopping list. As much as Hua had gone without this far in life, he deserved some small niceties.

The Realtor worked for a small office in Gardiner. Robin and Cam would view the house as Richard and Lynn Taylor, and if things worked out well, they'd make the purchase while Hua remained in the background. Just before closing time, Robin called the office and asked to speak to Elizabeth Terrin, the agent listed on the sign. After the introductions ("Don't call me Liz!"), Robin expressed interest in the house on the oddly-named Bobby Road.

There was a pause as Elizabeth collected her wits, but as soon as she recovered, she went into her sales pitch. "That's a lovely property. I've always wished someone would come along who appreciates its possibilities."

"We took a look at the outside this morning," Robin said. "It might work for a project we have in mind." Unbidden, Mark's way to a favorable deal came to mind. "Of course we're considering several locations."

Apparently used to such opening salvos, Elizabeth focused on the positives. "May I ask what you plan to do with the property?"

"A small artists' colony where talented people can come and spend a few weeks or months while they work on a project. The house has to be large enough to allow several of us to work in our preferred media."

"That sounds so interesting!" Her tone was a little over the top. "What medium is your specialty?"

"Photography pays the bills," Robin replied, "but oil painting feeds my soul. My husband works in metal, so the cement-block building behind the house would be a good place for that noisy metal cutting and messy welding."

"You've certainly chosen a great spot. Anyone with an artist's eye will love sketching in that courtyard edged with fruit trees."

It was time to cool her enthusiasm. "It's a bumpy mess. It will take weeks of work to flatten it enough to even make a spot to set a chair out there."

"True," Elizabeth allowed, "but surely you saw the beautiful architectural lines in that house."

"We also saw gnawed electrical wire, gable rot, and antiquated plumbing. I'm pretty sure I heard critters skittering around inside."

Elizabeth must have sensed that enthusiasm alone wasn't going to make a deal. "Well, I can tell you the place is bank-owned, and they're willing to dicker. The price you saw online is just a starting point."

"Good, because it's at least twice what the place is worth." Robin imagined the woman calling the bank as soon as they ended their conversation, prepping them to accept whatever the Taylors offered. "Could we stop in tomorrow to meet with you?"

"Of course," Elizabeth replied. "I'm excited to hear your plans for the place."

When the call ended, Robin admitted she'd learned a few things about dealing with people from observing her father's methods. While she wouldn't excuse the things he'd done, she was familiar with how he'd used a sentence, a smile, or a glance away at just the right moment to manipulate others. *Even a snake has lessons to teach.*

Once the appointment with the Realtor was made, Hua, Robin, and Cam looked at the research on their proposed target, Beverly Comdon. Though he claimed he'd be more efficient with "exquisite computing equipment," Hua had already confirmed Chris' contention that "Judge Bev" used her charity, Rehabilitate Louisiana, to manipulate young men into her service and her bed. His easy access to the judge's personal files disturbed Robin, who until he came along had operated under the delusion there was some privacy left in the world. He showed them an array of men with similar builds and coloring whose time was served doing "job skills training" on Comdon's estate.

Seeing the judge's picture on screen, Cameron ran a hand through his hair. "She's a lady, you guys."

"I'm a lady too," Robin replied. "Do we have any more right than men to break the rules?"

"Well, no, but she's old. I couldn't grab hold of an old woman and shove her into the van."

"Oh." Robin knew Cam well enough to see that manhandling a woman, especially one his mother's age, would be a problem for him. "We can talk later about our approach."

"I can't push an old lady around," Cam repeated. "It wouldn't be right."

"Forget it," she said soothingly. "I'll go out and get us something to eat."

***

Just when Robin thought she was getting good at being

unobtrusive, she made a dumb mistake. The *IN* driveway to McDonald's was hidden behind some other signs, and she drove past it. Since the *OUT* drive was clear, she pulled in there and quickly turned into a parking spot. She was reaching over to retrieve her purse when a police cruiser pulled up beside her. The siren made a single *whoop* sound before the cop shut it off and got out of the car.

Robin's mind bubbled with panic. Her first thought was *Run!* which was ridiculous. Her second thought was *Where are the papers for this car?* The only other time she was stopped in her life, she'd been so nervous she couldn't find her insurance slip. The cop had been understanding, and later she'd found it in the glove compartment, right where it was supposed to be.

The officer was almost to the car, and she bit her lip to keep from screaming. *I'm traveling with a fake driver's license. I don't know if I can prove the car is mine. I'm supposed to do important stuff tomorrow morning. I cannot get arrested. I can't do this!*

"Good afternoon, ma'am. Could I see your license, registration, and proof of insurance?

With fumbling fingers, she managed to get the Lynn Taylor driver's license out of her wallet. Opening the glove box, she said a little thank-you to Cam. Right on top, encased in a plastic sleeve, were all the necessary documents. She had a little trouble getting them out, since her hands felt like stones attached to the ends of her arms. When she handed them over, she noticed that the cop was looking at her intently. Did she look as evasive as she felt? She'd read about training they took to help them judge dishonesty in a person's behavior. She had to look like a criminal, because that's how she felt: guilty, guilty, guilty.

"You pulled in the OUT drive," he said.

"I'm sorry. I missed the first one, and the other one was

clear."

"I'll be right back." Taking her papers, he returned to his car, where she knew he would run the information to find out if she had any outstanding warrants. What if Thomas Wyman had put our some sort of "find this woman" alert? The cop might receive more information than she wanted him to have. There was nothing she could do about it.

As she waited, advice from two very different sources played in her head.

You're a pretty girl, her father had told her once. *Learn to use your looks to get what you want.*

Em's scratchy advice sounded too. *Everybody likes to feel important. Focus on them and they stop thinking about you.*

The officer returned and handed back her documents. "Everything's in order, Mrs. Taylor."

"Ms.," she corrected, lowering her lashes. "We're separated—kind of a trial."

His eyes showed immediate interest. "I see." He waved at the entry and exit drives. "Those signs are there for a reason, Ms. Taylor. Ignoring them could cause an accident."

Robin turned her best smile on. "I'm a little distracted with moving and—everything. Thank you for being nice about it."

The line between his brows softened, and he took a step back. "It's pretty easy to miss the signs with so much stuff along here."

"Listen, I know you're busy, but I'm new to the area, and I wonder if you can direct me to a good Thai restaurant. After I get my roommate a Big Mac, I'd like some spring rolls for myself."

"Your roommate is a fast-food junkie?"

Guessing what he hoped to hear, she included a pronoun in

her answer. “She sure is.”

When the cruiser pulled away, Robin had directions to a restaurant, and more importantly, no ticket for an illegal turn. She also had an invitation to become the cop’s friend on Facebook, which would never happen.

***

“I almost got a ticket!” she said when she returned to the hotel with their food. She gave a brief account, ending with, “Andy must be good. There hasn’t been a red flag yet.”

“Who is Andy?” Hua asked.

“The guy who made us into Richard and Lynn Taylor. He doesn’t work cheap, but he’s really good.”

Hua looked slightly offended. “Get me the proper equipment and I will do this for free,” he said. “You won’t need Andy again.”

Robin had bought Thai food for herself and Hua, but Cam refused to eat it, suggesting it was every bit as likely as Chinese food to contain cat meat. She’d bought him a Quarter Pounder with Cheese, which he ate in four bites while she set out steamed rice, jasmine tea, and an assortment of wonderfully fragrant dishes in neat cardboard boxes with wire handles. Apparently unwilling to even watch his friends eat foreign food, Cam took his fries and the oversize Coke to the motel parking lot, mumbling something about checking the tires on the car. When he was gone, Hua and Robin addressed Cam’s reluctance to go after Judge Comdon as they ate their meal. Hua used a pair of chopsticks that for some strange reason had been included with their food, and they both laughed at his clumsy efforts. Robin ate her food with an all-American Spork.

“If Cam won’t manhandle a woman,” Robin said, “we’ll have to get her into the van some other way.”

Hua slurped some noodles, chewed, and swallowed. "You might purchase a gun."

Robin frowned. "I know it's wimpy for a kidnapper to say, but I don't want to get into using weapons. It makes things seem wrong." She shivered. "I guess I should say *more* wrong."

Hua didn't argue the point. "Drugs? Perhaps Rohypnol, such as is used in many crime dramas?"

"She's almost seventy. I'd hate to cause her to have a stroke or something."

They ate in silence for a while. "You could change the method," Hua suggested. "Approach her at home."

"I'm sure there's security at her house." She set her carton aside. "We need to find a neutral spot where we can isolate her long enough to make our pitch."

A knock sounded on the door, and Robin rose to look through the peephole. Cam's face was all she could see, and he grinned in a way that indicated he had a surprise. When she opened the door he stepped aside, revealing Em Kane behind him. Apparently dressed for a trip to the Arctic, she wore heavy boots with felt liners; a wool coat in large blocks of red, black, and white; mittens that reached almost to her elbows; and one of those hats with fur-lined flaps everywhere. Em hadn't been kidding about disliking cold weather.

There was more. Beside Em on a short leash was the stray that had facilitated Senator Buckram's abduction. He sat quietly next to Em, eyes fixed on Robin as if he knew it was an important moment. His tail thumped hopefully on the floor beneath him.

Foregoing comment on Em's outfit Robin said, "You kept the dog?"

"Bennett," Em replied. "I named him after a supervisor I had once—same eyes."

Robin stepped back. "Please, come in."

"I'm almost done outside," Cam said. "A few more minutes." He disappeared down the hallway as Em entered the room.

Introductions were made, and Hua bowed graciously, giving "Ms. Em" his chair. They offered her food. Em said she'd already eaten but her companion was always hungry. After asking permission, Hua took what remained of the pad prik, opened the container so it was flat, and set it on the floor. The dog devoured the food in two snuffling bites and looked to Hua for more. "He eats enough to feed a third-world village," Em said fondly. "The other Bennett could eat too."

"I thought you were going to take him to the Humane Society."

She shrugged. "I figured if I was going on the road by myself, it might be good to have him along."

"About going on the road," Robin said. "How did you find us?"

"I have my ways." Robin guessed that meant she and Cam had been in touch.

"What's your plan?"

"I'm going to help you." Her tone was belligerent. "Maybe you don't always need me to make a diversion, but I can man your base when you find one." Though her voice was gruff and her words confident, there was a plea in Em's eyes. Despite the downside to having a grumpy, seventy-plus woman with a bad hip in the group, the thought of being able to draw on Em's experience made the knot between Robin's shoulders loosen a little.

"We found our base today, so you came just in time." She

looked at the dog, who seemed to be listening with interest. "And now our gang has a mascot too."

"I like this Bennett," Hua said, reaching down to scratch the dog's ears. "He is a very nice animal."

That cemented Hua's place in Em's esteem. "The better you know people, the more you like dogs," she told him.

The KNP crew has a house mother. And a pet.

"What will be your clown name?" Hua asked.

"I'd like to be called Loonette," Em said. "She's sort of a Canadian version of Pee Wee Herman."

"Did she have a dog?"

"A cat, I think, but I'm sticking with Bennett." She patted the dog's sleek head.

"Em, we've got a new target, but Cam's got issues because it's a woman."

"I could have predicted that," Em responded. "If she's about the same age as his mother, he won't want to mistreat her."

"Bev Comdon is nothing like Mrs. Halkias," Robin said. "In fact, she's the worst kind of cougar."

"Likes 'em young, eh?" Em snorted disdainfully. "Never understood people who can't act their age and not their shoe size."

Robin explained how the judge manipulated young men into her program. "We need to figure out how to get to her."

"But Robin says no weapons or drugs," Hua said.

"And Cam won't grab her because she's female," Em sneered. "Boy scouts and nuns, that's what this gang is made of."

Robin felt defensive in the face of Em's derision. "We are what we are, Em."

"I guess." Taking Robin's cookie, Em broke it in half and crunched it between her dentures. "Now that I'm here, we'll put our heads together and come up with a way to teach an old cougar new tricks."

***

Elizabeth Terrin was much as Robin had imagined from her voice on the phone, fortyish and enthusiastic to an almost irritating degree. She pooh-poohed the treacherous driveway as a minor problem that required only a little gravel, though she left her car on the road and tiptoed in bright pink, leopard-print boots around the pond-sized puddle. As she showed them through the house, Cam obeyed Robin's instructions and said little. He nodded wisely when Elizabeth waxed eloquent on the property's possibilities and managed not to let on that he'd been inside before, which Robin saw as real progress toward understanding the role little white lies play in everyday life. Once she'd done more griping about the price, which the bank obligingly dropped again the next day, they began the purchasing process. Elizabeth sparkled at the prospect of unloading a place her office had listed for decades, and when they met to make a formal offer a few days later, the bank's representative seemed equally pleased, though being a banker, she was much more decorous about it.

One problem Robin faced in the negotiations was Elizabeth's overly-developed desire to be helpful. A kind soul who didn't seem able to grasp that her newest clients didn't want her around, she launched a campaign to "integrate" them into the small community of Gardiner. In addition to shopping coupons and informational pamphlets, she offered contact information for a host of local organizations that would "love some new blood."

Em, who had been introduced to the Realtor as Cam's

stepmother, had an idea, as usual. "Try to sell her something." She straightened the yarn snaking from her current project to the skein at her side. "She'll move in a different direction quicker than a cat when the broom comes out."

The next day, when Elizabeth called with the suggestion that "Lynn" accompany her to the Chamber of Commerce After-Hours that evening, Robin followed Em's suggestion, though her face burned with embarrassment. "I can't come tonight," she said, "but I would like to meet everyone soon. I have several ideas for changing the face of Gardiner, and it won't be all that expensive."

Elizabeth hesitated. "Changing Gardiner?"

"I'm thinking our artists could do murals or statues for each of the businesses in town. It will help them offset the cost of the retreats, and for twenty, maybe thirty thousand each, your people will have original art on their buildings."

"Thirty thousand dollars? That sounds like a lot."

"For original art? Not at all. I was thinking your office could be the starting point, since you have that nice side wall with the empty lot next to it. I'd do the work at a discount—say, eighteen thousand. I'm thinking a scene from the Napoleonic Wars, but of course you'd have a say in that. I love creating battle scenes—so full of action, you know? Life and death—everything is there."

"A battle scene." Elizabeth's voice was faint.

"Once people see what you've got, we'll start signing up the other businesses. It might take them some time to get the money together, but we'll need to get the house ready and the artists on site, so it should work out great."

"Eighteen thousand dollars."

"Plus the paint, of course. And good brushes—I can't work with substandard equipment."

"Well." The Realtor's tone was cool. "We'll talk about it once you're settled, shall we?"

"Of course. I just had to share my idea with you because it's such a great deal for both of us."

"Umm. I'll be in touch, but I think everything we need to do right now is all caught up." She hung up so fast that Robin giggled. "Em, I think you just guaranteed Ms. Terrin will go out of her way to avoid talking to me ever again. But what if she'd loved the idea of spending thousands on a Napoleonic mural?"

"We'd have figured something out," Em replied. "Sometimes you have to go out on a limb, because that's where the fruit is."

***

For two weeks, Robin used the time she wasn't working on the sale to do the shopping she'd been putting off. First she took Hua to a second-hand store some distance down the freeway from Gardiner. Though his taste ran to the flamboyant, she stressed the need to blend in. They bought several plain outfits and one he promised to wear only at home. Eyeing the emerald green silk shirt, rhinestone-studded black jeans, and fringed leather vest, she hoped he meant it.

At least an artists' colony allows for the possibility of someone who looks like an Asian Michael Jackson.

Once he had decent clothing (and his own economy-sized bottles of ginger biloba shampoo and conditioner), Hua and Em took her car to Cedar to get the van they'd left in Robin's storage unit. Though Hua had no driver's license, he promised to drive carefully on the way back to Kansas, ignoring all distractions. When they returned Em admitted he'd been pretty good, though she commented that following Hua was like "chasing a chipmunk across the back forty."

Without telling either the bank or the Realtor, Cam began

work on the house. Each morning Robin drove him out to Bobby Road and dropped him off, laden with tools bought at the local hardware store. He spent the first few days assessing what needed to be done and fixing minor problems, loose boards, broken locks, and corroded hinges. Each afternoon when Robin picked him up, he was filthy, odiferous, and undeniably pleased with himself.

Once Hua returned with the van, the two men began buying larger items and transporting them to the property. The small electrical generator they'd bought for the first KNP came in handy for running power tools, since they couldn't turn the electricity on until the purchase was complete. "Now I can really do something," Cam told them after he and Hua bought two new toilets, a sink, and an array of accessories. "I'll get the plumbing working so the bathrooms are usable. It's good that we've got our own well." Robin noticed how he'd slipped into speaking of the house as "ours," long before that was true.

Due to his farm background, Cam seemed to know a little about every aspect of home ownership, and his confidence amazed Robin. "It isn't like you're going to call somebody in for every little problem," he said, unaware that most people she knew did exactly that. Because he was Cam, he was a little compulsive, focusing on a problem with a single-mindedness that recalled their early meetings in the workout room. A couple of times Robin sat in the car entertaining herself for an hour or more while he finished his to-do list for the day. For Cam, tomorrow wasn't here yet, so it was beyond consideration.

Hua began serving as Cam's gopher, hauling tools and turning spigots on command, which left Robin free to make lists and worry about things that might not happen. In the evenings Hua extended the Taylors' excellent though imaginary financial background, so her fears their loan would be denied didn't materialize.

Robin and Em spent their days cruising the area, learning the roads and locating stores where they could buy furniture when they were ready. By the time they officially became owners of the house on Bobby Road, the four new tenants had three working bathrooms (the upstairs wasn't yet operable) and a list of places that delivered home furnishings within their area.

Relocating was easy, since none of them had much to bring in. Em's first impression of the house was important to the other three, and as they showed her around, they each painted word pictures of its future. Though both Cam and Hua offered to share their respective wings with her, Em politely declined. The upstairs floors she deemed unsuitable due to her physical limitations. Finally, after sticking her pointy nose into this place and that, she announced, "I'll make an apartment out of the two parlors if nobody objects. The bath under the stairs is small but it's close, so I won't wake you all when I get up to pee in the night." Once she proposed it, they agreed it was the perfect place for Em.

With Hua in what he called the terrace apartment and Cam claiming the "hero wing," Robin was left the whole second story to herself. She took one room at the front of the house for general use, and a small one beside it for a bedroom. Not that she had a bed; only Em had one so she didn't have to sleep on the floor. The others would get beds as time and funds permitted. Robin insisted anything with fabric had to be new. "There's enough mold, dust, and bugs in this place," she insisted. "We aren't bringing more in."

Which meant she needed to do more shopping. *Was there ever a time when I looked forward to it?*

Mental unease and physical discomfort made the first night long for Robin. The house was cold, since Cam had refused to build fires in any fireplace until a chimney sweep was called in to clear the debris and check for broken flue pipes. The hardwood floor was uncomfortable despite the layers of blankets she spread out. The wide, mullioned windows were cracked in several places, so when the wind blew, the glass rattled and drafts swept the room.

With her nose chilled and her shoulders and hips squished against the adamant surface, she questioned every decision she'd made since that first day, when Cam had asked for her help. She couldn't count all the places she'd gone wrong. Her latest worry was that they'd be easier to find with a house, three vehicles, and a mortgage. Would Private Investigator Tom Wyman track them down tomorrow or the next day, call in the local police to surround the house, and capture them all? If he did, Robin knew she'd be responsible for ruining four lives. As she finally drifted into sleep, her last thought was how creepy the absolute quiet was. A house far from traffic, far from people. *How in the world did I ever end up here?*

The first order of business on the morning of their first full day in their new home was to scrub the whole place. Robin had bought buckets, sponges, brushes of all shapes and sizes, and anything else she thought looked useful for cleaning. Everyone pitched in, and Robin found having something to do—lots to do, in fact—lessened her worries and made her more optimistic.

That was despite the physical problems they faced. They had electricity, but the hot water heater was inoperable. That meant heating the icy well water in pans on the stove. Hua took responsibility for that, making many trips back and forth to add warm water to their buckets before returning to his own cleaning chores. Soon the strong smell of bleach was everywhere, but Em, wearing rubber gloves that came almost to her elbows, said that was better than mold and mouse droppings

After their cold first night, Robin called a local chimney sweep and offered a bonus if he'd come to the house right away. Next she called for firewood, promising the man an extra twenty dollars if the wood arrived that day. When the chimney sweep showed up, she put Cam in charge of dealing with him, and she was pleased to see that it wasn't long before the two of them were kneeling at the hearth, peering up and discussing fire safety. Later she heard footsteps on the roof and slightly alarming sounds from various rooms. When he was finished, the sweep pronounced all the chimneys usable except one and promised to return when the parts he needed were available.

Though they all looked forward to warmer temperatures, another problem arose when evening came and the temperature dropped. Neither Robin nor Hua had experience with fire-keeping. "That's okay," Cam said. "I'll show you."

Making a fire wasn't too difficult, Robin found, but keeping it burning was a problem. Used to setting a thermostat and forgetting it, she let her fire go too long without fuel the first night and had to start over again. She also learned that wood heat meant being either too cold or too hot. Near the fire, she felt like a piece of toast, but five steps away she felt brisk drafts from the poorly-insulated windows. When she woke in the morning the fire was low, and she hated getting out from under her pile of blankets to stoke it and re-warm the room. *There will be a furnace in that creepy, spider-filled basement by fall,* she promised herself.

"Cleaning will warm us up!" Hua said when she arrived in the kitchen with a blanket wrapped over the old felt bathrobe she'd found at Goodwill. She wore two pairs of socks inside her slippers to insulate her feet from the dank, cold floors. Hua seemed not to mind the cold, apparently adjusting his activity level to the need for warmth. Cam too accepted the chilly morning cheerfully, already hauling in more wood and leaving a trail of bark and sawdust in his wake.

Em announced that the rooms she'd chosen, being interior and fairly small, had warmed quickly and retained the heat well.

Still, she wore her trapper hat and heavy wool socks, and Robin noted she hadn't entered the kitchen until Hua warmed the room by lighting all four burners on the gas stove.

Needs were revealed as they cleaned, exploring corners and venturing into small spaces. At Cam's suggestion, Robin used clear packaging tape to cover the cracks in her windows. With so many problems to address, new glass wasn't high on the list, and the tape did a decent job of keeping out the wind.

The roof of Hua's wing leaked in several places. Cam found a stack of extra shingles in the shed behind the house, and between the top ones, which had dried up and cracked, and the bottom ones, which had rotted into the ground, there were enough good ones to make the repairs. Once they determined exactly where the leaks were, the two men climbed onto the roof to fix them. Between the pounding of two hammers, Robin heard them talking and laughing. *A displaced Asian and an asocial farm boy—men love having something to fix.*

Wiring was another problem they were forced to address immediately. Appliances had to be used one at a time, because more than that made the lights flicker. Some rooms had no electricity at all, since animals had chewed through the wires that ran along the outside walls. In addition, like many old houses, there simply weren't enough outlets for modern living. Robin's bedroom had only one, which didn't work, so she dressed and undressed by flashlight. The wings had more outlets than the main section, being slightly newer, but none located on the exterior walls worked.

After many calls and a wait of several days, they got an electrician to come out and make rudimentary repairs. He shook his head at the "cobbled up" system, claiming it was the result of several successive amateur installations. Robin accepted the estimated cost with a suppressed sigh and scheduled him to come out with a full crew and redo the wiring for the whole house. They simply couldn't operate without electricity.

There was a plumbing scare too. The third day of their residence they smelled something odd—nasty, actually—and discovered water backed up in all the downstairs drains. Once again Cam was the hero, tapping and listening along the septic pipe until he located a massive clog. He cleared it by shoving an old metal fencepost from the nearest joint in the pipe to the spot where the clump blocked the flow. "Hasn't been used in so long the stuff hardened up," he reported. "Should be okay now there's water going through all the time."

The hot water heater was replaced a few days into their occupancy, and the first rush of hot water through Robin's bathroom faucet was like a gift from Heaven. *It's a gift, all right. One we paid plenty for.*

Critters had made nests everywhere in the house, and though most were abandoned, some were still occupied. The residents had to be relocated, and naturally, they objected. Mothballs were scattered to repel the squirrels, and Bennett made himself useful by chasing off those who persisted. Traps were set for the mice, and Cam spoke of getting a cat or two. Worst, to Robin's way of thinking, was the possibility of snakes, indicated by a skin Hua found behind the toilet in his bathroom. Cam assured her that once the lawn was mowed regularly and the presence of rodents lessened inside (she noticed he didn't promise they'd leave entirely), snakes would no longer find the house attractive. Determined to make that happen, she spent fifty bucks on a used push mower at the Buy/Sell Gardiner site. When the weather warmed and things started growing, she intended to mow every week until no self-respecting snake would slither anywhere close to her property line.

Then there was the staircase, once beautiful but now dangerous due to weak and broken boards. Hua proposed a temporary solution: putting inexpensive parquet flooring over the existing steps. By purchasing close-outs and odd lots, they were able to make the steps usable though not very attractive, since one didn't always match the next.

Though there were times Robin rued the day they'd seen the house, it slowly became livable. Days spent in hard labor made for sound sleep, with neither childhood nightmares nor visions of private detectives invading her nighttime hours. Each improvement brought a sense of fulfillment for all of them, and something as simple as a toilet that flushed for the first time in a decade was likely to get appreciative applause. Those incidents brought them closer, and Robin felt for the first time in her life what the word *home* means.

Her weekly calls to Shelly were both comforting and disquieting. She didn't want to give away where she was; it was best that Shelly didn't know. She did share their adventures with the house, however, making a story about elderly Cam's mother joining them with her Asian caregiver. They were flipping a house, she told her friend, and she was finding it an enjoyable experience.

"My mom is still always knocking out a wall or digging up the yard," Shelly said. "I didn't inherit her love of table saws, but maybe some of it rubbed off on you."

"Your mom was great," Robin said. "I always felt like I'd been adopted when I was at your house."

I often wished I could be, she thought before the disloyalty of it hit her. *I'd never have left Mom and Chris. But Mark?*

"Your dad was great too."

Shelly laughed. "Mr. We-Should-Get-There-Early-So-We-Get-A-Good-Parking-Spot?"

"Trust me, Shel. He's a great dad."

The pause that followed told Robin her best friend understood a little of what she'd lived through. "Yeah. I'm lucky to have nice parents." Knowing Robin, she didn't let the moment get squishy. "But that doesn't mean I'm not embarrassed when they both wear tennis shoes out to dinner."

When the call ended, Robin thought about the odd "family" she was now a member of. Em with her knitting bag and saggy pants, Hua with his Michael Jackson outfit, and Cam with his stutter and his many rituals. As work on the house progressed and they'd begun to shift from four disparate individuals to a group focused on common goals, Robin began to feel more optimistic about the future. Thomas Wyman had apparently given up the search for them. They had a base—a home—and they were learning each other's strengths. Robin felt for the first time in her life what the word *home* meant: not just a spot to sleep and eat and keep your things, but a place where someone was always ready to share your joys and listen to your fears. Having a home helped meld them, so they'd be ready to take on the target they'd chosen—ready to show another miscreant the error of her ways.

Chapter Fourteen

They held their planning sessions in Hua's rooms, which he'd transformed with paint bought in the discount aisle. Gone was the grime, and in its place were elegant pastels that shifted pleasantly from wall to wall. While Cam had chosen basic office-type furniture for his wing, Hua had opted for classic pieces, the more ornate the better. To see what he'd learned about Judge Beverly Comdon, they stood arched around a battered refectory table that held his computer, oversized screen, printers, scanners, and other geeky machines Robin couldn't name, much less operate.

The downside of Hua's fascination with technology was that he often spoke in geek, peppering his conversations with terms like *bots, click-jacking*, *IP activity,* and *algorithm*. When he waxed poetic about the packet-sniffers he'd sent after the data, Em ordered, "Cut to the chase. We just want to hear what you know about the old biddy."

"Robin's source seems to be correct," Hua said obligingly. "Judge Comdon is a wealthy woman who seldom goes anywhere alone." He showed them a photo of the judge at an event. "Along with her personal assistant and a couple of law students, there is always a nice-looking, very fit young man in her entourage."

"And these men are convicted criminals?"

Hua pointed at a photo. "This one was caught selling heroin. His sentence was six months in Rehabilitate Louisiana." Clicks sounded as he brought up a second picture. "This one stole an elderly neighbor's money when he was supposed to be looking after her." He leaned close to read details. "He spent five months with the judge."

"Old Bev likes a certain type." Em pointed at the pictures one by one. "When a boy who's tall, dark, and handsome walks into her courtroom, she makes him an offer he can't refuse."

Robin leaned in to see the screen better. "When does her latest victim's sentence end?"

"Actually he was released last week," Hua said.

"She'll be looking for new blood," Em predicted. "We have to move fast."

Robin gestured at the screen. "I thought I'd approach some of these men and see if they'll talk to us."

"They won't help you take her down," Em said. "She has the juice to send them to prison."

"Well, if one of those pretty young men won't go on record, how do we convince her she's in trouble?"

Em tilted her head to one side. "Cam's pretty."

Robin turned to Hua, who shared her disbelief. "But Cameron has no—what are these—people skills."

"He wouldn't have to interest her for long, just enough time for her to embarrass herself," Em said.

Robin frowned. "Could we teach him enough to get her interested?"

"That would depend on whether he's willing to learn."

"I don't think—" Hua thought better of what he'd meant to say and stopped.

"Nothing ventured, nothing gained," Em said cheerfully. "Let's ask him."

They crossed the main house and went down the ramp to where Cam sat at his computer, lost in something called *Virgins of Calamara*. They had to wait until he finished a level so they could get his full attention. Even then he turned to them reluctantly, eager to get back to vicarious death and destruction.

Taking what she hoped was a persuasive slant on the proposal Robin asked, “Cam, you don’t want to have to force Judge Comdon into the van, right?”

He rubbed the front of his T-shirt. “I can’t push an old lady around, Robin. It wouldn’t be right.”

“Do you think you could flirt with her a little?”

Judging by his reaction, she might have asked the question in the ancient Calamarian language. “Flirt?”

Robin glanced at Hua helplessly, and he took a stab at it. “If you make her like you, maybe she would go somewhere to be alone together. Then Robin could talk to her, like she did the others.”

Cam’s frown cleared and then appeared again. “I don’t know how to flirt.”

“We’ll help you practice.” Robin turned to Hua. “Show him. Flirt with me.”

Hua’s smooth forehead wrinkled. “I have not done such a thing ever.”

She sighed in frustration. “Okay. You be Judge Comdon. I’ll be Cam.”

Cam snickered. “Hua’s going to be a girl?”

“It’s just a demonstration.” She turned to Hua and deepened her voice. “Oh, Judge Bev, it’s great to meet such an important person. And you’re very attractive too.”

“I saw her picture,” Cam interrupted. “She looks like Olive Oyl from the Popeye cartoons.”

"That's part of flirting. You say nice things, even if they're a little exaggerated."

"That's not exaggerating. It's a great big lie."

Robin rolled her eyes. "Just try, Cam." She turned back to Hua and said in the same gushy voice, "It must be exciting to travel all over the state meeting people."

"I would never say that," Cam put in. "I don't like meeting people very much."

"We're trying to put the idea into her head that you could travel with her."

Cam considered. "Do I have to leave my games here?"

"You're not really going to—"

"You should get him an earwig," Em suggested. "Then you could tell him exactly what to say."

"Can just anybody buy those?" Robin asked.

Hua shrugged. "Almost everything is buyable on Amazon."

"The problem will be how he says what you tell him." Em made her voice into a fair impression of Darth Vader. "That robot warrior voice of his won't work."

Cam didn't seem at all upset by the characterization, so Robin asked, "If Hua gets us an earpiece and Em and I show you how to flirt, will you try this new way, Cam?"

He turned back to his game and picked up the controller. "Sure, Robin. As long as you tell me what to say."

***

Hua hadn't exaggerated when he said he was an excellent cook. Stuck in Buckram's apartment twenty-four seven, he'd watched cooking shows from pure boredom and learned a great deal about food preparation. Claiming good meals deserved better than paper plates and plastic forks, he insisted they needed decent china and cutlery. Since he didn't ask for much, Robin searched until she found an almost complete set of each at Goodwill. Hua was inordinately happy when she brought home the two dusty boxes, and she felt pleased that some nameless donor hadn't seen the value in keeping Grandma's good tableware.

"We must plant a garden," Hua announced. "Fresh food is best for taste and health."

Cam agreed, and the two of them chose a spot behind the house that looked as if it had been a garden long ago. They badgered Robin into buying hoes, rakes, and other garden tools, and Cam visited the local feed store for advice on what grew well in the area. He returned with packets of squash, beans, peas, carrots, and broccoli, along with a bag of onion sets and one of seed potatoes. He and Hua could hardly wait until the date of the last frost, April 7th according to predictions, to begin the project.

The team for the Comdon Caper (Em insisted on calling it that) was Cam, Robin, and Hua. Keeping in mind Mink's warning to always have an escape plan, Robin designated Hua as backup. He would stay on the fringes of the operation in the van, watching for trouble, warning them if he suspected problems, and picking them up in case they needed to make a quick escape. Em's assignment was minding the house and the dog.

In the days before they left Kansas there was a flurry of activity. Hua and Cam thinned and weeded industriously in their small garden so Em wouldn't have to while they were gone. Robin paid as many bills ahead of time as she could afford to, worried about what would happen if she were unable to return. "I'll manage if you three have to go on the lam," Em said, knowing her concerns without being told. "I'll do what I can to divert the cops so you'll have time to get out of the country."

"And if we're arrested—"

"We've talked it through a dozen times, Sweet-cheeks. I close this place down and Bennett and me get a bus ticket out of here and start over somewhere else. If they arrest you, the rest of us do what we can to help."

She made it sound simple, but it wasn't. If Robin were caught, there might not be much the others could do. She couldn't imagine Hua, Em, or Cam executing a jailbreak. While Em was capable of plotting one, carrying it out with a couple of amateurs and a three-footed cane seemed unlikely.

A few days before the Comdon KNP, Robin left the house in Em's car. The "pond" at the end of their driveway was drying nicely as spring progressed but it was still a hazard. Gunning the engine at just the right moment to make it up the incline, Robin watched for oncoming traffic. Not that there was much of that on Bobby Road.

Cam had proposed a half-circle drive that began and ended at either end of the property, where the slope was much gentler. "We won't have to drive through that mud hole, and it will look nicer too." Again it pleased Robin to see Cam's growing confidence. Unless there was a stranger around, his stutter had almost disappeared, and his knowledge of practicalities meant the others often depended on his advice.

Too bad the flirting thing isn't going so well.

Hacking into a popular blog hosting site, Hua had discovered the identity of the blog writer who'd complained about the "sinful" practices of a "certain lady judge." The blogger was Ethel Simpson, grandmother to a young man who'd been one of "Bev's Boys." The blog was her attempt to let the world know about the judge's "wicked" practices without smearing her grandson's name.

When she arrived in Baton Rouge late that night, Robin went straight to the bar where Hua said Elmer Simpson worked as a bouncer.

Simpson was hesitant to talk about Judge Comdon, but the promise of anonymity and the offer of a hundred bucks helped. Robin hung around until the crowd thinned and he was free to talk.

"Tell me about the Rehabilitate Louisiana Program," she asked when he finally sat down at a table across from her.

He shrugged, elaborately casual. "I did work around the judge's place—lawn stuff and like that."

"Did your work include sleeping with the judge?" He opened his mouth to deny it, but Robin had her own lie ready. "I've already spoken with your grandmother."

He grinned sheepishly. "Gram thinks I was this innocent kid who fell into the clutches of an evil Maggie May type." He touched his shirt pocket, where a pack of cigarettes showed.

"Would you like to take this conversation outside?" she asked.

He grinned, showing white, slightly uneven teeth. "That would be good."

Once they were in the alley behind the bar, Elmer lit one. Waving the smoke away from Robin with his free hand, he began to relax, and the story came out. "My college roommate and I had this little business going, selling computer equipment that fell off a truck, if you know what I mean. When we got caught, he went to jail—like directly to jail—because it was his second strike. I was scared, and when Judge Bev offered to get me into her rehab program, I jumped at the chance." He grinned. "I could tell she liked me, you know?"

Taking a drag on his cigarette, he went on. “I took the deal: six months in the program. If the judge was happy with my work, she said I’d get a stipend.” He chuckled. “I didn’t even know what a stipend was.”

Tilting her head to one side, Robin said, “You must have had an idea something funny was going on.”

He shrugged. “I had my suspicions.”

“You signed up anyway.”

His tone said Robin was a little slow. “It was that or jail time.”

“Then what happened?”

Elmer looked away. “I checked in with the judge’s personal assistant, who showed me to the guest house and told me what my duties would be. As soon as she left, the judge showed up.” Taking a final drag on his cigarette, he crushed it against the brick wall of the building. “It didn’t take long to figure out the rest of it.”

“But you stayed?”

“Hell, yeah.” He smirked as if to ask who wouldn’t. “Two weeks later we were in Cabo.” He leaned against the wall. “Gram saw it as a big sin, and she hated that I never went back to school, but to tell you the truth, I had a ball. I never lived that high before, and all I had to do was pretend I liked the old biddy.”

“And did you?”

He rolled his eyes. “Bev is a real piece of work. Still, she lives good, so I got to live good too.”

“When your six months’ sentence was up, you parted amicably?”

“I don’t know what that word means, but we parted.” Turning

away, he lit another cigarette. “She gets bored easy, and I was kind of sick of putting up with her crap.” He shrugged. “The others said the same thing.”

Robin stopped breathing for a second, and she barely managed to keep the excitement in her voice under control. “You’re in contact with other men who went through the program?”

Elmer looked at the glowing tip of his cigarette. “One night the guy who’d been with Bev right before me came in here. I’d seen a photo of them together, and I just had to introduce myself.”

“Did the judge tell you not to talk about your time with her?”

He sniffed disparagingly. “She used to say it would be the word of a law-breaker against the word of a judge. I don’t think she ever thought her boys would get together and compare notes.”

“Could you put me in contact with some others who’ve been in the program?”

Elmer frowned. “You aren’t going to make trouble for them, are you?”

“Not at all.” Robin opened her purse. “I’ll give you fifty bucks for each name.”

He dug his phone out of his pocket. “I got a couple right here.”

The first name on Elmer’s list, Vic Unser, was slightly less cheerful about his time with Beverly Comdon than Elmer had been. Unser had been arrested for car theft, though Hua reported there was uncertainty about how much he was involved or if he even knew the car was stolen. Robin located him at his workplace the next morning, a slightly musty-smelling grocery store on the outskirts of the city. Unser was in the break room, drafting a work schedule for the coming week. When he learned her purpose, he got up to close the door on the busy scene behind her.

"I don't like to talk about it." Like Elmer Simpson, Unser was taller than average, with dark hair, wide shoulders, and the kind of symmetrical face that appeals to the majority of humankind.

"Your name won't be mentioned," Robin assured him. "And your time is worth a hundred dollars." She set two fifties on the table. "I only need to know if what I've been told is true."

Unser rolled his eyes. "Is it true she tricks guys into her sleazy rehab program, treats them like personal sex toys, and tosses them out a few months later? Yeah, it is."

"You didn't know that was going to happen?"

He rubbed a knuckle under his nose. "I guess I should have. People talked about the guy before me, but I didn't get that I was the next in a long line." He glanced around the room. "I was lucky to get this job back."

"Did the judge treat you well, aside from demanding your, um, cooperation?"

"Not bad, I guess. Good food, a nice room—" He looked away. "Not that I got to sleep there very often."

That brought a distasteful picture to mind, but Robin asked, "Do other guys feel the same way?"

He made a noise of disgust. "Rafael, the guy before me, was kind of a weirdo."

"Weird how?"

"From what people said, he actually liked the old girl. He was heartbroken when she let him go."

“Did you ever do anything that might be considered job training?”

He huffed sarcastically. “She’d say things like, ‘The pool needs skimming, Dear Boy,’ and we were supposed to hop to it.” Unser’s face flushed. “You were always ‘Dear Boy’ to her, like you didn’t have a name she could bother to remember.”

With Hua’s help Robin located Rafael Cardenas, currently working second shift at a small factory. When she called, he was less than cordial. “Why do you want to know about the señora?”

“We want to be sure Rehabilitate Louisiana is legitimate.”

Rafael became belligerent. “Señora Bev is a great judge. She does many good things for the people.”

“Mr. Cardenas—”

“Leave me alone, or I call the police.” The call ended abruptly.

“You should have guessed at least one of them would take her side,” Em said when Robin reported in. “Leave Mr. Cardenas his happy little fantasy and go to the next name on your list.”

That was Ricky Miller, who directed her to a pool hall where he was in the middle of a game when she arrived. Though he looked at her like she was lunch, Robin remained businesslike. “I’m here for information, Mr. Miller. I don’t need a drink and you don’t need my number.” Without explanation, she set a hundred-dollar bill on the lip of the table. It disappeared into his pocket with hardly a second’s lapse.

A chain smoker with no job and no prospects, Ricky’s story wasn’t much different from the others. He’d come before Bev Comdon on a robbery charge. When she’d commented on his muscles, he’d sensed her interest and flirted a little. “I got seven months in the judge’s rehab program,” he reported grimly. “I thought I got a gift, but it was a different kind of hard time."

"You regretted taking the deal?"

He shrugged. "I guess it was better than the alternative." A speculative gleam appeared in his eye as he added casually, "I got a pretty interesting recording if you're willing to pay for it."

"What's that?"

He shrugged. "This guy Elmer was one of Bev's Boys. He works at a bar."

"I already spoke with him."

"Well, he don't know about this. One night three of us met up, had a few beers, and started comparing notes on the old girl—what she liked, what she said in private moments. It was pretty funny."

Despite a feeling of revulsion Robin managed, "And?"

Ricky's eyes took on a nasty gleam. "I had my phone, and I recorded about ten minutes' worth." He picked at a piece of tobacco stuck on his lip. "For five hundred I'll send you the file."

Robin took her wallet out of her purse. "Send it."

***

Later that night in her hotel room, Robin found herself stuck between sleep and wakefulness. The room was tasteful but institutional, and she found she missed her space at home, filled now with items from second-hand stores that spoke to her, no matter what their style. She'd added modern touches to the old-fashioned floral wallboard by hanging dollar store posters and a set of brushed-nickel shelving. In her bedroom she'd installed a sleigh bed that took up most of the space and needed a board under one foot to balance it. Her sitting area had two mission oak dressers and a Duncan Phyfe-type table with Danish straight chairs on either side. It had been satisfying to make the space hers without worrying whether a landlord would deduct from the security deposit or her father would comment on her "stupid" choices.

But home was far away. She was here to do a job.

Except I don't think I can.

It's the kind of thing Mark would be thrilled to have found.

Was she becoming her father, using whatever means she could devise to get what she wanted?

"Sit right there and look real sad." Mark pointed to a bench outside the county courthouse. "If someone stops to talk to you, don't say a word, understand?"

Six-year-old Robin nodded, having learned it didn't pay to argue. Mark had taken to punishing Chris when she displeased him, knowing she couldn't bear to see her brother suffer.

People passed, glancing at the tearful child alone on the bench. A few stopped to ask if she was okay. If they were male or old or plain, Mark appeared and identified himself as her "daddy." When they went on, he returned to the shadows.

Finally a pretty young woman stopped. "Are you all right, honey?" Remembering her instructions, Robin said nothing. "Are you waiting for someone? You don't look very happy."

Mark appeared, apparently solicitous. "Sorry I took so long, Babe." He turned to the woman. "I had some, um, business inside, but I didn't want her to—" He stopped, as if unwilling to explain.

"She seems upset, poor thing."

Mark's smile was rueful. "She hasn't spoken since her mother—" He paused and swallowed. "—left us." Turning again to Robin he said, "Mommy's in heaven now, right, Babe? We'll be okay, you and me."

The woman's hand went to her heart. "I'm so sorry."

His chin rose heroically. "Thanks. We're new here, so I don't know the procedures. Don't even know who to ask." Another pause, another swallow. "Things are pretty tough right now."

The woman paused, no doubt taking in Mark's boyish good looks. "I have to get back to work, but if you two would like to meet later for coffee—" She smiled at Robin. "—or a soda, I'm a good listener."

"That's so sweet of you."

Mark would show up alone, armed with a lie about his daughter getting a chance to spend time with a friend from school. He'd say he came alone because he needed so much to talk to someone. Of course it would end up going much farther than that.

He'd been in a good mood that day as they left the courthouse. "You see how easy it is to get what you want, Babe? That's how the world works. Your old man is showing you so you don't turn out to be a sucker like her."

She imagined the Comdon KNP, the lies she would tell, the fake smiles she would plaster on her face. How she would urge her innocent friend Cam to lie. Pushing those thoughts away, she drifted into a troubled dream in which Mark followed her around, saying over and over how clever she was. In the background, peeping out from behind a chair or a tree—even a refrigerator once—was a disapproving Thomas Wyman, Private Eye.

Chapter Fifteen

Robin rationalized her nightmares away by giving herself a strict lecture. The accusations against Judge Bev were true, and the KNP was justified. She called to tell Hua and Cam to meet her in Monroe, Louisiana, where they would intersect the path of the judge's current speaking tour. When Robin fretted to Em about the two men traveling south on their own, she made a rude sound. "I swear you can't breathe without something to worry about, girl. They've got GPS, and they're doing better at acting like normal people than I ever expected they would." Shaking her head she added, "Who'd-a thunk it?"

Though their lives were pretty weird by "normal people" standards, Cam could answer when a stranger spoke to him and Hua no longer stared at his surroundings as if he'd just stepped off a spacecraft. They were learning to blend in.

Well, sort of. Hua still asked questions that were hard to answer in public, like the time a sales clerk in all black clothing with an assortment of piercings in her face waited on them. While she was still in hearing range he'd asked, "Robin, do you think she might be undead?" Cam still stuttered when asked a question he wasn't sure how to answer, since he couldn't shake his early teaching that lying was evil. When someone asked seemingly innocuous questions like, "What are your plans for the weekend?" Robin always interceded, because Cam was liable to answer, "We're planning something secret, so I can't tell you."

Hua had obtained a set of earwigs, and they'd practiced until Cam remembered not to talk back when Robin gave instructions. While he was no Don Juan, he repeated the words and tried to copy Robin's intonation. There was a lag between what he heard and when he repeated the line, but Em said his stunning good looks would go a long way toward covering his limitations.

Judge Comdon was scheduled to speak at the university law center, and she'd booked a room in a downtown hotel for the night. There was no handsome young man along on the trip, which was a stroke of luck. Em thought introducing Cam in a new setting, where the judge might be in an adventurous mood, would increase their chances of success.

Robin and Cam arrived two hours before Comdon's speech in order to look the location over. Like many conference rooms, it had a narrow, raised dais at one side and space for a few hundred chairs. Forty-five minutes before the event, the techs tested the sound equipment. Ignoring the repeated, "Test, test, test," and the scuff of fingertips across the mic's surface, Robin led Cam to a spot in the front row where he'd be in Comdon's direct line of sight. "Now don't be polite and give up your chair," she warned.

"But what if somebody can't see over me?" he asked. "I'm pretty tall."

Pretty. Tall. It's what I'm counting on.

"Just this once it's okay to ignore what other people need. Ms. Comdon should notice you, and when she does, make sure you smile right at her, okay?" Reaching up, she took hold of his chin and made him look directly at her. "Eye contact. Smile. Got it?"

"Okay." He spread his lips experimentally. C-3PO might have done it better.

"No playing games on your phone. From the moment she arrives until she leaves, I want you looking at her as if she's wearing skin-tight latex like those witches of Bardot or wherever." As Cam frowned she added quickly, "She won't be. Just imagine it's a warrior princess up there and smile at her."

"I don't—"

"You're flirting, remember? It's how I'm going to get to talk to her." Robin patted his arm. "She needs to know that what she's doing is wrong, right?"

"Yeah." Cam ran a hand through his hair.

Robin smoothed it for him. "She won't talk to me, but she's going to want to talk to you."

Still reluctant, he nodded. "Okay, but stay close." As she walked away, Robin turned to look back. Cam was mouthing words, and she read his lips, "Stay. Smile. Flirt."

Beverly Comdon was a tough-looking woman in her sixties who wore bright red lipstick and suits cut to hide her flat chest and backside. As she passed Robin's chair at the back of the room on her way to the podium, the scent of jasmine perfume wafted from her. Comdon spoke on the judicial system in Louisiana, tailoring her remarks to students who hoped to join the ranks of lawyers and judges at some point in the future. She claimed the law was the bones of society, providing a framework on which all other bits fastened, grew, and prospered. Justice was the basis for liberty, equality, and freedom. Her voice was compelling, her arguments persuasive. The audience was rapt.

Robin had to fight the urge to shout the truth. This audience of young, idealistic students had a right to know how little real justice mattered to this particular jurist.

No. That's not how we decided to do it.

It was easy to note the exact moment when the judge saw Cameron. He sat smiling up at the platform, as ordered. Though the smile was neither warm nor sincere, Robin hoped it would do in a pinch.

It did. Beverly stopped mid-sentence but covered the flub in a practiced manner, making her pause into a little cough. After that, her gaze often returned to Cam. If he'd been an ice cream cone, he'd have turned to a puddle under the heat she sent his way.

When the speech was finished, Robin saw Comdon look for Cam in the crowd, but he had disappeared, as instructed. They'd whetted the judge's appetite and then snatched the bait from sight. She'd be unwilling to let him slip away a second time.

Comdon and her entourage arrived at their hotel an hour later. Looking tired, the judge emerged from the limo, but she brightened when she saw Cameron standing nearby. Putting up a hand, she signaled a halt. Those around her obeyed as if she were an old-time wagon master, some confused, others glancing knowingly from their boss to the newcomer.

She took a few steps toward Cam. "Weren't you at the lecture hall earlier?"

"Yes," Cam replied in the manner of a middle-school thespian. "I wanted to get a picture with you, but there were too many people." Comdon didn't notice his emotionless delivery. She probably hadn't yet registered that this godlike creature was capable of speech.

When Cam's comment finally penetrated, Comdon said briskly, "Well, then. We'll get you a photo now."

A young man with acne and pigeon shoulders made a soft comment in the judge's ear. When she nodded once, the man stepped forward and spoke to Cam. "Um, do you mind showing some ID?"

"Show him your license," Robin said. Cam complied with the request. "Now raise your arms so he can frisk you if he wants to." Again Cam obeyed, and the intern did a hurried search to assure he had no weapons. When the man returned the license and backed away, Comdon stepped forward and took Cam's arm. He recoiled slightly at the touch of a stranger, but Robin had warned it might happen, so he didn't shake her hand off.

"We need an attractive background." Dragging him along, she went down the sidewalk a short way, talking as if she and Cam were old friends. Finally she turned back to the group. "Gail, take a photo with the awning behind us." To Cam she said, "That way your friends will know where you were when we met."

The woman named Gail dutifully took Cam's phone and snapped two pictures, showing them to Comdon for approval before handing the phone back to Cam. Comdon released his arm with obvious reluctance and said something in a low tone that didn't come through well in Robin's earpiece. When Cam nodded and flashed his not-quite-real smile, she knew they were in.

"She wants me to come up to her room at eleven o'clock," he said when the judge's party had gone inside. "Room 1076."

"Great. Did she say why?"

He shrugged. "She said she might have a job for me."

Robin guessed the man who'd taken Cam's ID was at that moment vetting him. The judge liked young men, but she wasn't stupid enough to invite a complete stranger to her room. If he didn't check out, Cam would arrive to find someone else in the room and face some serious questions. There wasn't much chance of that. A computer search would tell them the judge's new interest, Walter Danner, was a waiter at a local restaurant with no wife, no kids, and a high school education.

It had been necessary to burn one of the false identities she'd bought from Andy to give Cam the background Judge Bev liked for her boys. That was okay, because Hua was learning how to create authentic-looking forgeries. The cost of the equipment he'd ordered made Robin cringe, but it would be worth it to be able to recreate themselves as needed.

They hoped Judge Bev wouldn't be able to resist a handsome

young man with an apparent crush on her. If she could convince herself that twenty-year-old delinquents weren't faking their affection for her, Em argued, she might well be able to believe this handsome young man had a big case of hero worship.

If Em's correct, Judge Comdon will get more than she bargained for.

At precisely 11:00 p.m., Cameron knocked on the door of Room 1076. He had his earwig in again, though he complained it felt funny. Robin heard Comdon's pleased little growl when she opened the door.

"I wondered if you'd show," she said. "You didn't seem all that interested."

"Tell her you are very interested."

"You are very interested."

Robin shut her eyes. "Cam, say, 'You are a very interesting woman.'"

"You are a v-very interesting w-woman." He might have been reading an eye chart, but he did recall what he was supposed to do next. "Is there anyone else here?"

"No. I thought we'd get to know each other before we discussed the job I have in mind for you."

Barrier Number One down. Tell her you—" Catching herself, Robin rephrased. "Say, 'I'm glad we can talk, just the two of us.'"

When he repeated the words Comdon said, "Me too, Dear Boy."

Robin heard the door close and hoped Cam had been able to stick the lump of putty she'd given him into the lock. That was Barrier Two, but she wouldn't know if he'd managed it until she tried to enter. If he'd failed and the door was latched, Robin would have to show her face to gain entry. She had a story prepared, but it would be better if she could slip in unannounced.

"Say, 'I've admired you for a long time, Judge Comdon.'"

Obediently Cam repeated the sentence, and Comdon said, "Please, call me Bev."

Cameron's pause was longer than usual. "Okay, B-B-Bev."

The stutter told Robin she had to hurry, but she was almost as nervous as Cam. This KNP was different than before, and things could happen they hadn't foreseen. Someone from Comdon's staff might knock on the door. Comdon might scream for help. Cam might freeze.

Heck, I *might freeze! And the list goes on.*

To calm herself, Robin went over the steps they'd already completed. Having determined the old hotel didn't have cameras in the stairwells, they'd avoided surveillance by reaching the tenth floor the old-fashioned way. As soon as they learned Comdon's room number, Robin had rented a single room a few doors down from Bev's where they could change clothes. They were as prepared as they could be, and Cam had done his part. It was time for her to do hers.

She took a last look in the mirror. Baggy jeans and a loose sweatshirt blurred her frame, and she'd flattened her chest with elastic bandage. A ski mask in her pocket would go over her face just before she entered Comdon's room. She'd covered every bit of skin and placed the voice-changing device under the scarf at her neck. Now she had to traverse the distance between the rooms, put on the mask, and hope Cam had managed to disable the latch. Holding her breath, she checked to make sure the hallway was empty. Then she left the room, holding the door so it made only a soft click as the latch engaged.

To Robin's great relief, the door to Room 1076 opened easily and silently. Cam, wearing an expression of complete horror, was literally backed against a wall. His hands were raised to his shoulders, as if in surrender. Bev Comdon was touching his chest and crooning something about big muscles. Robin closed the door firmly and snapped the dead bolt into place.

Comdon turned, and her eyes widened. "What is this?"

"Bozo," Robin said encouragingly. The reminder of their mission snapped Cam into action, and he pulled the desk chair out and set it close to the judge. "Sit."

Comdon's eyes narrowed as realization set it. "You're going to be sorry—" she began, but Robin interrupted.

"Sit down and shut up."

With a glance at Cam, she obeyed. "Who are you?"

"We're members of a group that helps people like you correct their mistakes."

"I don't know what you're talking about."

"Then we'll begin by listing your recent sex partners." Taking out her phone, Robin began reading the names of Bev's many young men, paired with the crimes they'd been convicted of.

After a half-dozen names, Comdon interrupted. "Those men were part of a rehab program. I did nothing improper."

"All your participants seem to be of a certain type. If their photographs were made public, you'd have questions to answer."

Tapping the chair arm with a bright red fingernail, Comdon glared at Robin. "And I'd answer them. In the end you'd look like what you are: a bunch of amateur blackmailers."

"You take advantage of men who come into your court."

"Prove it."

"Your Rehabilitate Louisiana program—"

"—gives young men a chance to stay out of prison," Bev interrupted. "I doubt one of them will go on record against me and take the chance his case will be re-examined."

Her smug expression brought Em's warning to mind: "This old gal's been operating this way for decades. You're going to have to hit her hard to soften her up."

The tape of Bev's Boys laughing about their time with her—laughing at her.

Robin had played Ricky's recording once, shuddering at the casual unkindness with which the men compared notes on their time with Judge Bev. Making her listen to what they'd said about her would be cruel, perhaps worse than making Barney Abrams think he'd been cut with a knife. Half-drunk, Bev's former lovers had been merciless in their recollections.

Cam looked nervously at his watch. They didn't have all night. Navigating to the file, she hit *PLAY*.

There was the sound of laughter, and then Vic Unser's voice came. "She liked to, um, get together in the pool, you know? She'd turn off all the lights, and then I had to find her in the dark."

Comdon's face paled.

Ricky spoke next. "Yeah, we played that game too. She always had champagne for after, and she wanted me to drink it out of her navel. It was kinda gross, you know, because she's all wrinkly and stuff."

Elmer's deep laugh came through the tiny speaker. "There was this one time when I just wasn't in the mood, you know? She had some Viagra, and we both took some. It was—"

"Turn it off."

Robin obeyed. "What did you expect? Do you think men want to hang out with a woman old enough to be their grandmother?" She leaned toward the woman. "You *are* a grandmother. What would your family think if this became public?"

Comdon licked her lips. It took two tries before her voice worked. "What will it take to keep that quiet?"

"You have to admit what Rehabilitate Louisiana really is, and we're going to record what you say."

"And what happens to this recording?"

"Two possibilities. We could release it to the media. The media would love the Bev's Boys thing."

Anger flared again in Comdon's eyes. "You'd ruin a distinguished judge's career for spite?"

Robin snorted disdainfully. "You call what you've done distinguished?" Comdon turned her gaze away, and after a moment, Robin went on. "Second possibility. We keep your secret, if you agree to our terms."

"What terms?"

"First, there's a fee."

The hard look returned to Comdon's eyes. "It always comes down to money. What does your silence cost?"

"Five hundred thousand dollars."

"Ridiculous!" Comdon's manner became that of a practiced negotiator. "Too much. I'll fight your lies in the press. I might suffer embarrassment, but you'll end up in prison."

"We'll take our chances. As you said, it's your career."

"Which is nearly over." Bev ran a hand through her over-bleached hair. "It isn't worth half a million for me to keep going."

It was exactly what Robin hoped she'd say. "We'll take a hundred thousand if you promise to retire."

Comdon saw immediately that she'd been had. Her jaw jutted angrily for a few seconds, but in the end she nodded. "All right. I'll get the money together tomorrow—"

"You can transfer the funds to this account right now." Taking a tablet computer from the waistband of her jeans, Robin navigated to a site Hua had set up.

"I don't know how—"

"Don't lie, Judge. In your speech today you bragged about how you like to keep up with technology."

With a sigh of irritation, Bev took the tablet from Robin. Minutes later it was done. Robin scanned the room, looking for signs they'd been there, but found none. "Go, Bozo." Cam obeyed, clicking the deadbolt off and disappearing into the hallway.

Pausing at the door, Robin reminded Comdon, "This evidence will remain ready for distribution, and we'll be watching you. Once you retire, don't dip so much as a toe into public life again. Don't support political candidates. Don't consult for law firms or become a lobbyist. Don't advise other jurists or write articles for law journals. Retire to your home in Baton Rouge and grow flowers or something."

Comdon didn't answer, but anger shone in her eyes.

Removing the putty from the latch, Robin wiped the door handle down with her gloved hand. "Stay where you are for ten minutes." Then she closed the door firmly behind her.

Back in their room, Robin took off the disguise and stuffed it into the small suitcase she'd brought along. Cameron changed into a business suit, folding his jeans and polo shirt into the briefcase that completed his appearance as a traveling executive.

Robin changed too, after texting Hua a single word: DONE. Before she put the phone down, the message signal dinged, and words appeared: YOU SHOULD GET OUT NOW.

Fear shot through her, but she tried to not show it. “Cam, we’ve got to go.”

He looked up, his expression concerned. “What happened?”

“I don’t know, but Hua says to leave.”

They’d planned to stay in the room until Comdon and her staff checked out in the morning. Now Plan B kicked in. If the rooms were searched, Robin needed to be in hers, without the tall, dark-haired man Comdon would describe as her attacker.

“Cam, take the stairs down, leave by the side door, and wait in the car. Get in the back seat and lie on the floor. If I’m not there in an hour, call Hua. You and he will have to decide what to do.” As she spoke, Robin added the smaller bits of her disguise to the contents of Cam’s briefcase: the mask, the voice changer, and the gloves. The shoes and black sweat suit she’d worn wouldn’t fit, so she rolled them into a ball and stuffed it into a plastic laundry bag. “Toss this into the first trash can you find.”

Cam seemed torn, but in the end he did as she said, checking the hall before he slid out the door and closed it quietly behind him. When he was gone, Robin went to her suitcase and removed a bra, a shirt, and some toiletry items. She strewed them around the room to suggest a guest who expected to be alone and undisturbed. Five minutes later, when a knock sounded on the door, she was dressed in a full-length flannel nightgown.

“Who is it?”

“Hotel security, ma’am. We had a report of intruders and we’re checking to see everyone’s okay.”

She looked through the peephole, where a skinny young man

stood holding his identification badge up so she could see it. Robin opened the door a few inches and peered around it. “Did you say there are intruders?”

“We’re not sure, ma’am. A guest on this floor called in a report of someone trying to get into her room.” He peered over her shoulder. “Do you mind if I look around?”

“Why?”

“It’s for your protection, ma’am.” His tone was patient but there was a hint of irritation. “If you let us in, then we know there’s not some guy in there holding you hostage.”

She pretended to think about it. “I guess it’s all right.” Backing away, she allowed the man, whose badge said GERALD, to enter. As she did, she heard another man speaking to a guest somewhere down the hall, making the same reassurances and asking that he be allowed to check the room.

Gerald walked through, sticking his head into the bathroom and the closet with cautious determination. “Seems like everything’s okay,” he announced.

“Okay?” Robin exclaimed. “You’ve got criminals threatening people in your hotel and it’s okay?”

“Well, no. I just meant there’s no one here bothering you.” He chewed on his lip. “Actually there’s probably nobody bothering anybody, but when a guest says there’s a problem, we have to check it out.”

“I might head to the airport early,” she said. “My flight’s at five, and I’d just as soon leave if there are rapists in the building.”

“Ma’am, no one said anything about—” Noting Robin’s determined expression, Gerald abandoned his argument. “If that’s what you feel comfortable with, I’ll be glad to call you a cab.”

"I have the number in my phone. I'll just ask them to come now instead of later."

When Gerald was gone, Robin leaned against the door, trying to quell her rising panic. *You can't faint right now. You have to find Cam and let him know you're okay.*

Ten minutes later, she took the elevator to the lobby, suitcase in hand. The desk was unmanned, but she set her room key near the computer and turned to go. As she neared the door, a man rose from a chair along the wall and came toward her.

Thomas Wyman.

She read all sorts of things in his eyes. Recognition. Anticipation. Pleasure. "Ro—" He scanned the area and started again. "Miss—"

"I'm sorry. I don't speak to strange men in hotel lobbies."

Wyman grasped her arm with his left hand. "Do you know how many laws you've broken tonight?"

Just then Gerald stepped out of the elevator with a second hotel employee. Turning to him Robin said, "Do you people allow women to be terrorized in their rooms *and* harassed in the lobby?"

He hurried over. "Sir, the lady is a guest of this hotel."

"Not anymore," she said hotly. "I'm never coming back here again. First I'm woken from a sound sleep and told I'm in danger of being raped, and now I have to fight off this creep." She added as if it had just occurred to her, "Could he be one of the intruders you're looking for?"

Wyman's expression revealed discomfort. "I didn't—"

Gerald put a hand on Wyman's arm, and the other man stepped between him and the door. "Sir, if we could see some identification, this can all be cleared up quickly."

Wyman looked at Robin with an expression she couldn't read—frustration? "I wasn't bothering her."

Ignoring him, Robin spoke to her rescuer. "I'd appreciate it if you keep this man here until I'm gone."

"Of course." Gerald said. The second guy moved aside to let her pass, watching Wyman as if he might try to tackle her. "Would you like to stay inside until your cab arrives?"

"I told the driver I'd wait at the corner," Robin replied. Leaving Wyman squirming under the glare of the two employees, she left the hotel. As soon as she was away from the doors, she turned left and hurried to the parking garage. Minutes later, she and Cam had left Monroe behind. As Cam drove, Robin kept turning to see if a black Mustang had come up behind them. What if Wyman showed the hotel people his P.I. license and convinced them to call the police?

Don't think about that right now. Think about marshmallows and playful otters.

Hua was already seated at a booth when they entered a diner ten miles north of the city. He'd ordered a full meal, and Robin wondered if he'd be able to sleep with his stomach stuffed with spaghetti, garlic bread, and Mountain Dew. "Everything went well, yes?" he asked as they sat down.

"It was good that you sent the warning. Once we got it, we managed pretty well."

Hua's smooth brow wrinkled in consternation. "If you received a warning, it was not from me."

Digging out her phone, Robin retrieved the message and read it more carefully. "The sender's unknown."

Always an optimist, Hua said, "We have a friend, then. This is good, yes?"

Robin stared at the message. "Honestly, Hua, I have no idea."

***

"We didn't find anyone, ma'am," the night manager reported. "More times than I can count, we've had inebriated guests try to enter the wrong room." He gave a little laugh, but his expression revealed hope his distinguished guest wouldn't blame the hotel for whatever intrusion she thought she'd experienced.

"I'm sure you're right," Judge Comdon replied. "It just frightened me, that's all."

She had called security not in fear, but in a fit of pique, angry that she'd been duped, robbed, and humiliated. At least she'd been smart enough to report an attempted break-in and not tell what had actually happened. Why had she done it? She'd been desperate to get those recordings, both of them, and silence her supposed admirer and his able assistant with threats of prosecution. That had been stupid, and now she was glad it hadn't come to anything.

Once the humiliation abated a little, Bev looked at things more clearly. The money meant little; she'd always had plenty of that. Retiring from the bench was something she'd considered for some time. It was a monotonous, thankless job, and more and more often these days she wanted to scream obscenities at everyone in the courtroom, from the friendly, bear-like bailiff to the pompous young lawyers to the criminals dumb enough to get caught.

If the two strangers kept their promise, she could retire with no blots on her reputation. The only thing she'd really miss was the chance of having a dark-haired hunk appear before her, a chance to toy with him for a few months and move on to the next. Bev sat on the edge of the bed, stroking the silky coverlet absently. What made her angriest about the intruders was the destruction of her fragile fantasies. The memories of blissful times with her boys were ruined. She was an old fool, willing to let—no, require—young men to pretend they were infatuated with her. The truth was disgusting—pitiful: Her “boys” chose her only as an alternative to prison and a felony record. Behind her back, they’d compared notes, mocking her for their own amusement.

“Not all of them.” She said it aloud as a memory arose. One young convict had been sad to leave, even hurt by her eagerness to move on to the next candidate. What was his name? Robert? No. Rafe? Rafael. He’d been so admiring, so convinced that she was strong and admirable. Rising, Bev went to the mirror and touched the face of the haggard woman who peered back at her. Rafael might enjoy a reunion, maybe a trip to Cabo, even without a prison sentence as the alternative.

Chapter Sixteen

"I can't imagine how Wyman found us," Robin said when she called to tell Em what had happened in Montrose. "And who sent the warning?"

Em thought about it. "Who has your phone number?"

"That's exactly what I asked Hua. He doesn't know."

"If the message helped, then whoever sent it isn't your enemy. Could it have been Wyman?"

"No way! That creep can't wait to lock Cam and me up."

"Well, someone's on your side. If Cam had been in that hotel room, and if they'd found your disguises when they searched, you'd both have been arrested in two shakes of a lamb's tail."

That didn't make Robin feel better. It seemed every day or so the circle of people who knew about their crimes became wider. Though she trusted Em, Hua, and Mink, she believed the old saying, "Two can keep a secret if one of them is dead." In addition to those who knew exactly what she was up to, there was Shelly, who knew Robin wasn't where she claimed to be, and Chris, who knew she was doing things he wasn't supposed to ask about. She had no idea how much Wyman had reported to Abrams.

If we had a brain among us, we'd forget KNPs, start new lives, and hope no one connects us to Abrams, Buckram, or Comdon.

But Chris had already mentioned a possibility for their next target, and what he'd said piqued her interest.

As Mark used to say, *In for a penny, in for a pound.*

They got a motel room fifty miles north. The draining away of adrenalin left Cam and Robin in need of rest, and Hua wanted to assure that no statewide alarm had been raised before they crossed the state line. When they reached their room, Cam fell across the innermost bed and almost immediately went to sleep. Hua spent a few minutes on the computer, reported no alerts for them, and then curled up in a chair and slept, leaving the second bed for her.

It took Robin longer to settle down. She'd managed to hide it, but her post-KNP wooziness had kicked in on the way north. Though it was less severe than before, she'd been careful as they entered the motel, stepping cautiously and using handholds to keep herself steady. Lying on the overly-soft bed, she imagined some CSI tech finding a single hair or a partial fingerprint in Comdon's room that would identify Cam and set the FBI on their trail. Listening to the even breathing of the other two, she wondered how they managed peaceful slumber. Em contended the rest of them didn't have to worry about anything: Robin did enough of it for all of them.

Fear of the future was part of her nature, and though Em scoffed, Robin thought it wasn't such a bad thing. Unsuccessful criminals are the ones who can't imagine what might go wrong, Mink had warned.

It's true I'm a worrier, but that's a positive thing. I'm really good at dreaming up worst-possible-case scenarios so we can be ready for them.

***

The charity for their third donation was a drive to build a no-kill animal shelter, which pleased Robin's animal-loving heart. Hua made an anonymous bundle of cash and wrapped it for delivery, including a note that said an elderly resident of the parish wanted to save "kitties" and "doggies" in the area. Depositing the box at a

FedEx drop-off, Robin imagined with satisfaction how far fifty thousand dollars would take the shelter toward its goal.

The same day, Beverly Comdon announced she would retire at the end of her term. *Happy pets and better justice for the people.* It was the result Robin had imagined when she started this craziness.

Their half of the money wouldn't last long with a house that needed major work and four people who needed to eat regularly. Once they got home, Robin went to work on a budget, using pencil and paper. Having seen Hua operate, she would never again believe in private computer files.

Their costs thus far were high, but most of their spending had resulted in tangible property. The house had been a steal at $92,500, but making it livable was proving as expensive as she'd feared. Doing much of the work themselves was a savings, but they'd paid for experts when necessary, including a contractor to install the furnace she dreamed of on cold mornings. The dining and living rooms were completely empty. Robin worried sometimes about what the workmen who came and went told others about the new residents on Bobby Road, who had very little furniture and not much in the way of personal possessions.

Most evenings they met in Em's sitting room. Furnishing it had been Robin's job, since Em refused to shop. "Just get me things that are useful," she ordered. "Too many people these days spend money they haven't got to buy things they don't want to impress people they don't like." Robin had found a futon, a recliner, a rocking chair, and two end tables that made Em's main room cozy and inviting for an hour's chat before bedtime.

To hide a bowling-ball-sized hole in her wall, Em crocheted an afghan in red and pink blocks and set it into a vintage picture frame. Once she had her new furniture Em delighted in playing hostess, offering aromatic coffees from the Keurig she'd brought with her from Georgia. Hua was the only one interested, but the two of them took an inordinate amount of time choosing their flavor of the evening.

Em had also brought a selection of old board games with her, and they often played cards, Rack-O, and Aggravation, cheering or groaning as they won or lost ground. As the fire crackled, banishing the evening chill, they learned each other's ways and came to enjoy each other's company. Even the shadow of her father's abuse faded as Robin laughed and joked with the others. It was what growing up should have been like for all of them.

Once he'd obtained the necessary paper and printing equipment, Hua proudly showed them the identities he had created for himself. The documents looked authentic to Robin's untrained eye, and he assured them most computer searches would affirm that they were. One set listed his real name and country of origin—the only false claim being he'd become a United States citizen at eighteen. The other identity presented Hua as Ci Vu, the descendant of Hmong parents from Manitowoc, Wisconsin. "I hope no one expects me to speak Hmong," he said cheerfully. "I could perhaps manage, 'Yes,' 'No,' and 'Where is the train station?' but nothing more."

Hua also made them a website. Though Robin thought it was dangerous to identify themselves online, he insisted it would be useful if they became separated and had to communicate using an unprotected server. KNP.org appeared to be a site for a children's charity that hadn't yet received 501(c)(3) status. The splash page promised further information in the future, but visitors found little else of interest. Hua explained that the pages of a website under construction could be accessed only by administrators, so they could communicate in private.

Often when they met in Hua's wing, Robin listed in her head the cost of each printer, scanner, modem, and disk drive. When the cost of the supplies the machines required was added, it was scary. Monthly bills concerned her too. “This place consumes electricity like a couch potato eats chips,” Em had once commented as she watched the meter tick steadily upward. Internet access was expensive, as were groceries. Cam had an appetite to match his size, and Hua rivaled him in eating, despite being half his weight.

And then there were Em’s liquor bills.

“I feel bad for people who don’t drink,” she commented one evening as she splashed some Dewar’s into a glass. “When they wake up in the morning, that’s as good as they’re going to feel all day.” Behind the old Sinatra quote was an admission of Em’s constant pain and the knowledge that prescription painkillers did little to ease it.

But Medicare doesn’t pay for Scotch.

Travel was expensive too. So far they’d driven to their KNP’s, which was cheap and fairly anonymous, but the target Chris offered next was in California. Robin shuddered at the thought of listening to Cam and Hua discuss *A-Team* reruns for the hours that trip would entail. Flying would be fast and less nerve-wracking, but there was the money worry again.

Before leaving Cedar, Robin had closed her bank account and used the $730 in it to clear her bills. They’d drained Cam’s savings by visiting several ATMs in the dead of night, gleaning $6,000, which included what was left of the money Abrams’ crooked cousin had paid Mrs. Halkias for her property. They’d taken $50,000 from Abrams and kept $25,000, almost all of which had been spent on false identities and their second KNP. From Buckram they’d gotten $75,000. Their $37,500 portion had provided the down payment on the house. The $100,000 from Bev Comdon, split with the animal shelter, left them $50,000 to use on repairs and house payments. She figured and re-figured, stretching what they had, but they’d need another cash infusion soon. Whatever Chris had found in California had better be good.

One night after the game boards had been put away and the men had gone, Em broached the subject of money. "I haven't wanted to be nosy," she said. Robin had to hide a smile, since Em generally asked anybody anything. "How are we set financially?"

She shrugged. "We're managing. I've set up a schedule for repairs and renovations on the house, so it will take a while to get a downstairs bathroom big enough for a tub. I know it would help your hip, but—"

She waved the apology away. "It'll come when it comes. Money's tight, isn't it?"

"A little," she admitted. "Those boys of ours can eat."

Em shifted in her chair. "I told Hua to funnel my retirement payments to your bank account. He'll work his magic so it's hard to trace the connections."

"Em, you shouldn't—"

A raised palm stopped her. "I'm having more fun with you three than I've had since I left the Bureau. I don't mind tossing into the communal kitty."

"Well, I appreciate—"

Em's second interruption was even gruffer. "Don't thank me. Money's like butter, no good unless it's spread around." Jutting her chin she added, "I mean to have my say in exchange for my contribution though."

Robin swallowed. "Okay."

A crooked finger jabbed in her direction. "You're a young woman. You should be having lunch with that girlfriend of yours in Green Bay, sipping alcoholic drinks that taste like soda pop, and shopping for crazy-expensive purses. You gave all that up to hang around with an old woman, an escaped alien, and a mental defective. I want you to promise that anytime you feel the need, you'll walk away, whether it's for a day, a week, or a month. Go have some fun." She folded her arms. "Don't ever think we can't manage by ourselves for a while."

Neither Cam nor Hua ever questioned that Robin would make decisions for the group indefinitely. Em understood that Robin's normal life had been swept away by a single event, and she still hadn't found her footing.

It wasn't that she blamed Cam. What they were doing felt right. But she did sometimes miss the days when she could go to a movie on a whim or take a drive without watching to see who might be following. There were moments when she thought longingly of heading to the nearest Steak 'n Shake to get a sundae without telling a soul where she was going or why.

Overwhelmed with gratitude, Robin stepped toward Em with her arms outstretched. The glare she got stopped her cold, and she dropped her arms. "Someday I might do that."

"And spend a little money on yourself," Em finished. "Those Salvation Army sweat pants you wear every single day are starting to get on my nerves."

***

"This one could be a double," Chris said to introduce the target for their next KNP. Robin had placed their orders at the counter of a gourmet sandwich shop while he chose a table where his wheelchair was out of the traffic pattern. "You can decide if you want to approach one guy, the other guy, or both of them."

Robin had fetched drinks—a Coke for him and a mix of tea and lemonade for her—and she sipped as she nodded her understanding. He was getting used to the idea of KNPs, though he still wasn't sure what they involved. At first he'd claimed what they were doing was dangerous and refused to give her information. "That's too bad," she'd told him, "but we have someone who's very good with technology. He doesn't have your experience, but at least *he's* willing to help."

"Rob, I spent three years developing sources that ensure my privacy. Someone who's just starting out could get you into trouble poking around."

"Then point us in a direction," she argued. "We'll use what you tell us to make things better." In the end he'd agreed. Today's lunch was the launch of a new KNP target.

It was easy to see that the idea of taking overt action appealed to Chris, though he still worried for Robin's safety. Mink had voiced some of the same concerns when she'd called to report successful completion of the latest chapter of her "book." When speaking with either of them, Robin was careful to minimize any possible dangers and stress the good they were accomplishing. In fact, Robin's references to her "team" made them sound more like Delta Force than the haphazard amateurs they actually were.

Once Chris accepted their mission, Robin sensed he buried his dread under something more positive, anticipation. Chris's desire to stop the bad guys was every bit as strong as hers. *Our way of making up for Mark's dirty tricks.*

The guy behind the counter called out, "Robin!" and she went to pick up sandwiches served on tin plates and accompanied by deliciously dill-y pickles. As they ate, Chris handed over what looked like a photo album. Robin scooted close to make it appear they were looking at family photos.

"Do you remember Mark's charity bit?" Chris asked, his hand tapping the album cover.

"No. What was it?"

"He used to go to churches, small ones where the pastor

wasn't likely to be tuned in to the outside world, and tell them he was heading to Africa on a mission. He'd say he had all the money he needed except for a few hundred dollars, and he just couldn't stand to cancel the trip for such a small amount." Chris rubbed his forehead. "I got to take up the collection in my ball cap. He made me smile and thank everyone who donated."

"I missed out on that one."

"I think the word got around and he had to stop." Opening the photo album, Chris pointed to a picture of a handsome man in a sharp suit. "This is Yardley Niven, pastor of the Deep and Wide World Church of Our Triumphant God."

Robin dipped her veggie wrap in the spicy sauce, took a bite, and swallowed. "I always wonder why that last part gets tacked on. Isn't it a given that churches are about God?"

Chris grimaced. "That point is debatable with Pastor Niven. This church is all about him."

Pointing to the man next to Niven she asked, "Isn't that Uncle Bill, from the old sitcom?"

"His name is Dennis Parks, but he's so well known as Uncle Bill that he pretty much goes by that now."

"He's still acting?"

Chris grimaced. "Depends on what you call acting. He travels with the pastor and supports the Deep and Wide Church. Uncle Bill has that folksy, down-home air about him, and when he tells how Pastor Niven is changing the lives of people around the world, believers can't wait to drop money into the collection plates or mail a check to headquarters."

Frowning at the pastor's expensive haircut and massive diamond pinky ring she asked, "This guy does good works?"

"That's his story." Chris leaned back in his wheelchair. "Turn the page and take a look at Niven's home."

It was an aerial shot of a house that covered the space of a football field. There were swimming pools at either end, a terraced garden, and stables with a fenced paddock out back. "Wow."

"The pastor also has a private jet, a fleet of very nice cars, and a second home in Spain."

Robin turned to the next page, where another aerial picture showed a run-down building set in a packed-dirt yard. "That's the orphanage Niven operates in Haiti."

"That's an orphanage?" Anger rose in her chest, but Em's voice sounded in her mind: *Stay cool.* She needed to learn the facts, consider them dispassionately, and then act with courage.

"How many people actually research the places they give money to?" Chris said. "All Niven needs is a registered address in Haiti." He jabbed an accusing finger at the photo. "That's it."

The long, low building looked more like a shed than a benevolent institution. "How many kids live there?"

"Fifty, though it doesn't look like there's room for twenty. A journalist friend of mine stumbled across this place when she went down there to report on a hurricane. It wasn't the story she was sent to get, but it made her furious. She pitched it to her editor but something else came along and he decided to move on."

"Sad." Examining the ramshackle building closely, Robin saw nothing to indicate any intent to improve the place. "How does he get away with calling that a benefit for orphans?"

Chris shrugged. "They're not starving on the streets of Port au Prince. I guess that's something."

"But if I donate money, that isn't what I picture contributing to." She turned back to the first picture. "How does this so-called pastor live in a house like this and let fifty children live like that?"

"A combination of charm, brass *cajones*, and sleight of hand," Chris replied. "If you signed up to support Niven's Haiti Crusade, you'd get something like this." He paged through until he found a flyer showing a much nicer building with a highly polished door. Smiling workers stood on the steps, surrounded by well-dressed, apparently happy children. "You have to read the fine print to learn that the Deep and Wide Church supports orphanages *like* this one." He underscored the word with his finger. "The website has lots of that kind of wording. Niven doesn't lie outright. He just lets people believe he does great things with their money." Chris gestured at the photo of the elaborate house. "As you see, he spends most of it on himself."

Holding her wrap to one side to avoid dripping juice on it, Robin examined the picture of the men. "Uncle Bill goes along?"

"I'm not sure how much he knows. Bill does his part onstage, but I don't see any indication he has an active role in the running of the organization."

She had no patience for that argument. "Before he agreed to represent the church, he should have looked into its work."

"Come on, Sis. Do you think all those aging actors who push investment opportunities, reverse mortgages, and guaranteed life insurance bother to research the products they're selling?" Chris dragged a French fry through some ketchup. "The money's good, and they get to step back into the spotlight for a while."

Robin thought of retired baseball players who'd lost her respect by doing crappy reality shows or hawking questionable products and ventures. "It's all about attention."

"Yup." Chris closed the album.

"What kind of guy must Pastor Niven be?"

His mouth turned down at the corners. “Yardley Niven is the type real pastors wish would disappear in a puff of smoke.”

***

“We’re doing two KNPs at once?” Em seemed surprised but not averse to the idea.

Hua projected Chris’ pictures and documents on a large screen as Robin explained how Niven and Uncle Bill operated together to bring in millions for the Deep and Wide Church.

“They’ll require different approaches. It’s possible Bill doesn’t know the church fails to do what it claims.”

Hua gestured at the photograph of Niven’s estate. “Nobody could live like that without knowing it costs a great deal of money.” He zoomed in. “Mr. Uncle Bill has a cottage on the property—there.”

“Some cottage!” Em muttered.

Hua advanced the slideshow, projecting a picture of the two men shaking hands.

“Bill’s a figurehead, maybe *shill* is a better term,” Robin said.

“Then why mess with him?” Em asked. “Get the fake preacher.”

Robin sighed. “If we open Bill’s eyes to what’s really going on, we might be able to use him to get to Niven, who seldom goes anywhere without security.”

“What do you have in mind?”

Robin grinned. “To start with, we need a clueless little old lady. Can you think of a candidate?”

“I’ve got the little old lady thing down,” Em replied. “All I have to work on is the clueless part.”

Chapter Seventeen

Uncle Bill watched idly as the crew tore down the set for the taping just completed. They'd held a week of outdoor revivals under a huge white tent in Columbia, South Carolina, the last stop on their spring tour. The spot was beautiful, with flowers, shrubs, and trees blooming as far as he could see, creating color for the eye and soft scents for the nose. People worked busily around him, ignoring his presence, but he was used to that. Bill floated on the outskirts of the Deep and Wide Church, not a preacher, a singer, a tech or even a roadie.

Bill's job was making the largely over-sixty crowd feel nostalgic. When they heard his highly sanitized stories about his old TV show, they imagined there was a point in the past when everything in America was wholesome and good. "Back then," people were polite. Dialogue was clean. Kids were well-behaved. Folks cared about their fellow men. God was the center of all. Bill often reminded the audience of the final moments of each episode of his sitcom, when the family gathered, ate a meal together, talked casually and respectfully to each other, and prayed. No matter what had gone wrong in their lives in that week's story, those last few seconds made everything right again.

He never acknowledged that those scenes of peace and joy were all script and no reality. The audience didn't want to know that sweet Amelia was actually a ten-year-old she-devil, or that Momma Kate had to be watched so she didn't fill her water glass with Beefeater Gin before taping began. His audience didn't want their fantasies corrupted with anything like truth.

Once Bill had taken the folks on his redacted stroll down Memory Lane, Yardley would step into the limelight. Waving his Bible and waxing poetic, he'd compare those "good times" to the terrible state of today's world, so scary, so different. When he had them feeling just right, Pastor Niven told the folks how they could make things better "for God's children." Wallets slid from pockets and purses clicked open as people bought into the dream of making one small, dark corner of the world a better place.

There were moments when Bill was bothered by what he'd become, because he knew the donated money was spent on luxurious living for Yardley, his family, his staff, and for Bill himself. He'd heard the joking comments about Yardley owning nothing; the church bought every stitch of his very expensive clothing, every vehicle in his garages, every bottle of fine wine, and every meal. Bill shared in all of it, because Yardley, as he often said with a chuckle, was generous with other people's money. The casual assumption they were entitled to the lion's share of "God's seed money" didn't sit well with Bill. Still, he was pleased to be part of something so big, so noteworthy.

When the sitcom died in the late nineties, he'd spent a decade trying to duplicate the biggest success of his career. His beloved character had been like a member of the family, people said. Uncle Bill could be wise, he could be irritating, but he'd always been loving, like a real uncle. But Bill had been the victim of his own success. Casting directors said it was difficult to break the actor Dennis Parks out of the Uncle Bill shell he'd created. Though some character actors successfully transitioned to new roles, his character was too memorable, too lovable. Aside from a few jobs where he simply recreated the same persona, Parks had been finished in Hollywood before the millennium changed.

Then something wonderful happened. Bill met Yardley Niven at a basketball game, and they'd started talking. Niven was on the way up, having recently snagged a spot on one of the all-religious cable channels. He was putting together a team to entertain and edify believers, and he understood the show-business aspects of religion for the masses. He'd already signed a couple of successful gospel singers and located an open-air venue in California that looked great on television. He'd been looking for a face familiar to older audiences, a trusted sidekick to provide authenticity for a charismatic but unknown preacher.

Suddenly Uncle Bill was back. By some oversight, his studio contract hadn't excluded him from using the name for his own devices, so Dennis Parks disappeared completely into the character he'd played for years, a little older, a little wiser, and eager to do good in the world. If Uncle Bill was in favor of Niven's overseas missions, many who'd seen his face every week for twelve years felt it must be all right—no, better than all right. It was something they wanted to support.

"Excuse me."

He turned to find an elderly woman at his elbow, leaning heavily on a three-footed cane. She wore a shapeless dress, support stockings with black lace-up shoes, and an enormous straw hat that hid her face until she looked directly up at him. Despite the shade the hat provided, she wore the kind of wrap-around sunglasses that fit over regular eyeglasses. Her closeness brought an odor that reminded him of long-ago locker rooms and strained tendons—Cream-something.

Putting on his automatic smile Bill said, "Yes?"

"I wanted to let you know you're the best part of the Deep and Wide Worship Hour."

"Well, thank you, but Pastor Niven does the real work."

"But you're his strong right arm, like he said." She cleared her throat. "Would you sign my bulletin?"

Bill never tired of being asked for autographs. "Of course."

The old woman leaned an elbow on the cane and began rummaging in her purse. "It's right here." A few seconds later she said, "I know I put it–I wanted to ask you but I was afraid. Then I said to myself, 'Bernice, you might never get another chance.'" As she spoke, she continued to dig through the bag. The image of a gerbil hunting through wood shavings came to Bill's mind.

"I can get you another one."

She looked near to tears. "But I wrote down what you said about the children in Haiti and how they have toys now and can go to school." Giving up on her purse, she glanced around. "Maybe it's on my chair." Her face cleared. "I'll bet I laid it down to find my sunglasses and forgot to pick it up." She put a hand on his arm. "Will you come with me? I know exactly where I was sitting, back there in the corner."

Bill walked with her, matching his pace to her slow gait. She leaned heavily on his arm, keeping up a running patter on the way about how she'd driven up from a town to the south to hear Pastor Niven speak. "You're the main attraction as far as I'm concerned," she said coquettishly. "I always thought Uncle Bill was *so* handsome on TV, but you're better looking in person. And you haven't aged a bit."

In the far corner of the tent, she stopped. "It isn't here. I know I left it–" She pointed outside the tent, where a sheet of folded paper lay on the ground next to an equipment van with its sliding door yawning open. "Oh no! It's blowing away."

"I'll get it," he offered.

The woman smiled up at him. "You're so sweet!"

Bill walked toward the van. When he bent to pick up the paper, something stung his neck. It was the last time things made sense for quite a while.

***

As Em pulled herself into the passenger seat of the rented van with a grunt of effort, Robin looked at the limp figure Cam had dragged into the cargo area. "Are you sure he'll be all right?"

"He'll be fine." Em settled her cane between her seat and the door. "The dose is pre-loaded and the syringe dispenses automatically. I told you a million times, any amateur can do it."

"Further proof the world really is a scary place." Robin concentrated on breathing normally. *No emotion. Just do the job you came to do.* Turning onto the street and entering traffic, she followed the GPS commands, doing her best to ignore the fact that she'd taken another step in a direction she didn't want to go. Even Mark hadn't stooped to drugging his victims. She had now surpassed her father's iniquity.

When Em proposed drugging Uncle Bill, Robin had argued against it, citing the possibility of allergic reaction or a heart attack. Em insisted they—and Robin didn't want to know who "they" were—had come a long way with such things. "He'll have a slight headache when he wakes up. Otherwise it'll be like a pleasant nap." In the end, Robin had given in. For their plan to work, Bill had to be unconscious for several hours.

Robin soon wished it were she who'd been rendered unconscious. She was a nervous wreck from the moment Bill fell into Cam's arms until she delivered him to what she hoped would be an eye-opening experience. First they drove to a small airport where Hua had arranged for a pilot to fly them to their destination in secret. She had invented an elaborate story about taking her sick father, a former missionary, back to the place where he could die among the people he'd served. The pilot didn't believe it for a minute, but he didn't care, either. Accepting half the money he'd been promised (Hua would provide the other half when they returned safely), he ushered them to a small plane that was literally held together with baling wire in places.

They waited until deep night before taking off. Though Robin understood why, it made the whole thing scarier. Did the pilot have adequate guidance equipment? Would the landing site be well-lit? Observing his nonchalance as he started the engine and went through his preflight checklist, she knew better than to voice her concerns. *No turning back now.*

The plane sounded like a poorly-calibrated wind-up toy, and the ride was bumpy and noisy. The pilot amused himself by singing not-so-current popular songs. As he attempted a Miley Cyrus tune, Robin hoped they wouldn't come in like—

Don't think about that. Think about puppies in a basket and angel food cake.

Though it was dark, she imagined the water below them. Was it the Atlantic or the Caribbean? If the pilot screwed up, either body of water would easily swallow them. And the landing—where would he set down in this mountainous area? Reminding herself of Em's advice, "Do your research and then trust the experts," she closed her eyes and surrendered to the hum of the motors and the pilot's occasionally correct interpretation of a lyric.

At sunrise they landed in a field that seemed dangerously short. Robin thought her teeth might shatter when the wheels touched the uneven ground, but for all his bad singing and larcenous motives, the pilot was good at his job. Leaving the engines running, he helped her get the "patient" into the wheelchair she'd brought along.

Humidity hit her like a slap with a wet towel as she stepped down the rough wooden ramp. The view around her was both breathtaking and terrifying. They were on a Haitian mountainside, green with low vegetation. No sign of civilization was visible: no houses, no people, and no vehicles.

Promising to return in four days, the man climbed into his plane, turned it around, and left Robin in a cloud of dust with her unconscious "father" slumped beside her. She had to force herself not to run after the plane, pleading to be returned to the land of bathrooms and Wendy's. Telling herself it was too late for that, she took out the DEET she'd brought along and began applying it to herself and Uncle Bill, covering all exposed areas. She'd already violated the guy's humanity; she wasn't about to expose him to the Zika virus too.

After twenty minutes of feeling more alone than she'd ever felt in her life, Robin heard a vehicle approaching. Soon an antique Land Rover bounced across the clearing as a cheerful, sunbaked driver waved a greeting. He seemed to expect Robin's still-unconscious companion. These people were part of the drug trade, Hua had admitted, low-level workers who broke the law in order to eat regularly.

The driver spoke no English. When he held out a hand, Robin gave him a second envelope Hua had provided. After a glance inside, he loaded Bill into the vehicle and put the wheelchair in the back. Bill groaned a little at the movement but didn't wake. Gesturing at the front seat, the driver indicated Robin should ride there. He turned the Land Rover around, and they bounced toward a road that seemed to go straight up. On the way, Robin got out at what passed for the local inn. Her prisoner went on, heading for the surprise of his life.

***

Uncle Bill awoke confused, and when he opened his eyes, nothing looked familiar. He lay on a pill-y, matted blanket in a room with no furniture, only rough shelving laden with woven bags and oversized tin cans. Beside him was a plate containing a slab of bread, some kind of fruit he didn't recognize, and a cup of water. Since his mouth felt like old wood, Bill drank the water all at once. When it was gone, he realized that had been unwise. He had no idea where the stuff had come from. It might be poisoned, or at the very least, unsanitary.

He tried to stand, but his head wasn't ready for that yet. The room tilted to one side, and he had to brace himself against the wall. The old woman who'd claimed she wanted his autograph had led him into a trap. Taking his wallet from his pocket, Bill saw that his money and ID were still there. This wasn't a robbery. Then he checked his pocket. His phone was missing.

Was he being held for ransom? That was frightening, since Bill couldn't think of anyone who might pay to get him back. Neither of his ex-wives for sure, nor his deadbeat son. His boss? After some consideration he decided Yardley would pay, if only for the publicity it would bring. He could almost hear a future sermon decrying those who'd kidnapped "our Uncle Bill" in order to impede the work of the Deep and Wide Church.

The place was quiet. Crawling to the door on hands and knees, Bill was relieved to find that it wasn't locked. In fact, it had no latch at all. Peering out, he saw an empty hallway. Since his head was still spinning, he went no farther. Pressing his back against the wall, he rested his head on his knees. What had happened? Why had he been brought here?

When he thought he could trust his legs Bill stood up, using the door frame for support. His head ached, and his back was stiff from the hard dirt floor. Rubbing it, he looked out into a hallway. To his right an exterior door sat crookedly in its frame. Rot at the bottom allowed dirt and probably cold night air to penetrate. Turning the opposite way, he went down the hallway. Two large rooms a few feet down faced each other, both filled with cots that were closely spaced and precisely aligned. There was only one inhabitant at present, a child whose eyes were glazed with illness. His arm drooped over the side of the cot and grazed the floor. The cots were all child-sized, and each had a thin blanket pulled over it, some arranged neatly, some less so.

Beyond the bedrooms was a dining area with a kitchen at the back. Dead insects littered the floor, and live ones scurried away at his approach. Stacks of faded plastic bowls rested on a long counter, and a dented tin bucket held what looked like an equal number of spoons. The room smelled of something old and yeasty, but he saw nothing that looked like food.

A small room off the kitchen held two adult-sized beds, an assortment of clothing hung on wooden pegs, and a battered dresser with a pitcher and basin atop it. This room had a door that locked from the inside with a metal latch. The occupants could close themselves in and keep others out.

At the end of the hallway was a second exterior door, even more deteriorated than the other. Opening the loose, rusty handle, Bill leaned out to see a bare yard where two dozen children between three and seven years of age waited in line, silent and wary. On the only tree in sight, a rope swing hung suspended from the single branch sturdy enough to support it. The others watched as the boy who occupied the swing went back and forth, his thin legs pumping. A wide-hipped woman with a turned-down mouth glared at them and at one point spoke in a tone of warning. Though he understood none of the words, Bill deduced from the pantomime she acted out that if the children displeased her, she'd cut the swing down with her knife. There was nothing else in the yard that remotely resembled playground equipment.

Removed some distance from the building was an extended shed with a door hanging crookedly against its frame. When a child hurried inside and closed himself in with a sharp bang, Bill realized it was an outhouse. In his youth he'd heard of one-holers and two-holers. If his guess was accurate, this was a four-holer.

Voices at the front of the house made him turn and retrace his steps. In the hallway he met a second woman, thinner than the other but no happier-looking. She held the door open as a second group of children came inside. These kids were older, perhaps up to age fourteen, and they'd apparently put in a hard day's work. Most stumbled along as if exhausted; all of them were sweaty and dirty. When the woman saw Bill, she spoke to the children, who trooped obediently into the dormitory rooms, boys to the right and girls to the left.

Approaching, the woman said something in a language Bill didn't understand. "Sorry," he apologized. "Do you speak English? English?" She merely glared at him.

He stepped outside, and the woman made no attempt to stop him. There was a dusty street, a couple of huts, and not much else. He had to get help, but where? Was he in Mexico? South America? Somewhere else? Wherever he was, he felt completely isolated.

Turning back to the woman he said, "Please. Get me out of here. Call my friends. They'll pay you."

One brow rose in disdain, and she rattled off several sentences, pointing sharply at the room where he'd been sleeping. He got the message. He was confined to quarters.

Sitting on the floor with his feet splayed in front of him, Bill ate the bread and fruit he'd ignored earlier. His stomach called loudly for more food, but no one came to offer anything.

With nothing to do and no one to talk to, the hours passed slowly. One child or another peeked in from time to time, some shyly, some looking mischievous. Most wore T-shirts of adult size, some so long that they looked like dresses. The older boys wore loose shorts and the girls had long skirts that were dirty and ragged around the bottom. Several times Bill tried to entice them to speak, but they glanced nervously down the hallway and disappeared.

The house again went silent, and he heard children's voices outside. Leaving his room, he looked out the window to find they were clustered in small groups, some watching passers-by, some talking in low tones, and some inventing games that required no equipment. No one approached the swing, where the wide-hipped woman stood like a centurion, forbidding its use. In the kitchen the other woman directed several of the older children with sharp commands as they prepared the evening meal. She glanced at him and then pushed one girl and slapped another in an apparent attempt to make them hurry.

Bill went back to the room. Where was he? How did he get here? Why had someone, presumably the old woman, arranged it? None of those questions had answers he could fathom.

Much later a shy girl brought his dinner, the same three items he'd had earlier. It was hardly enough to keep a man alive, but from her manner he guessed it was the best these people had. Bill thanked her, accompanying his foreign words with gestures so she'd understand. The girl bowed her head in acknowledgement and went on her way.

He heard sounds in the dining area as the children came inside and ate. As soon as they finished, they were sent to the sleeping rooms. Bumps and scrapes sounded from there for a while. Then the sounds quieted, and the night took control.

***

Three of the longest days Bill had ever experienced followed. He spent the first day hoping someone would come and explain what was going on. His stomach growled almost constantly in objection to his meager diet. His rear became numb from sitting on the hard-packed floor. If he left the building no one stopped him, but the half-dozen houses made of scraps of wood and metal were mostly deserted during the day. The few people he met going about their daily tasks smiled and nodded politely. None of them seemed curious about him. None of them spoke English.

On the morning of the second day, Bill started walking downhill, expecting at any moment to be stopped. Though a pack of half-starved dogs followed him hopefully, no one else paid much attention. A half-mile or so down a very rough road, he came to a coffee plantation set on the hillside. Hundreds of plants grew on both sides, their dark green, waxy leaves resembling small Christmas trees. Adult men and women pruned the plants with deft movements. The children from the orphanage gathered up the branches and took them away. This was where the people of the village spent their days.

Bill looked past the plantation, where the road descended even more steeply. Would someone stop him if he tried to continue down the mountainside? Could he manage the rocky descent without hurting himself? How far would he have to walk to get help? In the end, the steep path, the hot sun, the humidity, and self-doubt deterred him. At his age and with the extra forty pounds of fat he carried, it was best to stay where he was. No one had hurt or even bothered him. Aside from being hungry he wasn't suffering, and he admitted, he was curious about all this. Who were these people, and why had he been brought to this ungodly place?

The children's caregivers, who were more like guardians than givers of care, frowned whenever he showed his face. The girl who waited on him was sweet, but she answered his questions in her own language, speaking so softly he almost couldn't hear her. It didn't matter. He understood nothing of what she said anyway.

Having no other choice, Bill used an outhouse for the first time in his life. He was repulsed by the smell, leery of what might be crawling around in there, and surprised to find there were no partitions between seats. The holes were almost always occupied, so giggling boys sat on either side of him each morning. He was grateful the girls understood he didn't want their company.

Sometime after noon on the third day, a man approached where Bill sat in a tiny spot of shade beside the front door. He looked like a character from an old movie, a caricature of the

Hispanic sleazebag in a white suit no longer white. His hair was greasy and lay in clumps alongside his face, and a well-chewed toothpick hung from one corner of his mouth. None of that mattered when the man greeted him. “Good day, sir. I am Martìn.”

Though the accent was strong, Bill was thrilled to hear English. Rising, he brushed the dirt off his rear, though his clothes were by now past saving. “Thank goodness! I can’t even figure out what language these people are speaking.”

“Creole, sir. Many Haitians prefer it to French.”

So he was in Haiti. A shadow crossed Bill’s mind, but he pushed it away. “Listen, I don’t know what’s going on, but I can pay. Just tell me how much it will take to get me home.”

The toothpick shifted to the other side. “You don’t like it here?”

“I didn’t mean that. It’s just that I have...work to get done.”

“The women. They have treated you well?”

“Fine.” He frowned. “There isn’t much here for those kids. Don’t they have school or something?”

His visitor huffed derisively. “Educating these children would be a waste of time and money, my friend. They are trash, collected from city streets after their parents abandon them.” He nodded toward the road. “Here they are taught meaningful work.”

“At the coffee plantation.”

Martìn nodded vigorously. “Work is good. Without it they will become troublemakers, you know?”

Bill shook his head. “The women aren’t exactly kind to them.”

“Here is not like the U.S.A.” He leaned closer, and Bill caught the stink of his suit. “Their job is not to fill their heads with words and numbers. We are preparing them for life.”

Though afraid to ask, Bill had to. “Who do you work for?”

“The Deep and Wide Church of Our Triumphant God,” Martìn said proudly. “We are one hundred percent supported by the congregation of Pastor Yardley Niven.”

Chapter Eighteen

Robin waited the full four days before rescuing Uncle Bill. Though she worried about him, she let anger harden her heart. He had to understand the hopelessness and poverty of the lives of the orphaned children. That was Step One of the KNP.

That didn't mean she was content with her choice. Sleep came in short snatches, and even then she dreamed terrible scenarios: Bill died of ptomaine from eating local food. The pilot never returned to pick them up. And for some reason, Thomas Wyman appeared in Haiti, his stern face showing disappointment in her behavior.

The last day at evening, she had the man with the Land Rover drive her up the mountain to the orphanage. The two women sat on the ground near the front door, and they looked up without much interest as the engine ground uphill. Walking past them, she found Bill in the orphanage store room, looking listless and depressed. When Robin appeared in the doorway, he gestured at their surroundings. "You wanted me to know about this."

"Yes."

He licked his lips. "We ask folks for money to run an orphanage, and this is it."

She nodded.

"I take it Yardley knows?"

Robin shrugged. "Not how much of the money Martìn keeps for himself, but he knows enough." She looked around. "He provides no funding for education, barely enough for food and supplies. I guess just keeping these children alive and giving them work to do proves he's doing God's will."

"I should have known," Bill said. "I should have asked." He jabbed a bag of what looked like beans with a finger. "These kids work like dogs. They're fed just enough to keep them able to do what they're told. They get no medical care, no affection, not even a goddam ball to play with." His head drooped, and he propped it with a hand. "I'll never be able to get up on that stage and play kindly old Uncle Bill again." He met Robin's gaze. "Unless I do something about this place."

Robin was relieved, even pleased. Bill was the man she'd hoped he would be, which meant the rest of the plan might work. "In that case," she asked, "Are you willing to participate in a little benevolent blackmail?"

***

The Deep and Wide Church had its own jet, despite media types who carped about the expense. Niven explained publicly that his ministry required periods of calm with which to commune with God, and what better place was there than a mile above His magnificent creation? Privately he admitted he couldn't abide sitting next to some overweight mouth-breather or hear someone's bratty kid whining from the row behind him through an entire flight. The church could afford to spare him the irritations of ordinary travel. And on his own plane he could drink without some old bat giving him dirty looks every time he ordered another round.

When *God's Wings* touched down, a single gray Lexus waited on the tarmac near the church's slot. Uncle Bill leaned against it, his face telegraphing amiability though he wasn't actually smiling.

Yardley Niven exited first, as he always did. Admirers often showed up to celebrate his return home, and he believed they wanted to see him when the door opened, not some personal assistant. He always appeared surprised to find a fan or two on the tarmac, but he never let on he was disappointed if there was no one waiting. It wouldn't do to seem taken with his own celebrity.

Today there was only Bill. "Hey, Buddy. Where'd you go last week? The text you sent was pretty vague."

Bill chuckled. "Met an old girlfriend and we had an interesting week." He gestured at the car. "I got back just ahead of you, so I thought I'd wait around and give you a lift home."

"Great." Niven stopped as the limousine driver got out to open the car door. "Who's this?"

"I can't pronounce his name. I've just been calling him Charlie, like Charlie Chan."

When the young Asian man reached out a hand to take the bag Niven carried, he brushed it away. "I'll keep this one with me. You can see to the rest."

The chauffeur moved to obey, and Bill nodded at the obviously heavy case. "Is that the take?"

Niven smiled. "It's a good one too."

"I guess you'll claim about a third of it."

For a moment Niven thought he detected criticism in the tone, but Bill's expression was as benevolent as ever. "Since when did you care about the business end of things?"

A shake of the head indicated he didn't. "As long as there's money for pizza when we're done."

Niven laughed with him. "Right. This will definitely build up the pizza fund."

Bill's week off must have done him good, because he seemed energized, chatting nonstop as they left the airport. It took some time before Yardley realized they'd made a wrong turn.

"Charlie, or whatever-your-name-is, this isn't right."

In answer the driver pulled the privacy window closed. Niven glanced at Bill in consternation and then tried the door handle. It didn't work.

"Hey! Stop this car right now!" Turning to Bill he asked, "Where did this guy come from?"

"I don't know, Yard. I called my service and told them what I needed, and he showed up."

After trying his door handle several more times, Niven reached across Bill and tried his. Same result. "Disabled," Bill said. "A safety feature for when there are children or drunks in the back."

Pulling out his phone, Niven pressed several buttons. "It says there's no signal."

"He's equipped the car with some kind of jammer."

Bill was too calm. The old guy was obviously stunned, emotionally incapable of handling the present emergency. That meant Niven had to take the lead.

But what was the right way to go? Yardley had never been much of a fighter. He couldn't think of a way to make the driver stop the car. He guessed the purpose of the abduction wasn't to harm or kill them, or they'd already be hurt or dead. He'd have to depend on his strongest suit: persuasion. Whatever the Asian guy had in mind, Yardley would talk him out of it. *When God is your sidekick, you can talk anybody into everything.*

When the vehicle finally slowed, they could see rows of storage units through the darkened windows. There were several gentle turns then a sharp one followed by a complete stop. Niven got a glimpse of metal walls before all light was extinguished.

"Where are we?"

"I lost track. Too many turns."

All was silent for a few minutes, but finally they heard the locks click. The doors opened on either side, and a low mechanical voice ordered them to get out. A large man in dark clothing pushed Niven toward the back of the car, and he felt his way along until several lights came on, illuminating lawn chairs set side by side.

"Sit," said a mechanical voice.

Niven squinted, but he was unable to penetrate the gloom. Drawing himself up to full height, he spoke in the voice of the old prophets. "Whoever you are, you'd better let us go. I have friends all over this state, and when they hear about this, there'll be nowhere you can hide!"

Despite the bravado, Niven heard the tremble in his own voice. A third figure had joined the first two. The abduction was well planned, and they were isolated in an unknown spot. Bill had gone silent beside him, frozen with fear. He'd be no help. Yardley was on his own.

***

"Bubbles." Spoken in Robin's deep metallic voice, the name sounded silly, but Hua knew what to do. Approaching first Niven and then Bill, he found their phones and put them into his pocket. Niven made a grab at his, but Cam swatted his hand away.

"I'm warning you, when the friends of the Deep and Wide Church find out—"

Robin stopped Niven with a firm voice. "They aren't going to find out, Mr. Niven, because you aren't going to tell them. Now sit down in one of those chairs."

Bill obeyed immediately, though Niven glared at him. "I'll

never agree—"

"Shut up."

It had been so long since anyone ordered him to be silent that Niven obeyed out of pure surprise.

"Now sit down, or my men will tie you to the chair."

Niven glanced at Bill, whose eyes urged cooperation. He sat, his jaw jutting like an angry three-year-old.

"You have been brought here to answer for misrepresenting yourself to the people of your congregation."

His nostrils flared. "You're mistaken, sir."

"No mistake. You're the worst sort of charlatan, the kind that preys on people to make yourself rich."

"Those who donate to my causes get a full measure of blessings in return."

"What blessings?"

"First, they have the peace of knowing they do God's work."

"Are you kidding? You spend the money on yourself."

Niven's tone turned silky. "My followers don't mind that I have nice things. They know how hard I work for God's kingdom on Earth."

"Your house is the size of Disneyland."

His chest strained against his silk shirt as he quoted, "Ezekiel 28:4: 'By your wisdom and by your understanding you have gotten yourself riches, and have gotten gold and silver into your treasures.'"

"So your 'understanding' bought you a Lear jet and a dozen expensive cars?"

"'Whosoever hath, to him shall be given, and he shall have more abundance.'" Niven raised a sardonic eyebrow. "That's from Matthew, in case you prefer New Testament citations."

"We prefer people who don't use scripture to justify greed. Doesn't it say in Luke that life shouldn't be about possessions?"

Niven wasn't about to let anyone best him in religious disputation. "Proverbs 8:18: 'With me are riches and honor, enduring wealth and prosperity.'" He looked up, his expression pious. "My Heavenly Father sees my work, and I am rewarded."

Robin's anger rose at the glib responses. "Didn't Jesus warn that it's hard for a rich man to enter the kingdom of heaven?"

Niven smiled. "That depends on the rich man's approach. Matthew again, sixth chapter, verse 33: 'Seek first his kingdom and his righteousness, and all these things will be given to you as well.'"

Behind Robin Cam shifted his feet. The interview wasn't going well, and she feared the preacher's easy recitations of Scripture were having an effect on him.

"You cheat the people who give you money," Robin charged. "You cheat the children your followers think they're helping. I can't think of a pastor who represents God's kingdom on earth less than you do."

Smoothing his hair at the sides with both hands, he replied, "At least I don't kidnap innocent people and hold them hostage." Robin went silent and Niven went on, sensing his advantage. "You didn't bring me here to hear me quote the Bible. How much do you plan to charge my wife for my release?"

"Your wife has nothing to do with it." He seemed surprised, and she went on, "We'll take the money you're carrying with you."

Niven looked at Bill as if confused. "Money?"

"The cash you carry yourself so no one knows how much you actually collect from your revivals."

Obviously distressed to hear they knew about his secret practice, Niven tried for outrage. "You'd steal money earmarked for the poor and disadvantaged of this world?"

Robin's spirits rose at the plea in his tone. "They'll get more of it our way than they will yours."

As Niven huffed in anger, Robin imagined the sermon he planned to write about the evil men who'd robbed him. He was probably already considering just the right words, tragic pose, and sorrowful expression.

With a sigh that confirmed her suspicions Niven said, "All right. If you've got what you want, then let us go."

"We're not finished." Again he looked surprised. "You're going to confess your sins, pastor, and we're going to record it."

"You can't be serious."

"Take a look at this." She handed him a folder of documents Bill had provided: emails, letters, and photos, including one of Niven shaking hands with Martìn in front of the orphanage.

"What does that prove? We have a lot of work to do on the program, but helping those children is God's work. You'll never convince me to say I've done anything wrong."

"Believe me, we will. You'll admit you know exactly how underfunded the orphanage in Haiti is. You'll explain how you divert massive amounts of your congregation's gifts to yourself. And you'll agree that will change. Those kids will get better housing, a school, decent food, and caregivers who actually care."

He made a noise of objection, but she ignored it. "If you do that, we'll keep the recording you're about to make private. If you fail to live up to your promise, we'll send it, along with the file I just showed you, to the media. They'll like nothing better than to get their teeth into someone like you. I predict that even if you stay out of prison, the resulting investigation will dry up your revenue." She paused to let that sink in before adding, "There are lots of pastors who actually do the Lord's work. Your contributors will switch their allegiance to them."

Niven seemed to mentally dissect the proposal. "What I say will remain secret?"

"As long as you do as we say."

"I have to maintain a certain standard of living," he protested. "It's expected."

Robin sighed. "We'll allow you the tithe you suggest to your followers: ten percent of the intake."

"Before or after expenses?"

From behind Robin, Hua spoke. "After."

"I can't live on that."

"Sell Disneyland," Robin suggested. "Get a nice place in a subdivision."

He actually gasped in horror at the thought. "I've worked hard for what I have."

"You can keep any money you earn yourself, like for the book you're writing about your blessed life."

"How did you know about that?"

Oops! Bill's eyes widened at her accidental mention of what he'd told her on the way home from Haiti.

She made her voice even sterner. "What difference does it make? The profits on that mighty work of fiction will be yours. The ten percent will apply to what the church itself brings in."

After a few moments Niven said, “Let’s get it over with.” Robin guessed he was already figuring how he’d get around their demands, but old Yardley didn’t know everything.

It took a long time to record the confession. Niven quibbled and excused himself at every turn, cloaking his dishonesty in convenient scriptural passages and insisting his “flock” wanted to reward him for the excellent work he did for the Lord. “If I got sidetracked, it was because I wanted my family, my friends, and my employees to have secure futures.”

“Your family’s future certainly looks secure.”

“If you interfere with the Deep and Wide Church, I’ll have to lay folks off,” he argued. “You’ll be taking away the livelihoods of many good people.”

“Have them do something useful instead of waiting on you and your spoiled kids.”

He didn’t give up the argument that he “blessed” his donors. “People who give to us feel they’ve made a difference in a world too big for them to comprehend.” His hands formed a globe and then expanded to demonstrate the size of modern problems.

“That’s good,” Robin responded, “because you’re going to make that difference happen for real.”

He frowned. “What do you mean?”

“Designate someone other than yourself to control church finances.”

He looked up, confused. “Someone—?”

“—less likely to succumb to the temptations of Mammon.” Robin paused as if considering. “There must be someone who knows your organization’s stated goals, who can see what’s needed and achieve real benefits.”

"My wife would—"

"Spend the money on those fat little sausages you call your offspring. Someone else."

"Such as?"

"How about Uncle Bill?" She made it sound like she'd just thought of it. "Bill, if Yardley here put you in charge of his financial operations, do you think, with the help of competent professionals, you could do some good in the world with it?" She lowered her mechanical voice in warning. "If you fail us, you'll be responsible for the destruction of his career as well as your own, and we *will* be watching."

Bill said his line perfectly, as if he'd never considered the prospect until that moment. "I guess so." He looked at Niven as he said it, his gaze telegraphing, *What else can I do?*

"Good. Within forty-eight hours, Mr. Niven will draw up documents making you partner and CFO of his enterprises. He'll allow you full access to records and finances." Turning to Niven she went on, "Bill may choose from existing staff or hire a new financial manager, as he sees fit. As soon as you email copies of the signed documents to us, we'll put the confession you just made into long-term storage." She handed Niven an index card on which Hua had printed an email address. "Several times each year we'll require you both to prove you're abiding by the agreement."

Niven tapped the card against his knuckles before sliding it in the pocket of his shirt, a signal of capitulation. Robin stepped back, relieved to have the hard part done.

Cam switched off the lights and took Niven by the arm, leading him back to the limousine. Robin stopped Bill before he got in. "Are you going to be able to handle this?"

He grinned. "Actually, I'm kind of excited about it."

"I hope he doesn't throw too many roadblocks in your way."

Glancing at the limousine, Bill shook his head. "Yardley isn't really a bad man. He wanted to lead people to the Lord, but he got caught up in the fame and the money. He'll go along, though we'll have a time explaining all this to his wife."

That opinion was borne out by what Robin heard Niven say as Bill got into the car. "I can't tell the harpy she has to cut back, Bill. Think you could talk to her about it?"

***

At the headquarters of the Deep and Wide Church of God the next morning, Yardley Niven closed himself in his office with Uncle Bill. "I need your help, buddy," Niven began. "We've got to get around these people somehow, and we have to do it together."

"Why, Yard?"

The pastor's face showed disbelief. "What do you mean, why? They want to ruin us."

"That's not true."

All night Bill had considered the most important argument of his life. During his stay at the orphanage, he'd admitted to himself he was compliant in Yardley Niven's dishonest ministry. He'd accepted Yard's easy assurance that there was enough money for both good works and good living. He'd ignored his nagging doubts when old men in scuffed shoes and raveled sweaters contributed fifty dollars "for the children." He'd suspected some of them didn't have enough money to buy groceries for themselves at the end of the month. In the end Bill hadn't felt good about himself for a long time. If he could turn the Deep and Wide Church into an entity that actually helped others, he might still find a little self-respect.

Now he steepled his fingers and rested his chin on the tips.

"Yard, what do you want your legacy to be?"

Niven's first reaction was the canned speech he'd sold to himself long ago. "When I face the Final Judgment, I want to be able to report to my Lord and Savior that I brought thousands to Him, that I showed them His love and caring."

Bill said nothing, but an arched brow registered doubt.

Niven tried again. "I know it's kind of a show, Bill, but we do bring people to God."

"Then why do I drink too much Gray Goose? Why do you need another vintage car or another woman whose name you don't remember the next day? If we were really doing what God wants us to, we'd be okay without booze and sex and new toys. Isn't that what you preach to your followers?"

Niven looked away, unable to meet Bill's gaze.

"The way I see it, the people who toss money in the collection plates give you—give *us*—the chance of a lifetime. You've built this great church, and there's a regular pipeline of money coming in. You work hard, and you started telling yourself it was okay to enjoy the benefits of that work. Am I right?"

Licking his lips, Niven said, "People expect us to project a successful image. It gives them confidence."

"Sure, sure. But you've had it good for a couple of years now, and I don't see that it's made you happy." He raised his hands, palms up. "I know *I* feel funny about how we live."

"It isn't about the money, Bill. The bigger we get, the more people hear the message we offer. When they hear it, if their hearts are right, they want to help spread it to others. That's why we need a large organization."

"But *this* large organization only feeds itself. How about we try using the money the way we say we will?"

"We have a good thing going here," Niven said stubbornly. "Why change it?"

"I don't see that we have much choice." Bill rubbed his chin. "From what I heard last night, these people can make things pretty uncomfortable for you." Niven's eyes hardened and he added quickly, "Not that I'm any better off. If that confession hits the news, I'm either the crook that helped you steal from God or the guy who's so dumb he couldn't see it."

Bill scratched his head in a gesture reminiscent of his TV character, whose aw-shucks wisdom always came in a self-deprecating manner. "Since we have to change things, I say let's do it right. Cut personal spending to reasonable levels and put the money where it can do some good." He made the next thought seem like it had just occurred to him. "Heck, you might end up a saint, or whatever Protestants have that's equal to it." He leaned forward earnestly. "You've got the power to change lives, Yard. Money rolls in when you ask for it. Let's do some good with it."

Across the wide, cherry wood desk, Niven's expression turned thoughtful. "Janie won't like living on less."

"She'll change her mind when her husband starts getting featured in articles about today's great philanthropists." Bill pointed a finger at him. "If anybody can put a positive spin on this situation, it's Yardley Niven."

The pastor scratched at the side of his face. "This could be a plus for me, Bill. It could be a big, big plus."

***

"Three hundred and twenty-four thousand, sixty-two dollars, and eighty-six cents." Hua's tone revealed disbelief. "I have counted it twice."

Cam's face creased in a frown. "Pastor Niven makes a lot of money."

Robin grimaced. "If you'd seen those kids taking turns on their one and only swing—I wish we'd been harder on him."

"We get what we get." Em hobbled down the ramp with Bennett at her side and a cup of coffee in her free hand. The cash Hua had laid out included all denominations, crumpled wads of ones, folded fives, and crisp, new tens. One twenty had a note paper-clipped to it: BLESS YOU PASTER FOR THE WERK YOU DO.

"Even after we split with the orphanage," Robin said, "we can pay the debt on this mausoleum off."

"And keep the wolf from our door for a few months," Em added.

"Uncle Bill emailed this morning," Hua said. "He's taken over management of the orphanage and replaced Martìn and the two women. He is working on convincing Mr. Niven that if the Deep and Wide Church operates more philanthropically, there could be a Nobel Prize in his future."

"Whatever." Robin was grumpy. She'd had no physical response after the Niven KNP. Her breathing remained normal, her steps steady. Instead of seeing that as a positive, she'd stared at the ceiling most of the night, wondering if she'd become a conscienceless monster who hurt others without a shred of mercy.

"As long as those kids get treated better, we did good," Cam said. Robin waited for Em to add that the end justified the means, but for once she kept her clichés to herself.

Did their targets' behavior warrant the treatment they received? For Robin it boiled down to "maybe." She had to believe she was better than Mark, had to focus on the good they did and not the methods they used. She decided as long as she felt empathy for her victims, she was not her father, who'd cared only about himself. Retreating to her room, she called Shelly. Talking to her friend made her feel normal, though she had to be careful what she said. Shelly's comments about hairstyles, movies, and the latest diet advice were like a lifeline back to the old Robin. It wasn't that she missed her former self, but it was sometimes nice to pretend that the most important thing in her life was deciding whether it was time to try bangs again.

An hour later Robin started downstairs, dressed for a walk outside. When they'd first come to Kansas, she'd been nervous in the rural setting. The quiet, the absolute darkness at night, and the surrounding trees had been new to her and therefore unsettling. She and Hua had wondered aloud if there were bears in the woods, but Em scoffed at their fears. "Take Bennett with you and go for a walk," she'd urge. With the dog for security, she had explored the property and found nothing more threatening than an irritated raccoon. After that Robin had decided she liked the woods. Walking among the trees was both relaxing and energizing, better than any spa treatment she'd ever experienced.

Since she'd left her shoes by the back door, Robin's steps were silent on the stairs. Halfway down, she heard Em talking on the phone. "It went okay," she said to some unknown person. "They got home last night."

Robin stopped dead. Who was Em talking to? Hardly daring to breathe, she listened. "Don't worry about that right now. Just take care of yourself, and we'll get you up here when the time is right." There was a pause as the other person spoke. Then Em said, "I know. Do what they tell you to, and everything will work out."

Tiptoeing back up the stairs, Robin waited until she was sure the call had ended before coming down, slipping into her shoes, and going outside. The shady woods cooled her skin, but her mind struggled with what felt like betrayal. Em claimed she had no family, no friends, yet she was telling someone about their travels. What was she up to, and what should be done about it?

In the end Robin decided Em had the right to have friends and to speak with them on the phone about daily things. The comment about them getting home might serve only to reassure an acquaintance that she wasn't alone. The promise to "get you up here when the time is right" was more puzzling, but it was vague enough to mean nothing, like when people say, "Let's have lunch sometime."

No reacting from emotion. Play it cool.

The sinister scenario came to mind only because she was a worrier. Not only was Em completely trustworthy, she didn't owe Robin any explanations. She let the trees absorb her tension, and by the time she returned to the house, her shoulders were relaxed and her smile genuine.

Chapter Nineteen

Making a list for her weekly trip to the grocery store, Robin went to Hua's apartment to ask what he needed for upcoming meals. The pocket doors that separated the wing from the main house were usually left open, but she never entered without announcing her presence in some way. When she tapped lightly on the door frame, Hua jumped as if he'd been slapped. He touched a computer key, collapsing the image on the screen.

"What are you doing," she teased, "plotting the takeover of the US government?"

He smiled, but it was a weak attempt. "No plot, Robin. Only wishes."

There was such sadness in his tone that she approached and put a hand on his arm. "What's wrong?"

Instead of answering he touched the screen, recalling the image he'd minimized. A dozen somber-faced children stood in a line, holding numbered placards to their chests. Below the picture was a list of information that corresponded to the numbers: names, ages, and attributes. One said CHE, 10, TRAINED IN HOUSEKEEPING. Another said, LOUISA, 8, EXCELLENT ENGLISH.

It took a second. "These children are for sale?"

He nodded. "As I was sold to Senator Buckram."

Shock made her words come in clumps. "Where—? Can they—? How did this get on the Internet?"

"This is the deep web, the internet not catalogued by Google." As usual when Hua lapsed into computer jargon, Robin struggled to keep up. "Much of the information here is unstructured data gathered from sensors and other devices. It does not reside in a database that can be scanned. Often pages are temporary, removed before search engines can crawl them."

She understood that keywords helped Google, Yahoo, and the like find information. It was weird to think there was information out there, a lot of it, not meant to be easily located.

"Some areas of the deep web are accessible only by special software that allows people to share information anonymously via peer-to-peer connections rather than a centralized computer server." Hua shrugged delicately. "I spent much time trying to find this site, and now—" He gestured. "You see."

"Doesn't the government stop things like this?"

"They try to. The Defense Advanced Research Projects Agency, known as DARPA, works with researchers from companies and universities to devise search tools that provide new ways to analyze and organize data pulled from the deep web."

"But as of right now—"

"The only way to locate a site is to know the exact address. Criminals pass the information to other criminals. For the authorities, it is like searching a dark football stadium with a key-fob flashlight."

Robin couldn't look away from the faces of twelve frightened children. "Who does something like this?"

"These are the people who brought me to this country."

"They're still operating after all these years?"

Hua's smile was grim. "Do they not say success brings success? They call their business All-Hands, and the woman in charge is Linda Billings. She is perfect for the task of training slaves, being—" He searched for a word. "—single-minded."

"You want to go after her."

He put his hands up, palms out. "I know I said I would help with your KNPs, but I feel quite strongly about this." His usually sweet expression turned hard. "I will stop this woman."

Robin was still staring at the screen. ""No, Hua. *We* will stop her."

***

Robin realized right away she shouldn't have spoken for the others. Going after a member of a human trafficking ring wasn't the same as kidnapping cheaters and scaring them semi-straight. For starters, they'd be up against hardened, professional criminals. It would take all the skill they could muster to isolate Linda Billings and convince her to leave the organization.

Hua explained another problem. "Human trafficking is a difficult crime to prove. Of the 2.5 million victims worldwide, the United Nations found that forty percent of countries surveyed had fewer than ten convictions in 2014. Many reported no convictions at all."

Still, any blow struck against the group seemed worthwhile to Robin, and Hua was determined. That evening in Em's sitting room, Robin proposed Linda Billings as the next KNP target.

"This is very different from what we've done before, and much more dangerous," she warned. "Hua knew Linda Billings, but it was years ago. We don't know what's changed since then. Even if we're successful, she's just one cog in the machine. Without her, the organization will go on."

"Better to light a candle than curse the dark," Em argued. "We do what we can with what we've got."

"One bad guy at a time," Cam agreed. "Or bad lady, I guess it would be."

"These people won't hesitate to kill anyone who gets in their way," Em said gravely. "We need to have our poop in a group."

"If it turns out the case is beyond our abilities," Robin promised, "we'll accept that and move on."

Not that Hua would do that. Not that he could.

Though All-Hands was an international organization, Linda Billings controlled incoming "goods," for the Southeastern United States, overseeing training, sales, and distribution for their "candidates." Sixty-five years old, she currently lived somewhere in Florida, from what Hua could determine. "They choose isolated places," he said, and his eyes darkened at the memory. "We had no idea where to go if we ran away, and they told us there were wild animals in the area. If we escaped the beasts, Linda said, the police would put us in jail forever."

"Disgusting," Em commented. "Show us what you've got on Mrs. Billings."

Hua produced his tablet, and a few efficient taps brought up the photo of a well-preserved woman with light hair and a long face. She had beautiful eyes, but Robin thought her mouth revealed a hardness that belied her otherwise gentle appearance. Knowing what Billings did for a living might have colored her perception.

The slave dealer presented herself as a semi-retired entrepreneur who matched competent staff with elite clients. Her website invited visitors to write a short essay describing their needs. One tip-off to the dark side of her business was that no salary for prospective employees was ever mentioned.

Em made the initial contact, which involved filling out a form. She'd developed several alternate identities in her days at the Bureau and kept a few as "rainy day necessities." To contact All-Hands she became a wealthy woman named Jane Canty who wanted *an English-speaking female to take care of my home in a way that satisfies my demanding standards.* When asked who had recommended the site, she filled in the name of Senator Buckram's deceased manager, Paul Dotsun.

A day later Em received a reply suggesting she fill out an "ancillary document" outlining her exact needs.

"It's a test." She rubbed her hands together. "If I say the right things, I'll get some sort of personal contact."

"Don't go too fast," Robin cautioned. "We need time to set things up."

"I'll tell them I'm visiting my children and won't be back in Florida until next month. If they're interested, they'll wait."

She was correct. Once she'd submitted the second form, Em got a phone call. With acting chops that made Robin grin with admiration, the fake Mrs. Canty whined about her greedy family, her distrust of anyone under thirty, and the lack of loyalty among those who would in another age have been pleased to be good servants.

Mrs. Billings was very understanding, and soon they had plans to meet in person at the Tampa airport, where they would discuss All-Hands' proposal to address Mrs. Canty's needs.

Ending the call, Em watched Bennett gobble the lima beans Hua had picked out of his soup. "Is there anything he won't eat?"

"It is very efficient, having this dog," Hua commented. "There is no wasting of food."

"When you're done spoiling him, get me a flight from here to Detroit and then on to Tampa on the twenty-third. Billings will check my itinerary, just as she's already checked my bank account and my identity." When Robin looked surprised Em finished, "She hasn't stayed in the slave game this long by being sloppy."

***

"I think I've solved a problem," Linda Billings told her son as she ended the call. "I've got a customer who's perfect for the twins."

"Oh yeah?" Luther sounded unimpressed, and she wished for the hundredth time he cared more about the business. She wasn't getting any younger, and she wanted him to take a more active role. Though he favored her in looks—blond hair, blue eyes, and a tendency to roundness—his slightly mean and definitely shiftless disposition came from his father. Luther was, she had to admit, too dumb to plan and too lazy to care.

It had been a mistake to accept the twins. Mai was delayed—or whatever you were supposed to call it nowadays, and Jai was too rebellious for her own good. Linda kept them in line, because she didn't take crap from any of her charges, but it took constant effort. She was tired of being the tough one all the time.

Lighting her last cigarette of the day and blowing the smoke to one side with an audible puff, she navigated to the site on the deep web where her business associates let her know what was going on. She was scheduled for a shipment in forty-nine days, which meant she had to clear the house by then. That was doable. The girls had been whipped into shape, and she already had nibbles on several of them. It was almost too easy with girls: housemaids, nannies, and "companions." She sometimes wanted to ask, *Who are you trying to kid, pervert?* Of course she didn't. Repeat business was like a gift; you didn't even have to work hard for it.

"So what you got going?" Luther asked from the couch.

"This old woman is afraid she's losing it. She wants someone to make it look like she's okay so her son doesn't stick her in a nursing home and take control of her money."

"She wants the twins?"

"I'll offer them to her as a two-fer."

"You're going to *give* one of them away? That's stupid!"

Billings turned angry eyes on her son. "Who are you calling stupid?"

"Losing money is stupid. Sell Jai to the old lady and the retard to Greg's guys."

"If we separate them, Jai will kill herself. Mai can keep house while the woman teaches Jai to do her accounting."

"If Jai kills herself, so what? No refunds."

Billings pounded a fist on the table. "I make the decisions, Luther. Stick with what you do best: following orders."

"I'm just saying—"

"You're always 'just saying,' and it never contributes one positive thing to the conversation. I'm sick of it." She kneaded her forehead. "I'm tired of arguing, tired of figuring all this out. I'm really tired."

"From what? All you do is sit around and think about stuff."

"If I died tonight, you'd be in jail by tomorrow, because I think about all the 'stuff' you don't. You just run your big mouth."

The sound of a key in the door distracted them. When it opened, Luther said, "Hey, Gary. My mother says I got a big mouth. Is she right or is she full of crap, like always?"

Apparently used to this sort of thing, the newcomer said, "Nice out there tonight. Real pretty."

***

When Em entered the airport Starbucks, Linda Billings rose and approached, her hand extended. Em had dressed the part of Mrs. Canty, wearing an expensive but slightly outdated dress, shoes that reminded her with each step why she mostly wore tennis shoes these days, and an inordinate amount of costume jewelry. After they introduced themselves, they bought drinks and sat down at a small table in a comparatively quiet corner. There was some small talk, and Em knew she was being judged, so her answers were carefully worded. Without going too far, she managed to hint she was stingy, misanthropic, and convinced that anything she wanted from life should be handed to her without question.

When the general conversation wound down, Em realized it was decision time for Linda Billings. Had she been convincing enough?

"I can help you stay in your home, Mrs. Canty, but you need to understand that the service we offer isn't the usual employer-employee situation." Billings moved her coffee cup rhythmically back and forth a quarter turn as she spoke. "I'm sure you'll agree there's nothing worse than a domestic servant who tattles on you or leaves just when you've got her properly trained."

"That's exactly what I told you on the phone," Em commented. "I want a girl who's loyal."

"What if I offered someone who can't leave?"

"And why can't she?"

"Because you own her." Behind the counter, a stack of trays fell to the floor, making a tremendous clatter.

Em winced but remained focused on Billings. "I own—"

"We provide competent personal servants that buyers may use as they like."

"Where do you—? Where do they come from?"

Billings took a sip of her iced coffee. “Does that matter?”

“I guess not.” Em feigned confusion. “You want to sell me a person.”

“Yes.”

“And she’ll do whatever I need her to?”

“We have a young woman at this time who has great potential.” Opening a folder she’d brought along, she placed a photograph on the table. “This is Jai, who is very intelligent. In the future, if you become...unable or reluctant to deal with financial matters, she is capable of taking them on—with permission from you—and continuing your affairs exactly as you wish.”

“But you say she would belong to me. What does that mean, um, legally?”

“There is no ‘legally’ here, but practically? It happens all the time.”

“But surely she needs papers, identification—”

Billings’ expression turned amused. “Where will she go? Who will she see?” She chewed at her lip, choosing her words carefully. “No one is searching for this girl. She has no past, and her future is whatever you decide it will be.” She let her companion think on that for a moment before adding, “Some of our clients even adopt them. If that’s the way you choose to go, we can help with reasonably believable documentation.”

Em huffed a laugh. “That would certainly surprise my son. Competition for his inheritance!”

Setting a second picture beside the first, Billings went on. “This is Mai, Jai’s sister. Mai isn’t very bright, but she can do simple household tasks, and she doesn’t mind hard work.” She cleared her throat. “We’re prepared to offer both girls for the same price."

Em frowned peevishly. "You want me to take two foreign females into my home?"

Billings' sales patter rose to the next level. "In two weeks' time you'll wonder how you did without them. Our people are trained to be obedient. Though Mai is...less than gifted, her presence keeps Jai in line."

"What do you mean by that?"

Her mouth tightened. "We find that if we discipline Jai, she becomes defiant, but if we even threaten to punish Mai, Jai immediately turns submissive."

Imagining the beatings and deprivation used to keep the girls compliant, Em struggled to keep her expression blank. "I would own two human beings?"

"We don't think of it that way," Billings said smoothly. "You're more like a mentor to them—a godmother." She sipped at her drink, letting the kinder motive sink in. "These children come from impoverished areas of backward countries. You will give them lives they could never have imagined."

"As slaves?"

Billings put the plastic lid on her drink with a snap and made as if to rise from her chair. "Perhaps you aren't the person I thought you were."

"No, wait," Em reached out a hand. "I didn't mean to imply disapproval. It's just unexpected, that's all." Billings sat back down as Em asked, "What would these, um, workers cost me?"

"Seven thousand dollars."

Em made a yelp of alarm. "Are you kidding?"

Billings remained calm. "Think about it, Mrs. Canty. You're

getting a lifetime of service for less than the cost of a year's work from a cleaning company. And the girls will protect you. No one can say you're incompetent or unable to stay in your home as long as they're looking out for you."

Em let herself appear half-convinced. "What if they don't work out?"

Billings shrugged. "There are no refunds. Some clients re-sell unsatisfactory workers. Or you can make other arrangements." Her direct gaze said what her words didn't, and Em suppressed a shiver. Billings went on, "You can even release them if you like."

"Wouldn't they report me—and you?"

Billings raised her brows. "Any risk would be yours. Our children don't know where they're kept during training." Her smile absolved All-Hands of responsibility. "Once you've paid our fee, what happens to them is your choice."

"I'm going to have to think on it." Crushing her cup, Em looked around for a recycle bin, the result of Robin's influence. "You make a good case, but I never considered something like this."

"It's easier than you think," Billings replied. "One secure room in your house is all it takes. Once they're used to the situation, our people almost always accept their lot and stay put."

Em rose. "I'll be in touch. It was...interesting to meet you."

Billings rose too, leaving her cup and other trash on the table for someone else to clear away. "I'm sure you understand that this information may not be shared with others." Her eyes turned a colder shade of blue. "That wouldn't be good for you, no matter what you decide about my offer."

Chapter Twenty

Over the course of the next few days, Em negotiated with Linda Billings. She played her role well, first claiming she was unsure about the whole thing, then abruptly changing tactics to argue the price, insisting she should get a break since she was taking an obvious problem off the slavers' hands. The fact that she managed to whittle it down to five thousand indicated the girls were more of a problem than Billings admitted. "She's had trouble with them," Em commented. "There's two things in life one can never be prepared for: twins."

As the deal firmed, Billings gave Em advice about how she should deal with her "employees." Some buyers used physical intimidation to keep them in line, she reported. Others chose gifts and rewards for good behavior and still others, fear tactics. "Our children believe the American police will lock them up if they catch them," she explained. "They tend to be very quiet whenever anyone else is around, which is good."

Once the details were agreed upon, Billings said the girls would be brought to the parking lot of a box store outside Tampa. There Em would pay the entire fee in cash and take ownership.

"Isn't that an odd place to pick up slaves?" Em asked.

"Involuntary household staff," Billings corrected. "And no one pays attention to what happens in those places."

"Should I bring someone to help keep them under control?"

"We give them a little something to calm them down. It will last long enough for you to get them home and secured."

"I have a hard time keeping my mouth shut," Em told her friends. "It's like she's peddling Roombas."

"We're going to do what we can," Robin promised.

"If we stop Linda, that's something," Em agreed. "That is one cold-hearted woman."

***

Robin stood in the box store parking lot, pretending to be on the phone as she watched Em, who waited in a rental car for the delivery of two slaves. How had they gotten to this point? Robin felt like she'd descended the ladder of depravity, from a low-level shyster to bigger crooks to perhaps the worst type of all, those who sold their fellow human beings without a shred of guilt or pity. She'd been ashamed of her father all her life, but this was worse, a ring of people who profited from the suffering of others. How did one become involved in something so evil?

The plan for tonight was simple, which Robin hoped meant it was workable. Em would pick up the girls she'd arranged to buy. Once she had them safely away, Cam and Robin would make a decision, based on who the delivery person turned out to be. If Billings herself showed, they'd take her hostage and demand a ransom. If she sent a flunky or came with an escort, they'd follow them back to their base of operations and wait for a chance to get Billings alone. Em had pressed as hard as she dared for the woman to make the delivery herself, claiming she preferred someone she had seen before.

Billings was driving the car that pulled up next to the rented Mercedes. Getting out, she came to the window and peered in to assure herself that Em was alone.

"Have you got it?"

Em handed over a mailing envelope. Billings reached inside, flipped through the stacks of cash, and nodded satisfaction. "I'll get them."

Going back to her car, she opened a back door. At her gruff

command, two girls connected by a zip tie around their wrists exited the vehicle. Clumsily they followed Billings to Em's car and climbed into the back seat. Though their hair was neatly braided and their clothing was clean, there was a hollowness in their cheeks that indicated poor nutrition.

"Thank you, Mrs. Billings," Em said, putting her car into gear. "I hope this works out for me."

"I'm sure you'll do very well together," Billings replied. "Just don't be afraid to assert your authority."

As the Mercedes left the parking lot and turned onto the street, Billings returned to her car. Before she could start the engine, Robin rose from the back seat and touched a piece of pipe to her neck. "Give me your phone," she ordered in her metallic voice. After a moment Billings obeyed, glaring at the reflection in her rearview mirror. Robin wore a transparent Halloween mask that blurred her features, and she held the pipe in her left hand, out of view. Billings' cold eyes made Robin's heart thump in her chest, and the audacity of what she was doing settled over her like a cloak of doom. This woman was part of a heartless organization responsible for the suffering, even deaths, of many innocent victims. If she screwed up, they would descend on her and her friends with the full weight of their evil. For a few seconds terror took hold of her, and she wanted nothing more than to bolt from the car, escaping Linda Billings' gaze and the threats it implied.

"When I get the man to set his package down, you reach in and take the jewelry-store box, Babe."

"I don't want to, Daddy. I'm scared."

"Scared doesn't mean you don't do something," Mark said, pinching her arm until she winced. "Now do what I told you to do or I'll give you something to really be scared of."

Saved from panic by the urging of a man she despised, Robin

pocketed Billings' phone. "Drive."

***

As she left the parking lot, Em assessed the condition of the girls she'd just rescued from slavery. It was obvious which was which, since Mai showed clear signs of Downs Syndrome. Jai had intelligent eyes, high cheekbones, and the look of someone who'd been brave almost longer than she could bear. Despite the drug they'd been given, she met Em's gaze with angry defiance.

Trying to put them at ease she said, "We're going somewhere safe. Do you understand?"

After a moment Jai said in perfect English. "Of course I understand. That doesn't mean I believe you."

The house Hua had rented for them stood on stilts over the gulf shore. Parking on the slab beneath, Em said, "Would you like to come inside?"

Jai considered for a moment before giving a tight nod, and Mai readily followed her sister's lead. Leading the way up the stairs and into the house, Em gestured at the zip tie that bound the girls together. "Let's get rid of that first." Rummaging noisily in the silverware drawer, she came up with a knife. When Mai's eyes widened in fear, Em turned the handle toward Jai. "You cut it."

When it was done, Jai didn't return the knife but held it to her side. Em shrugged. "Keep it if it makes you feel better. Would you like some tea?"

"No."

"Suit yourself. I'm having some." Filling a pitcher with water, she set it in the microwave to heat. As it hummed and counted down the time, Em took an unopened package of cookies from the cupboard. "Hungry?"

Mai's eyes said she was. Jai's revealed nothing.

"I suppose they kept you half-starved so you'd be easier to handle, but you're finished with that now. You can eat anytime you want to." She opened the refrigerator, which Robin had stocked with food, and stood aside so they could see. "Take what you like, now or later."

Jai regarded Em with distrust. "What do you want with us?"

"Nothing, Jai. We want nothing from you."

"We? I see one old woman. How will you stop us from leaving here?"

Em grinned. "I have no intention of stopping you, but you might consider what's best before you go running off into the dark. Best for you, and best for Mai."

Jai seemed ready to cry for a moment, but she regained control. "We must go home."

"If that's what you want, we'll help you do it." The microwave dinged its signal, and Em removed the hot water. "In the meantime, wouldn't you like some cookies and tea?"

***

Robin had steeled herself for this part of the abduction, expecting chillingly specific threats from her captive and even a possible escape attempt. Though Billings blustered like a school-yard bully, she made no attempt to swerve off the road or grab Robin's "weapon." She made vague, almost childish statements about how her captor would be sorry he'd "messed with" her, and he was going to "get it." Robin found her muttered defiance easy to ignore, as long as Billings drove where she told her to and did what she demanded.

When they pulled up at the unit, Cam came out from the shadows to open the door, the hood of his jacket pulled close around his face. “Drive inside,” Robin ordered. Billings obeyed, and Cam closed the door, shutting out much of the light. When he turned on the trouble lights, Robin ordered, “Get out of the car and take a seat in the chair.”

Billings moved slowly, as if she were frozen with fear. Switching on the recorder she'd set up earlier Robin began, “Mrs. Billings, we're aware of how you make your money.”

Billings seemed to make an effort to pull herself together. “You mean my employment agency.”

“You traffic in human beings.”

Billings remained calm, though her face was flushed. “We match workers with employers who need them.” Fingering the collar of her shirt she added, “We recommend a weekly salary and humane living conditions.”

“The ‘workers’ are brought here against their will and held as prisoners.”

Billings shook her head. “We give them a life they could never have imagined.”

“One where they can be beaten, starved, even killed by their masters.”

“Things like that seldom happen.”

Robin tried to steady her voice. “Seldom is good enough for you?”

Billings rubbed a hand across her forehead. “Can we skip the moralizing? Why am I here?”

Turning slightly, Robin booted the laptop she'd set on a small stepladder. After some fiddling, Hua's face appeared on the screen. Though he remained calm, his jaw shifted slightly when he saw Linda Billings.

"Would you tell us what you know about this woman?" Robin asked.

He swallowed before answering. "When the men who took me from my home brought me to this country, she trained me to serve as a houseboy. Then she sold me to Senator Buckram."

As Hua spoke, Billings began rubbing her chest. "You got any water?"

"Um, yeah." Digging in her backpack, Robin located the water bottle she'd brought along. "Here."

She took a long drink, at the same time kneading her chest as if something inside it wanted out. Suddenly her face contorted, and she slumped forward. "Don't—feel—good." The bottle clattered to the floor, and a moment later, Billings toppled after it.

Though her first reaction was concern, Robin had taught herself caution. "Watch her, Cam. It might be a trick." He nodded, and Robin stepped forward, calling the woman's name.

Billings lay prone, her face to the floor and one hand under her. The other hand was limp at her side. Neither had been used to break her fall. Robin felt her neck. No pulse. Linda Billings was dead.

Chapter Twenty-one

"Do not be upset," Hua told his friends from the computer screen. "Mrs. Linda Billings was not a nice person. The world is better without her."

"But we killed her, Hua. We scared her to death." Robin was close to panic. She couldn't look away from the prone form of the woman whose death she had caused. Her throat felt parched, but her water bottle rolled beside Billings, still in motion from the force of being dropped.

Cam also stared at the corpse, but he seemed more intrigued than guilty. "When my dad had his heart attack, the doctor said he probably had chest pain for months and didn't tell anybody. I'll bet Mrs. Billings did too."

"She smoked all the time," Hua put in. "I remember how her breath smelled when—" He stopped himself. "It's bad she died tonight, but she would have anyway, tomorrow or the day after."

Tomorrow would have been better. I've never watched anyone die before.

Having always thought that in the movies the hero accepted the death of a villain way too easily—one quick check and a sorrowful expression—Robin tested Billings' pulse again. She was still dead.

"What are we going to do, Robin?" Cam's right hand wiped at his shirt front, and his gaze remained two feet to her left, as if she were a stranger he'd just met. This was the ultimate failure of Plan A. Though they'd plotted escape routes and meeting points, they had never discussed what to do if a target died in their custody.

Cam's question was like a weight that fastened itself around her ankles, dragging her down, down, under the earth. The voices in her head piled atop her: *What now, Robin? What's the plan, Robin? What should we do, Robin?*

She wanted someone else to say what came next, because she really didn't know.

In a tiny, tiny miracle, Hua granted her wish. "Do you have her phone?"

"Um, yeah."

"See if her thumbprint opens it."

"Her—?" Panic circled her brain, and she didn't see what Hua was getting at.

"Robin! Take Linda's phone out and open it with her finger. It's usually the dominant thumb, so start with her right one."

Numbly Robin obeyed. Billings' hand was still warm, and she shivered as she took hold of it. "It worked!" she said a second later. "The main screen is up."

"Okay, look for a bank logo. If our luck holds, she will have her password and account login stored."

She was beginning to understand what Hua intended. Could it possibly be that easy?

"I think that's a bank logo." She touched the icon, and a screen opened.

"Type an *L*," Hua advised. "If her ID begins with her name, as many do, the rest will fill in automatically."

"It didn't work."

"*B* then."

"That's it! The information came up."

"Okay. Click and get into her account. You might need to enter the thumb print a second time."

A few seconds later Robin said, "Wow."

"Can we get the amount we planned on from there?"

"And more."

"Take $500,000. That's the maximum one-time transfer allowable under most bank rules."

With trembling fingers Robin typed in the amount and the rest of the information required to move Linda Billings' money from her account to theirs. Her finger hovered for a moment when the COMPLETE THIS TRANSACTION? prompt came up. "Hua, she's dead. She can't change now, so is it fair to take her money?"

His response came in the softest tone possible. "Was what she did to me fair?"

Taking a deep breath, Robin pressed the button that affirmed the transfer. She watched in dread for a few seconds before the screen informed her that her transaction was complete. Would she like to do another?

No. What I'd like to do is lie down for a while.

Hua had a different idea. "See if there's another bank icon on the phone."

Navigating to the menu she replied. "There is, but—"

"What is it you often say? 'In for a penny, in for a pound.' We should hinder these people as much as possible, yes?"

Sighing, Robin took up Billings' rapidly cooling hand. "Yes."

The second account had over $400,000, and she took almost all of it, promising herself the whole amount would be spent to fight human trafficking. When that was over, somewhere under all the shock and regret, she felt the scales of justice tilt a tiny bit in the direction of humanity.

Then she picked up on what Hua was saying. "—so you must find Billings' house and help them."

"What did you say?"

"The other slaves," he repeated urgently. "When Linda fails to return, her people will run away. They will not leave anyone behind who knows what they have done."

Her nerves felt like they were being squeezed in a vise. "They'll kill them?"

"Yes."

It was almost too much to comprehend. There was a dead body on the floor beside her. More lives were at risk if she didn't act quickly. And she had only Cam for help.

No. Cam is the only one here, but Hua and Em are with us. Sort of.

"Hua, can you make the records of tonight's meeting disappear from her devices?"

"Her people will do that as soon as they realize she's missing."

"Great." Taking out Billings' phone, Robin erased all recent calls except one that said MARY'S NAIL SHOP. Wiping her prints away, she tucked it into the pocket of the woman's pants. "Cam, here's what you need to do." As she explained, his nervous gestures accelerated. When she said, "—move the body," he ruffled his hair repeatedly, and when she warned, "—stay away from cameras," he rubbed both hands along his shirt front as if trying to scrub the color out of it.

"I d-don't think I can do that, R-Robin," he said when she finished.

"You have to." She glanced around the storage unit. "Talk to Hua until you're done. He'll help you remember what to do." Cam trusted Hua as much as he trusted Robin, and Hua seemed unaffected by Billings' death. Even from a thousand miles away, he could keep Cam calm enough to do what needed to be done.

"Find her address." While Cam searched the car, Robin called Em to report what had happened. "I need as much location information on Billings' house as the girls can provide."

"You're not going out there, Robin."

"I have to. Hua says when Billings doesn't return, her men will kill whoever is left."

Em sighed. "At least you have Cam with you."

"Um, right." *What you don't know might hurt me.*

"I'll put Jai on. She can tell you what you need to know."

Jai's English was good, though Robin strained to understand some of the words. "We are locked in one room—all girls. Linda likes shipments all one kind." Robin's resolve hardened at hearing people referred to as "shipments." If she could get there in time, this shipment would not be dumped like bananas gone bad.

"How many girls and where is this room?"

"Without us, six. Our window is by a tall blue light with a metal cover—pretty, you know? But for prison."

A grate to prevent escape through the window and a security light to reveal who was outside.

"What will you do to Luther?" Jai asked.

“Who’s Luther?”

“Linda’s son. He says if there is trouble, he will throw a grenade into our room and run.” Her voice turned hard. “He laughs when he says this, like it would be so funny.”

“Does Luther really have a grenade?”

“I don’ think so. It is a joke, you know?” Jai added in a hopeful tone, “Perhaps you will surprise him. Luther is very lazy, like—a worm, is it?”

“Slug,” she corrected absently. “Does someone stand guard outside the house?”

“I don’ think so.”

“So Luther will be there alone?”

Jai considered that. “Sometimes there is Dave and Gary, but I don’ see them today.”

“Two, possibly three men in the house, and six girls in the one room.” Robin wasn’t sure how to ask her next question. “Is there a chance one of the men might have a girl, um, with him?”

Jai gave a mirthless chuckle. “Linda says virgins get more money. If one of them did something to us, she’d take off his...man thing, you know?”

That was both creepy and a relief. “One more thing, Jai. Do these men have weapons?”

“Yes.” She sounded surprised. “Luther say everyone in America is, um, strapped.”

It just gets better.

An hour later, Robin left the car on the road and took a diagonal route through the woods south of Linda Billings’ residence. As the fishy smell of the gulf wafted toward her through the trees, Robin tried not to let herself wonder if Jai knew what she was talking about. The house was situated on the Gulf of Mexico, and Em had consulted a Florida atlas in order to describe the terrain. "It's mostly swamp," she'd said. "The nearest neighbor is a bird sanctuary, which means only pelicans and cormorants are around to see who comes and goes on the beach at night."

Billings' house was long and low, with a crushed-stone drive closed off from the road by a six-foot metal gate. A Florida privet hedge screened the front from view, and trees protected its sides. As Florida homes go, it was neither noticeably large nor particularly fancy, but the advantage to human traffickers was obvious. There wasn't much chance anyone would accidentally hear or see what went on there.

Robin searched for surveillance cameras near the turnoff. None. Though the gate served as a barrier to vehicles, she easily scaled the crossbars and dropped to the other side. Crouching in the shadows, she wished she'd checked for a gun in Billings' car. She could have come armed and at least pretending to be dangerous. At the last possible moment she remembered her phone and shut the ringer off. It would be dumb, possibly fatal, to announce her presence by a random call from some telemarketer.

The girls' room was easy to locate. Nothing but darkness behind the sturdy window grate. At the back of the house, light poured out of several windows. Robin crept to the border of a small swimming pool and peered through a sliding-glass door partially obscured with vertical blinds.

At one end of the room a man sat in a recliner, watching TV and smoking. Beside him on a small table was an oversized bowl of popcorn, a jumbo can of beer, and an overflowing ashtray. He resembled Linda Billings in coloring and facial structure.

Luther.

She saw no sign of anyone else. *Maybe I got lucky and the others have the night off.*

“Stand up slow and then don’t move a muscle.” A jab at her ribs indicated the speaker had a gun.

Robin froze for a second, unable to obey. When the speaker jabbed her ribs a second time she rose, as ordered. Without being told to, she raised her hands.

“Let’s go inside and see what Luther wants to do about you sneaking around on his patio.”

Her numbed brain functioned enough to make an attempt at an excuse. “I wasn’t sneaking. Sometimes I use the pool when nobody’s here.”

He thought about that. “Where’s your suit?”

She tried for a casual tone. “I don’t wear one.”

“Huh.” He sounded interested but didn’t change his mind. “Let’s go.” Taking a handful of Robin’s hair, he slid the door open and pushed her inside.

***

“I don’t like doing this,” Cam told Hua’s image on the phone.

“What have you done so far?”

“Nothing. Robin said you’d tell me what to do.”

Hua licked his lips. “You have to put Mrs. Billings in the back seat of her car.”

“But she’s dead.”

“I know that.”

“I don’t want to touch a dead person.”

“You don’t want Robin to get into trouble, do you?”

"No."

"Then we have to get this done." Hua considered for a moment. "You told me about your dad butchering cows, right? You helped with that."

"I didn't like it."

"But you did it for your family. We are your family now, so we will do this together."

There was a long pause, but finally Cam said, "Okay."

"Good. Set the phone down and drag the body into the back seat. Let me know when you're done."

Hua heard a car door open and some faraway grunts. When Cam returned he said, "She feels cold. And she's really heavy."

"I know. Now you're going to drive her car to the store where she met Em. Obey all the signs and travel at exactly the speed limit, so you don't get stopped on the way. Got it?"

"I always do that."

"Good."

"Can we leave the phone on so you can talk to me?"

"Sure." Hua hoped Cam's phone was fully charged.

As he drove, Cam reported everything he noticed along the way. At another time it might have been interesting, but since Hua was anxious to get their task done, the play-by-play was a little discomfiting.

"That guy's got a '55 T-bird for sale. The wire wheels look okay, but the tires are shot. Top's in pretty bad shape too. Body needs work."

Driving on he said, "It smells really nice down here, Hua, did you know that? I think it might be orange blossoms, but whatever it is, it's nice. I like flowers."

"Really." Cam seemed to have forgotten he had a dead body in the back seat.

A minute later he said, "Hey, they've got the new Captain America movie. I really want to see that. I wonder if they'll have a matinee tomorrow."

"I doubt you'll be in Florida tomorrow," Hua said. "You'll be coming home as soon as this is done."

When Cam reached the parking lot Hua said, "Find a spot with no video cameras and park there."

Cam didn't speak for a while, but finally he said, "I found a panel truck with a spot beside it."

"Good. Wait until it is clear then drag Linda out of the back seat and drop her by the driver's door."

"Drop her?"

"So it looks like she collapsed." When he didn't answer Hua added, "It won't hurt her, Cameron. She's dead."

"Oh. Yeah."

"Is anyone around?"

"There's a woman with two little kids. They shouldn't be out this late, and besides, it just started to rain."

"Good. Rain will wash away evidence the body was moved."

A few seconds later Cam said, "Okay. Nobody's here."

"All right. As quickly as you can, get her out, drop the keys beside her—are you wearing your gloves?"

"Yeah. Robin said to."

"Okay. Leave the driver's door open, but close the back door.

It has to look like she came there to shop and died suddenly." Hua tried to sound encouraging. "When you're done, walk away. Toss the gloves into the nearest waste container."

"How do I get back to the van?"

"It's safest if you walk, but you said it's raining. I can bring up the bus schedule."

"I kind of like walking in the rain," Cam said. "Can you stay on the phone, so we can talk?"

"Once you get rid of that corpse, Cameron, we'll talk as long as your battery lasts."

***

When Robin half-fell into Billings' beach house, the man in the chair looked up in surprise. A painful tug on her hair stopped her just inside the door, and she turned to see her captor. Almost as big as Cam, he was much less attractive, both in appearance and expression. It was easy to imagine his photo on a TV screen with the caption: CAN YOU HELP POLICE LOCATE THIS MAN?

The TV watcher spoke in a voice that matched his wimpy looks. "What you got there, Dave?"

"I was heading out to secure the boat and saw her peeking in the window.'"

"Huh." Luther turned in the chair to examine Robin. "What are you doing here?"

She tried the pool story, adding details she hoped made it more believable. When she finished he merely repeated the question. "What are you doing here?"

Concluding her energy was better spent thinking of a way to escape, Robin went silent. If Dave loosened his hold on her hair, if Luther looked away for a split second—

But they were used to handling captives. Dave's grip

remained firm, and Luther's eyes never left her face.

Despite the uselessness of regret, she spent a few seconds there. Though Mink had repeatedly advised they have a Plan B, she hadn't predicted something as weird as Billings' death. Now her desire to rescue the captives had resulted in an action that was well-intentioned but ill-conceived. And she would pay for it.

Should have called the police, even the fire department. The girls would be rescued and I might have lived through the night.

"What do we do with her?"

Luther's pale blue gaze rested on Robin. "Are you alone?"

"No. I called the police, and they're on their way. They'll find the girls—" She glanced down the hallway, realizing too late she'd revealed too much.

Your need to explain just clinched your death sentence.

A twitch showed in Luther's cheek. "Get her phone and ID."

Dave's hands searched her roughly, lingering briefly on her breasts before moving on to the pocket where the phone rested. She shivered in fear and disgust. "No ID. Just this." He tossed it to Luther, who checked the log. "Well, will you look at that? You didn't call the cops after all." He frowned. "How did you find us?"

"My friends know where I am. You're going to be arrested."

"If you had friends, they'd be here with you."

She'd played it all wrong. Em would have played dumb; Robin had *been* dumb.

After staring at her for a few seconds, Luther made his decision. "Take her out to the end of the dock and drown her."

Perfectly at ease with the command, Dave grabbed Robin by the neck. "No marks if you can help it," Luther warned. "It should look like suicide."

"Gotcha."

Robin started fighting then, but she didn't stand a chance. Dave simply put one hand over her mouth, the other around her waist, picked her up, and backed out the sliding door. She caught at the frame but only managed to scrape several layers of skin off her hands as he pulled her through with a strong jerk. Behind them Luther returned his attention to the TV. The last she saw of him, he was reaching for his beer.

Dave made his way clumsily over the sand, avoiding Robin's flailing hands and staggering a little as she threw herself from side to side.

Why did I come here alone? Why wasn't I more careful? Why did I ever think I was in any way qualified to take on professional criminals?

Don't count your mistakes. Think!

There was nothing she could do. In minutes she'd be drowned in the waters of the gulf. When her body floated to shore, Cam, Hua, and Em would know she hadn't committed suicide, but who would they tell? How would they explain their presence in Florida without admitting their own crimes? Worst of all, Luther and Dave would disappear once they realized Linda wasn't coming home, leaving six more corpses behind.

Suddenly Dave lurched to one side. At first she thought he'd stepped into a hole, but it was more than that. Something—make that some*one*—had hit him with the force of a football tackle. He fell hard onto the sand, almost squashing Robin beneath him. A second impact forced him to release his hold, and she rolled out of his grasp and pushed herself to her feet. What had just happened?

Grunts of exertion sounded, and she realized that Dave was wrestling with another man. Robin took a step toward the writhing figures, but it was too dark to see more than shadows. The newcomer was doing his best to keep the big man from getting to his feet.

Should she join the fight or seize the opportunity to escape? As she hesitated, the smaller man gasped out a command. "Robin—get help!"

Though her mind grappled with the impossibility of it, she recognized the voice: Tom Wyman.

"Go!" he urged, but the sound changed as a blow turned it to a grunt of pain.

However much she'd have liked to do as Wyman ordered, Robin saw no way to comply. Luther had taken her phone, and they were too far away from other residences to get help in time.

She was the only help Wyman was going to get.

Dave outweighed the detective by at least forty pounds. He had two hands, and he was without doubt the more ruthless of the two. It was up to her to help Wyman. She stepped forward and kicked at Dave's ribs, but her soft leather flats were useless as weapons. She needed a club.

On both sides of them, the high-tide line that deposited seaweed and shells stretched dark on the sand. Robin ran along it a few feet, looking for a rock or a sturdy piece of wood. Behind her the dull thud of a fist connecting with flesh sounded, and Wyman groaned in pain.

Faster!

Her toe hit something hard and she picked it up. It was a cowrie shell, too small and fragile to do her any good. A moment later her foot found something larger. Moving aside the soggy, slimy seaweed, she felt a fist-sized clump of coral. It was as good a weapon as she was likely to get. Behind her Wyman's breath came in gasps. Dave muttered a curse that signaled imminent victory.

Holding the coral in her fist, she hurried back. Dave had gained the upper hand and rolled over, straddling Wyman and pinning him to the ground. As he raised his fist to deliver a crushing final blow, Robin whacked him just above the ear, throwing her weight into it as if it were a tennis stroke. Dave roared in pain, his body teetered, and his hands fell to his side. She raised her makeshift weapon again, but he fell to the sand before she could deliver a second strike.

Wyman immediately pushed himself free and rose to his knees. "Here," he panted, pulling a zip tie from his jeans pocket. "Fasten his hands behind him before he gets his wits back."

Dave was already stirring, but with only a little fumbling

Robin wrapped the tie around his wrists and pulled it tight. Wyman put a second tie around the man's feet, though how he accomplished the task with one hand, she couldn't imagine.

When Dave was immobilized Wyman said, "We need to keep him quiet."

As if to demonstrate that need, Dave began making gibberish sounds. It wasn't loud, but he had not gone conveniently silent, the way bad guys do in the movies once the good guys defeat them. Pulling off her stretchy headband Robin asked, "Will this work?"

"We'll make it work." Wyman sat down on the sand and pulled off a shoe and sock. "Sorry, buddy." He stuffed the sock into Dave's mouth and put the elastic band around his head to hold it in place.

As Wyman pulled his shoe back on Robin said, "He was going to drown me."

"I figured," Wyman said. "It's a good thing Em called me, huh?"

Chapter Twenty-two

Though Robin's mind boiled with questions, there was no time to ask them. Wyman dragged Dave to an overturned rowboat and rolled him under it. "Now he can't scuttle along the beach and escape." Muted thumps from the boat indicated Dave's unhappiness with his makeshift prison.

Wyman staggered back to where Robin stood, his breathing still labored from the fight. Even in the dim moonlight, she could see his lip was bleeding. "Thanks for the rescue," he said.

"Likewise."

Gesturing at the house he asked, "What have we got in there?"

"Six victims of human trafficking. The woman in charge of selling them—well, she isn't coming back. Once the others realize that, they'll kill all six girls and take off."

"Who's guarding them?"

"I only saw one guy."

"We need to call the police."

She surveyed the remote location. "Luther will kill them before help can get here."

Wyman's silhouette showed against the white sand, and she saw him nod. "Okay. You and I take him out now and let the cops do cleanup afterward."

Across the beach, the sound of a sliding-glass door grating along its sandy track caught their attention. Ducking to a crouch, Wyman and Robin watched as Luther peered into the dark.

"Dave?" he called softly. "Dave?" When there was no response but wind and water, Luther's body tensed. Sliding the door closed, he clicked the lock into place.

"He's going to do it." Robin was up and heading for the door before Wyman could respond. When she reached the patio he was beside her, his presence reassuring even though she had no idea what they should do. Skirting the pool, she put her eye to the gap between the blinds. Luther sat at a computer, and his hands moved quickly over the keyboard.

"Destroying evidence," Robin whispered. "The girls will be next."

Wyman took hold of her arm and put his mouth close to her ear. "Go around to the front. Ring the bell, knock, make a lot of noise, and then hide. I'll go in this way and get them out."

She didn't stop to ask how he'd get in, but hurried away, avoiding lawn chairs and shrubbery with no grace at all. As soon as she was separated from Wyman, Robin felt oddly alone and isolated.

The door at the front of the house was wide and well-lit, with glowing sidelights that allowed those inside to see who waited on the porch. Since her presence hadn't scared Luther earlier, Robin doubted it would now. He knew she was unarmed, and he thought she was alone. He had to be convinced reinforcements had arrived.

With that in mind, she filled the pockets of her jeans with a half-dozen of the decorative stones that edged the driveway. Stuffing them in her pockets, she rang the doorbell for as long as she dared, pounded on the door a few times with her fist, and retreated behind a magnolia bush.

Luther came to the door and looked cautiously out the sidelight, his expression concerned. He held a gun in one hand.

Rising from the shadows, Robin launched the first of her missiles, which bounced harmlessly off the door. Luther stepped back, but when he saw the stone on the porch, he seemed more irritated than afraid. She threw a second rock, this time with better luck. It broke a sidelight panel with a sharp *ping* and fell onto the tiles inside. This time Luther glared out at the apparently empty yard.

When a crash resounded behind him, Luther turned, but Robin pitched another rock at the sidelight, bringing his attention back to the front. Her missile didn't break through, but the rattle did its job. Luther's mouth formed a swearword, and she sent yet another rock his way. That one broke a second pane of glass, sending shards tinkling onto the foyer floor.

More sounds at the back of the house forced Luther to make a decision. After glaring out the sidelight for a few more seconds, he turned and disappeared. As soon as he was gone, Robin left her hiding place and peered through the glass pane she had broken. Luther stood between the foyer and the TV room, with his back to her. He held a gun held loosely in his hand as he watched two men locked in a fierce struggle. One was Wyman; the other man brought to mind Jai's mention of someone named Gary. She should have warned Wyman there might be a third threat.

I have to get inside and help him.

Getting in wasn't difficult, since one of the stones she'd thrown left a hole big enough for her to simply reach through and unlock the door. Quietly she let herself in, avoiding the shards of glass on the tile floor. Luther calmly watched the men battle. Robin guessed he hoped Gary could subdue Wyman so he didn't have to risk a gunshot, but the gun would no doubt be the final decider of victory.

She had to take Luther out while he was distracted, but once again she was without a weapon. Near the door, a shadow box held an assortment of solid glass bird figurines. Choosing the one that best fit her hand, a plump woodcock, she moved toward Luther.

Something alerted him, or perhaps he remembered the distraction at the front of the house. Whatever the cause, Luther turned, saw Robin, and raised the gun at her. Before he could fire, Robin dropped the figurine and dived past him, seeking cover. She landed on the floor of the TV room with an impact that took her breath away. Her legs still worked, and she was already crawling behind the couch when Luther fired twice. *Bang! Bang!* The noise was deafening. Behind the sofa Robin lay panting, with ringing ears and more than a little panic in her brain. She'd never felt anything as terrifying as a pistol pointed at her by a man with no qualms about killing her.

As terrifying as Luther's action was for Robin, the interruption proved lucky for Wyman. From her position she could see that the two combatants were both surprised by the gunshots, but Wyman recovered first. Swinging his left fist up, he drove it into the taller man's chin with a force that sent his head snapping back. Gary's eyes lost focus, and Wyman turned sideways and punched his opponent in the gut with his elbow. He followed it up with a second punch to the face. Gary dropped to the floor, making no attempt to break his fall.

Luther turned his attention—and his gun—toward Wyman, who stood exposed not ten feet away. There was nowhere he could go to escape the next bullet, and Luther's expression revealed satisfaction in that knowledge. Wyman's face showed certainty that death was imminent.

No!

Pressing her back against the wall, Robin pushed the sofa hard with both feet. It lurched forward, catching Luther on the shins and unbalancing him. The shot went wide, and in the millisecond that followed, Wyman stepped forward and made a side-kick worthy of a Ninja Turtle. The gun flew from Luther's hand and landed on the floor a few feet away. Robin scuttled out on hands and knees to retrieve it. Gary was trying to stand up, and Luther crouched as if ready to attack, but she ordered, "Stay where you are. I took firearms training at the Y."

They elected to believe her. Speaking to Wyman, who stood with both hands on his knees as he struggled to recover from his second to-the-death contest of the evening, she said, "We need to release the girls. They're probably terrified after all this ruckus."

"They'll be less scared if a woman shows up," he panted. "I'll take the gun, and you go."

Having met Linda Billings, Robin doubted a woman would be all that reassuring, but she did as he suggested, glad to give up the gun and the responsibility that came with it.

Down a hallway off the kitchen was a door fastened closed. It took a while, but eventually she found the key hanging on a hook near the refrigerator. Unlocking the padlock, she opened the door and called softly, "Don't be afraid. I'm here to help you."

There was no answer, so she felt around and found the light switch. Illumination revealed a dozen army cots, half of them occupied, and dark eyes that examined her distrustfully. "Who speaks English?" After a moment, a girl raised her hand. "My name's Robin. What's yours?"

"Boonsri."

"Boonsri, please translate what I say for the others."

The girl nodded, and Robin began. "Jai told us how to find you. She and Mai are safe, and you are all free." She paused to let Boonsri tell the others that much. As she spoke, tension eased in some of the faces.

Robin explained that Linda Billings was dead and the men who'd guarded them were captured. "This isn't what America is supposed to be like," she told them. "These are very bad people, who will be punished for what they did. You all should wait here. Help is on the way."

Leaving Boonsri to translate that, Robin went back to the living room where Wyman stood guard over Luther and Gary, who now sat on the sofa looking glum. Quiet had descended on the room, but evidence of the struggle was everywhere: a broken lamp, an overturned table, and the foul smell of a spilled ashtray.

At Wyman's direction, Robin tied Gary and Luther to a couple of kitchen chairs with some cord she found in a junk drawer. Once they were secured, Wyman went outside and retrieved Dave, who was disoriented but able to follow instructions. Once he was tied to a third chair, Wyman led Robin onto the patio, where they couldn't be overheard.

"How do you want to do this?"

Before she answered, Robin ran a series of questions through her mind. What was the connection between Em and Wyman? Why was he in Florida? Why had Em sent him here? Did he intend to arrest her along with the others? Her future depended on a man who seemed like a friend but could still be a foe.

"I don't—" She didn't finish. *I don't have a plan. I don't want to go to jail. I don't know what you want from me.*

Apparently understanding her confusion, he took the lead. "Here's my plan. First we get rid of any evidence of who we are. Then we move our cars. There's a dock about a mile from here where we can call the police and watch while they arrest these guys. Once the girls are safe, we can tell each other stories."

Rather dazedly, Robin agreed. She and Wyman brushed away their footprints and wiped down places they'd touched, though it bothered her that Luther's pale gaze followed their every move. He seemed to be memorizing their faces.

Taking their respective cars, they went to the spot Wyman had mentioned. As she drove Robin considered escaping into the night, but she guessed Wyman would simply find her again, as he had several times now. In addition to that she'd begun to trust him, at least a little.

When they reached the end of the old dock Wyman called the local police, giving a terse explanation of the situation and the physical address. He used Robin's burner phone to make the call, and when he was finished, took out the memory card and destroyed it with the heel of his shoe. Using Wyman's phone, Robin called Em and reported that she, Wyman, and the girls were okay. Em didn't react to the news that she and Wyman were together. She merely reported that Cam had done his part and reached the rental house without any problems. "He says next time he'd rather rescue slaves than haul around a dead lady."

Wyman pocketed the phone she returned to him and leaned against the rickety handrail. "Now we watch the fun."

"Great," Robin replied, at least she thought she did. Her voice sounded far away, like a call across the water. The next thing she knew, she was sitting on the dock, her back resting against a rough wooden post. A face hovered near hers, but it was hard to tell who it was until he spoke.

"Are you okay?"

Wyman.

"Did I faint?"

"Yeah, I guess so. You scared the—You scared me."

Her face warmed, and she was glad the darkness hid her embarrassment. "Sometimes after a stressful situation I get all swoony, like some Victorian invalid." She turned her face away. "I don't know why I'm such a wimp."

"Wimp? Robin, one of those guys intended to drown you in the Gulf of Mexico and the other one shot at you. Over the last what—two hours?—you've dealt with multiple crises. That's some pretty extreme stress."

"But the danger is over, so it's stupid to have these panic attacks or whatever they are." She ran her fingers through her hair. "Em talks about playing it cool, and I try, but—"

Wyman sat down beside her. "It's PTSD, Robin. Soldiers returned from a war zone deal with it a lot."

"Did you?"

He was quiet for a moment. "You aren't human if you don't feel a difference between everyday life and what you experience in a life-and-death situation."

"So I'm not a baby?" The words were out of her mouth before she could stop them.

"What do you mean?"

Without making a conscious decision, she told Thomas Wyman something she'd never told anyone before. "If I cried or acted scared, my dad used to say, 'Don't be a baby.' When he hit one of us Mom would tell me, 'Don't cry. It makes him worse.'"

His voice was soft. "You learned to be tough until the threat was over, but a person can't ignore that kind of emotion forever."

She sighed. "I guess not."

Holding out his good hand, Wyman helped Robin to her feet. "Tears, shaking, even fainting. They're completely understandable reactions to trauma."

"You've had traumatic incidents. I bet you didn't faint

afterwards."

There was a smile in his voice. "We all react differently." Leaning his forearms on the railing, he went on. "What's important, Robin, is that you did what had to be done. If you'd fainted earlier, I'd be bleeding out on the floor of that house now."

"Oh." That was as close as she wanted to come to reliving the last hours, so she changed the subject. "How did you get here, Detective Wyman?"

He took a deep breath. "You know I was hired to find Carter. What you don't know is that I figured out Buckram was shifty within about ten minutes of meeting him."

When she made only a grunt of agreement, Wyman went on. "Ms. Kane, Em, said she didn't know where her former neighbor was, but later she said he'd moved out west somewhere. When I finally found you at home, I got the feeling there were things you weren't sharing."

Robin's voice was tinged with humor as she asked, "Because of the cat in the closet?"

Even in the darkness she could tell he was smiling. "Did you know your nose gets red when you tell a lie?"

She frowned. "I'm getting better at it."

Now there's something to be proud of!

The headlights of several cars turned onto the road to Billings' house. The lights went out, one by one, and Wyman said, "I told them to proceed with caution."

Though they couldn't see what was happening, Robin pictured the police finding the frightened girls and the bound traffickers.

“What do you think those men will tell the police?”

“My guess is they’ll say nothing. People in their line of work don’t talk to cops, or they don’t live very long.” He chuckled softly. “Besides, they’ll be reluctant to admit three of them were taken by two unarmed attackers, a female and a male amputee.”

“You did pretty well, despite the disadvantage.”

“Thanks. I’ve been working on it.” His casual reply reminded Robin of her brother. Wyman had the same spirit as Chris, the will to maximize his abilities and ignore his disabilities.

“You were telling me how you came to play the knight in shining armor tonight.”

“Yes.” Wyman spoke softly. “One day when I went to the apartments, I learned that you were moving out. Em said you’d lost your job and planned to relocate, but I was starting to get a read on her. The more she doesn’t want to answer a question, the more corny sayings she tosses in. Since she was throwing them in like crazy, I wondered what she was nervous about.”

“So you hung around.”

“We got to be friends.” His tone of voice changed slightly. “Em was lonely, and I admit I used that. I’d stop by, and we’d chat. Her no-bakes are pretty good, don’t you think?”

She turned to face him. “No-bakes? Really?”

“Okay, okay.” Wyman’s teeth flashed white in the moonlight. “One day while Em was getting me a cup of coffee, I snooped through her desk. I found a sticky note with a phone number and your name written on it. It wasn’t the one I had for you in my notes, so I memorized it.”

“Which is how you got the number of my throwaway cell.”

“Yes.”

"But why did you care where I was going?"

He was silent for a while, and Robin got the feeling she wouldn't hear the whole truth. "You didn't seem like the criminal type, despite your family history."

"You know about my dad?"

"A little." He seemed embarrassed to know her secrets. "He's been arrested a few times in the last ten years."

"Good," she said. Looking across the water, she thought about Luther, probably under arrest by now. He too had been raised by a criminal parent, but he'd taken to it more than she had. Luther seemed to enjoy the role of controlling others through force and intimidation. Robin hoped she never got to the point where she did. If that meant panic attacks and frequent bouts of worry, she'd accept them. It meant she was still human.

Shifting his feet on the wooden planking, Wyman got back to his story. "I'd become more and more suspicious of Abrams, who kept calling to see if I'd located Carter Halkias. I started digging and learned his cousin bought the Halkias farm last winter." His face turned toward her in the darkness. "The commissioner cheated Carter and you got back at him somehow, right?"

"Mrs. Halkias was sick and he took advantage of her."

He clicked his tongue. "He's really mad at you."

"At me?"

"Well, you and Carter."

"He goes by Cameron now, or Cam." *Why do I trust this guy? He could still turn us in to the cops.*

Wyman nodded. "So Halkias was gone, you were leaving town, and I suspected Abrams was crooked. I told my client I'd found no trace of the guy, which was true. The case was over."

“Until—?”

“Until I caught Em packing for a trip.”

“I thought you said the case was over.”

“It was, but I had the feeling there was a lot I didn’t know. And besides—” He paused. “Em reminds me of my grandmother.”

“Your grandmother carries a snub-nosed .38 Special?”

Wyman laughed aloud. “Gram’s long dead, but like Em, she always refused to act like an old lady.”

“Why did you care if Em was leaving town?”

“I didn’t, except she tried too hard to convince me the trip was no big deal. It was the first time I’d seen her really nervous.” Now his grin lit the darkness. “Idioms and adages flew thick and fast.”

Robin imagined Em’s last-minute nerves as she prepared to abet two amateur kidnappers in the abduction of a senator. With their inexperience and her physical limitations, she’d had plenty to worry about.

“What did you do?”

A rustle of clothing indicated a shrug. “I didn’t have any other cases at that point.”

“You followed us to Richmond.”

“Yeah. You can imagine my surprise when the missing Carter Halkias and the supposedly-relocating Robin Parsons joined Em and took off together. I watched you guys for several days, but nothing I saw made sense. There was a van that needed work. There was a dog that needed a few square meals. And the last night? What I saw then was pretty freaky.”

“You saw...” She found it difficult to put into words.

"An abduction. I followed Em downtown and saw her set a guy up. I saw you and Car—Cameron pull him into the van and take off."

"And after that?"

"I was on foot when it happened. All I could do was follow Em home and confront her about what I'd seen."

"And she said—?"

Wyman put a hand to his chest in mock horror. "She said she was shocked. She'd been afraid to tell anyone what happened. She said she was going home to Cedar, where people didn't get abducted in dark alleys."

"But the fact she was there at all told you she was lying."

"Oh yeah." He chuckled. "Eventually, she told me everything except the names of the kidnappers, but I already knew that part."

"Why didn't you go to the police?"

Again she got the sense she wouldn't get the whole truth. "I'm not sure. I'd managed to get one photo of the abduction with my phone. With it, I identified the victim, one Senator Buckram. I called his office Monday morning and learned he was doing business as usual. That meant you hadn't hurt him, so I figured what Em had told me was the truth: You kidnapped the guy to teach him a lesson, just like you did with Barney Abrams."

"Some would say crime in the name of fairness is still crime."

Wyman turned to face her. "A lot of people think you can end hatred by killing other people too. That doesn't make it true, and I learned it the hard way. You don't hurt anybody, but you rack up points against the bad guys when you can. I admire that." He looked down the beach to where the police lights were now flashing. "They wouldn't be on your side, but I am."

Suddenly Robin felt a lot less tired. “I guess I should thank you, Mr. Wyman.”

He chuckled again. “*I* guess after all we’ve been through tonight, you might consider calling me Tom.”

Chapter Twenty-three

When Tom and Robin joined Em an hour later, she introduced them to Mai and Jai. Robin had to assure them several times that the other girls were safe; that Luther, Dave, and Gary, were under arrest; and that Linda Billings was dead.

"You kill her? Very good!" Jai told Robin when she first broke the news.

"No, I didn't kill her."

Jai looked at Wyman. "He did it then? Still good."

"Nobody killed her. She just died."

Jai thought about that. "Too bad. She needed killed."

As they spoke, Mai looked from one face to another, obviously confused. She understood only simple commands in English. Everything else Jai explained in their native language, Bijiang.

Em put a hand on the girl's thin shoulder. "Jai, help your sister understand that you're safe with us. Then try to get some rest."

Jai nodded, but she gestured at Tom and Robin. "You will tell them what I said?"

"I will."

Jai led Mai down the hallway to the room Em had assigned them, already jabbering and gesturing. When they were out of earshot Em said, "She says they won't go back to Vietnam."

Robin huffed in surprise. "What does she want to do—get a job at Epcot?"

“She says they’ll stay with us and do whatever we need done.”

“Stay with us,” Robin repeated blankly. “Because we need more people to take care of?”

“No concerns with those girls,” Em said. “Jai is a smart cookie and Mai does whatever her sister says.”

“But we can’t just keep taking people in, Em,” Robin argued. “We aren’t wealthy, we aren’t legitimate, and we aren’t an amnesty hostel for illegal aliens.”

“You just took a million dollars from those slavers. Hua can make the girls papers, like he did for himself.” As a final argument she added, “There’s plenty of room in the house.”

Wyman, who’d listened silently to the conversation for some time, cleared his throat. “That’s good to know. I was thinking you might be able to use the services of a former military, former private investigator.”

***

Tom Wyman prepared to leave the rented house early the next morning, promising to join them once he closed his apartment in Cedar. Robin did her best to convince him not to make such a drastic change in his life for them, but he was cheerfully adamant.

“What am I giving up?” he argued. “As far as private investigation goes, my partner and I have serious differences of conscience, so our future together isn’t looking good. Other than that I have an apartment I never liked much and a few guys I drink beer with and tell lies to on Friday nights.”

“That’s better than ending up in prison, which is probably what will happen if you join us.”

“You underestimate yourself,” he said. “Your KNPs actually do something about the blatant criminals who hide behind the law in this country. No one knows about them except your targets, and they can't tell without exposing their own crimes." He raised his coffee cup in salute. "It's pretty genius, I think."

Robin eventually stopped arguing, though she believed Tom was overly optimistic. Since he seemed determined to be a part of their enterprise, she gave him the address of her storage unit and a key to the padlock. "Haul your stuff out there and put it in with mine. That way you can have it all back in a month or two if you decide your urge to join us was misguided." When she walked him to his car, she thought of one more point that might dissuade him. "You're going to have to give up driving this car, because it's too identifiable. There's a shed behind our house you can leave it in."

"That sounds fair. I did hope I wouldn't have to give up my baby to become an official KNP operative."

Tom scrubbed at his chin, which needed a shave—or maybe not. Robin asked herself why she'd ever thought him scary-looking. Right now, with stubble or without, he looked pretty darned good to her.

***

They started north that afternoon, once they'd determined there was no police search for any of them. Cam and Em rode in the car, playing Mom and Sonny Boy on vacation. Robin drove the van, now identified as a floral delivery vehicle with the addition of a magnetized sign. Jai and Mai rode in the back, dressed as teenaged boys, their long hair hidden under knit hats. Though they were beginning to believe they really were free, Robin stressed to Jai the need to blend in until identities could be created for them.

The knowledge that Wyman would soon join them gave Robin a sense of security she hadn't felt in a while. She'd come to care deeply for Cam, Em, and Hua, but Tom offered something else. Intelligent, experienced, and decisive, he'd be a strong partner. That didn't seem to cover everything, but she was afraid to examine too closely what else he might be to her.

They'd planned to meet at a Denny's outside St. Louis. Tom wasn't there when they arrived. "It's probably taking longer than he thought to get his stuff into storage," Em said. "He'll be here soon, or he'll call."

As they waited, Em came as close to apologizing as she ever did. "I was going to tell you about Tom after this caper. I didn't like hiding things from you, but I wanted to be sure he fit with us before I brought him in."

"He's the one who texted the warning during the Comdon intervention."

She nodded. "He tried to talk to you that night, but he said you weren't ready to trust him."

"So he's been watching over us, like a fairy godfather."

Em shrugged. "It seemed good that someone more physically able than me was keeping an eye on you."

"Was he around for Niven and Uncle Bill?"

"No." Em sipped at her coffee and winced. "Hot!"

Robin thought she was more worried about admitting her lies than she was about the coffee. "You called him after we got back."

"The boy was like an ant in my underwear," she said defensively. "He was all worried about you." When Robin said nothing, she went on, "He's getting a prosthesis, so he had to spend a week in Cleveland. He'll soon have two hands again and be fit as a fiddle."

"Good to know." Robin drank the last of her orange juice, letting Em squirm a little before she admitted, "I guess I'm lucky he got back in time to rescue me."

"Like I said, he's very interested in what you're up to." She stirred more sugar into her coffee and tasted it tentatively. "Can't imagine what that's all about, can you?"

Robin poured dressing on her salad to avoid meeting Em's eyes. "I hope he lets us know where he is pretty soon. We have to move on."

Wyman never called, and after they'd waited two hours, they continued their journey home. "When he calls, I'll explain how to get to the house," Em said as she eased her way into the car. "We should have known he couldn't just pick up and leave Cedar in a few hours."

Robin's thoughts were darker. With time to think, Tom might have decided he'd been hasty in his decision to join with the daughter of a small-time criminal to engage in activities that were dangerous and felonious. If that was the case, she hoped Tom hadn't also concluded he had to put an end to their KNPs.

***

When they reached home, Wyman still hadn't called. Em at first excused him, but as the hours went on, she became angry and even apologetic. "I really thought he was telling the truth."

Robin dialed Wyman's number again. No answer. Checking the log, she saw it was her sixth attempt. Something was wrong.

"Should we leave while we have the chance?" Hua asked.

They had to consider it. If Wyman had lied in order to learn where their base was, the authorities might even now be closing in on them. Their best bet might be to disappear in the night and start over somewhere else.

"No." Though Robin didn't know what the truth was, she felt certain Tom hadn't infiltrated their group in order to betray them. "Something happened that changed his plans. We need to find out what that was."

She called Mink, who agreed to go to Wyman's apartment to learn what he could. Two hours later the lawyer called to report, "His landlord's had no notice Wyman is moving out."

Thanking Mink, Robin relayed to the others what he'd said. After a long pause Hua said, "Maybe he had an accident on the way to Cedar."

"Yeah," Cam said, "he could be in the hospital with amnesia or something."

Em stared out the window, her expression grim. "That's the lesser of two evil possibilities, my friends."

The chill that settled on the group brought the twins' fears back. Jai understood that Tom's failure to show meant trouble. Though Mai was less aware, her eyes followed her sister's every move, as if wondering what terrible thing loomed over them now.

Unsure what to do about Tom's absence, Robin decided to address a problem she could actually do something about. "I'll get a room ready for the girls." To Jai she said, "The upstairs is a little cramped. Since we didn't plan on having company, we stored some remodeling stuff in the vacant rooms."

"We are grateful for what you give," Jai assured her.

"There's no bed, but I bought every blanket and sheet they had at The Red Shield Store when we moved in. We'll use them to make the floor comfy until we can get you some furniture."

"Um, Robin?" Cam said. "Can we talk to you for a minute?" Hua had stood and moved to his side, his expression serious. Cam rubbed his shirt front as if scratching an itch.

"Sure." They went out into the hallway. Hua closed the door after them, shutting out Em's suspicious stare. For a few seconds neither man spoke, but finally Hua took a breath and nodded as if to encourage himself. "The girls can have my place."

Robin jumped to the wrong conclusion. "Hua, you're not going anywhere. Those slavers—"

"He's moving in with me." Cam put an arm around Hua's shoulders. "We're an item."

She was dumbstruck, and together they started explaining. "We've been talking about it for a while—"

"We don't want you to be shocked—"

"It isn't anybody's business but ours—"

"But it's okay, really."

"I can move all the computers. Everything will be excellent."

Finally catching up, Robin looked at them, standing with arms touching—at least as much as a six-foot plus man's arm matched with one who barely topped five feet. She chided herself for being slow. "I'm surprised, guys, but not shocked. You're adults, and you can sleep wherever you choose."

Cam punched Hua on the arm so hard that he staggered a little. "I told you she's cool."

Hua said formally, "We will move everything tomorrow. Then the twins can have their own space."

"No hurry," Robin assured. "Wherever they sleep, they're better off than they've been for some time."

When the girls were closed in their temporary bedroom upstairs and Em had been apprised of the men's secret, Robin retreated to her own room. Bad scenarios returned, playing like crime dramas with no happy ending. Was Tom under arrest somewhere? If so, she, Cam, and Em would soon join him, charged with multiple crimes. Hua, Jai, and Mai would be deported. If he wasn't under arrest (or afflicted with amnesia), Tom's situation was even worse. If it wasn't the police who prevented him from joining them, then who?

The next morning Hua supplied a possible answer. "I have been looking at text messages," he told them as he poured water over a bowl of Cheerios. Hua didn't like milk, and he claimed water was healthier anyway.

"Whose text messages?" Em asked.

Hua shoveled another spoonful in, chewed, and swallowed. "In order to be certain our targets do not violate the terms of the agreements, I monitor their communications." Waving his spoon he began, "It takes a little spear-phishing to get them hooked, but once you get a person to click on—"

"No hacker how-to's," Em ordered. "Just tell us what you found out."

Hua obligingly reported only the pertinent information. "Your first target, Mr. Barney Abrams, contacted your most recent one, Linda Billings."

"Abrams sent a message to Billings?"

Hua nodded. "She did not reply, due to her being dead, but it interested me that he was aware of her existence. It turns out Mr. Abrams contacted Thomas Wyman's partner, Ms. Cynthia Tinker, a few weeks ago. Their first meeting was face-to-face, so I don't know what was said, but judging from recent messages, Ms. Tinker followed Mr. Wyman to Florida."

"Abrams must have gotten suspicious when Tom said he couldn't find Cam," Em said.

"He hired the partner to watch him," Robin murmured. "Tom said they had philosophical differences."

"So Tinker followed Tom, which means she might have

stumbled into the mess at Billings' beach house. I wonder what she thought of that."

Em asked, "Hua, are you keeping track of Luther Billings and his buddies?"

"They were charged with harboring illegal aliens," he replied, adding glumly, "They pled not guilty and were released after posting bail."

Robin stared at him. "How do slave traders get out on bail?"

"Human trafficking is hard to prove." Em took a bagel out of the toaster, dropped it onto a napkin, and shook her burnt fingers. "The cops often charge trafficking suspects with harboring illegals in order to gain time to gather more evidence, but that's a charge for which bail is allowable. If they have the money, they get out."

"What about the scared girls who were locked in that house?"

Hua had an answer. "No doubt they've been told bad things will happen to them in the American justice system. It will take time and counseling to get them to reveal what they know."

Robin sighed. "What's the penalty for harboring illegal aliens?"

"It's fairly tough," Em replied, "but you can bet Luther and his buddies won't hang around to face their punishment."

Hua nodded. "They're already headed to another country."

"No," Robin said as the truth struck her. "They've got Tom."

There was a moment of silence as the others considered her statement. "How would they have found him?"

"I don't know." She rose and started pacing. "But we almost a million dollars of their money. They'll offer to trade Tom for it."

Em set the bagel aside. "They won't let him live, even if you give the money back. They'll kill you too."

"I know. They'll set up some sort of trap."

After a few seconds Cam said, "I thought Thomas Wyman was a really bad guy, but he isn't. He's pretty nice."

"It is my fault he is in this precarious situation," Hua said. "If we knew where this trapping of Robin will take place, we could arrive first and perhaps rescue Mr. Wyman."

Robin frowned at his use of *we*, but Em noticed and said, "He's right. They won't expect you to have help."

Cam had set his phone aside, the current game forgotten. "What are we going to do, Robin?"

"First we find out where he is," she replied. "Then we go get him."

While Cam checked out the car and packed items they might need, Hua and Robin studied Barney Abrams' communications carefully. An old-fashioned type, Commissioner liked email, while Cynthia Tinker preferred texting. Since Robin was better at decoding the often cryptic text messages, Hua set it up so she could scroll through those while he re-read Abrams' emails. Her first discovery came when she found Tom's initials.

FLLWED TW TO FL Tinker had sent three days earlier. In another message, Robin found TW FLLWD GIRL TO HOUSE. Farther down, she found COPS EVRWHR, and later, NO SIGN OF W-ARRESTED?

"She thought the police went to Billings' house to arrest Wyman," she told Hua. "The way the place is situated, she'd have had a hard time seeing who it was they took away."

"Mr. Abrams sent her an email the next morning." Hua read from his computer screen, "*Check out the house once the cops leave and see what you can find out.*"

"Oh, no," Robin moaned.

"What is it?"

"You said Luther and the other two were released on bail. What if they caught her out there?"

"That would be bad for her."

"And for Tom. If they made her talk, they got his name and address."

Hua shut the computer down. "We must go now. I can do the rest of this while you drive."

Em disapproved of the trip, and she made a final attempt to prevent it as they joined Cam at the car. "How will you find Tom? You don't even know where to start looking."

"We'll go to his place and work backward," Robin said, though Em's brows remained pinched. "I have to go, Em. He saved my life. I have to do the same for him, or at least try."

"It's the wildest of wild goose chases," Em insisted. "He could show up here a half hour after you leave, and you'll just have to turn around and come back."

"Best case scenario, Em. I won't mind a bit if we turn around at the Mason-Dixon Line." Robin gave Em a brief hug, and for once she didn't shy away. In her ear Robin said, "I know Tom might already be dead. But if Luther wants his money, he'll keep him alive long enough to lure me in."

"But remember—"

"I know. He wants us both dead."

"He probably already tried to beat your location out of the poor guy." Em spread a hand over her face, and Robin suspected she wiped away tears before she slid it down to her collarbone. “They won’t believe he doesn’t know it.”

“We have to find him before Luther decides he isn’t worth keeping around anymore.”

“I know,” she tried to smile. “I’m just sulking because there’s nothing I can do to help.” As Robin climbed into the car, Em called out, “We’ll keep the home fires burning, so don’t leave us in the dark.”

Chapter Twenty-four

For once Robin and Cam didn't have to argue Hua out of taking his turn driving. He worked on his tablet nonstop in the back seat of the RAV4, trying to eliminate places they didn't need to go. "Satellite shows the Billings' house is empty," he reported. "Not likely they'd remain there." A few minutes later he said, "Oh-oh."

"What?"

"You know the internet pays attention to searches and often shows news that matches sites where you've recently been."

"Yes. Shop for shoes on-line and you get ads from Zappos."

"Here is a news item from the Florida gulf coast. A woman's body washed up near the Billings house this morning."

Robin smacked the steering wheel with a hand. "Tinker!"

"The identification is confidential at the moment, but they say the victim is thought to be a woman from Georgia."

Massaging a knot that formed between her eyebrows Robin said, "They found out what she knew then drowned her, like they tried to do to me." After a second she added, "They'll probably blame Tom for it."

"It will seem the woman followed him, putting her nose into his business, so he got rid of her."

"That's how the police will see it." Robin's mind took the scenario one step further. If Tom were dead, he'd be unable to set the record straight. End of investigation.

"Robin, your phone's ringing," Cam said. The ID said UNKNOWN, but seeing that the caller was from Florida, she steeled herself for bad news. "Hello?"

"Is this the woman who breaks into people's homes and causes trouble?"

Robin recognized Luther's fluty, almost immature voice.

"Is this the guy who buys and sells children?"

"I've got someone of yours." His voice faded as he spoke to someone else. "Say hello to your girlfriend."

Tom's deeper voice came on the line. "Robin, don't do what he says. He's going to kill me whether you show up or not."

"Tom?"

"That was him," Luther said cheerfully. "Now he might be right about the killing part. I am seriously thinking of letting Dave slice him in a few places so we can watch him bleed out." He let that sink in for a moment. "Of course, you have the power to change my mind."

"What do you want?"

"You took a large chunk of our money, so here's the deal. Give it back, and we'll give you Detective Tom here in exchange." His voice turned dark as he added, "And I'll forget what you did to my mother."

"I can't get at the money easily. It's, um, tied up."

Luther's laugh belonged in a cheap horror movie. "Then rob a bank, or start a GoFundMe page. You've got until tomorrow night."

"Let's say I get it. What happens then?"

"You'll bring it—in person, alone—to a spot near Cedar. We'll get specific next time we talk."

Robin's mind went in a dozen directions as she tried to find an advantage. “Let me talk to him.”

“You heard him. He’s alive.”

“I want him to tell me he’s okay.”

She heard Luther speak to Tom. “Here. Tell your girlfriend you’re all in one piece.” He chuckled as he added, “At least that you got all the pieces you had when we caught up with you.”

“Robin? I’m okay.”

Knowing Luther was listening, she said what she had to. “I’ll get them the money. Don’t worry.”

“That’s good, honey. I’d like nothing better than to be back in your big old bed with the oak headboard.”

Though she had no idea what that meant, she played along. “Me too.”

The call ended abruptly, and she imagined Luther grinning malevolently at Tom.

“What did they say?” Hua asked.

She repeated it as exactly as she could in order to puzzle out for herself what Tom had tried to tell her. “The part about my bed is strange.”

“Why do you say that?”

“I’m pretty sure he’s never seen my bed.” She explained that Cameron had hidden in the bedroom on Wyman’s only visit to her apartment. “The door was closed, so how does he know I’ve got an oak headboard?”

“Perhaps he searched your apartment after you left.”

“She had everything put in storage,” Cam said. “I helped her take the bed apart for the movers.”

Cam grabbed the dashboard as Robin reacted, sending the van slewing toward the ditch. "The storage unit!" she said, steering back onto the road. "Luther said we'd meet at a spot *near* Cedar, not *in* it. Tom was letting us know they've got him at the unit."

"So we can go let him out?" Cam asked.

"It won't be that simple. Somebody, maybe all three of them, will be guarding him."

Hua's round face lengthened. "It's my fault your friend's life is in danger. I will make the exchange."

"That won't work, Hua. They want me to do it."

"I could dress in your clothing."

Robin suppressed a smile at the idea of the five-foot-nothing Hua pretending to be five-ten. "You and I don't look much alike."

Disappointment sounded in his voice, "If it were nighttime, perhaps it could work."

Robin rubbed her chin. "You should call Em. We're going to need everyone's help this time."

***

They reached Cedar at eight the next morning, which left them the whole day to prepare. Robin had Hua and Cam drop her off at a car rental agency and sent them to purchase items they'd listed as they drove. After renting a mid-sized SUV, she found a Goodwill store and bought a fluttery floral-print dress, a straw hat with a huge, floppy brim, and platforms so high she clopped like a horse. Dressed in her new finery, she drove to the Ur-Place Storage Lot.

As Robin parked the car, she paid better attention to the layout than she had before. The facility was big, with 192 units broken into sections of sixteen per square. Her original unit, #121, was situated at the back of a square at the end of the second row. Using one of her false identities, she rented a second unit in the same building, #124.

That done, Robin drove to a park where she and the guys had agreed to meet. Knowing it might be a long night she tried to nap, but her mind wouldn't stop churning. What if she'd misunderstood Tom's message? What if they'd already killed him? What if? In the park's smelly little rest room, she changed into shapeless black pants and a hoodie, what Em called her "caper outfit."

Cam and Hua arrived with a bucket of chicken and all the fixings. Robin tried to eat a little, telling herself she needed strength, but every morsel tasted like dirt. When they finished eating, the men transferred the items they'd bought to the rental then sat on the grass and played games on their phones. Robin sat under some trees, biting her nails and worrying.

Luther called at four, ordering Robin in curt sentences to come to the Ur-Place Storage Lot at ten that evening. When he gave her the code for the automated gate, she pretended to write it down. She tried to sound reluctant to meet in such an isolated spot, but Luther promised glibly that she and Tom would both be fine. *Yeah right!* Still, Robin was pleased to know she'd figured out Tom's clue. They were a step ahead of the bad guys.

Em and the girls arrived at six, proud of the fact they'd made good time despite what Em termed the "clunkiness" of the van. "It's about as comfortable as a buckboard on a two-track," she said, "but it goes down the road all right."

At six, car keys were exchanged. Em took the rental, Hua and Cam the van, and Robin drove the RAV. She arrived long before the appointed time, parked the car some distance away on a side road, and walked the quarter mile to the storage lot. The RAV was Plan B. If things went wrong, everyone in the group knew where it was and where the keys were. Those who could would escape.

Robin approached the security fence on the back side of the lot, climbed it like a grunt at boot camp, and dropped softly onto the grass. Listening for a moment, she heard nothing but birds making settling-in-for-the-night sounds. Moving into the shadows of one of the buildings, she found a spot where she could see the unit she'd rented long ago and hunkered down to wait for dark.

The temperature dropped as night fell, and she soon wished she could move and warm her muscles a little. Shivering in the cool night air, it was easy to recall the panic of that first KNP. There'd been the fear of discovery, fear of not being good enough to pull it off, fear of failure and its result, prison. She felt those things more strongly now. Added to them was the fear of dying.

Still, the present situation was different. She'd spent months learning how to think like criminals, how to beat them at their own game. She'd learned to consider every eventuality. She'd practiced setting her emotions aside in order to act with confidence. She'd even accepted the value of her father's lessons on how to play on the expectations of others. Though Mark had used "people skills" for his own ends, Robin tried to develop hers in pursuit of justice. Tom Wyman, a man of strong moral fiber, had seen the laudable intention behind their crimes, so she didn't think they were deluding themselves about the value of their work. If she used her father's teachings to make the world a better place, it was the ultimate rejection of him and his smug belief in Me First.

Her cell phone vibrated, and she answered softly. "Hello?"

"Where are you?" Luther asked.

"I'm in a restaurant on I-20, almost there."

"Do you have the money?"

"Most of it. I have to hit one more ATM before I meet you." It wasn't a complete lie. They'd brought enough cash to make a convincing show.

"Okay. Don't be late or he's dead." He ended the call.

As she slid her phone into her pocket, a car entered the lot. The light-colored Subaru headed down the row to the storage unit where Tom was being held. As it passed, Robin glimpsed four heads—three human, one canine.

The car stopped outside Unit #124. Two slight figures in hooded jackets got out and rolled the door of the unit open. From the back of the SUV they began unloading power tools and long, thin boxes marked *IKEA*. Soon boards started slapping against each other, a hammer pounded, and an electric drill whined.

It didn't take long for the door of Unit #121 to rumble upward, a few feet. Robin recognized Gary as he peered out, frowning in the direction of the noise. Ducking out, he closed the door behind him and approached the newcomers. When a dog met him halfway, growling in warning, he stopped. The woman who'd driven the SUV stepped out of the unit. "Behave, Dog!"

"Does he bite?"

She shrugged. "Only if you get too close."

Gary stayed where he was, but he pointed. "What are you doing in there?"

"My nephews are making me shelves," she replied.

"Shelves?"

"I collect dolls." As if he'd asked for details, she launched into a long explanation. "I find them everywhere, in catalogs, in stores, everyplace I go. I have dolls from all over the world.

They're beautiful, just beautiful. It's hard to decide which one is my favorite. You know, it's just hard to decide something like that."

Gary winced as the drill apparently hit something metal. "You're putting shelves in there. For dolls."

"My room at senior living is really small. A friend suggested I could adapt a storage unit and make a little doll museum." Her hands made a fan-like gesture. "You only get the full effect when you see them all at once."

"Dolls."

Gary, you'll never win a prize for sparkling conversation.

"Some of them are pretty special. I have an African Ndebele, some wonderful Matryoshka nesting dolls, and two rare American Girls. Would you like to see them?"

Robin gasped at the invitation. *What if he says yes?*

"Uh, no thanks." Gary took a step backward.

Her enthusiasm didn't flicker. "Stop by later, when the shelves are up and the dolls are set out."

He chewed at his lip. "Any chance you could come back and do this some other time?"

"I don't see why I should. It's a free country." Reacting to her tone, the dog gave a growl of warning.

He spit into the grass beside the road. "How long you think you're going to be?"

"I promised the boys' mom they'd be home by midnight. Kids these days are so busy, it's hard to find a time when they can help their old granny out." Her tone warmed again. "But it's going to be great not to have my babies shut up in boxes." As if it had occurred to her for the first time, she tilted her head. "What are you doing out here so late?"

For a moment Robin thought the boundaries of what one person is allowed to ask another had been overstepped, but age apparently excused nosiness. "A friend is bringing stuff he wants me to store for him," Gary replied. "He must have got held up."

"Well, I'm going to check on the boys," Em said, backing away. "Soonest begun, soonest ended." Bennett remained where he was, aware that he was on guard duty.

Returning to the unit, Gary took out his phone and made a call. Robin couldn't hear what he said, but after he did some explaining he listened, nodded, and slid the phone into his pocket. Almost immediately Robin's phone pulsed against her side.

She retreated to the next row of units before answering. With the noise Jai and Mai were making, pounding, grinding, and smacking bits of wood together, it wasn't likely Gary would hear her talking, but she didn't want Luther to figure out she was already at the lot.

"Hello?"

"Where are you?"

"I've got the money."

"We hit a little snag. It'll have to be later, around midnight."

"Why?"

"What difference does it make?"

"I want to get this over with."

"Me too, lady, but stay where you are. I'll call when things are settled."

Robin ended the call, pleased by the frustration evident in

Luther's voice. He was on the run. He had no money and no resources. His chance for escape was delayed by an event out of his control. She hoped that meant he'd make mistakes. Lots of mistakes would be perfectly acceptable.

When she returned to a spot with a slant-eyed view of Unit #121, Gary was pacing in front, a newly-lit cigarette in hand. He'd pulled the door down to about two feet off the ground.

The better to hide the prisoner. Robin wished she could see into the unit. Was Tom really in there? Was he all right? Were Hua and Cam doing their part?

Noise continued from #124, but Em came back outside and wandered toward Gary, apparently bored. Robin heard snatches of what she revealed: a recently-deceased husband, a move to a smaller living space, and a fondness for nesting dolls. He listened and nodded, though his expression revealed no real interest.

As they'd planned, Mai and Jai's pounding in their unit made it uncomfortable to remain inside the other. In addition to driving Gary out, the noise would cover sounds Hua and Cam made as they used metal snips to cut a hole in the side wall of #121. With luck, they'd get Tom out through the opening and into the rental car undetected. As soon as that was done, Em would get him and the girls out of there. Cam, Hua, and Robin would climb the fence, the guys would leave in the van, and Robin would call the police to report suspicious activity at the lot before driving away in the RAV.

Their plan hit a bump when two vehicles rounded the end of the row and approached the spot where Gary waited. Robin's heart sank. Luther was driving Linda Billings' car, and Dave followed in Tom's black Mustang. It was, as Em would say, "Time to book."

They stopped their vehicles and got out, but Dave left the Mustang's engine running. The low roar of the after-market pipes interfered with Robin's ability to hear what was said. She heard, "—tell 'em to get lost," but Luther shook his head. His hands moved as he explained something, probably that they couldn't afford to raise anyone's suspicions, since they planned to commit a couple of murders in the near future.

Dave had ducked into the unit, apparently to check on the prisoner, and he re-emerged, his face a mask of anger. "Gone!" she heard him say. In a typically human reaction, Luther had to see for himself. Gary followed him inside, and their voices rose with outrage when they saw the hole in the metal wall.

Em and the girls had accelerated their movements when Dave and Luther arrived. Em ordered Bennett into the vehicle and followed him in. Jai closed the hatch then squeezed in beside Mai on the passenger seat. They had to get out before their enemies realized the appearance of a slightly loony woman and her noisy helpers represented more than a minor delay to their plans.

Dave had already turned his gaze in their direction. "Stop!" he called. When Em paid no attention, he pulled a gun from the waistband of his jeans. Taking a position in the center of the road he aimed at the car, his stance indicating he was no amateur shooter. Robin gauged the distance between herself and Dave. Could she reach him before he fired at Em? With a heart-stopping pang of dread she realized she was much too far away to help.

Em had the situation under control. Ducking to her right, she pressed on the accelerator, and the engine responded with a roar. Robin got the idea, though she wasn't sure she could have done it.

What kind of crazy does it take to drive directly at someone who's pointing a gun at you?

Em's action was dangerous, but it also takes an iron will for an unprotected pedestrian to face a two-ton vehicle in a deadly game of chicken. Em was betting Dave didn't have that kind of courage.

She was correct. When he realized Em wasn't going to stop, he dropped his arm and leapt aside. The SUV sailed past as he rolled in the grass, took aim, and fired a couple of shots. Being hasty, they went wide. Em and her passengers were around the corner before he regained his feet.

"Gary!" he called. "Stop them before they get out the gate!"

Throwing himself into the Mustang, Gary drove off. It was pointed away from the front, and he sped past the spot where Robin stood, took the corner in a wild slide, and headed up the next row. Left in the darkness, Robin said a little prayer that Em got away before he caught up with her.

***

Chewing at her lip, Em entered the passcode for the entry gate. It seemed to take forever, but the arm finally lifted in a series of jerks that indicated great age and a lack of maintenance. She scooted under just as the Mustang rounded the corner at the far end of the lot and roared toward them. The arm dropped behind them, almost in free-fall, and the driver of the Mustang had to stop and re-enter the code. Making the most of those precious seconds, Em gunned the SUV's engine, strewing gravel behind her as she pulled onto the highway and headed for town.

Jai had taken a bottle of water from the cup holder and crawled into the back, gently pushing Bennett to one side as she offered Tom Wyman a drink. He looked terrible, with two black eyes and a split lip. The grimaces he'd made crawling into the car revealed painful body bruises, possibly broken ribs.

His sense of humor was intact. "Good to see you, Em. Don't be afraid to drive as fast as you like."

"Gary is through the gate," Jai reported. "What can we do?"

"Outrun him, I hope," Em replied. "If that doesn't work, we'll think of something."

"How good are you behind the wheel?" Tom asked. His swollen lips made the words sound slushy.

"As good as any; better than some. What you got in mind?"

"My car sits pretty low to the ground, but this thing has all-wheel drive. If you can get him to follow you off-road, it won't be long before he wrecks something."

Em knew what it cost Tom to propose wrecking his beautiful car. Still, it was better than waiting for the guy behind them to start shooting. "Let's do it."

"Okay," Tom said. "Instead of turning toward Cedar at the stop sign, go west. There's some open country out that way that should work for us."

Em did as he suggested. Within a minute he directed her to take a left down a dirt road. The turn was neither smooth nor fully controlled, but a glance in the rearview mirror told Em their pursuer had more trouble with it than she did. The Mustang's back end slewed wildly, and the driver barely kept it under control. As soon as he did, he accelerated and caught up quickly. Glancing at the mirror, Em saw his determined face close to the steering wheel, his hands in the ten-and-two position.

Dragging himself upright, Tom twisted to a position where he could look out the front window. "That field ahead should work. Are you ready for this?"

She ignored her throbbing hip and sweaty palms. "I was born ready."

Let's hope Loonette the Clown hasn't lost her skills.

Turning the wheel sharply, Em steered down an earthen ramp meant for farm equipment and bumped abruptly into the open field planted with sorghum. Steering along the rows, she heard W*hack, whack, whack!* as the plants surrendered to the car's grill and brushed along the undercarriage. The tires spun in the loose dirt and the vehicle bogged a few times, but she kept the accelerator pressed down and fought the steering wheel as it bucked in her hands like a wild steer. Somehow, they continued forward.

Behind her the driver of the Mustang hesitated, but in the end he made the decision they'd hoped for. Unwilling to lose them in the darkness, he turned off the road and followed.

"Good on ya," Em muttered. "Now all I have to do is find a place to hang you up."

It came sooner than she expected. In the center of the field was a low spot the farmer had filled in with rocks. The plants around it hid the hazard from view until the last second, and when her headlights illuminated it, Em yanked the wheel sharply to the left. Though they didn't hit it head-on, the SUV's right-side tires climbed up and over the edge of the pile, sending them all into space for a split second before they were jammed back into their seats again. Tom let out an involuntary groan, Bennett whined an objection, and Mai squealed in fright. Straightening the steering wheel, Em continued forward, hoping the man following their track was coming too fast to avoid disaster.

A few seconds later they heard it. Too low to the ground to climb over the rocks, the car's underside scraped along them, making a sound that signaled the imminent death of the oil pan. Even if their pursuer managed to get over the obstacle, he wouldn't get much farther before the car's engine seized.

At the other side of the field, Em drove along the edge until the headlights illuminated a gentle enough angle to cross the ditch and get back on the road. There she stopped for a second, turned off the lights, and rolled down the window. Behind them they heard the whine of an engine fighting its frozen axles. The Mustang was marooned in the darkness, unable to move.

"Now what?" Em asked Tom.

As he looked toward the stationary headlights that revealed where his car was dying, Tom's voice revealed regret. "We call the cops and report a car in trouble."

Chapter Twenty-five

Though concerned about Em and the others, Robin was all too aware of her own precarious situation. After the two vehicles sped away, complete silence fell over the lot, which meant any sound she made would alert Luther or Dave. It would be impossible to climb the metal fence without the vibration betraying her presence. She'd have to wait and hope they left.

"Somebody's still here," Luther said.

"What do you mean?"

"If the boys were in that unit making noise, and the old lady was distracting Gary, who cut the hole and got Wyman out?"

"The woman that was with him in Florida."

"She didn't come with the old lady, and I don't think she left with her." Robin sensed Luther's gaze searching the darkness. "I want her dead, but I want the money first."

What followed was a terrifying game of hide and seek. The lot was lit intermittently: the perimeter fairly well, the interior less so, which meant Robin had to stay between the buildings to remain unseen. Finding a spot where a burned-out lamp left almost complete darkness, she took shelter in the recessed doorway of a unit. Biting her lip to keep from sobbing, she cowered in her hiding spot while Luther called out from time to time, "Anything?"

"Nothing."

She hardly dared to breathe when one of them, Dave she thought, passed so near she could have reached out and touched him. Though the cloudy night was an advantage, the blackness around her emphasized her isolation. Her friends were gone.

They'd saved Tom, but who would save her?

The worst times were when Luther and Dave didn't talk to each other. It was difficult to tell where they were, close or far away, and Robin fought the panic every stalked creature feels—the instinct to run, even if running means discovery.

How long before they find me? How long before I die?

When a soft scrape sounded on the tarmac at the end of the row, she turned to see a glow that made her cringe. One of them had located a flashlight, and he swung it in a wide arc as he approached. Irrelevant thoughts tumbled into her head. She hadn't made her weekly call to Shelly. She'd meant to get tickets to a Royals game so Cam could experience the thrill of a live sporting event. She wasn't sure she'd put away the clean laundry Hua left neatly folded on the table in her room. She was going to die, and there was a lot she'd meant to do.

After a few seconds, a voice in her head, maybe Em's, maybe Mark's, maybe her own, told Robin to stop being a baby and think. Like many flashlights kept for emergencies, this one wasn't all that useful. Its yellowish light indicated weak batteries, and its compact size made the illumination angle narrow. Unless the person carrying it got within a few feet of her, he'd see only shadows.

Pulling the hood of her jacket over her head, Robin drew the strings tight, leaving only her eyes uncovered. Then she stretched herself, face inward, along the metal wall of the building. It was unnerving to turn away from danger, but she knew her chances were better as an amorphous, low form. Her enemies expected an upright or a crouched figure. She was, as Em would have phrased it, shaking like a shirt in a hurricane, but if she could remain silent, they'd walk right by.

I hope.

With only her ears for warning, Robin lay there, trying to slow her racing heart. Damp seeped into her clothing. Cold concrete sucked the heat from her hip and arm. Stealthy footsteps were close. Had Luther seen her? Was Dave creeping toward her, ready to pounce? Should she bolt from her hiding place and try to outrun them? Remain where she was? She took shallow breaths and forced her unwilling muscles to remain limp. The sound of footsteps passed, and after what seemed like an hour she heard Luther say, "Anything?"

Dave's voice came from farther away. "No."

As she blessed luck and lousy flashlights, Luther ordered, "We need to get the car."

"Yeah. The headlights will find her." Dave trotted off, but Luther remained where he was for a while, as if sensing Robin's nearness. It seemed his light eyes would penetrate the darkness from sheer will and discover her lying there. She counted her breaths, counted the seconds, counted her chances of surviving.

Too noisy. Too long. Too low.

Finally Luther moved away. She sat up, slowly and with great caution, and tried to decide what to do. Which direction would the car come from? Which way should she go when she made a run for the fence? No matter how she imagined it, her escape attempt didn't end well. She could almost feel Dave's hand gripping her ankle before she reached the top, pulling her back to the ground.

Still, she couldn't stay where she was until headlights trapped her against the building.

The slightest of noises to her left made Robin tense further. A figure traced the building, fingertips lightly touching the metal wall for guidance. Had Luther circled back? She stretched out on the ground again, hoping what had worked once would work again.

It didn't. A foot touched her foot. Then a hand squeezed it tentatively. As she coiled, ready to kick the hand's owner in the face, she caught the smell of ginger.

"Hua?"

"Robin." His voice was at her ear. "We've been looking everywhere for you." Stretching out a hand, he helped her to her feet. "Cam and I have devised a Plan B to fit this situation, but it requires all three of us."

She had trouble processing his words. "You've got a plan?

"We must make these men believe they have won. Then we will divide them and beat them."

Robin felt a sinking dread. "You want me to surrender."

He must have heard the dread in her voice. "Temporarily. We will rescue you."

In what universe do you two stack up against killers with guns?

"Come with me." As Hua led the way, Robin clung to what she'd learned. Mink's advice was to have a Plan B. Apparently Hua and Cam had that covered. Em said to always play it cool. Luther didn't know she had help, so if she struck the right note, he'd think he had the upper hand. Last came Mark's harsh lesson: *Do whatever it takes, Babe. Whatever it takes.* In a fight to the death there could be no hesitation, no holds barred.

"I put the money in the second unit," Hua was saying. "Lead them to it. When things start to happen, take a prone position if at all possible."

They reached the end of the building across from Robin's unit and stopped in the shadows. Luther's car was fairly well-lit by a lamp along the fence line. Dave was already inside. Luther was just opening the driver's side door when she stepped out with hands raised. Seeing her, Luther nodded to Dave, who exited the car, approached, and took her arm in a rough grip. "I owe you one upside the head, lady."

"If you want your money, you'd better hold off for a while." Her voice shook, but she managed to meet Luther's eyes directly. He came around the back of the car. "Where is it?"

"People think you have the same motives they do," Mark had often said. "If your story sounds like what they'd have done, they swallow it hook, line, and sinker." If her father was correct, Robin needed to sound as greedy, mistrustful, and selfish as Luther would be if he were in her situation.

"We thought we could get Tom out without giving up the money, but then you two showed up. My mom got Tom out, but she couldn't stop for me with your friend on her tail."

"Too bad," Dave sneered, but Robin focused on Luther.

"She left the money, in case I had to give it up to get Tom back." She nodded down the row. "Half of it's in there. You get the rest when I go free."

Luther glanced down the row. "The old woman left half a mil in that unit?" Opening the car door, he retrieved the failing flashlight from where he'd tossed it on the seat. "Show me."

As Robin started for Unit #124, her mind spun with questions. What was the plan? What could she do to help when "things start to happen?" Dave and Luther both had their guns in hand, and Dave held her arm so tightly she might need reconstructive surgery later. If she lived.

The door to Unit #124 was closed but not locked. Robin rolled it up, exposing a dark space littered with boards, a couple of hammers, and a cordless power drill—mute testimony to Jai and Mai's hasty retreat. In the center of the floor was Hua's chartreuse backpack. "Watch her." Luther opened the zipper and peered inside. "It looks like she's telling the truth."

"What now?" Dave asked.

"If you want the rest, you have to let me go," Robin said.

"Not necessarily," Luther answered.

At that moment steps sounded on the pavement outside the unit. "Hey!"

Hiding his gun at his side, Luther went to the doorway. Dave followed, dragging Robin with him. She almost fell when he stopped suddenly in apparent surprise. A tall figure in black stood at the corner of the building, his aggressive pose suggesting Wolverine in anger mode. When Robin noticed Cam's mouth moving, she realized he was counting. Hua must have estimated how many seconds he could risk standing there before one of the gunmen recovered and started shooting. At "one" he made a sideways leap and was gone.

"Get him," Luther ordered. "I'll watch her."

"That's one big SOB," Dave observed. "Bigger than me."

"Just makes him an easier target," Luther replied. "Now go!"

Dave sped away, rounding the building and disappearing into the night. Luther shined the flashlight on Robin's face. "Now about that other half-million."

"I told you. When I go free—"

The slap came from nowhere, and she reeled backward, trying to keep her feet beneath her.

"You're gonna try to negotiate with me?" A second slap stung her cheek and sent her staggering again. "Tell me where it is, or you'll find out what pain is, like your boyfriend did."

A cry sounded from some distance away, a single yelp that modulated to a groan. Had Dave wounded Cam? She hadn't heard a shot, but the gun might have a silencer.

That thought was interrupted by a third blow, with a closed fist this time. When she put her hand to her eye in response to the pain, Luther punched her stomach. The breath left her body with a *woof*, and she struggled to get air into her lungs again.

"Where is my money?"

Shock made her thoughts muddy, but Mark's voice reminded, *Whatever it takes, Babe.*

"I'll tell!" She made her voice tearful. "Don't hit me again."

Luther's voice revealed satisfaction. "That's a good girl."

She needed a new plan. If Cam was hurt—or killed, but she didn't want to think about that—only Hua was left to save her. There was no way he could come into the unit and get her. Dave might return at any moment. She had to get Luther out in the open, while he was alone and where Hua could—

What? Attack Luther? Disarm him and beat him into submission?

She had to try. "The rest of the money's in the other unit."

His tone was doubting. "How'd that happen?"

"When my friend got Tom out, he left it in case I needed it. As I said, we didn't trust you to let us go."

She heard the smile in Luther's reply. "That's the only smart thing you did tonight. Not that it's going to help." Bending slightly, Luther slid the backpack strap over one shoulder. With the gun in one hand and the light in the other he ordered, "Let's go."

Robin went first, her back rippling with anxiety at the

thought of the gun just inches from her spine. When they were almost to the car, they heard grunts of exertion, and a second later Dave appeared at the corner of the building, his face anguished. Leaning heavily on the structure, he panted, "Bastard kneecapped me."

Luther glanced nervously around. "You let him get away?"

Dave's expression turned resentful. "I can barely walk. How was I supposed to chase him down?"

"You," Luther said to Robin. "Help him into the car."

Robin obeyed, supporting Dave as he limped to the passenger side. Sliding the seat all the way back, she helped him inside.

"You still got your gun?"

"Yeah." His voice was weak.

"Keep an eye out for trouble. A few more minutes and I'll get you to a doctor." Dave tried to nod in acquiescence, but pain showed clearly on his face, and his head lolled back onto the seat.

As Robin closed the car door, Luther grabbed her by the hair, jerking her backward. "Hey!" he called to the night. "I bet you're out there watching, so here's the deal. You come out now, and I won't kill the woman." There was no reply, so he added, "She doesn't have to die quick. A bullet to her knee will do what you did to my buddy there, maybe worse." When there was still no reply he said, "Let's count it down. When I get to five, she gets a non-lethal bullet hole. I get to pick where. One. Two."

"I'm coming out." Cam's voice came from down the row. He appeared first as a dark form, then a clear image with hands raised in surrender. Robin held her breath. Would Luther shoot him immediately and end one threat?

He did not, and she let herself breathe again. Instead, when Cam was almost to the car Luther said, "Stop."

Cam obeyed. His eyes sought Robin's, sending a message she thought was positive. Hua was still out there somewhere. That was good, except now he had to rescue both her and Cam.

Luther had considered his options, and he dragged Robin to the driver's side of the car. Opening the door, he leaned in and pressed a button. The trunk lid popped open. "Get in," he ordered.

Cam did as he was told, stepping in easily and folding himself small enough to fit. When Luther ordered Robin to close the lid, she did so reluctantly. The next time Cam saw the sky, she was certain it would be only long enough for Luther to put a bullet in his head. To her surprise Cam appeared calm and even gave her a subtle thumbs-up sign as the lid closed over him.

"Now let's get the rest of my money," Luther said cheerfully.

Robin led the way into the open unit, which was lit by a small lantern. It was half full of the things she'd left behind in Cedar: her bedroom set, her living room furniture, and a tall bookcase filled with her mother's hardcover set of *Books That Changed the World*. She noted a few new items that must be Tom's. One was a weight bench that had ropes attached to it. Mottled with dark stains, the ropes had recently been cut. A small pool of something that looked like blood had settled under the bench.

"I haven't got all night, lady."

Though her throbbing face made it difficult, Robin tried to think. Her right eye was almost swollen shut, and her scalp burned where Luther had pulled out strands of hair. Still, she had to stall. Maybe Hua had called the police by now. Maybe Em would return for them when she realized they were late meeting her in town. Neither of those things was likely to save her or Cam.

Searching through the items as if unsure where to look, she said, "It's in a black gym bag. You might have to get him out of that trunk and have him show you where it is."

"Or I could put a bullet in there and see if that makes you any better at finding things."

"I'm trying!" she said angrily.

As she moved to explore the back corner, Robin noticed the hole Hua and Cam had cut to get Tom out. Could she dive through it and escape before Luther caught her?

"Don't even think about it." He took her arm and pulled her backward. As she went, Robin caught sight of an eye and a shock of black hair behind the headboard of her bed. Hua.

"There it is!" she said, pointing in the opposite direction. "Behind the bookcase."

As Luther leaned in to look, she twisted out of his grip. At the same time, Hua leapt out and swung at him with a softball bat Robin recognized as her own. Luther's instincts provided a warning, and he turned at the last moment. Hua's blow landed on his shoulder, and though he bellowed with pain and staggered backward, he was able to raise the gun and aim at Hua, who stood so close there was no way Luther would miss.

Whatever it takes.

With a swift motion, Robin pushed the bookcase, tipping it toward Luther. His eyes widened and he tried to step back, but he was too slow. The case fell forward and its weight carried him to the ground. Books tumbled out, burying him in philosophy, history, and economics. As Luther struggled to roll out from under them, Robin put a foot on his neck, holding him down. Hua hurried forward and took the gun from his hand.

"Are you all right, Hua?"

His chest heaved with exertion as he said, "I had to run very fast to get here before you, Robin, but your decision to bring

Luther inside was very wise indeed. Now can you find some things among your possessions to tie around his limbs? If I had known we would need it, I would have worn my Elvis scarf."

"Hua, Cam's in the trunk of their car."

"No, I'm not," Cam said from the doorway. I told you there's a release button in most cars now, Robin. You forgot, just like Luther did."

***

"Get three rooms somewhere north of Cedar and message me the address," Robin told Hua and Cam as they got into the van. "I'll pick up the others and be right behind you." To their great relief, she'd received a text from Em with a simple *OK*.

Robin drove the RAV to the park, where Em and Bennett stood next to the rental. "Everybody's okay?"

Em frowned as she got a glimpse of Robin's face. "We're good. You look a little worse for wear."

"You should see the other guy. Where's Tom?"

"Under that tree. Bennett and I will return the rental car and walk back here while you get him situated in the RAV."

"Is your hip going to let you do that?"

She looked offended. "It'll be good for me."

"Does Tom need a doctor?"

Em donned cotton work gloves and began wiping fingerprints off the car's surfaces as she spoke. "I did some triage. He doesn't seem to have a punctured lung or anything. It's probably best if we get out of Dodge and see a doctor later." Satisfied with her work, she let Bennett into the rental, followed him in, and drove away.

Taking a flashlight from the van, Robin found where Wyman lay on the ground. Though someone had wiped the worst of the dirt and blood from his face, he was a still mess. “Oh, Tom!”

He raised a hand almost to her face. “What happened to you?”

“Let’s just say I’ll live. Luther will too, if he’s lucky.”

“He didn’t believe I couldn’t tell them where you were. I’m not a good liar, but apparently I’m not convincing when I tell the truth either.”

“I’m so sorry,” she repeated. “It’s my fault.”

He laughed. “Hey, I got blown twenty feet in the air by a roadside bomb and lost a few pieces in the process. A little beating isn’t going to kill me.” He licked the split in his lower lip and winced. “Sorry about mentioning your, um, bed. It was the only way I could think of to let you know where I was.”

“Hey, it worked.”

Tom looked away. “Look, I know you and Cam are together, and I want you to know I won’t make any trouble. Not that I don’t find you attractive, but, I mean—”

“What makes you think Cam and I are together?”

“I’m a detective, remember? Shared apartment. Shared hotel rooms. Now that I’ve seen him, well, what girl wouldn’t want a guy who looks like that?”

When Robin giggled he asked, “What?”

Putting on a serious expression she said, “The guys are waiting a few miles north of here. Can’t wait to introduce you.”

***

They reached the motel with a PETS WELCOME sign out front at

2:00 a.m. Hua and Cam had been watching for them from a second story balcony and came down to help Tom out of the car. They half-carried him into one of two rooms they'd reserved on the ground floor.

Once he was situated on a queen-sized bed, Tom explained his capture. "They must have followed me to the lot. One minute I was carrying my weight bench into the unit, and the next I was on the ground with my face smashed against the concrete." He added, "They were going to put Robin and me in my Mustang and sent it over a hillside somewhere." He made a rueful grimace. "The car was a goner either way."

"Loss teaches us the worth of things," Em responded, "but I wish I hadn't been part of that lesson." She made a washing gesture with her hands. "Now we need to make our sleeping arrangements and get some rest."

That was tricky, but eventually it was decided that Hua and Cam would take one room while Robin, Mai, and Jai would take the second. Em would stay with Tom in the room they currently occupied. "I'm a decent nurse," she told Tom, "and I promise not to try to jump your bones."

Robin had noticed Tom's gaze resting on Cam from time to time. The fact he'd be sharing a room with Hua seemed to interest him more than casually, and he turned his eyes to hers. She responded with an impish grin, and before he remembered his split lip, he smiled back at her.

Chapter Twenty-six

“The kid’s good at a lot of things, but driving isn’t one of them,” Em told Robin when they stopped to eat the next afternoon. “I told him: if at first you don’t succeed, maybe failure is your thing.” She spun her coffee cup a quarter turn. “Hua behind a steering wheel makes me more nervous than you the day before a caper.”

“Tell him you want reports on the arrests of Luther and company. He can’t drive and stare at his phone.”

“Good one!” Em patted Robin’s arm. “How’s the patient?”

“He’s okay unless the driver ahead of me forgets what a turn signal’s for and I have to brake suddenly.”

“Cracked ribs make you wish you’d died, at least for the first few days.” It sounded as if Em spoke from experience. “We’ll make him comfortable when we get home.”

“We haven’t even got beds for Mai and Jai yet. Where can we put an injured man so he’ll be comfortable?”

Em made a *tsk* of irritation. “We’ll figure it out, Robin. Worry never changed a single thing.”

When they arrived at the house around four in the morning on Monday, Robin helped Tom up the front steps and into the empty room at the front of the house. Cam and Hua moved Em’s futon there while Jai and Mai collected sheets, pillows, and blankets. As they stood expectantly around him, Tom claimed his temporary bed was perfectly comfortable and he intended to get some real sleep. There was a flurry of activity as one or another of his hosts thought of something he might need. Soon he had within reach a glass of water, a box of tissues, a can of mixed nuts (for protein), a magazine (for gamers, but 'really cool,' according to Cam), and Em's extra cane, in case he needed to make a trip to the bathroom. When he'd assured them several times that he could think of nothing more he might need, they retreated to their own rooms to rest or sleep, as individual personalities allowed.

Robin rested but didn't sleep. As usual, her mind went over and over things. She was relieved she'd had no fainting spell after the events at the storage lot, but negatives nagged at her anyway.

We ruined that storage unit. Need to pay for repairs.

The police think Tom's been murdered. How will we explain it when he's alive and well?

What are we going to do with the twins?

Luther and the others must have told the police something. What was it?

And the most pressing question of all as she touched her bruised face: *Should we give up KNPs before we all get killed?*

Don't think about that right now. Think of peanut butter cups and snowmen.

Despite snowmen and Reese's, the questions circled endlessly in her head. The answers eluded her.

***

The next council meeting was held in Tom's room, in deference to his injuries. He looked a little like the king of Siam, with his subjects seated on the floor around him. Cam brought in a kitchen chair for Em, who sat next to Tom, her posture as erect as always.

They began working on solutions to the questions that had kept Robin awake. Em suggested Mink could arrange an anonymous payment for repairs to the hole in the unit wall. As the listed renter, Robin had been informed of a break-in by email that morning. She'd written back expressing dismay at the crime, relief that nothing was missing, and her intent to move her things to a more secure facility.

Next was a discussion of who needed to know what. "Luther and the others claim they were attacked by unknown assailants for unknown reasons," Hua reported.

"They'll take their medicine and keep their mouths shut," Em predicted. "Anything they admit makes them look incompetent, and in their line of work, incompetence isn't tolerated."

The next step was to let the police know Thomas Wyman, Private Investigator, was still among the living. Tom called the sheriff's department in Florida, gave his name, and said he had information for the person in charge of investigating Cynthia Tinker's death. It took a couple of transfers, but he finally heard, "Edgars, homicide."

"Detective Edgars. My name is Thomas Wyman."

There was a pause. "We've been looking for you, Mr. Wyman."

"I'm aware of that." Tom gave the account they'd prepared, claiming his partner, Cynthia Tinker, had learned of slaves being held in Florida. Though he'd tried to talk her out of it, she'd gone to investigate. "We had already ended our partnership," he explained, "since I'm moving out of state. I'm not sure what happened, but I was loading some stuff in a friend's storage unit when someone attacked me. Three men wanted to know how Cynthia had found out about the operation." He paused. "I didn't know the answer, which made things uncomfortable."

"How did you escape?"

"A woman came to store stuff in a unit down the row. She

was a talker, and while my guard was distracted, I used some tinsnips I found in the unit to cut my way out. I circled the building and begged the woman to help me get out of there." He chuckled. "One look at me and she knew I wasn't kidding about the danger."

"But one of them came after you."

"In my own car, which I would guess is totaled."

"It is. Where are you now, sir?"

"A hospital in Frankfort, Kentucky. Mrs. Cabot brought me here."

"That's the woman who rescued you?"

"Yes. I can give you her phone number, and she'll verify what I've said."

Edgars wrote it down. "I'll give her a call. What we'd really like to know, Mr. Wyman, is who beat the heck out of those traffickers sometime around midnight that same night and then called the police to come and collect them."

Tom grinned at Robin. "I guess it's your job to figure that out, Detective. I was long gone by then."

"Let us know when you're well enough to make the trip down here, Mr. Wyman. We'll need a deposition."

"Sure thing. I'm just sorry I can't tell you anything more about what happened."

When he hung up Robin asked, "Wasn't that a bit much?"

"I *am* sorry I can't tell them more," Tom said. "I'd love to brag to the whole world about my inventive vigilante friends."

"But you won't, will you?" Cam asked. "Robin says we have to keep it a secret, and Robin's usually right."

***

Cedar County Commissioner Barney Abrams was nervous. His morning newspaper reported the body of a private detective had been found in the Gulf of Mexico north of Tampa, Florida. Scanning the article, he found her name, Cynthia Tinker.

Damn!

Just after nine, his cell phone vibrated. Abrams set aside the doughnut he was eating, licking jelly off his thumb as he answered.

"Abrams."

"Commissioner, it's Thomas Wyman. I have new information on your case."

"I was under the impression you'd given up on it."

"We never like to give up, sir. It makes us look bad."

"What have you found, son?"

"I picked up the trail of a woman who befriended Carter Halkias. I think she knows where Halkias is."

There was a long pause. "If you get me that information, I'll double what we agreed on originally."

When Tom ended the call, he turned to Hua. "Do your magic. We need to hear Abrams' next call."

In seconds they heard Abrams' voice. "I have a job for you."

With grim expressions, they listened as Barney Abrams negotiated a deal with an unknown man for the murders of two people, a man and a woman. "I'll get you the details later. Just be ready to travel when I call."

"No problem."

“I want it to look like a mugging. Can you do that?”

The reply was a humorless chuckle. “Let’s just say it wouldn’t be the first time.”

“I can’t believe it,” Robin said when the call ended.

Folding her ever-present knitting in her lap, Em rested her hands on the soft yarn. “Most of the time, the leopard doesn’t change his spots.”

Cam asked, “What do we do now, Robin?”

“We get him,” Em replied for her. “We make your recording of Honest Abrams’ confession public.”

“Is that enough?” Robin asked. “He’ll say the confession was forced and he lied to save his life.”

Hua raised a finger. “But how will he explain the recording I just made of him hiring a hit man?”

Chapter Twenty-seven

After giving his deposition against Luther Billings, Tom Wyman took their evidence against Abrams to a friend in the county sheriff's office and also to an acquaintance at the local TV station. Between the deputy's eagerness to be part of a big case and the reporter's thrill at having a scoop, the investigation moved forward quickly. Abrams hadn't been as careful as he should have, and with the scrutiny of police and the press, his secrets soon came to light. Investigators discovered multiple property deals in which he'd partnered with his cousin to take unfair advantage of information he got in the course of his job. The cousin, sensing his more eminent relative was a shinier target for law enforcement to chase, turned state's evidence and admitted everything.

Most of Linda Billings' money went to Amnesty International, anonymously of course. In another interesting note, Em reported that an old friend in the FBI had launched an investigation into the affairs of Senator "Buck" Buckram. He'd left rehab after only a few weeks but had caught the attention of the Justice Department. The wolves were circling, both governmental and media, and questions were being asked that Buckram couldn't answer.

"Did you have anything to do with Buckram's downfall, Hua?"

He didn't look in the least ashamed. "I might have switched some private files to public. I made it appear his security man did it, so the two of them are now at each other's throats. The truth will come out."

"But we promised if he behaved we wouldn't—"

Cam looked up from launching torpedoes at undersea monsters. "Robin, the guy bought a little kid and kept him locked up for nine years. Besides, Hua didn't promise Buckram anything."

Tom asked, "When you made that promise, did you know he had a personal slave?"

"Well, no. His owning another person never entered my mind."

"He had sent a request to Linda Billings," Hua said softly, "looking for my replacement."

A wave of defeat washed over Robin. "We haven't changed a thing. It's all been a waste of time."

"No." Em was knitting a sweater for Mai, and she pointed a needle at Robin like a threatening sword. "We've accomplished a lot."

"Really?"

Em looked to Hua. "Tell her about the preacher."

"Pastor Niven recently made a trip to Haiti, and the Deep and Wide Church now fully sponsors its mission there. He speaks of building a second orphanage in Central America. He lives much more simply than before, and his recent sermons have been about the need among God's servants to guard against the sin of pride."

Wyman chuckled. "I'll bet that makes some of his fellow televangelists squirm! Robin, you might have affected a whole school of sharks by showing one shark the error of his ways."

"That is very good, right?" Hua asked.

"Okay, so we're running around fifty percent," Robin said.

"Even that is a great thing," Hua claimed. "Our greatest

success was stopping Linda Billings."

"During which she died."

Em pointed an arthritic finger at Robin. "Not your fault, Girlie."

"That's your opinion."

"Mine too," Tom said.

"And mine," Cam and Hua said together. Looking up from the curtains she was making from sheets, Jai nodded agreement, and even Bennett made a whine that might have been affirmation. Only Mai didn't chime in, and that was because she was in the kitchen, grinding something called mugwort that Jai had promised would relieve Em's hip pain.

Robin smiled. "You're saying we need to keep doing what we're doing?"

"As long as we can," Em said.

"As long as we're careful," Tom cautioned.

"As long as we work together," Hua agreed.

"And don't blab to anybody," Cam added.

Robin thought of Butler Mink. "As long as we always have a Plan B—and maybe a Plan C too." Raising her energy drink in salute, she proposed, "I propose that Kidnap.org moves forward."

Em raised her coffee cup. "Why stop now? We're hot as a firecracker, and the Fourth of July isn't that far off."

****

Dear Reader:

If you enjoyed this book, please consider placing a review somewhere others will see it. Authors rely on word of mouth to spread the news of a new book or series, and no one does that better than happy readers!

Thank you for supporting what we writers love to do!

Peg

Other books by Peg Herring

The Simon & Elizabeth Mysteries (Tudor Era Historical)

Her Highness' First Murder
Poison, Your Grace
The Lady Flirts with Death
Her Majesty's Mischief

***

The Loser Mysteries (Contemporary Mystery/Suspense)

Killing Silence
Killing Memories
Killing Despair

***

Clan Macbeth Historical Romance (medieval Scotland)

Macbeth's Niece
Double Toil & Trouble

***

Standalone Mysteries

Somebody Doesn't Like Sarah Leigh (contemporary cozy mystery)
Her Ex-GI P.I. ('60s-era mystery)
A Lethal Time and Place ('60s-era paranormal mystery)
Shakespeare's Blood (thriller)

***

Writing as Maggie Pill

The Sleuth Sisters Mysteries (cozy, set in Michigan) If you like lighter mysteries, and if you have sisters, had sisters, or know a little about sisters, you'll love Maggie's series.

The Sleuth Sisters
3 Sleuths, 2 Dogs, 1 Murder
Murder in the Boonies
Sleuthing at Sweet Springs
Eat, Drink, & Be Wary

67633768R00194

Made in the USA
Lexington, KY
18 September 2017